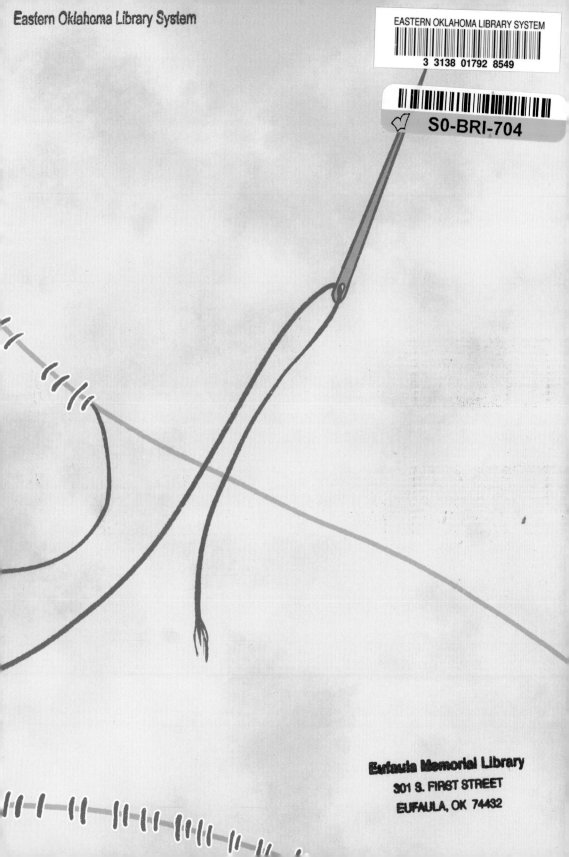

M Is for
MONSTER

M Is for MONSTER

Talia Dutton

Abrams ComicArts SURELY • New York

SURELY Curator: Mariko Tamaki
Editor: Charlotte Greenbaum
Editorial Assistant: Lauren White-Jackson
Designer: Andrea Milller
Managing Editor: Marie Oishi
Production Manager: Alison Gervais
Colorist: Avery Bacon
Inking Assistant: Raven Warner
Lettering Assistant: Lor Prescott

Library of Congress Cataloging Number
for the hardcover edition 2021949388

Hardcover ISBN 978-1-4197-6220-8
Paperback ISBN 978-1-4197-5197-4

Printed and bound in China
10 9 8 7 6 5 4 3 2

Abrams ComicArts books are available
at special discounts when purchased in
quantity for premiums and promotions
as well as fundraising or educational
use. Special editions can also be created
to specification. For details, contact
specialsales@abramsbooks.com or the
address below.

Abrams ComicArts® is a registered
trademark of Harry N. Abrams, Inc.
Surely™ is a trademark of Mariko Tamaki
and Harry N. Abrams, Inc.

ABRAMS The Art of Books
195 Broadway, New York, NY 10007
abramsbooks.com

ABRAMS COMIC ARTS
Surely

SURELY publishes LGBTQIA+ stories
by LGBTQIA+ creators, with a focus
on new stories, new voices, and untold
histories, in works that span fiction and
nonfiction, including memoir, horror,
comedy, and fantasy. Surely aims to
publish books for teens and adults that
lend context and perspective to our
current struggles and victories, and
to support those creators underrepre-
sented in the current publishing world.
We are bold, brave, loud, unexpected,
daring, unique.

For Mom, Dad, and Panda-Poodle

At first, the monster felt nothing.

The rest of us always feel something.

At every moment in time,
we are existing.

Nose itching, foot falling asleep,
even just the slight tickle of a hair
brushing against an arm.

It is possible that,
at the moment she awoke,
the monster was the only one
in history to remember
what it is like . . .

to not feel anything.

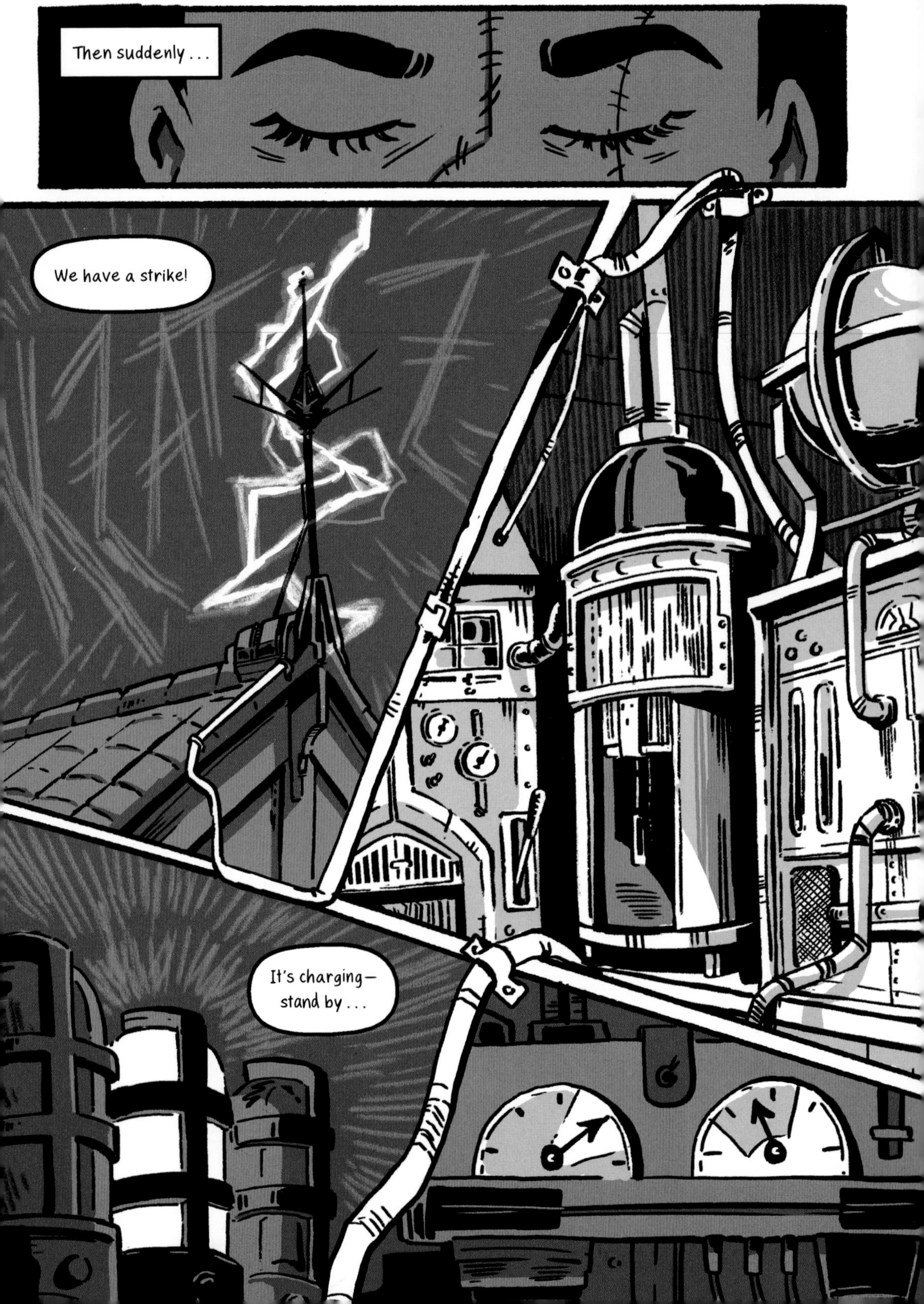
Then suddenly . . .
We have a strike!
It's charging—
stand by . . .

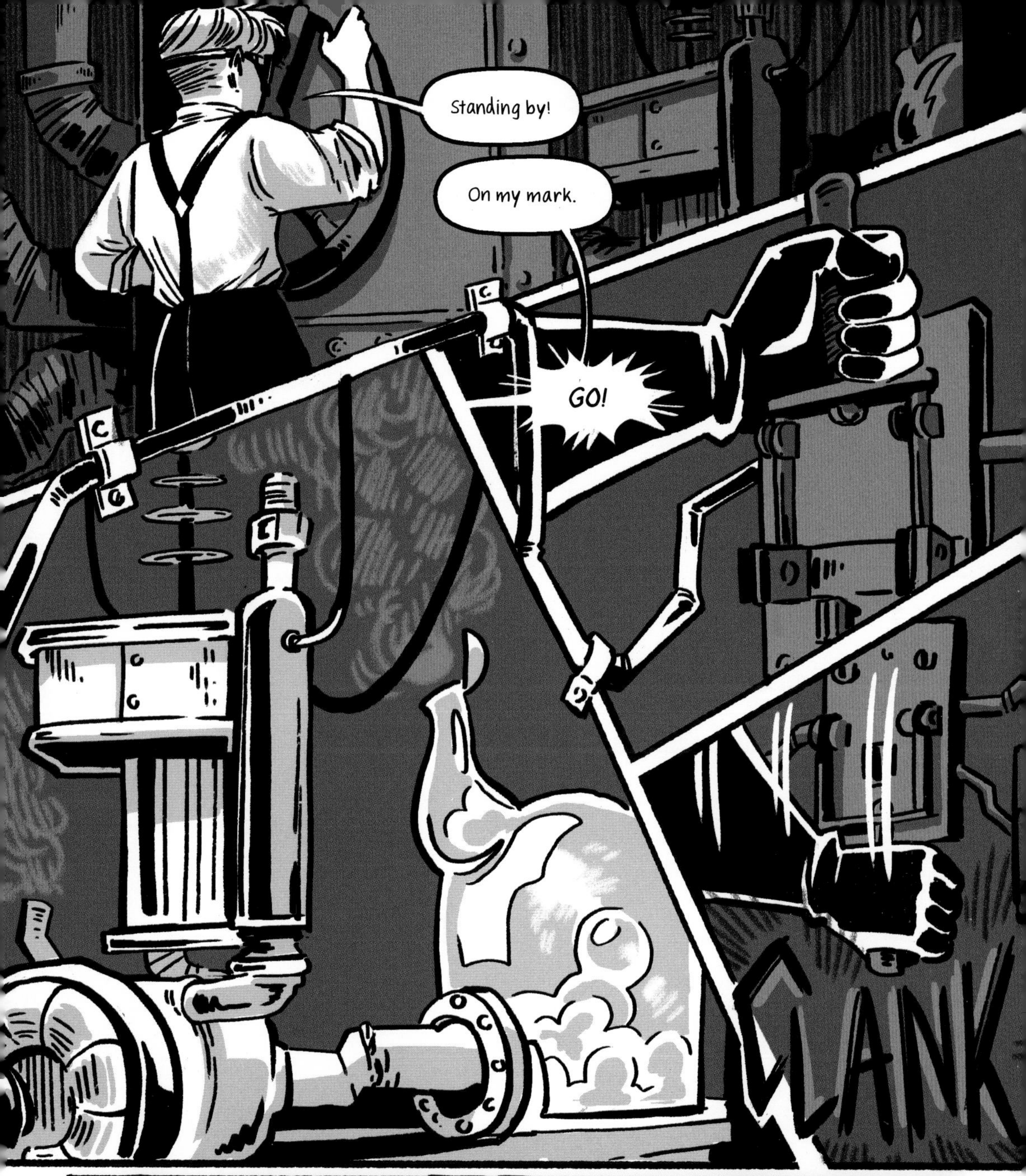
Standing by!
On my mark.
GO!
CLANK

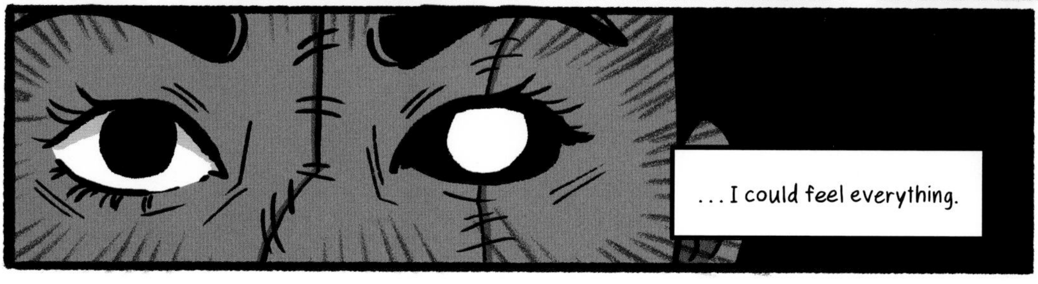
. . . I could feel everything.

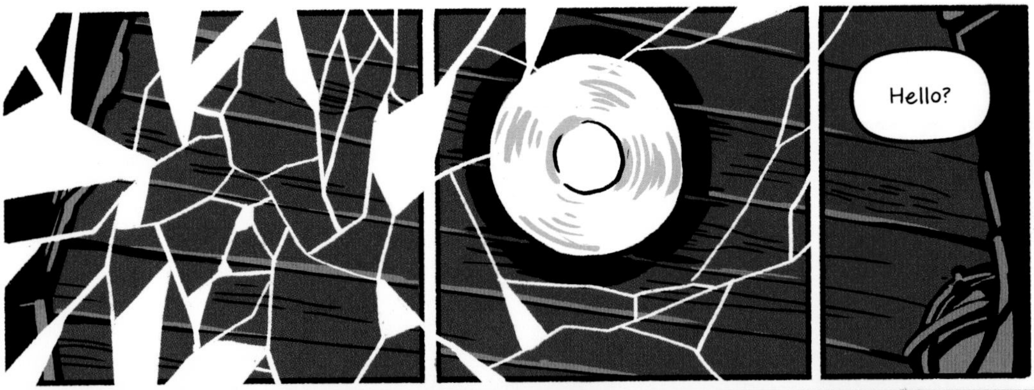
Hello?

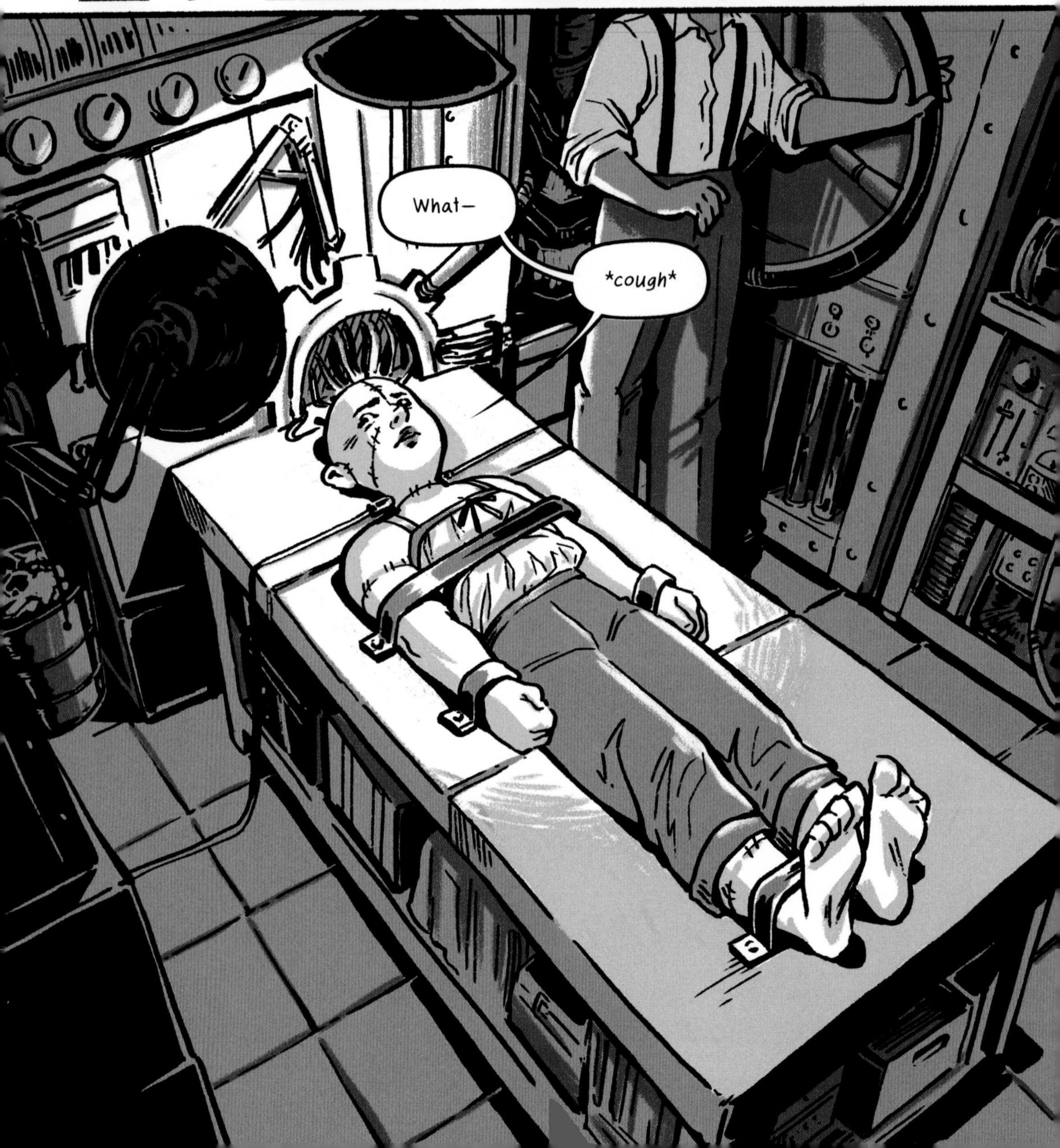
What–
cough

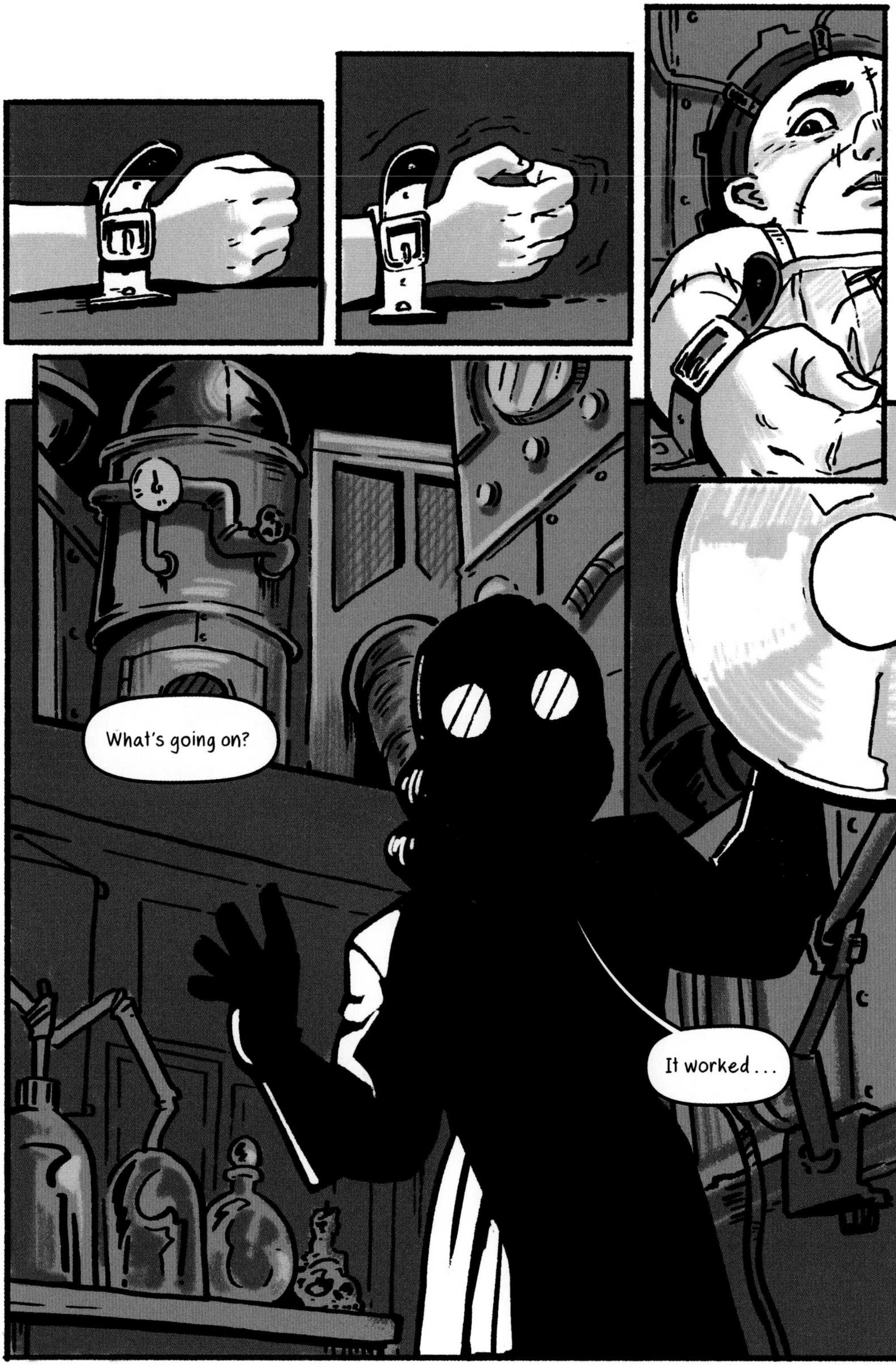
What's going on?
It worked...

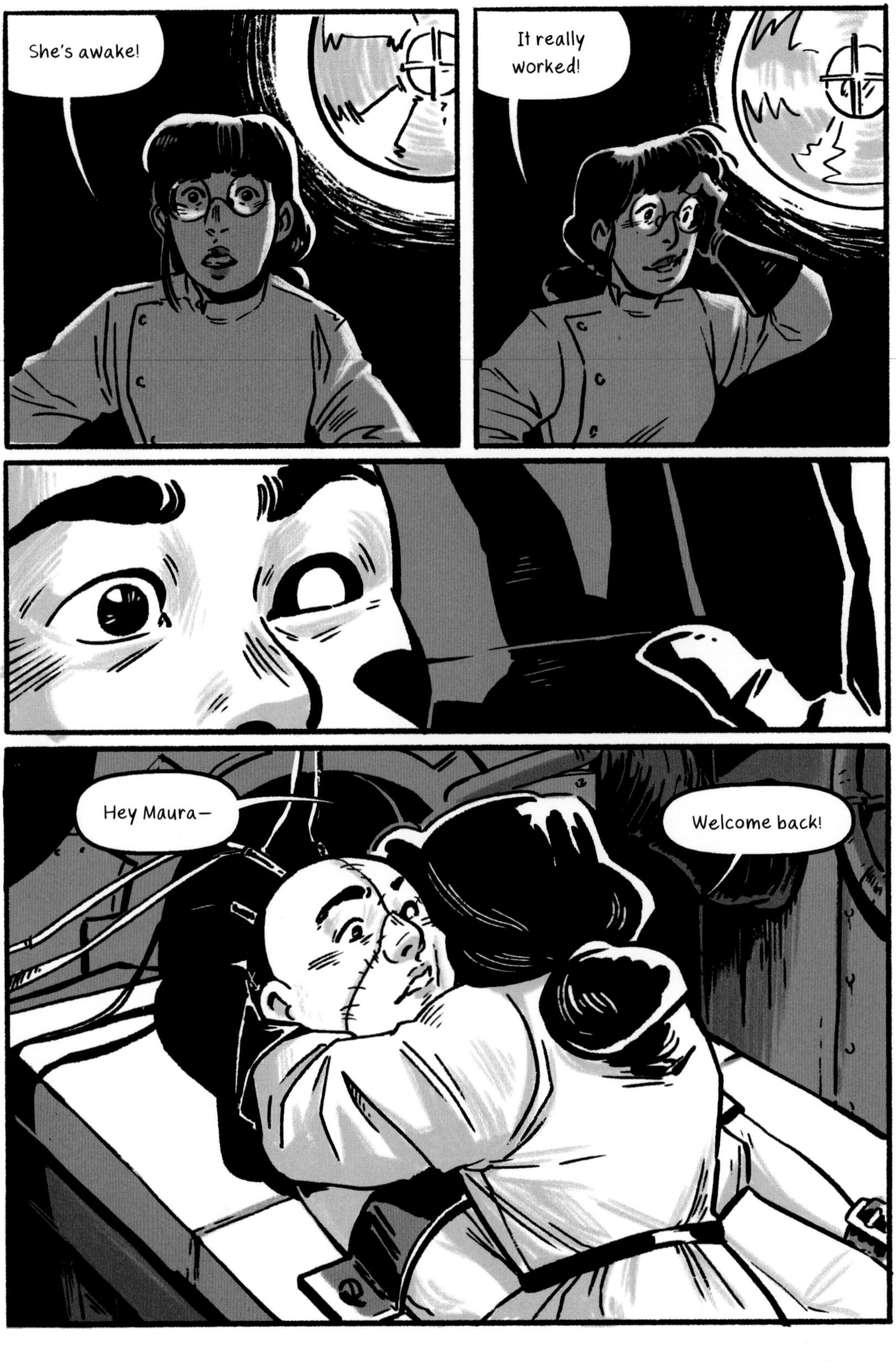
She's awake!
It really worked!
Hey Maura—
Welcome back!

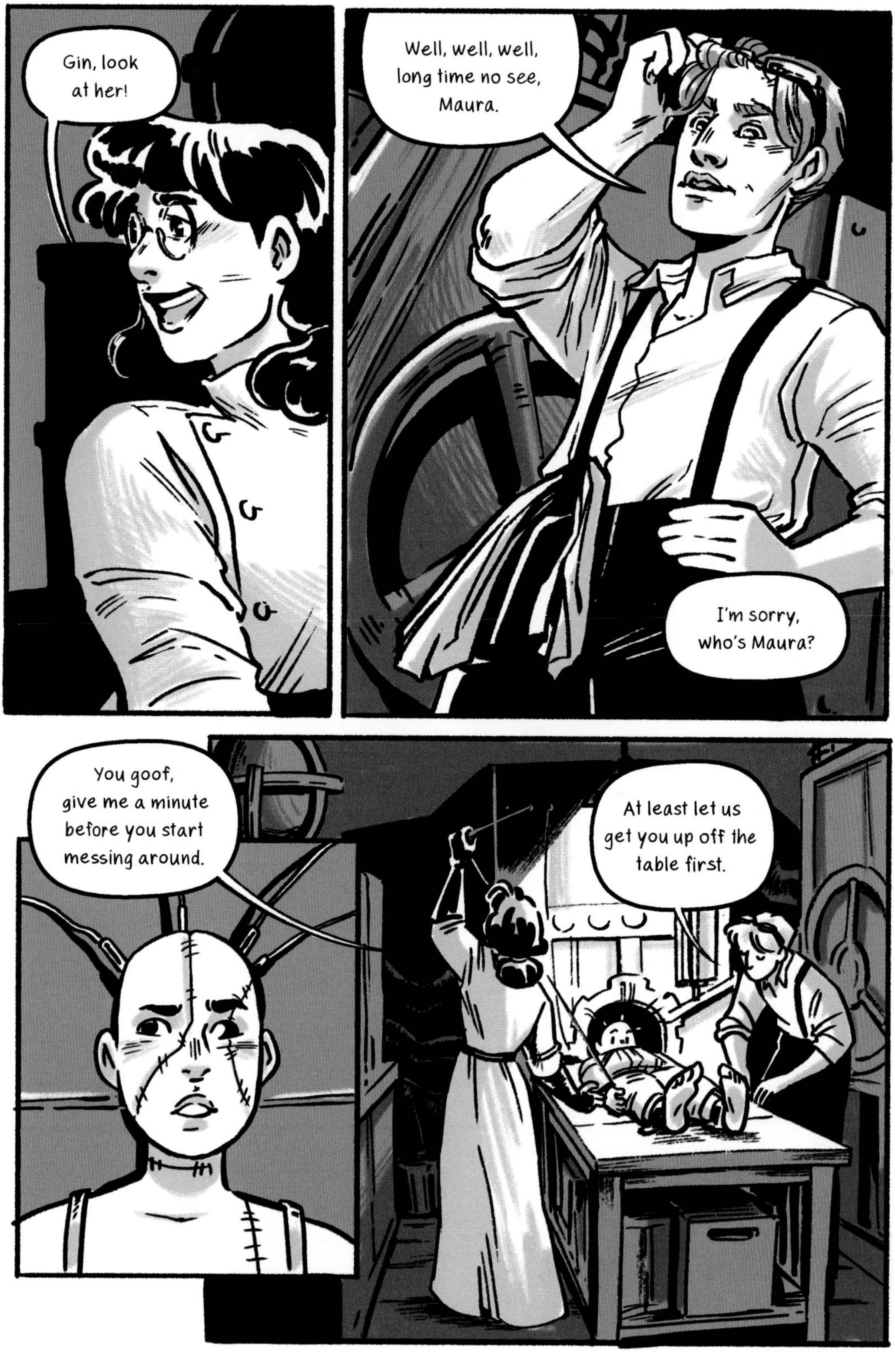
Gin, look at her!
Well, well, well, long time no see, Maura.
I'm sorry, who's Maura?
You goof, give me a minute before you start messing around.
At least let us get you up off the table first.

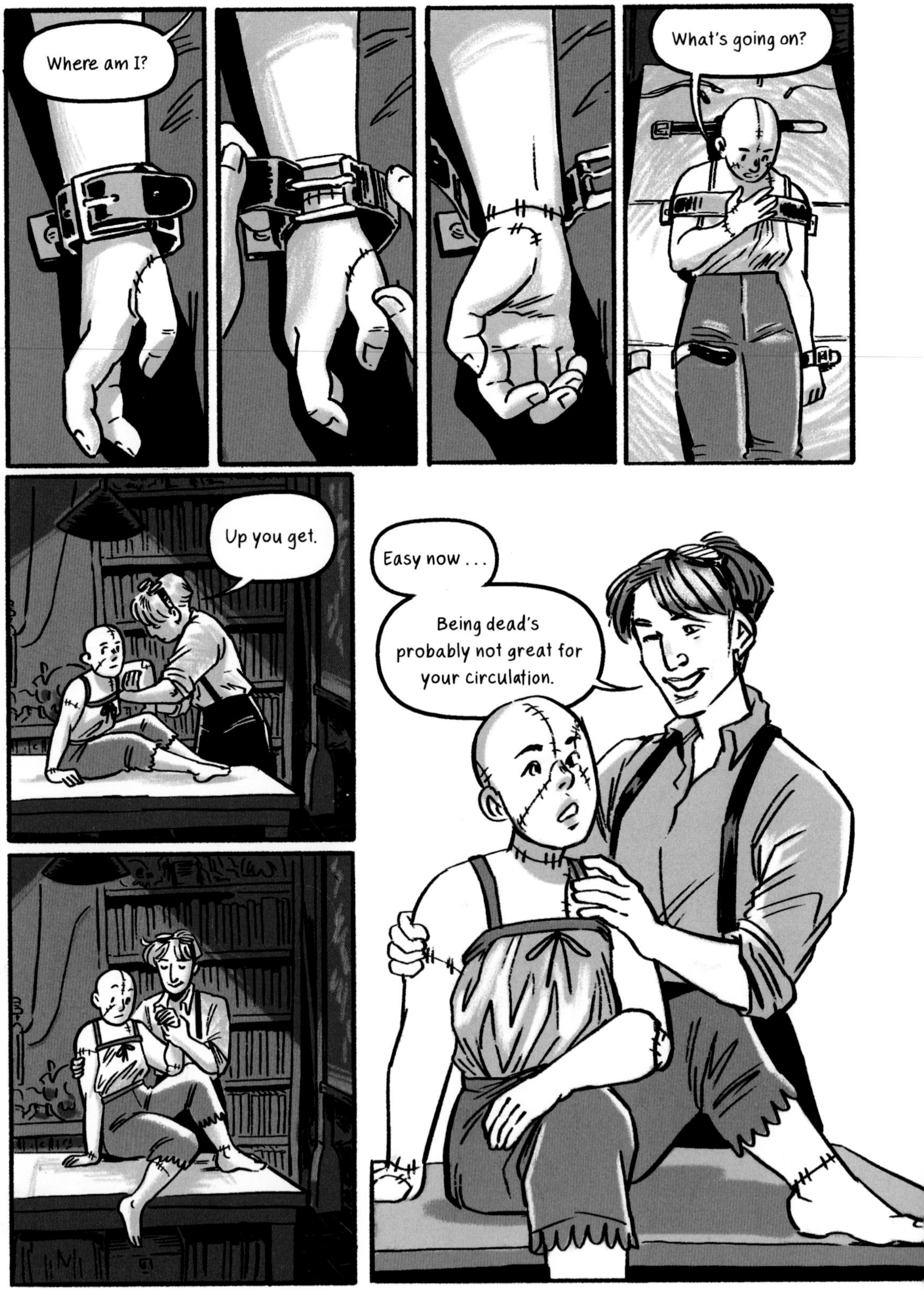
Where am I?
What's going on?
Up you get.
Easy now . . .
Being dead's probably not great for your circulation.

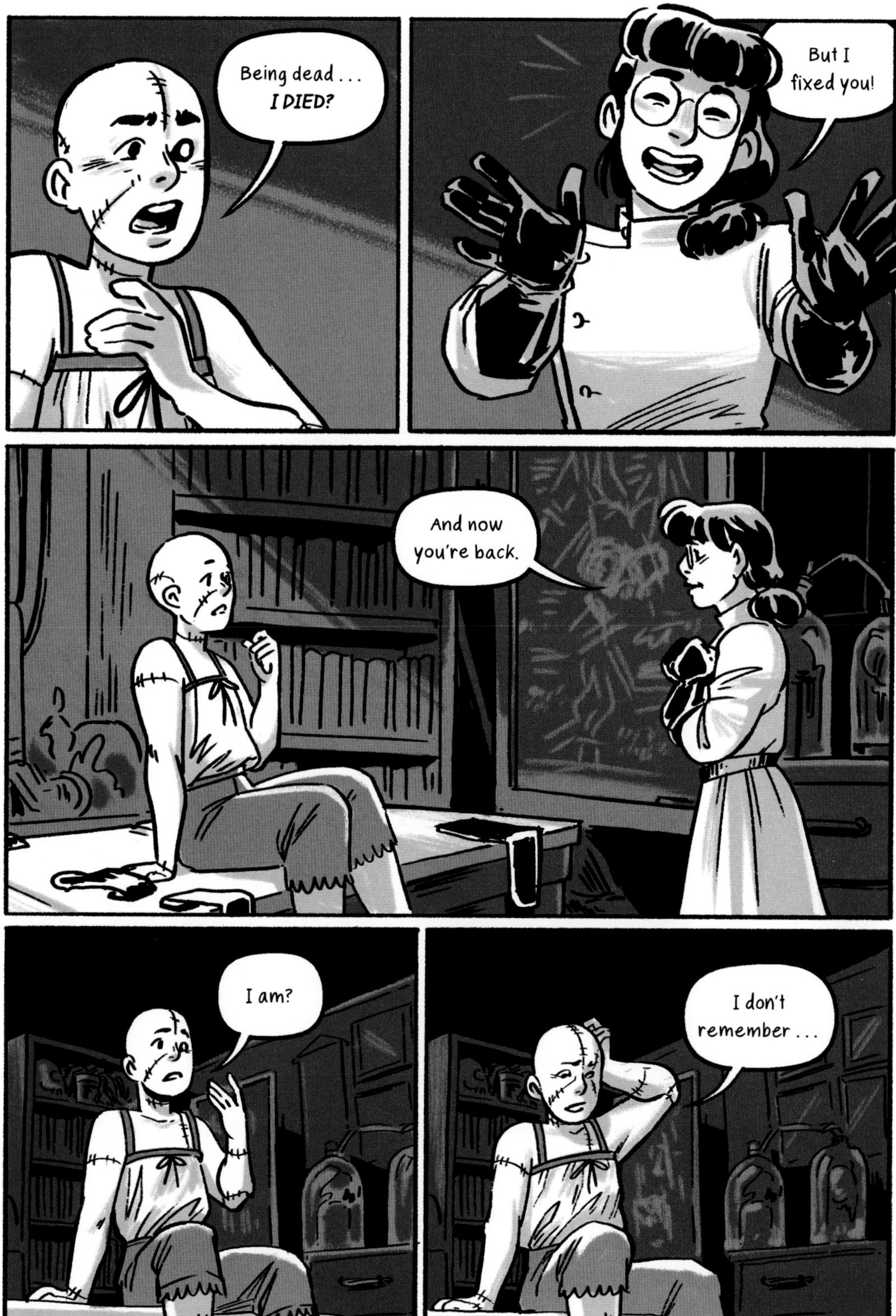
Being dead . . . I DIED?
But I fixed you!
And now you're back.
I am?
I don't remember . . .

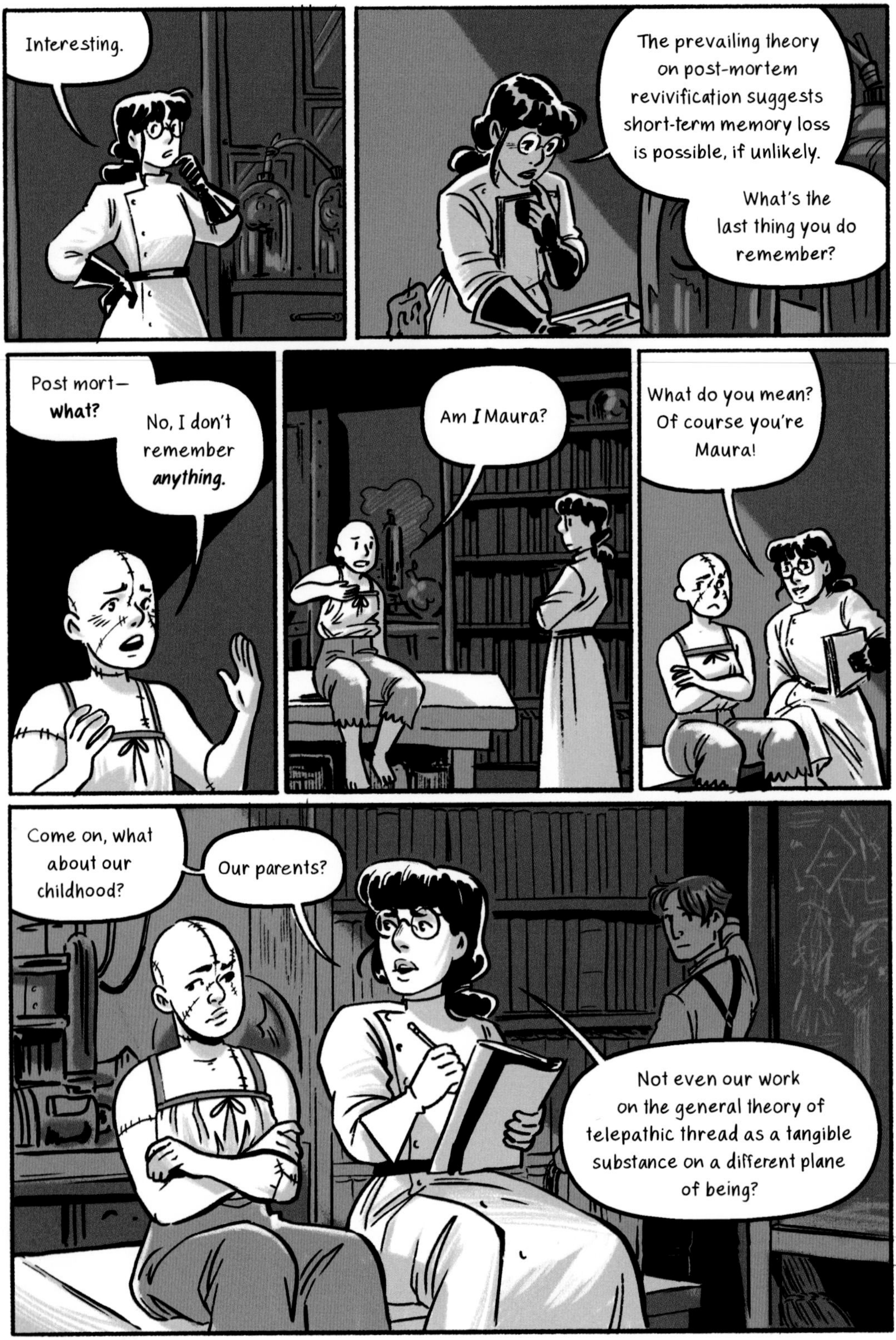
Interesting.
The prevailing theory on post-mortem revivification suggests short-term memory loss is possible, if unlikely.
What's the last thing you do remember?
Post mort— **what?**
No, I don't remember *anything.*
Am *I* Maura?
What do you mean? Of course you're Maura!
Come on, what about our childhood?
Our parents?
Not even our work on the general theory of telepathic thread as a tangible substance on a different plane of being?

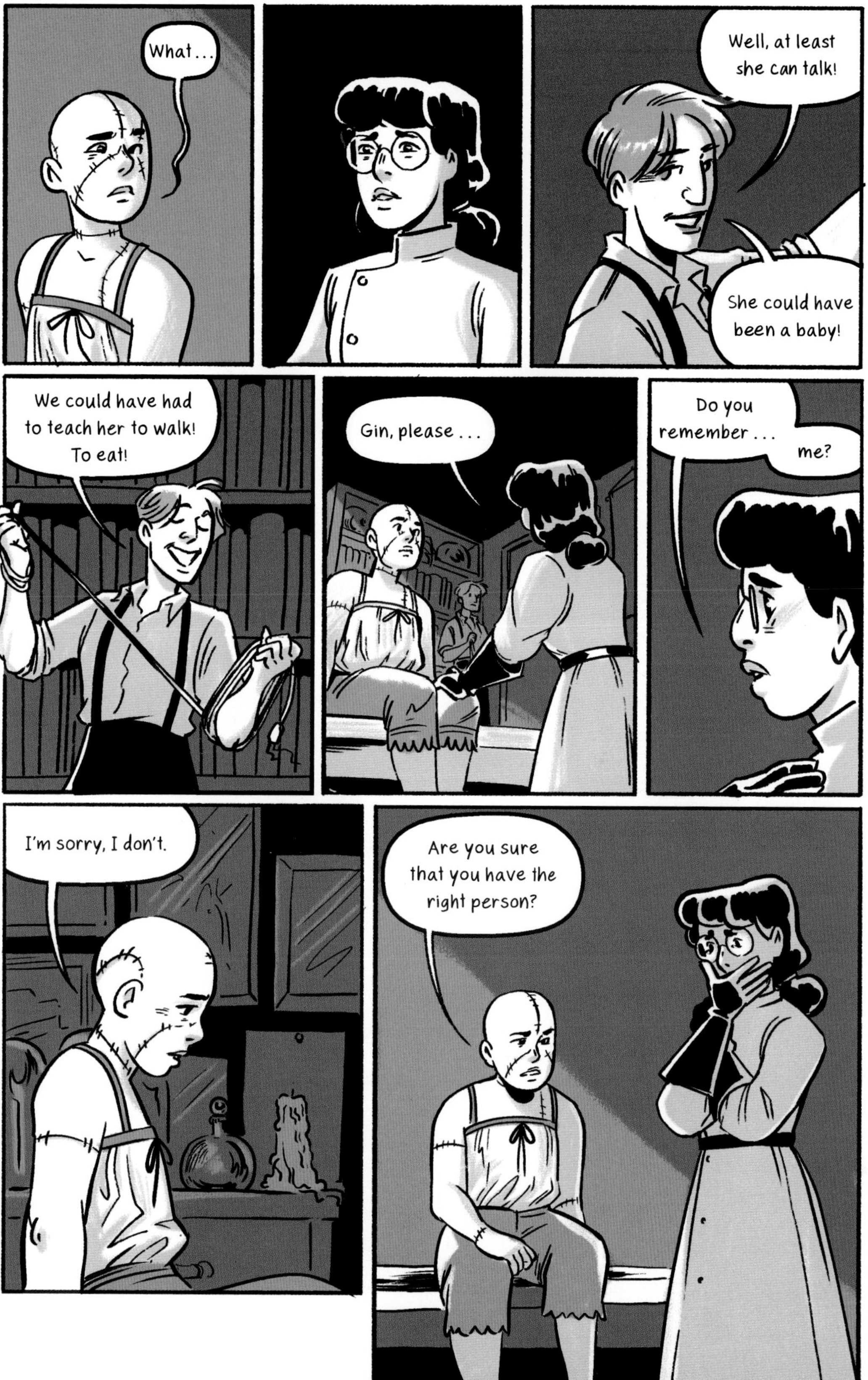
What...
Well, at least she can talk!
She could have been a baby!
We could have had to teach her to walk! To eat!
Gin, please . . .
Do you remember . . .
me?
I'm sorry, I don't.
Are you sure that you have the right person?

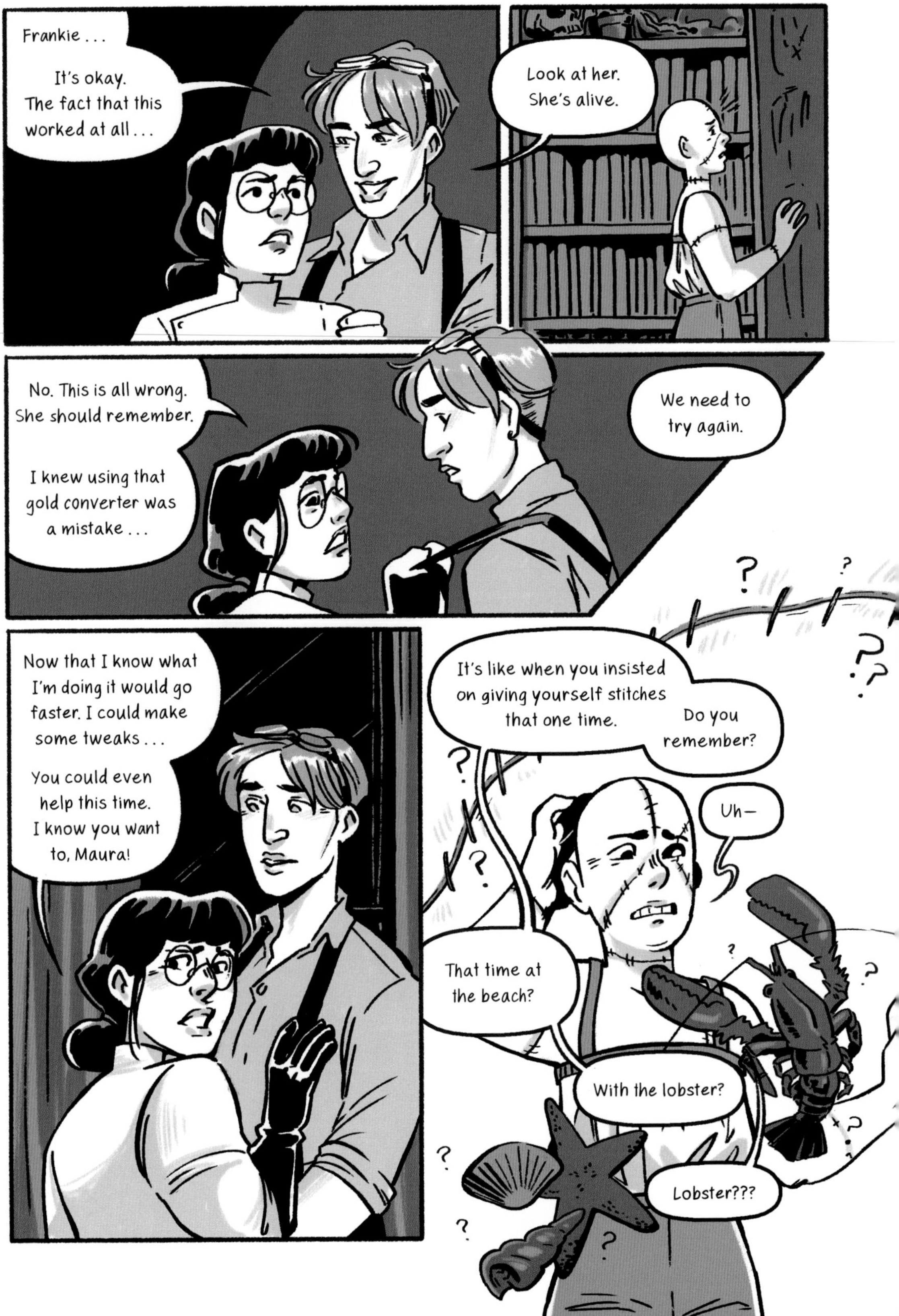
Frankie . . .
It's okay. The fact that this worked at all . . .
Look at her. She's alive.
No. This is all wrong. She should remember.
I knew using that gold converter was a mistake . . .
We need to try again.
Now that I know what I'm doing it would go faster. I could make some tweaks . . .
You could even help this time. I know you want to, Maura!
It's like when you insisted on giving yourself stitches that one time.
Do you remember?
Uh—
That time at the beach?
With the lobster?
Lobster???

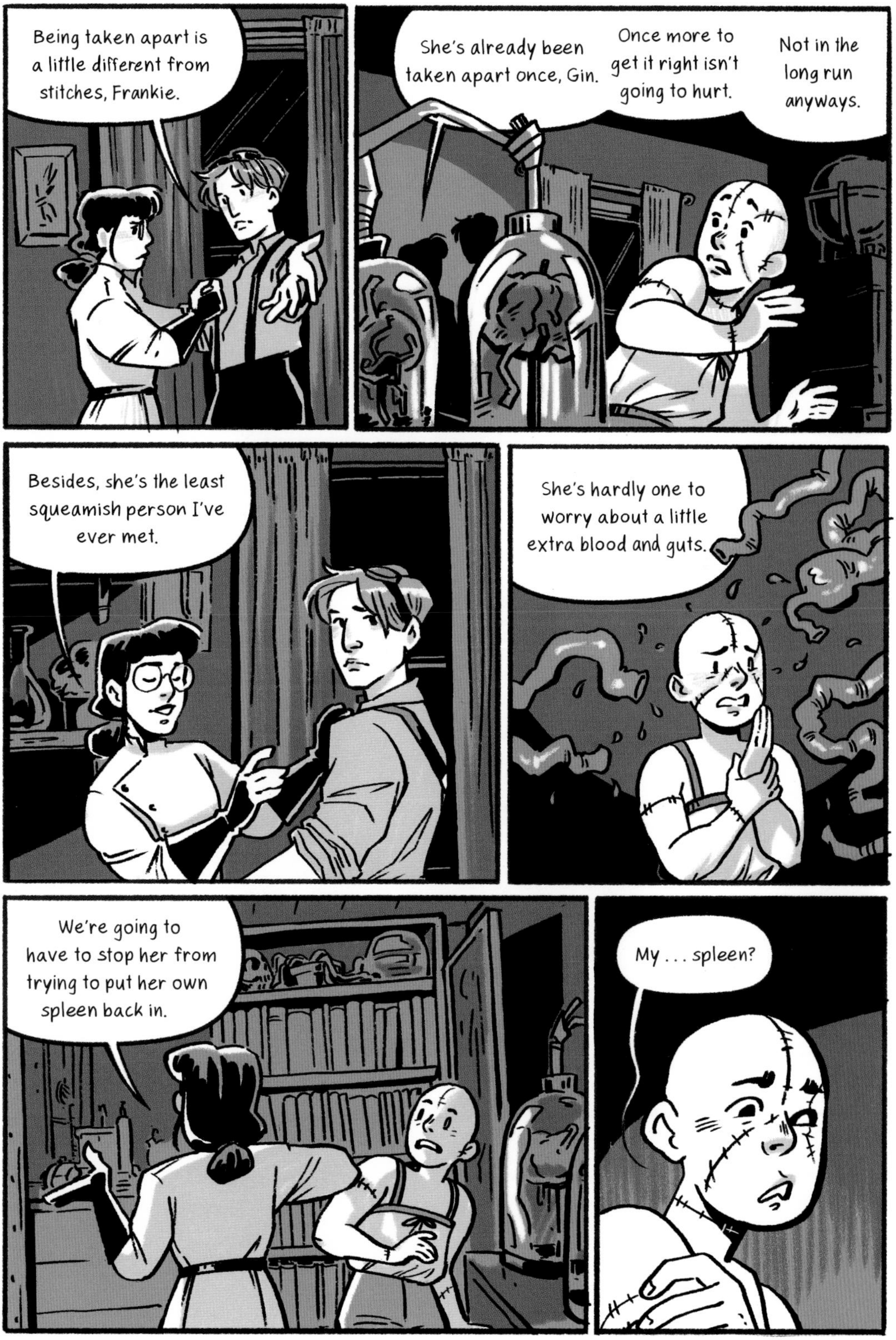
Being taken apart is a little different from stitches, Frankie.
She's already been taken apart once, Gin.
Once more to get it right isn't going to hurt.
Not in the long run anyways.
Besides, she's the least squeamish person I've ever met.
She's hardly one to worry about a little extra blood and guts.
We're going to have to stop her from trying to put her own spleen back in.
My . . . spleen?

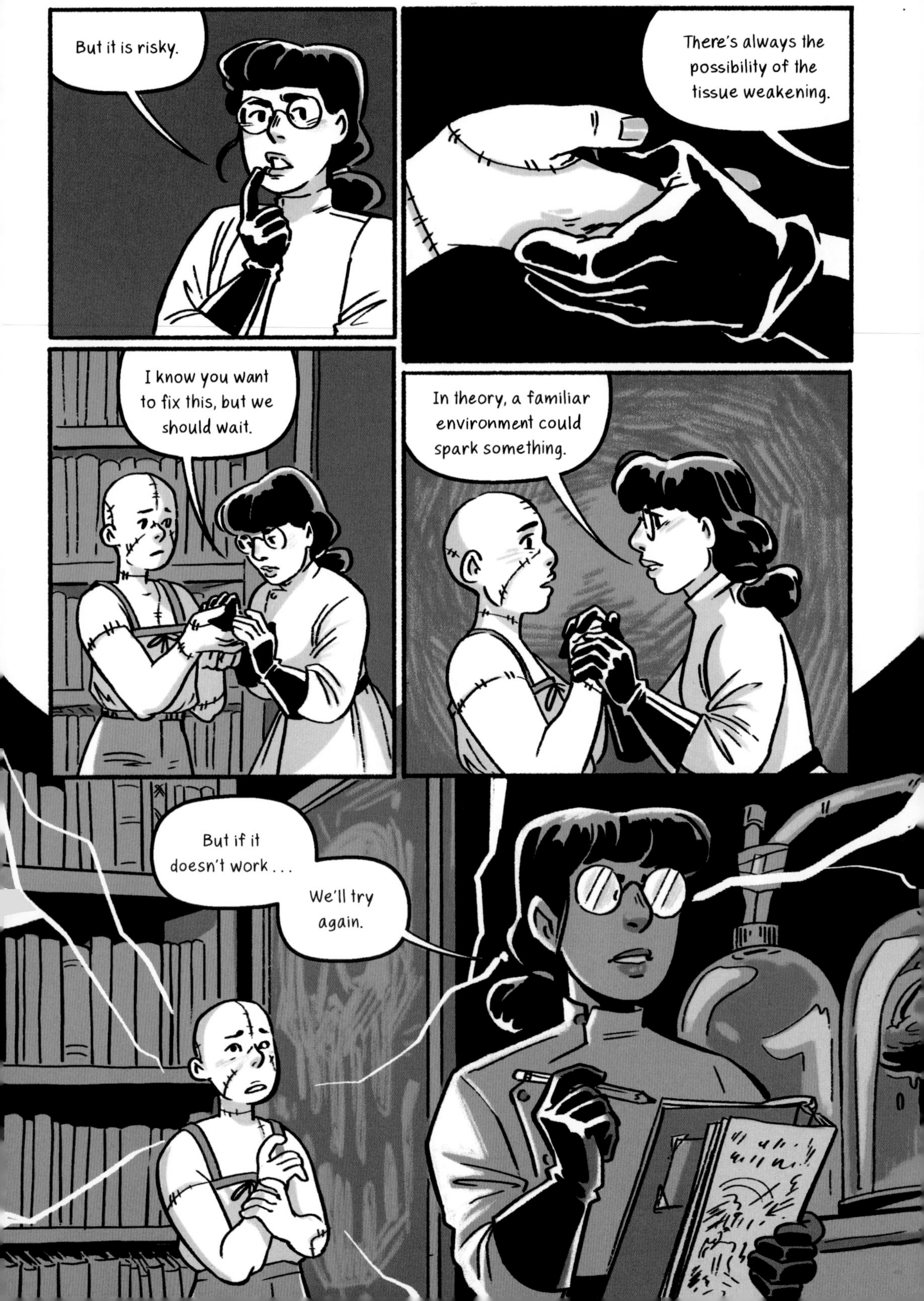
But it is risky.
There's always the possibility of the tissue weakening.
I know you want to fix this, but we should wait.
In theory, a familiar environment could spark something.
But if it doesn't work . . .
We'll try again.

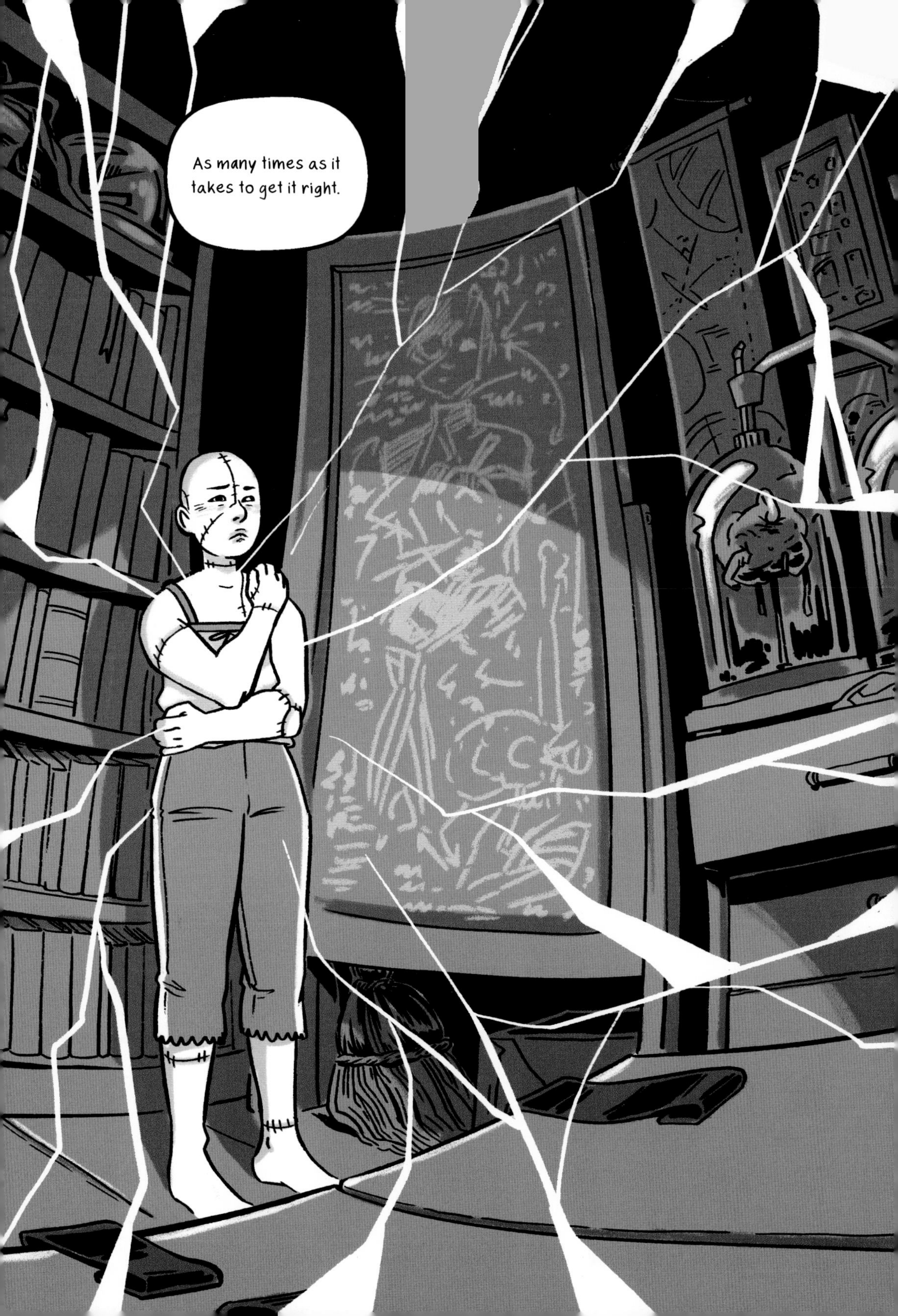
As many times as it takes to get it right.

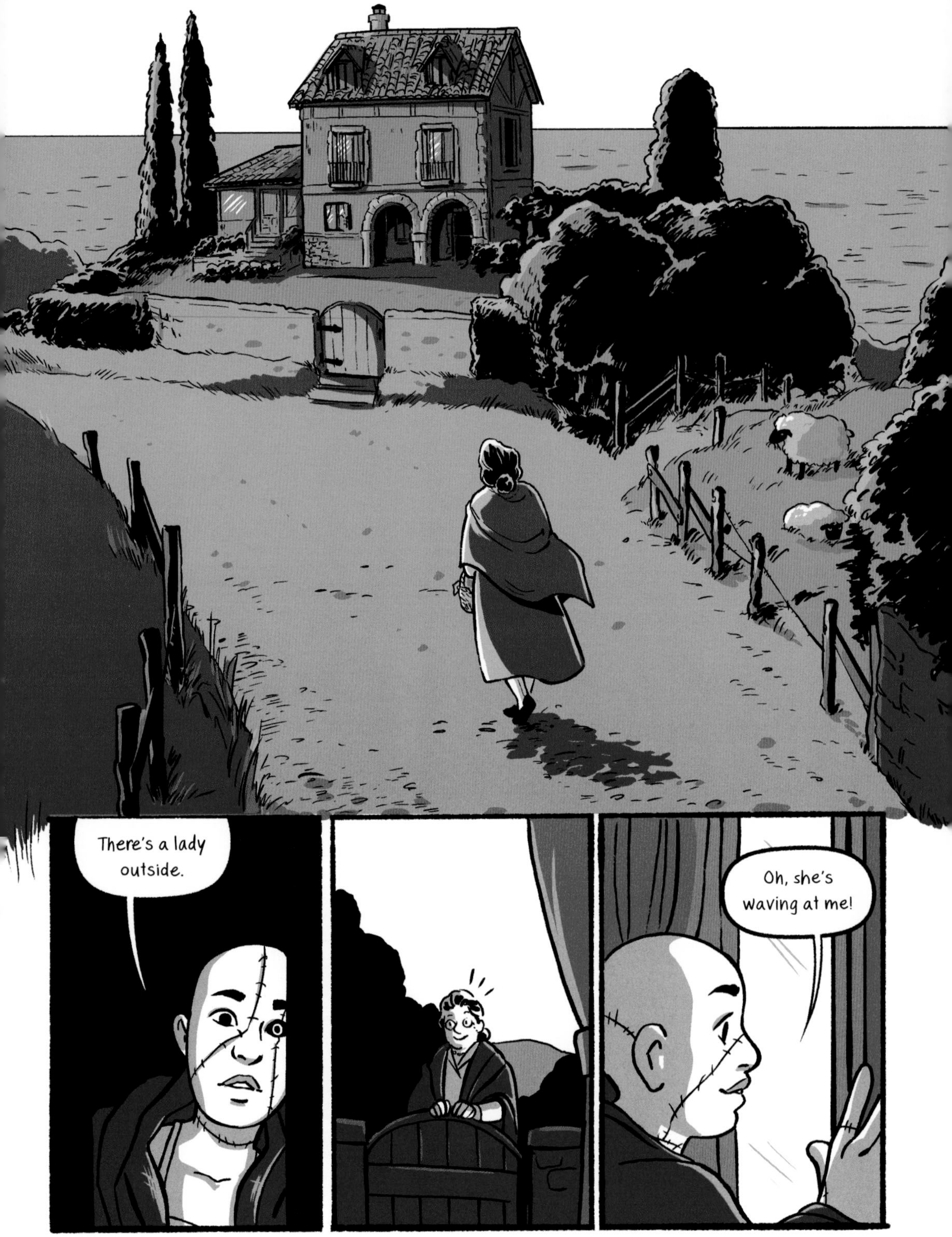
There's a lady outside.
Oh, she's waving at me!

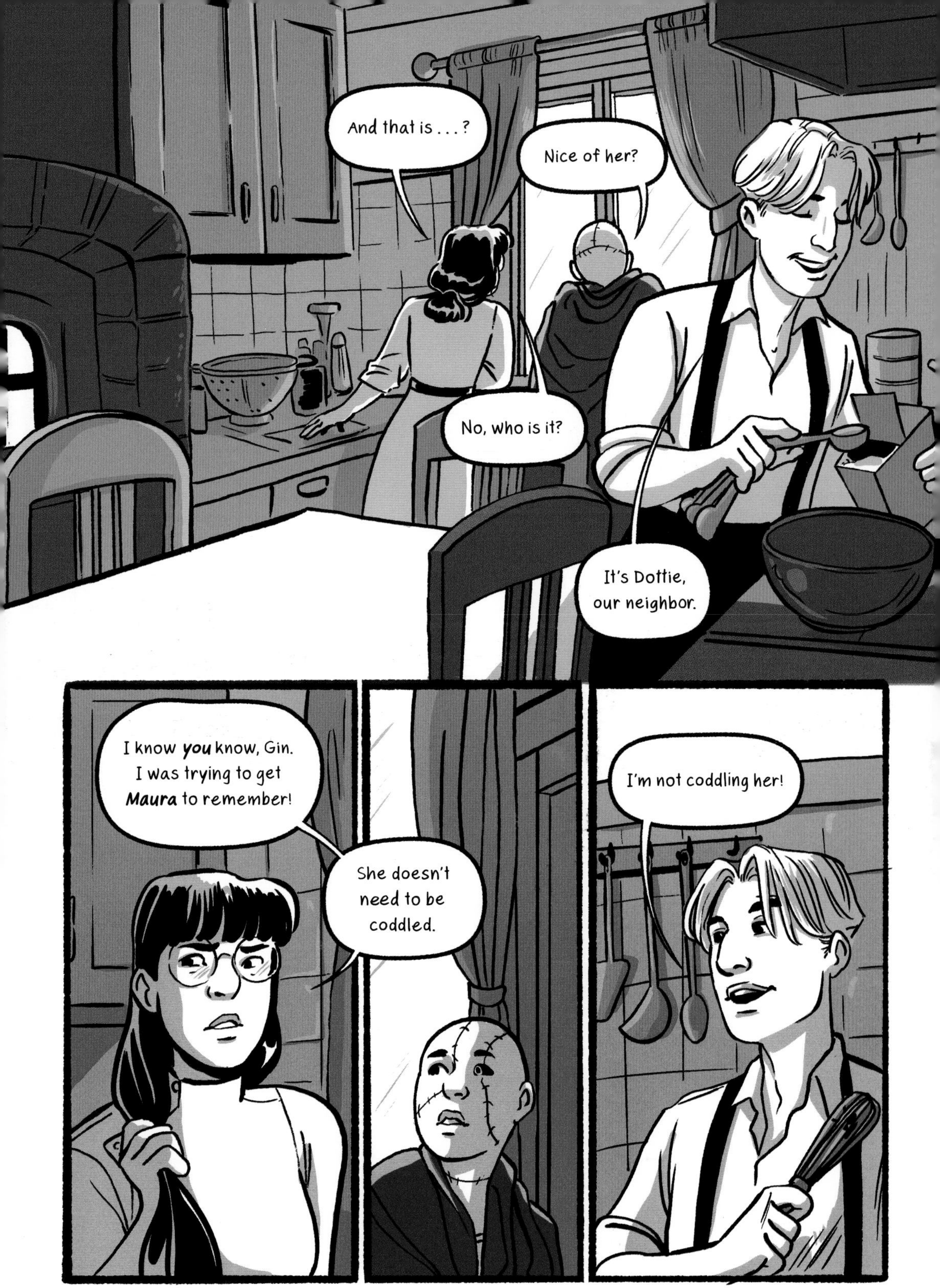
And that is . . . ?
Nice of her?
No, who is it?
It's Dottie, our neighbor.
I know *you* know, Gin. I was trying to get **Maura** to remember!
She doesn't need to be coddled.
I'm not coddling her!

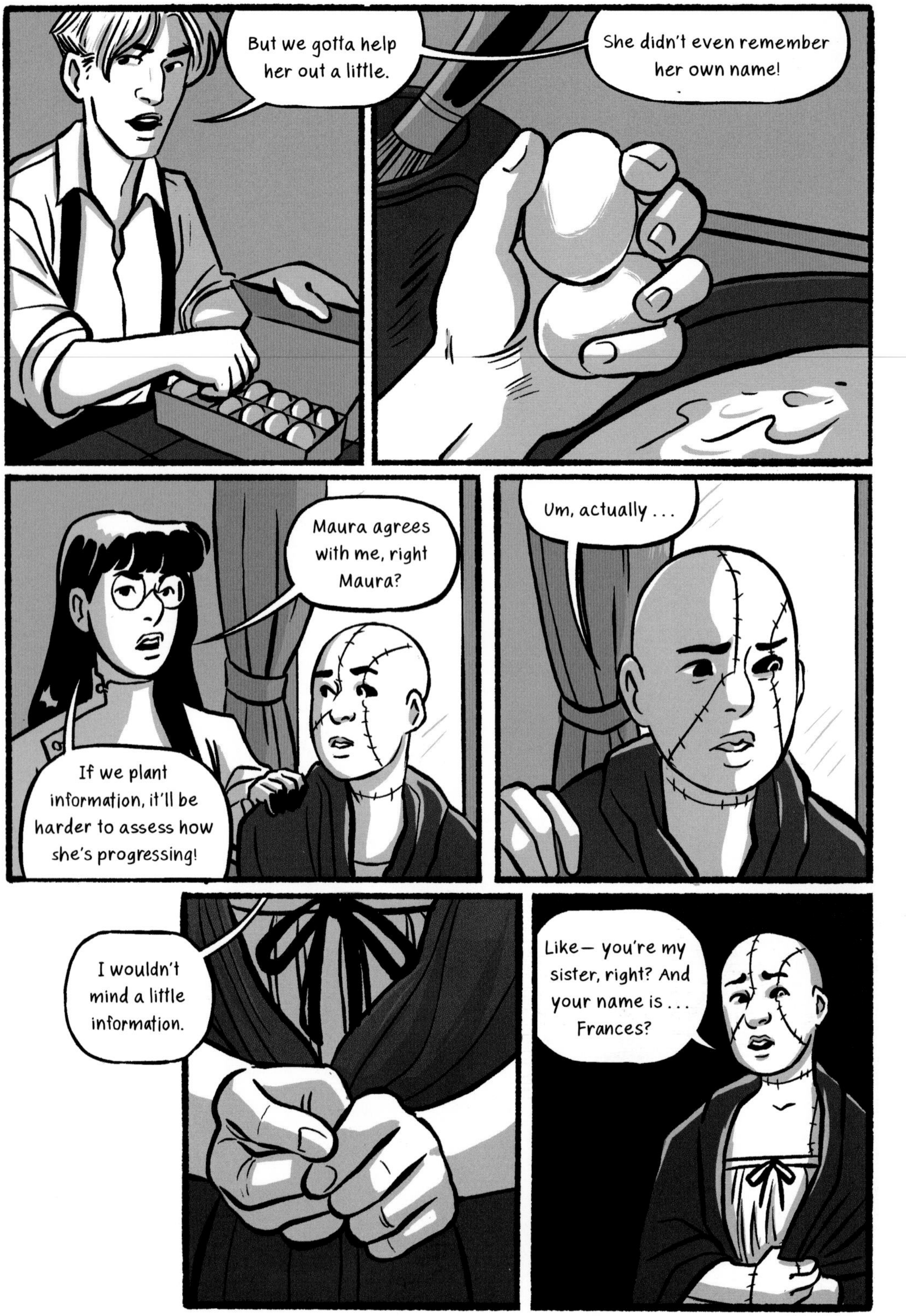

But we gotta help her out a little.
She didn't even remember her own name!
Maura agrees with me, right Maura?
If we plant information, it'll be harder to assess how she's progressing!
Um, actually . . .
I wouldn't mind a little information.
Like— you're my sister, right? And your name is . . . Frances?

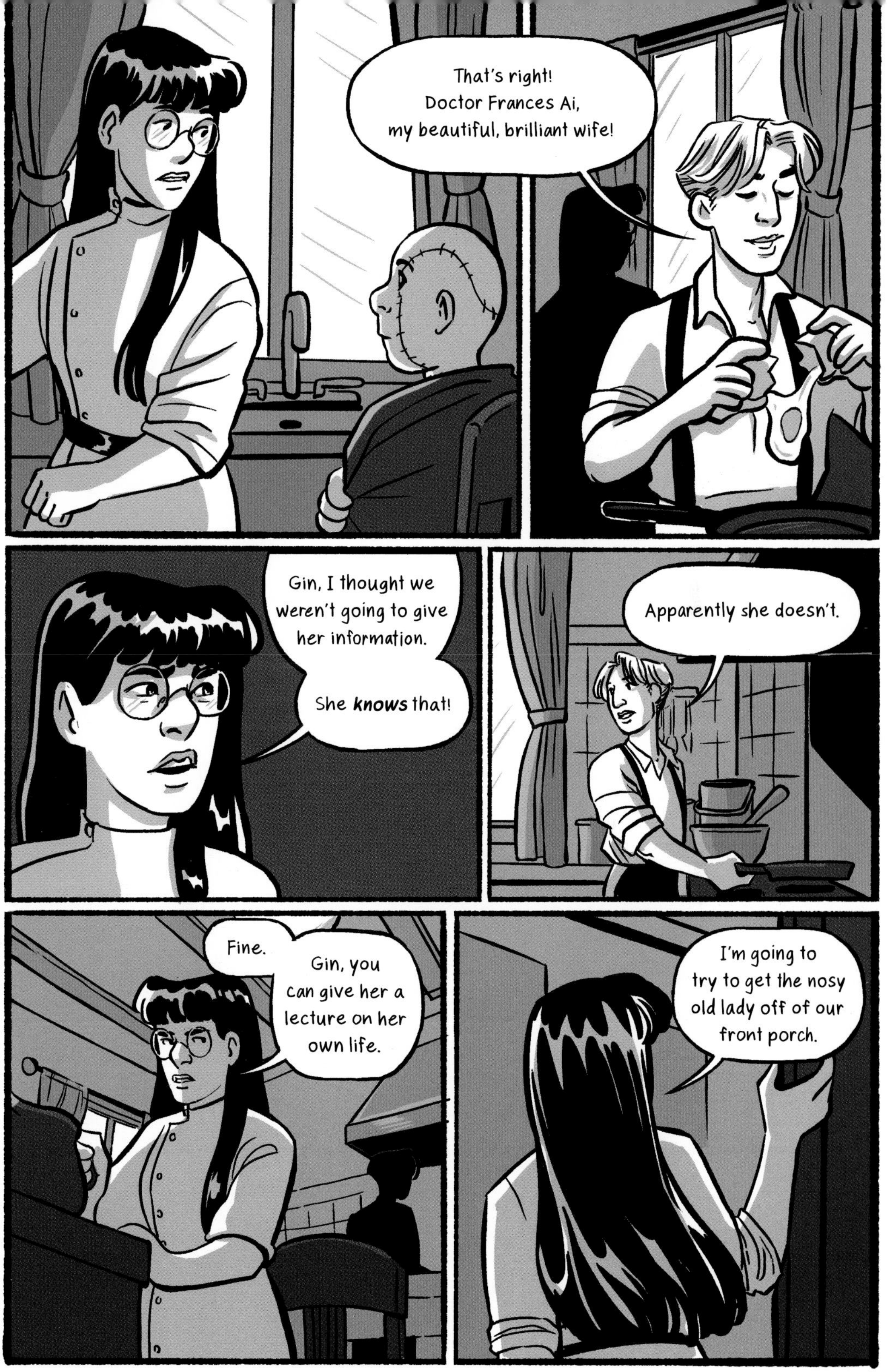
That's right!
Doctor Frances Ai,
my beautiful, brilliant wife!
Gin, I thought we weren't going to give her information.
She **knows** that!
Apparently she doesn't.
Fine.
Gin, you can give her a lecture on her own life.
I'm going to try to get the nosy old lady off of our front porch.

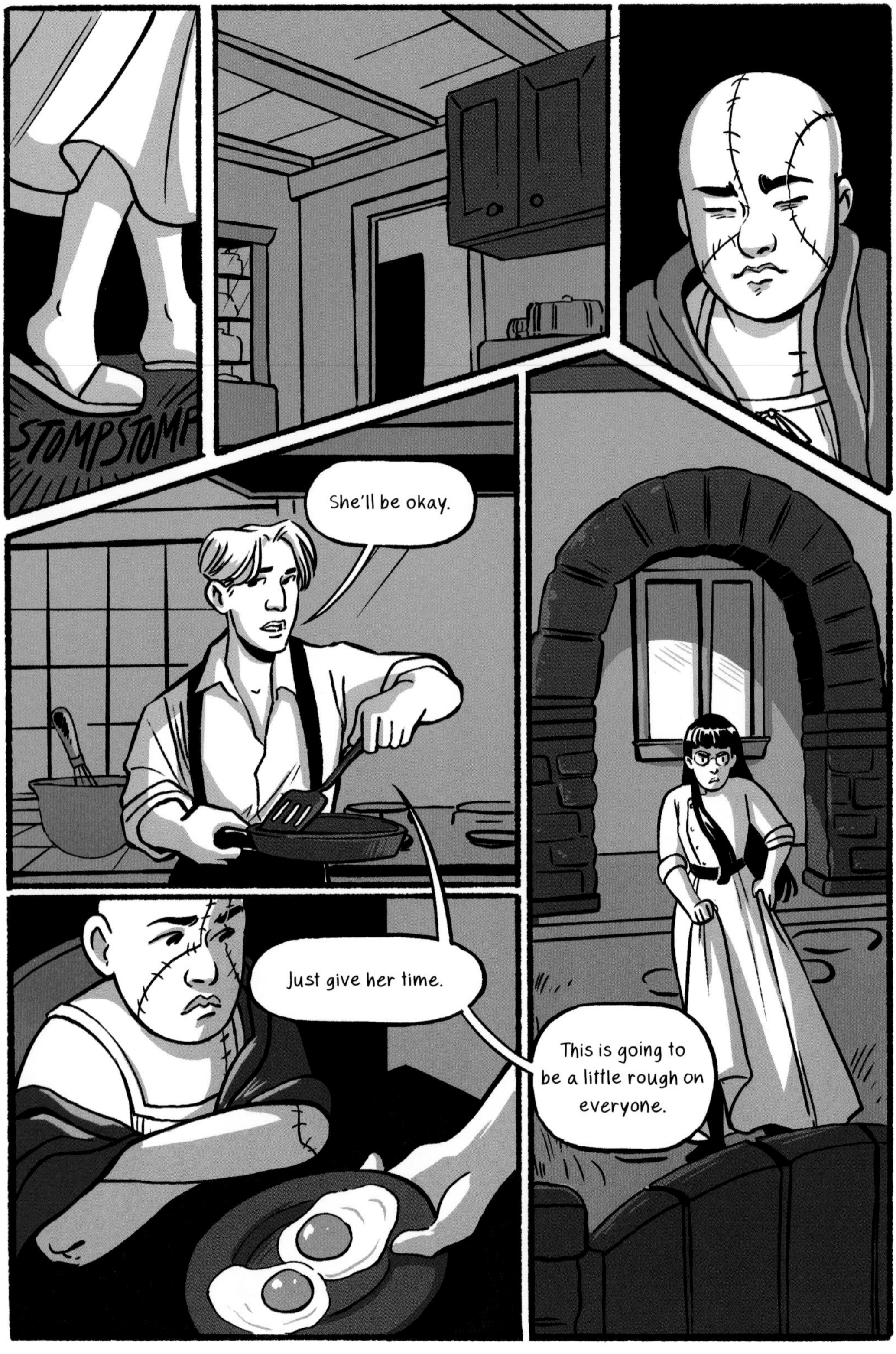
STOMPSTOMP
She'll be okay.
Just give her time.
This is going to be a little rough on everyone.

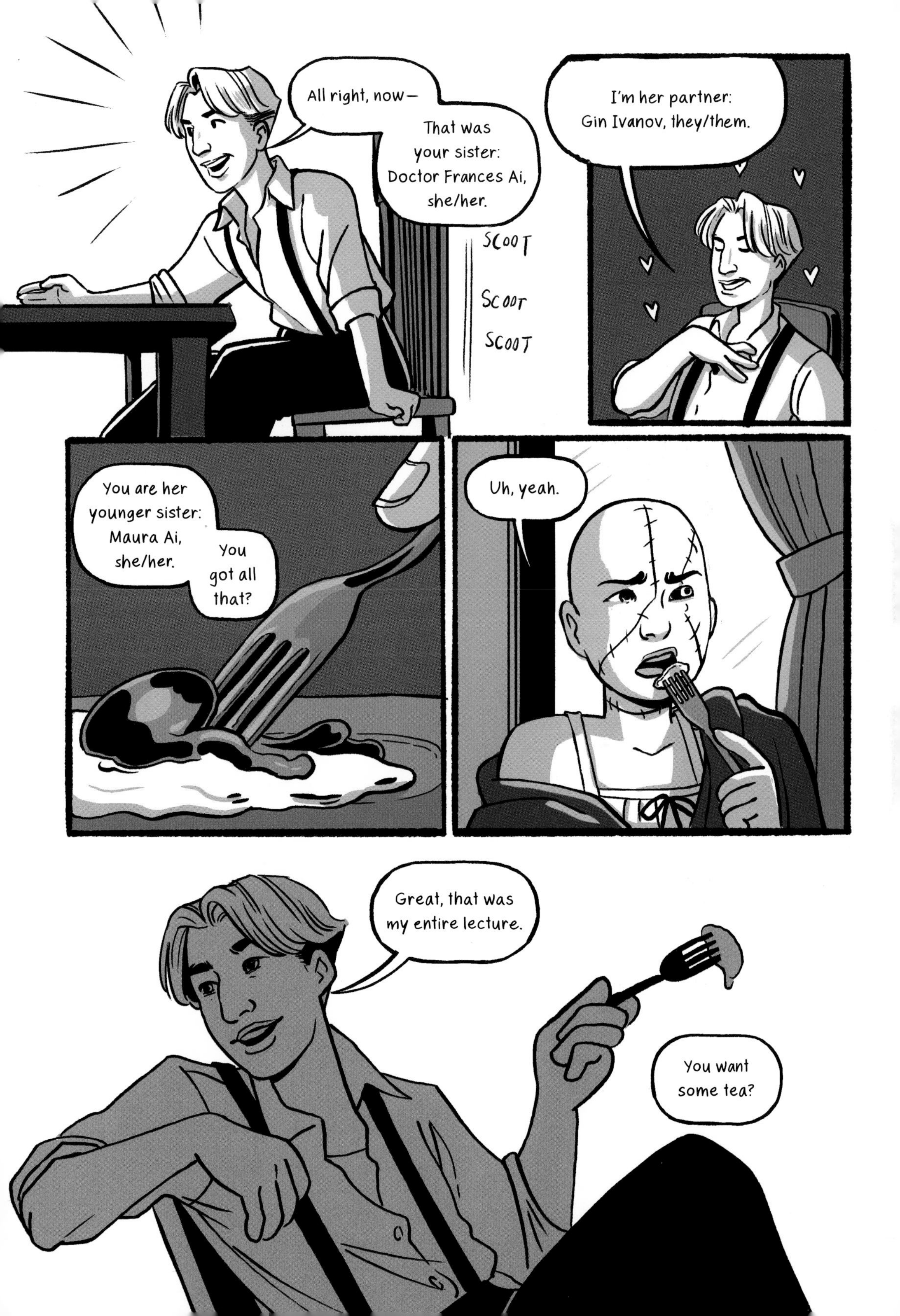
All right, now—
That was your sister: Doctor Frances Ai, she/her.
SCOOT
SCOOT
SCOOT
I'm her partner: Gin Ivanov, they/them.
You are her younger sister: Maura Ai, she/her.
You got all that?
Uh, yeah.
Great, that was my entire lecture.
You want some tea?

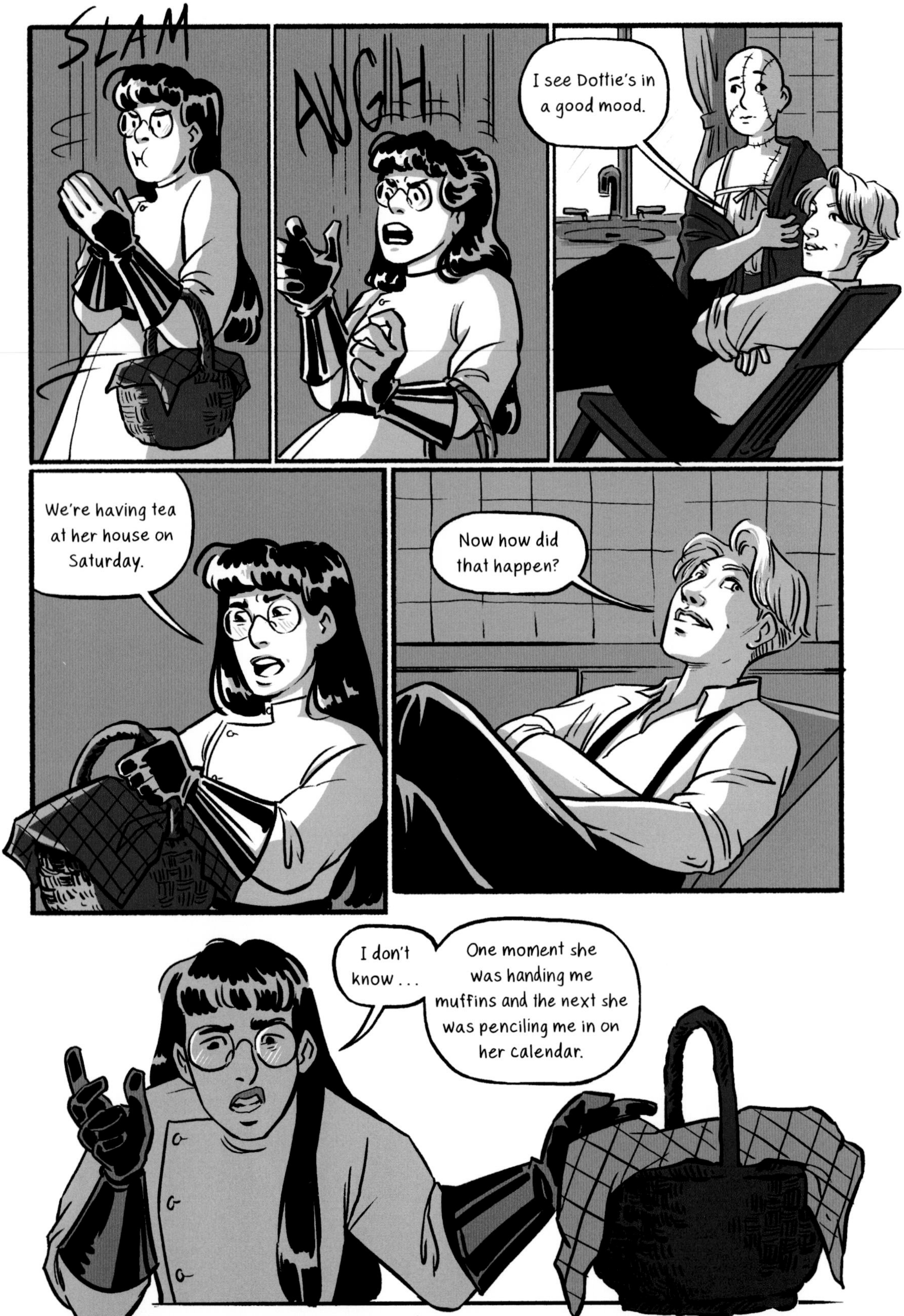
SLAM
AUGH
I see Dottie's in a good mood.
We're having tea at her house on Saturday.
Now how did that happen?
I don't know . . .
One moment she was handing me muffins and the next she was penciling me in on her calendar.

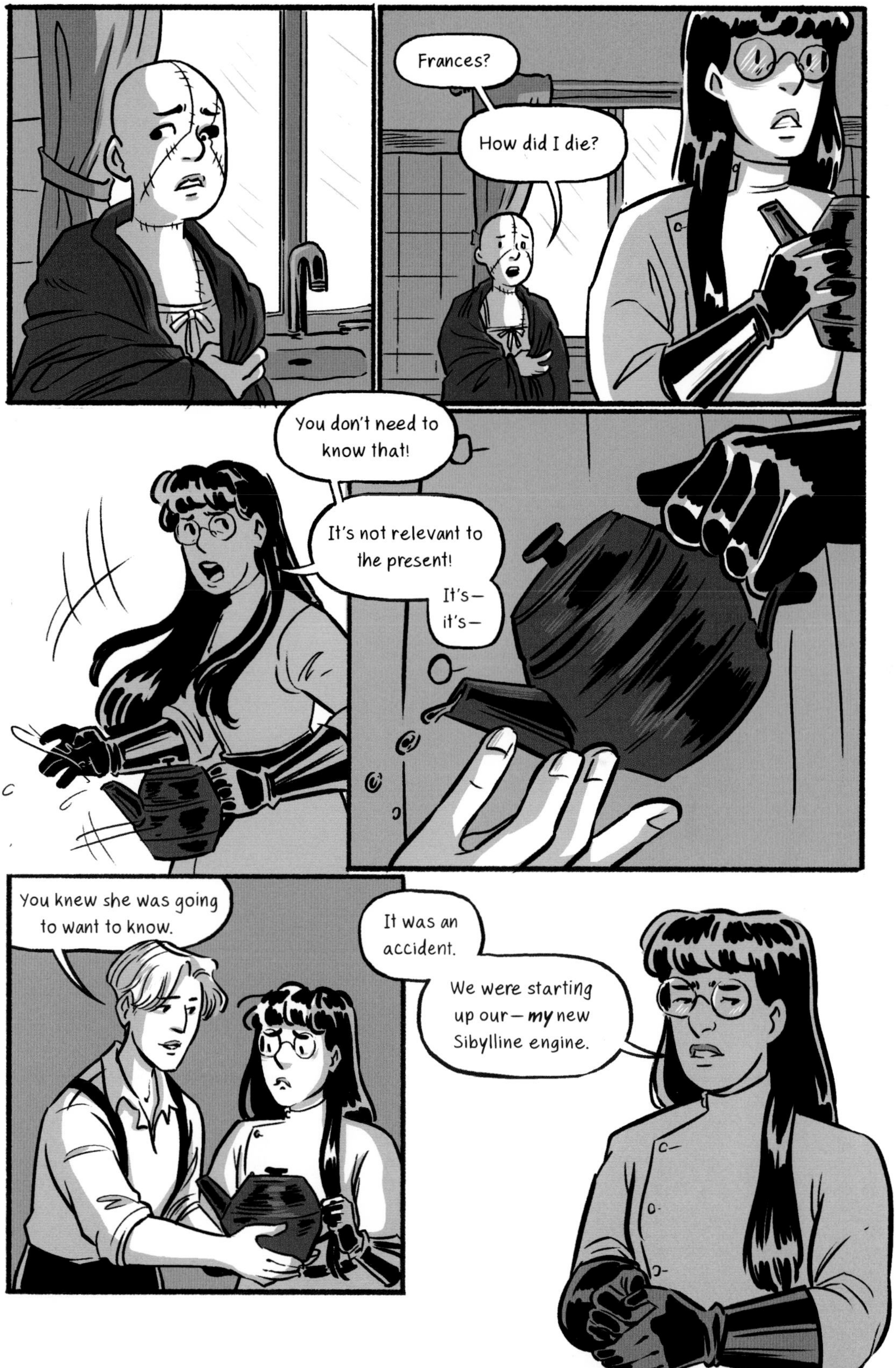
Frances?
How did I die?
You don't need to know that!
It's not relevant to the present!
It's— it's—
You knew she was going to want to know.
It was an accident.
We were starting up our—*my* new Sibylline engine.

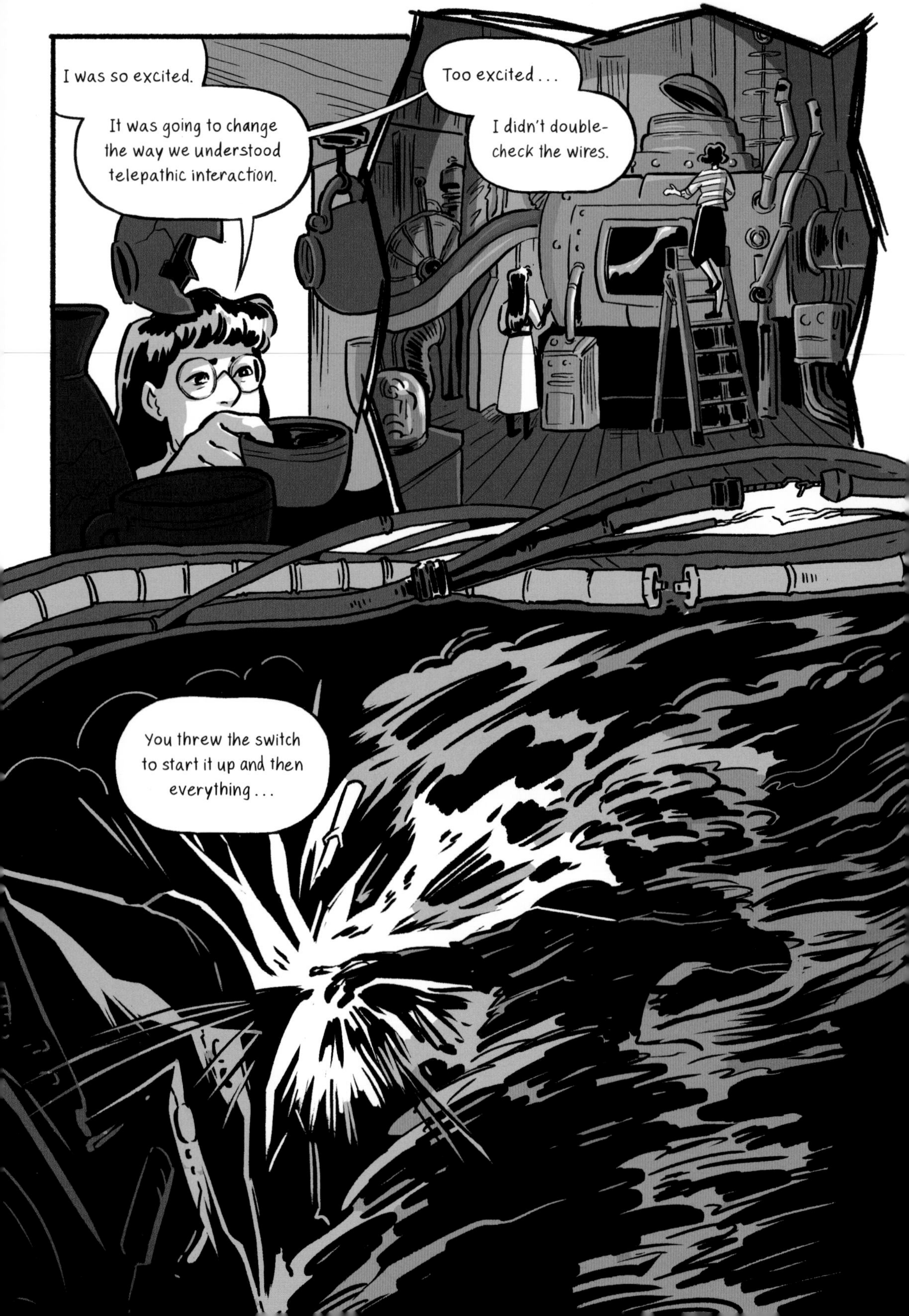
I was so excited.
It was going to change the way we understood telepathic interaction.
Too excited . . .
I didn't double-check the wires.
You threw the switch to start it up and then everything . . .

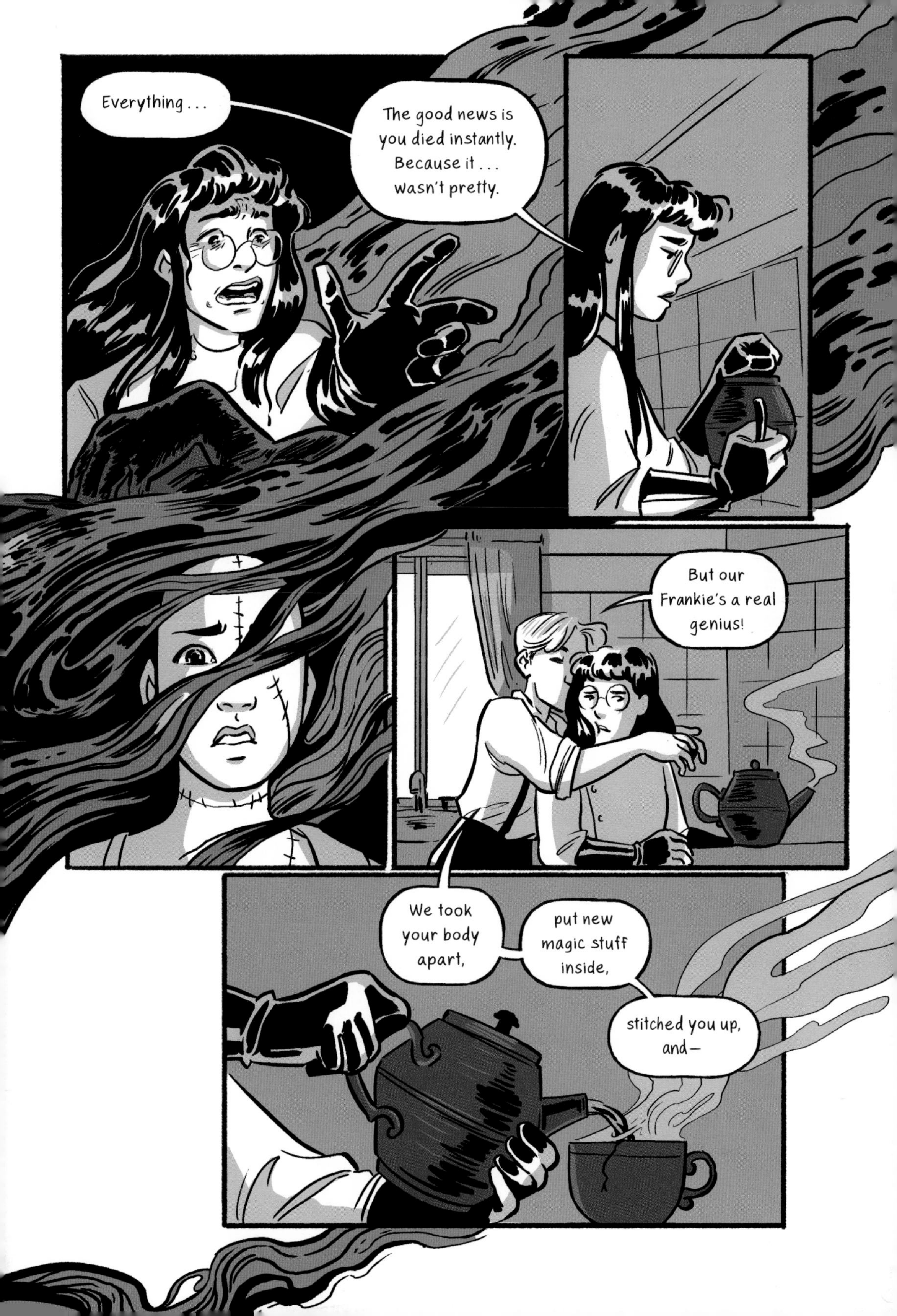
Everything . . .
The good news is you died instantly. Because it . . . wasn't pretty.
But our Frankie's a real genius!
We took your body apart,
put new magic stuff inside,
stitched you up, and—

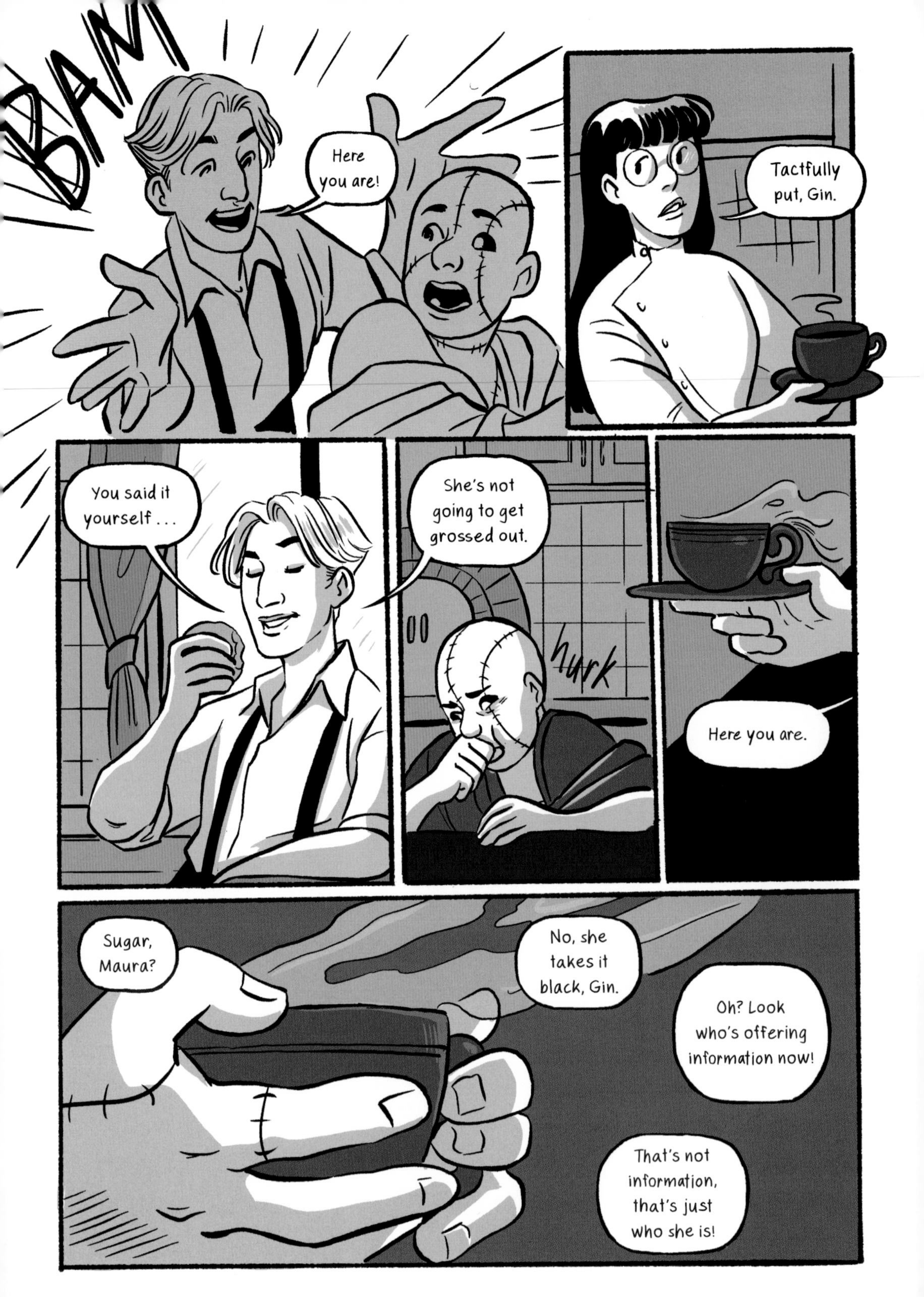
BAM
Here you are!
Tactfully put, Gin.
You said it yourself . . .
She's not going to get grossed out.
hurk
Here you are.
Sugar, Maura?
No, she takes it black, Gin.
Oh? Look who's offering information now!
That's not information, that's just who she is!

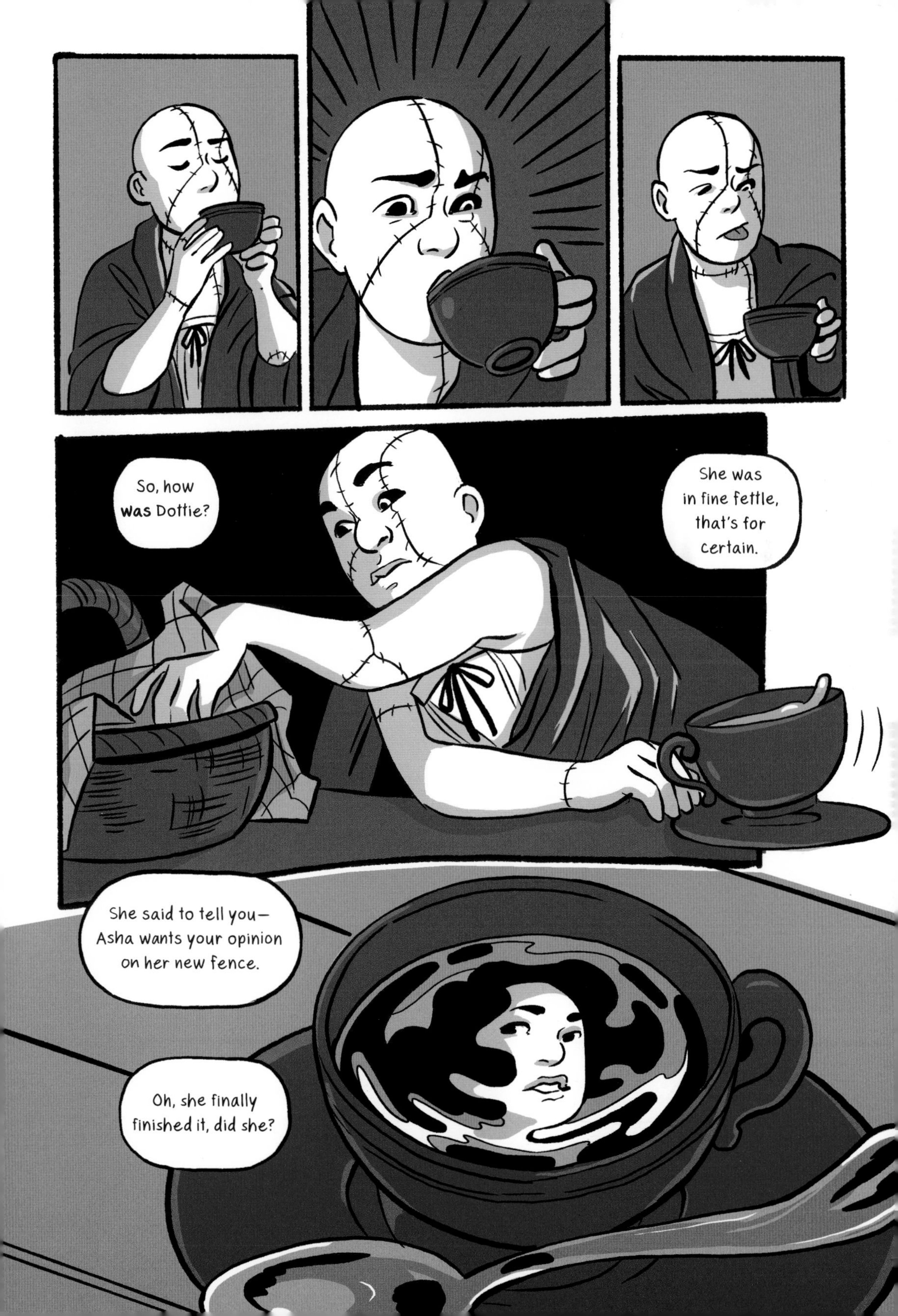
So, how **was** Dottie?
She was in fine fettle, that's for certain.
She said to tell you— Asha wants your opinion on her new fence.
Oh, she finally finished it, did she?

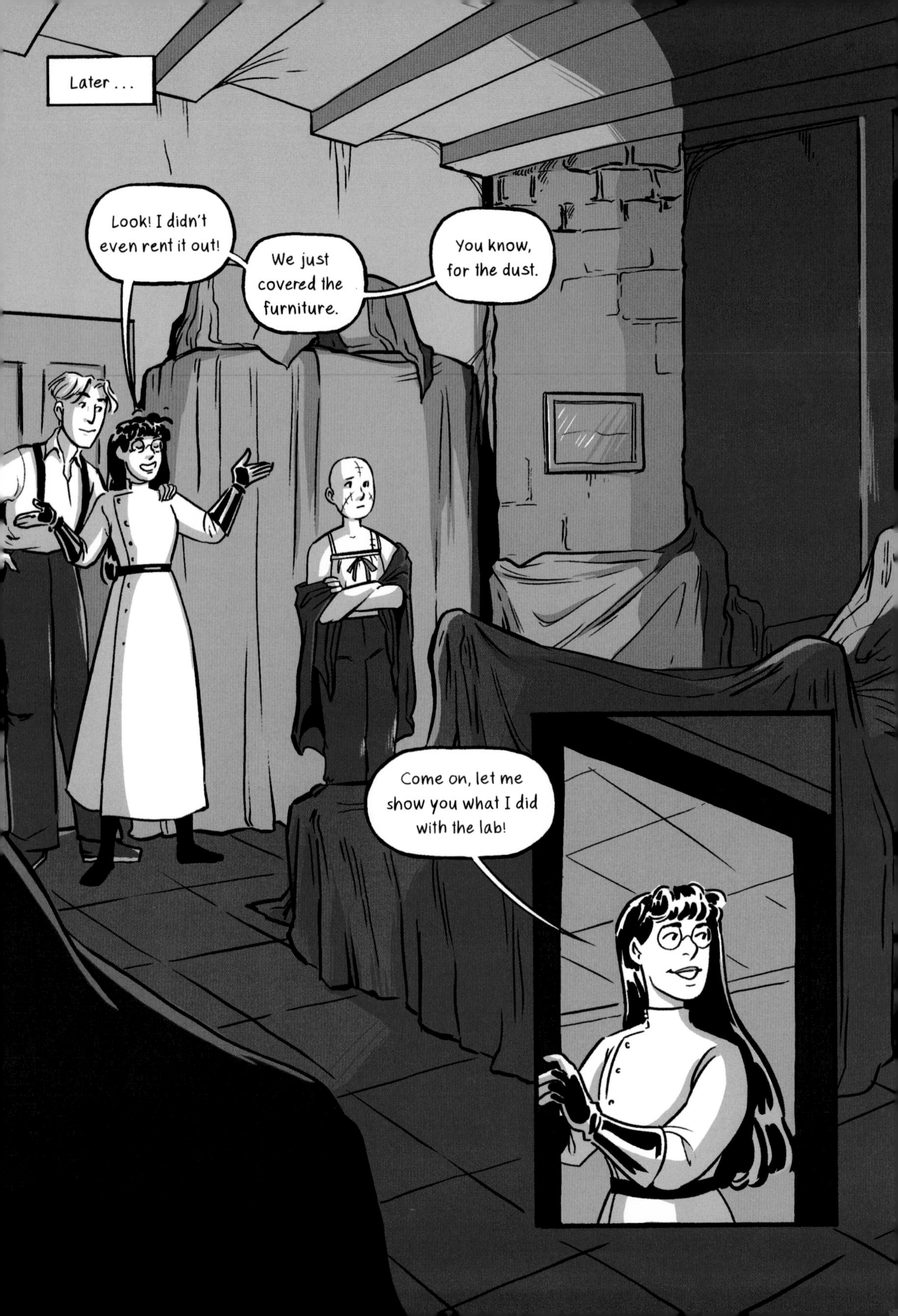
Later . . .
Look! I didn't even rent it out!
We just covered the furniture.
You know, for the dust.
Come on, let me show you what I did with the lab!

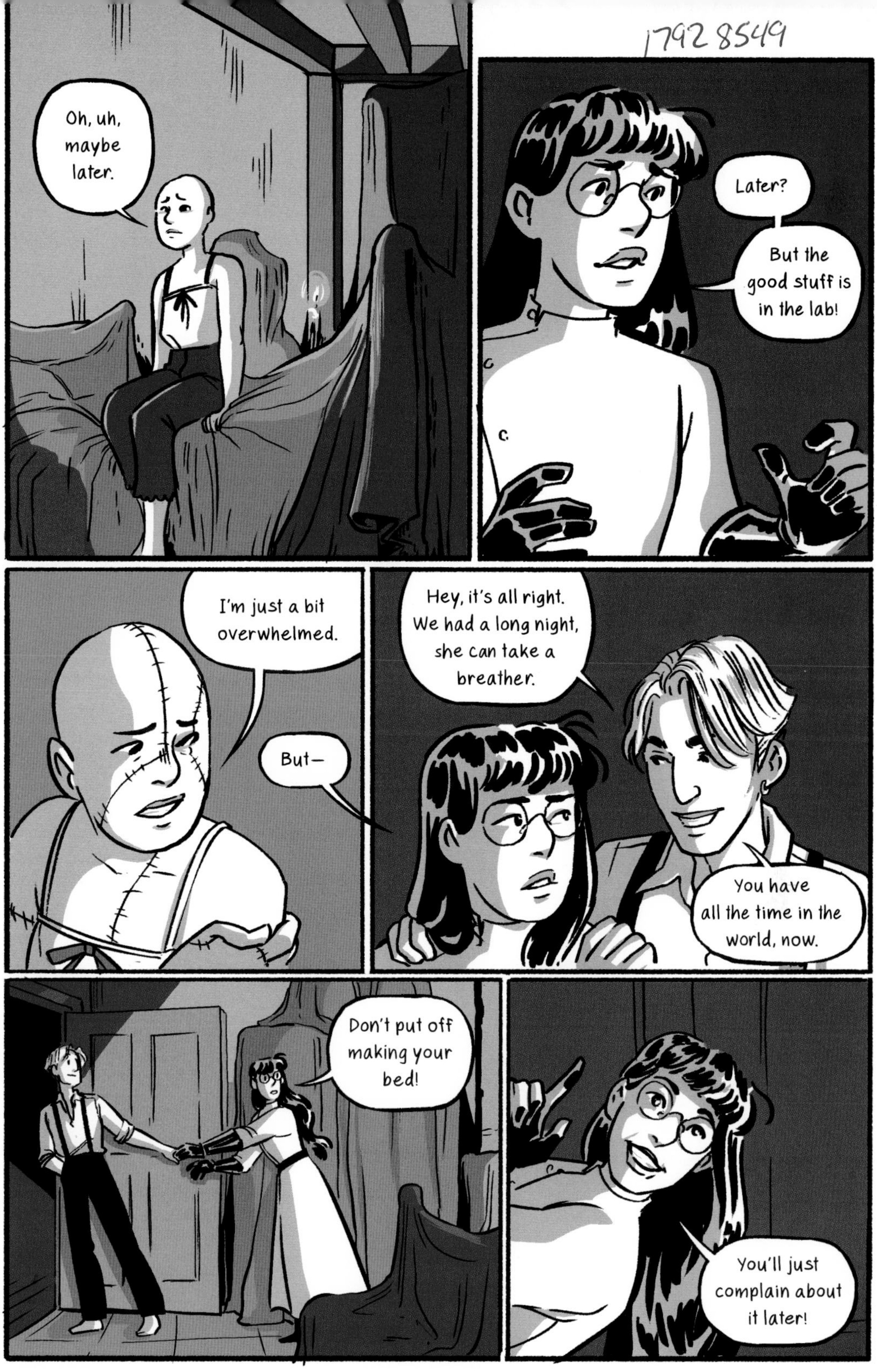

Oh, uh, maybe later.
Later?
But the good stuff is in the lab!
I'm just a bit overwhelmed.
But—
Hey, it's all right. We had a long night, she can take a breather.
You have all the time in the world, now.
Don't put off making your bed!
You'll just complain about it later!

17928549

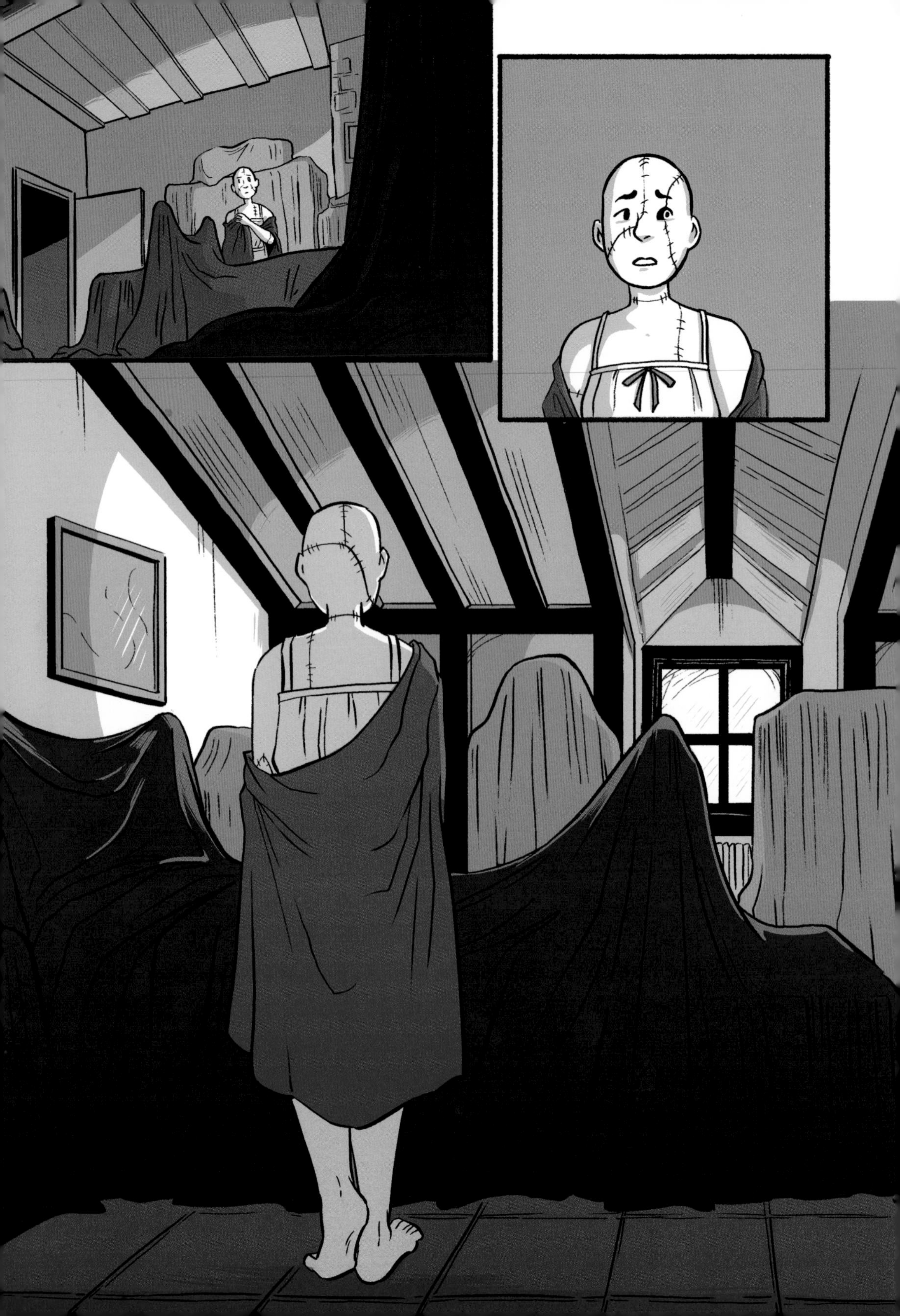

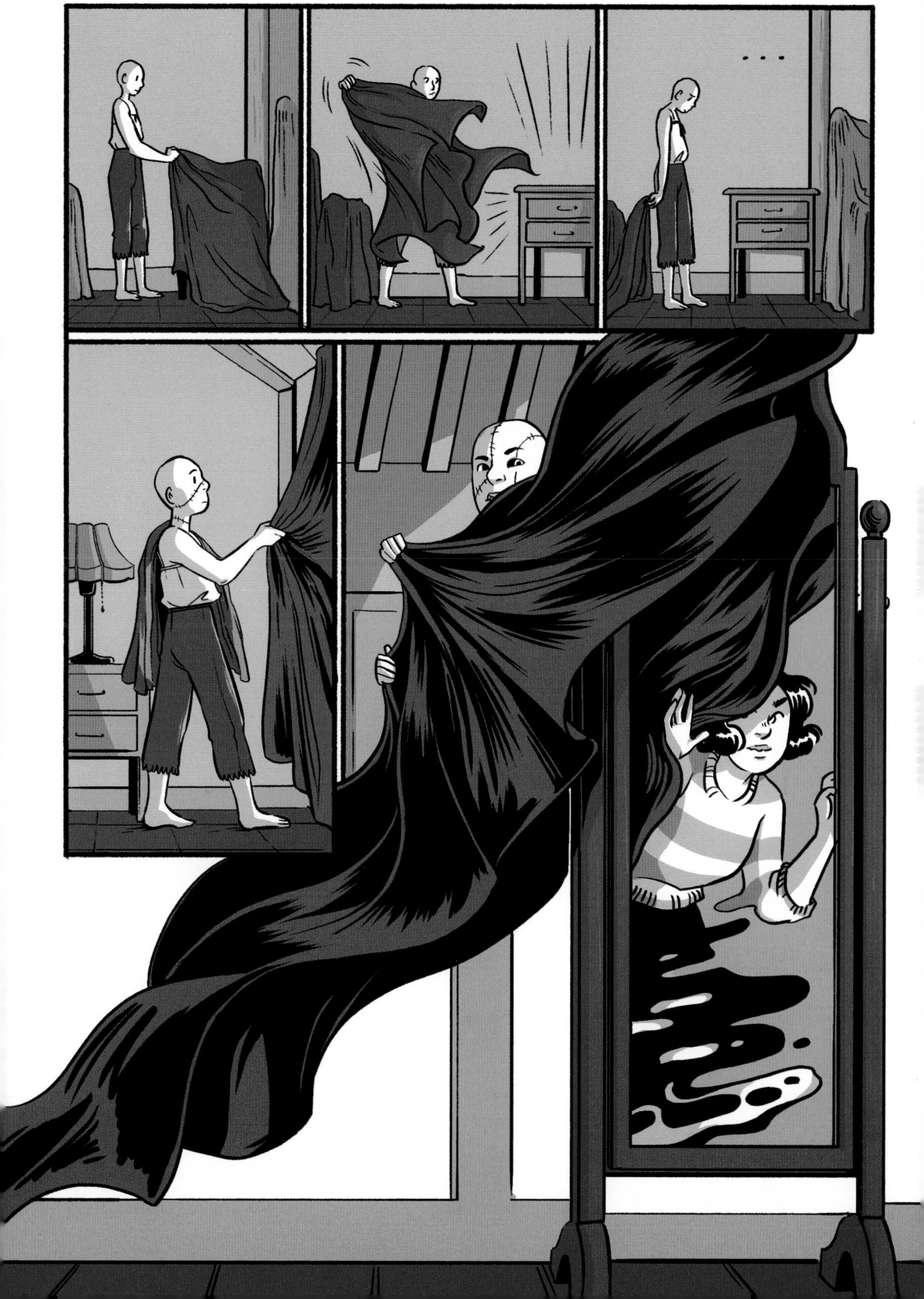
...

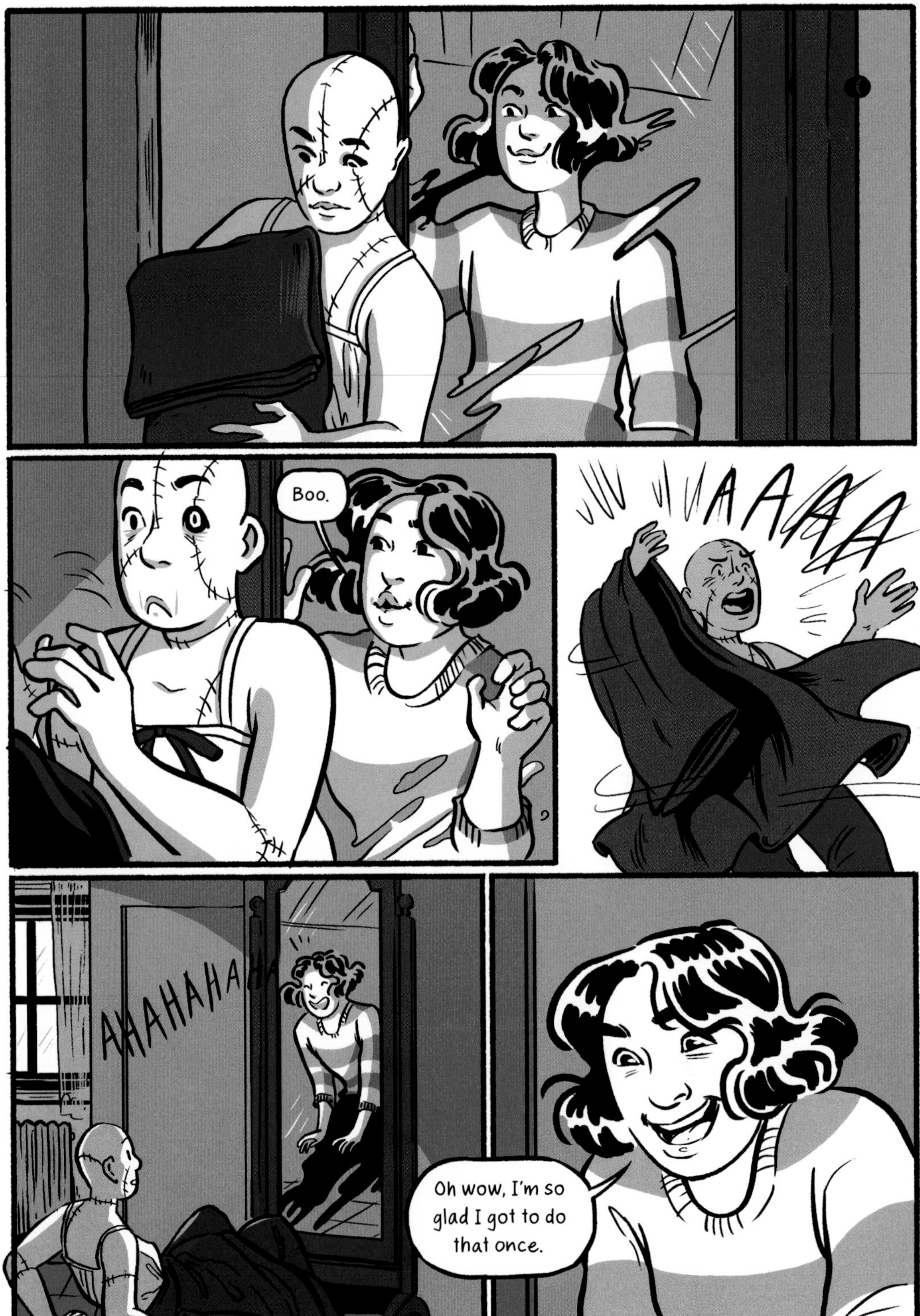
Boo.
AAAAA
AHAHAHAHAHA
Oh wow, I'm so glad I got to do that once.

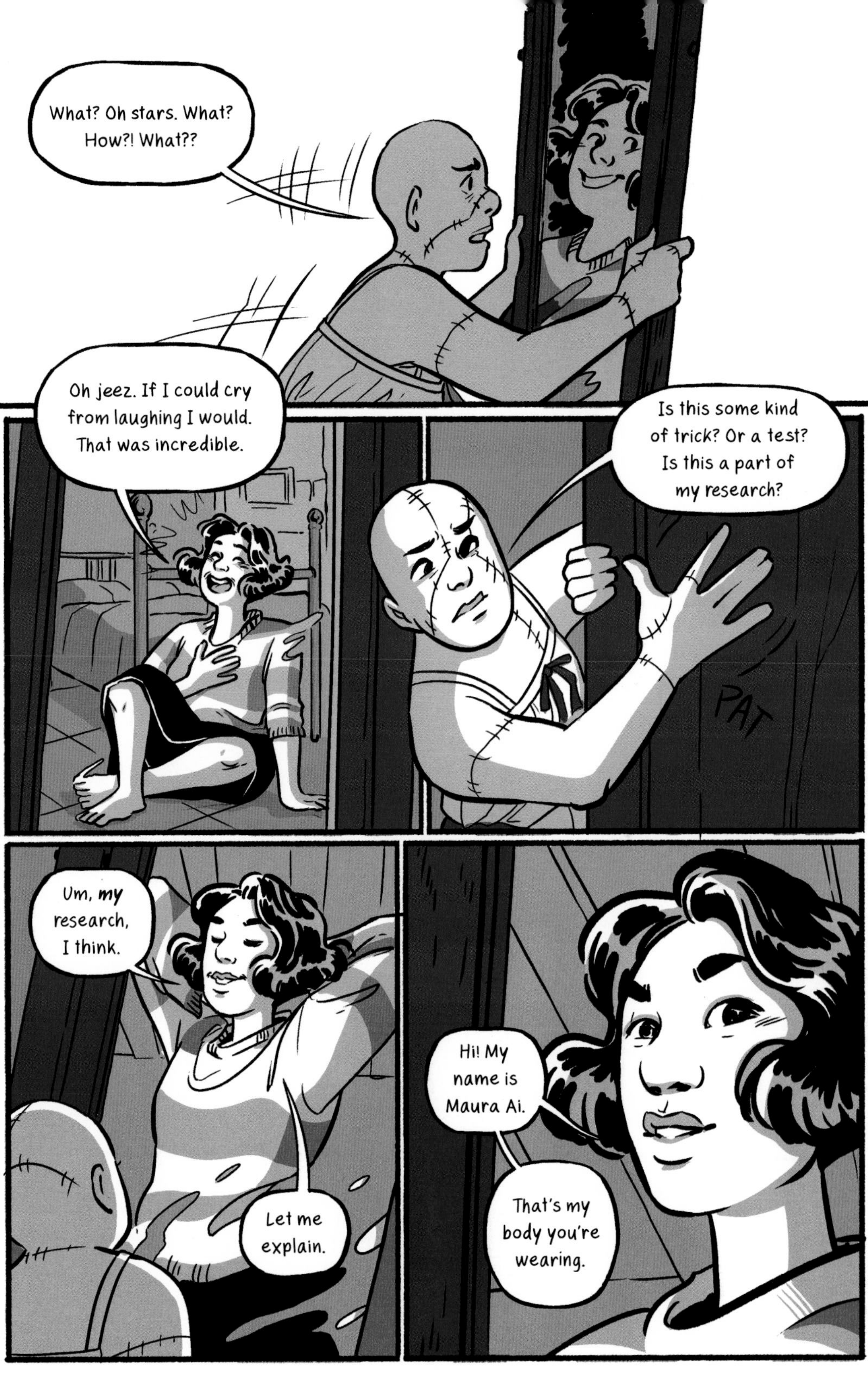
What? Oh stars. What? How?! What??
Oh jeez. If I could cry from laughing I would. That was incredible.
Is this some kind of trick? Or a test? Is this a part of my research?
PAT
Um, *my* research, I think.
Let me explain.
Hi! My name is Maura Ai.
That's my body you're wearing.

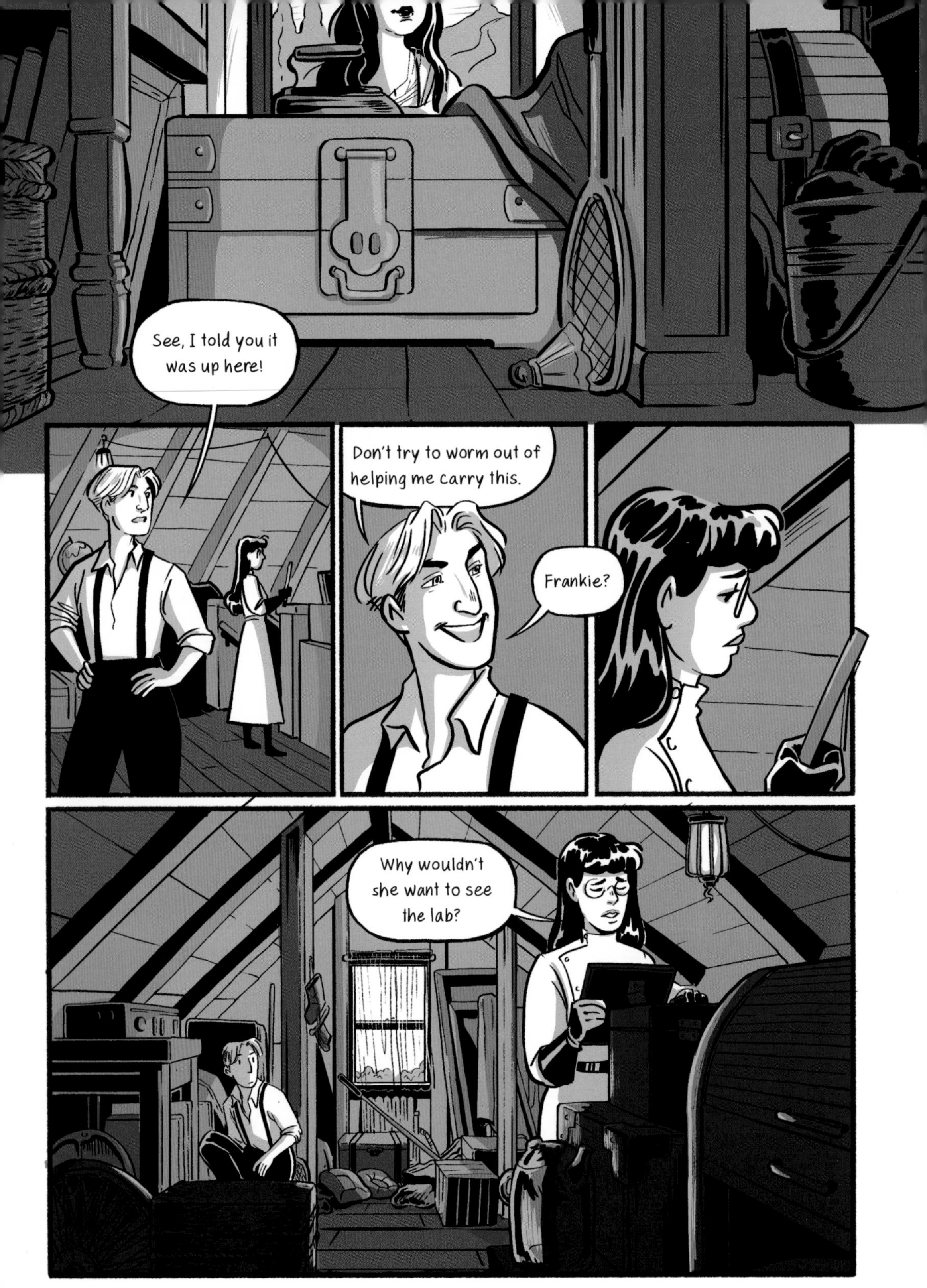
See, I told you it was up here!
Don't try to worm out of helping me carry this.
Frankie?
Why wouldn't she want to see the lab?

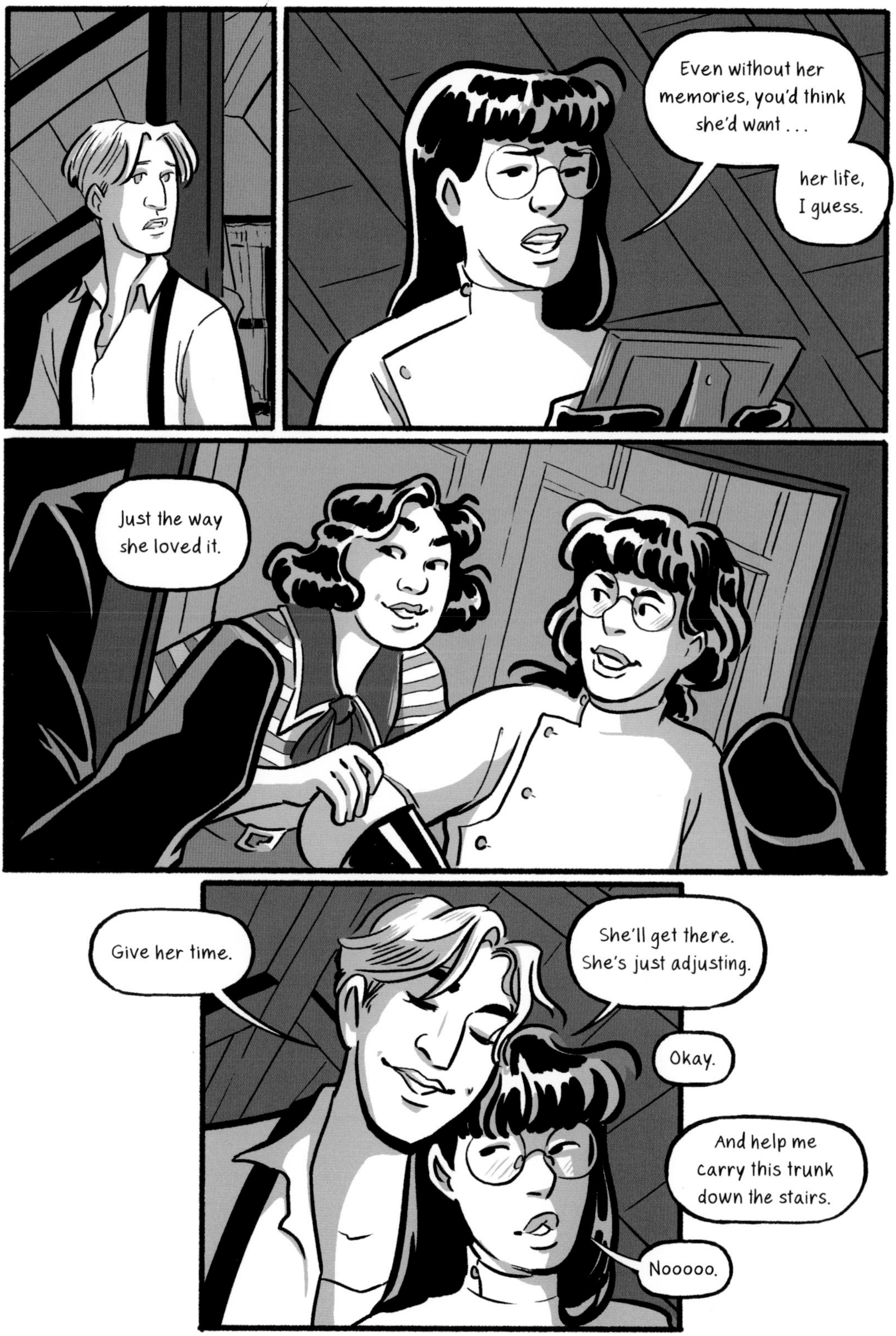
Even without her memories, you'd think she'd want . . .
her life, I guess.
Just the way she loved it.
Give her time.
She'll get there. She's just adjusting.
Okay.
And help me carry this trunk down the stairs.
Nooooo.

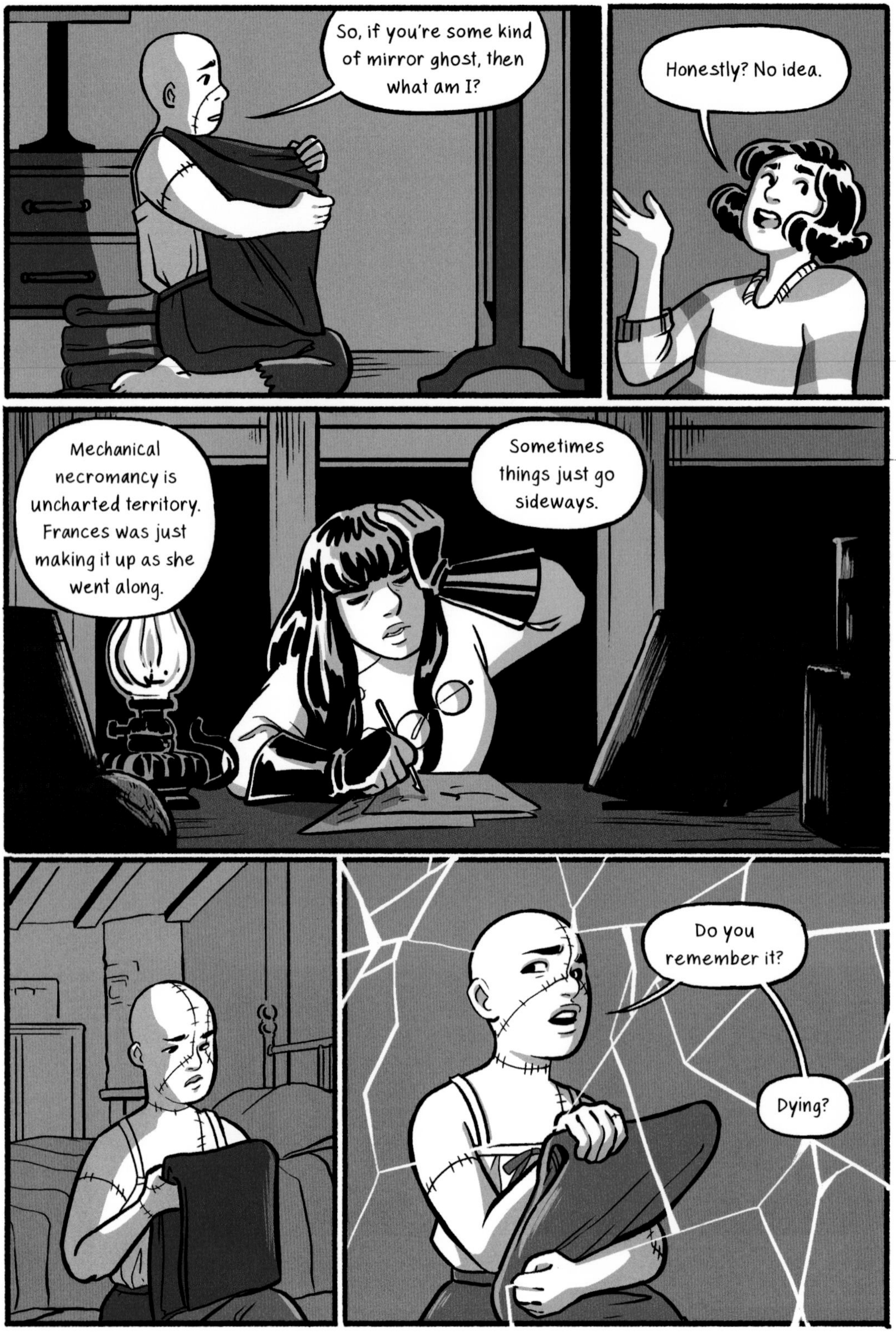
So, if you're some kind of mirror ghost, then what am I?
Honestly? No idea.
Mechanical necromancy is uncharted territory. Frances was just making it up as she went along.
Sometimes things just go sideways.
Do you remember it?
Dying?

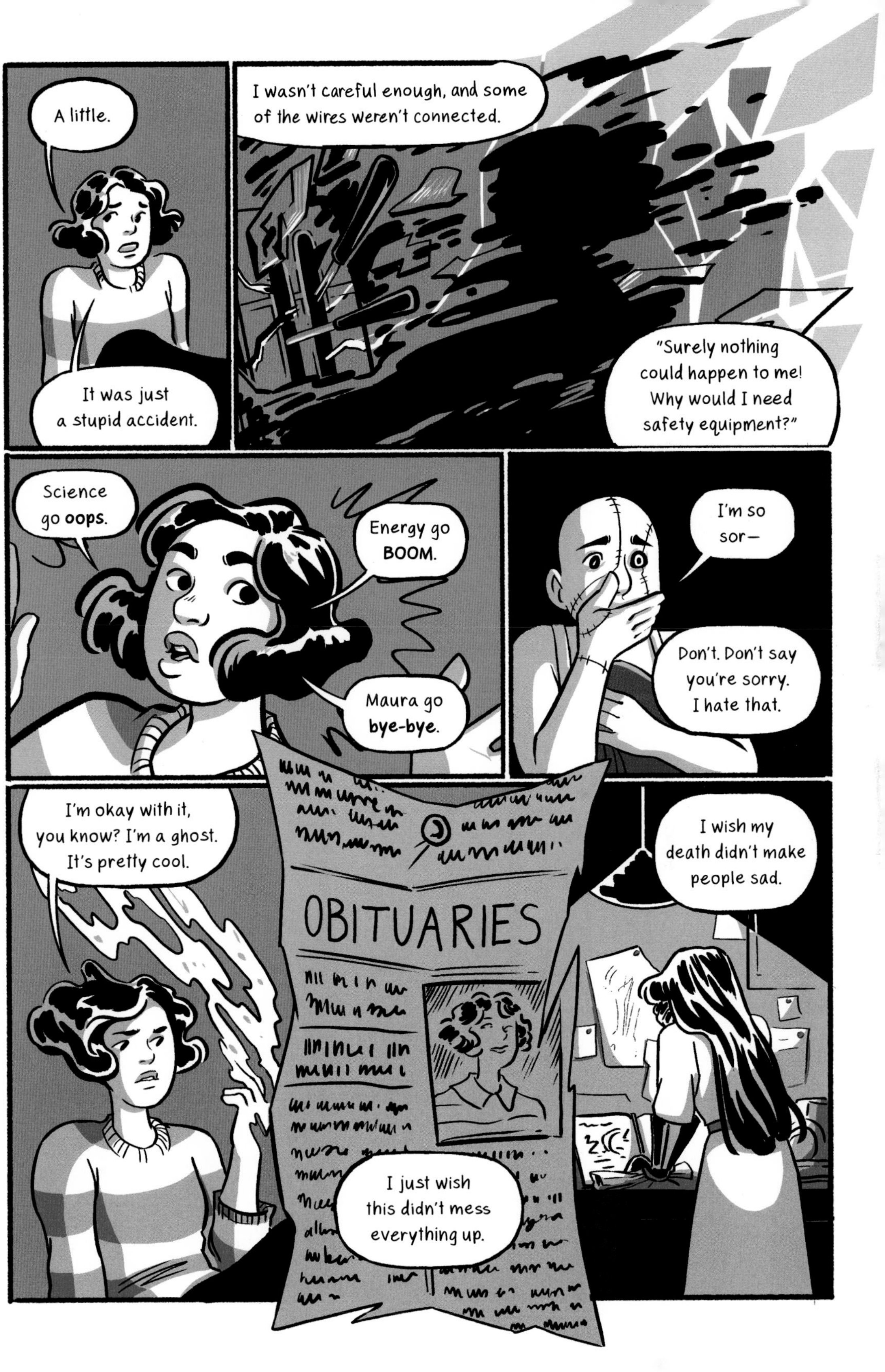
A little.
It was just a stupid accident.
I wasn't careful enough, and some of the wires weren't connected.
"Surely nothing could happen to me! Why would I need safety equipment?"
Science go **oops**.
Energy go **BOOM**.
Maura go **bye-bye**.
I'm so sor—
Don't. Don't say you're sorry. I hate that.
I'm okay with it, you know? I'm a ghost. It's pretty cool.
OBITUARIES
I wish my death didn't make people sad.
I just wish this didn't mess everything up.

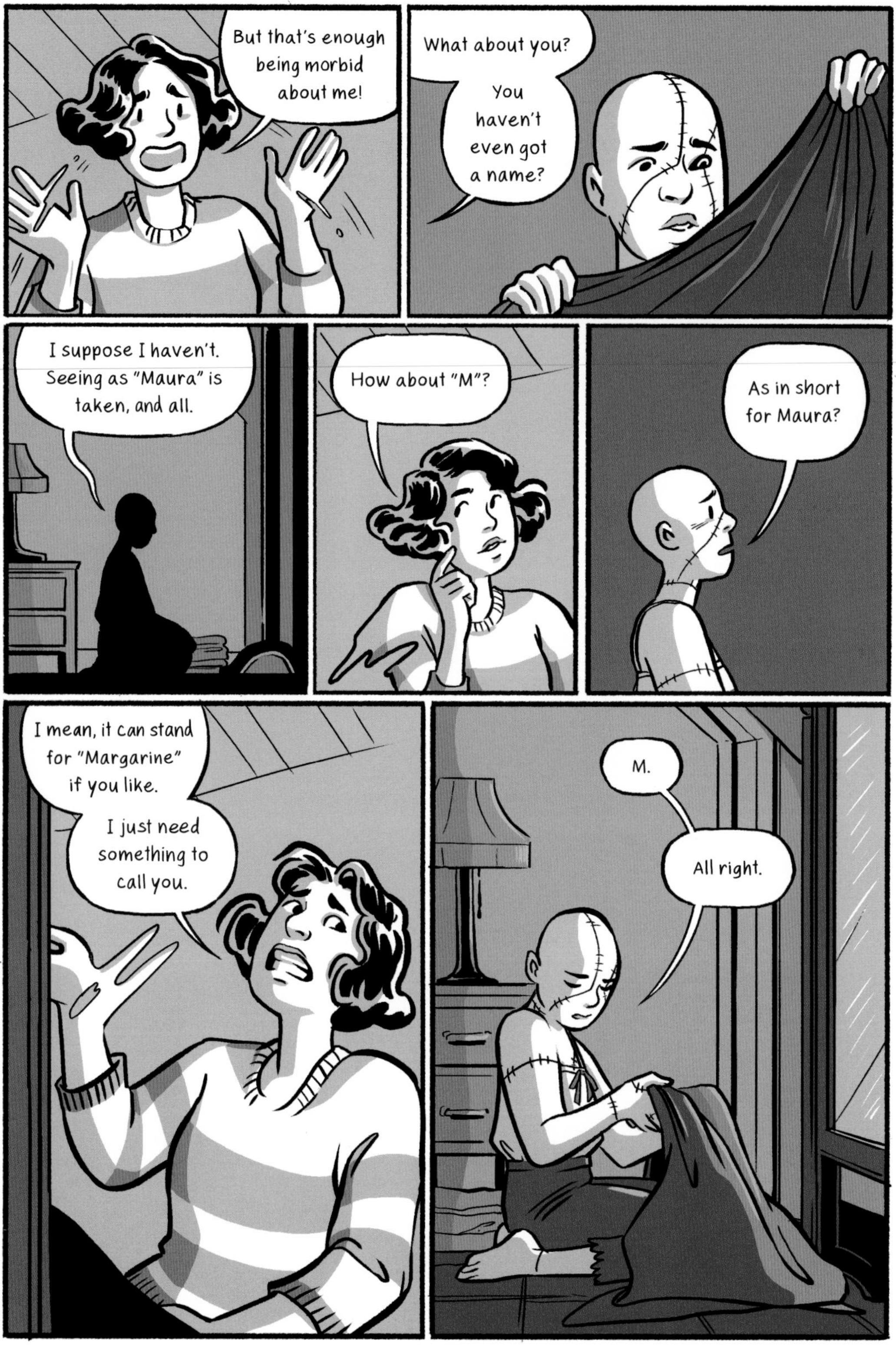
But that's enough being morbid about me!
What about you?
You haven't even got a name?
I suppose I haven't. Seeing as "Maura" is taken, and all.
How about "M"?
As in short for Maura?
I mean, it can stand for "Margarine" if you like.
I just need something to call you.
M.
All right.

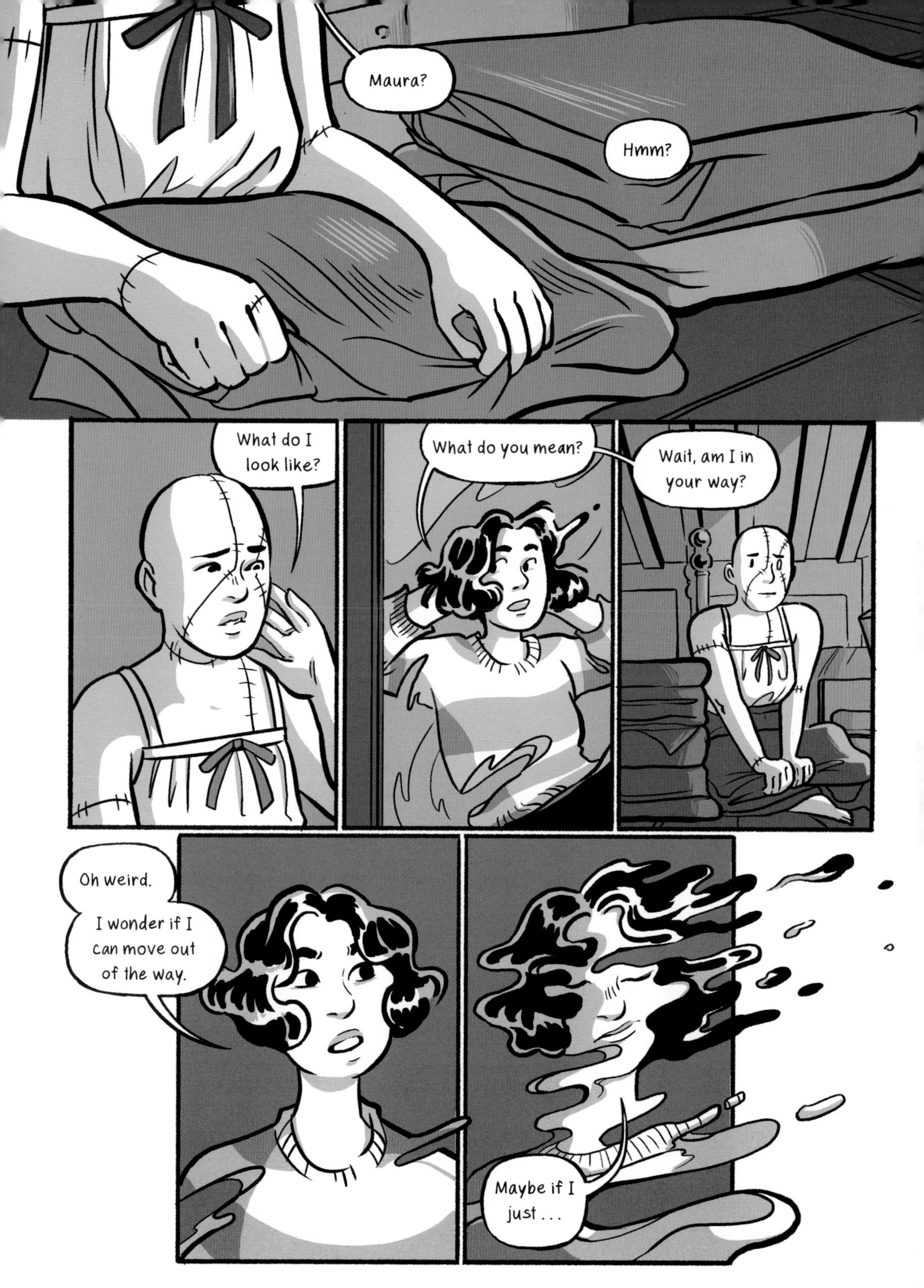
Maura?
Hmm?
What do I look like?
What do you mean?
Wait, am I in your way?
Oh weird.
I wonder if I can move out of the way.
Maybe if I just . . .

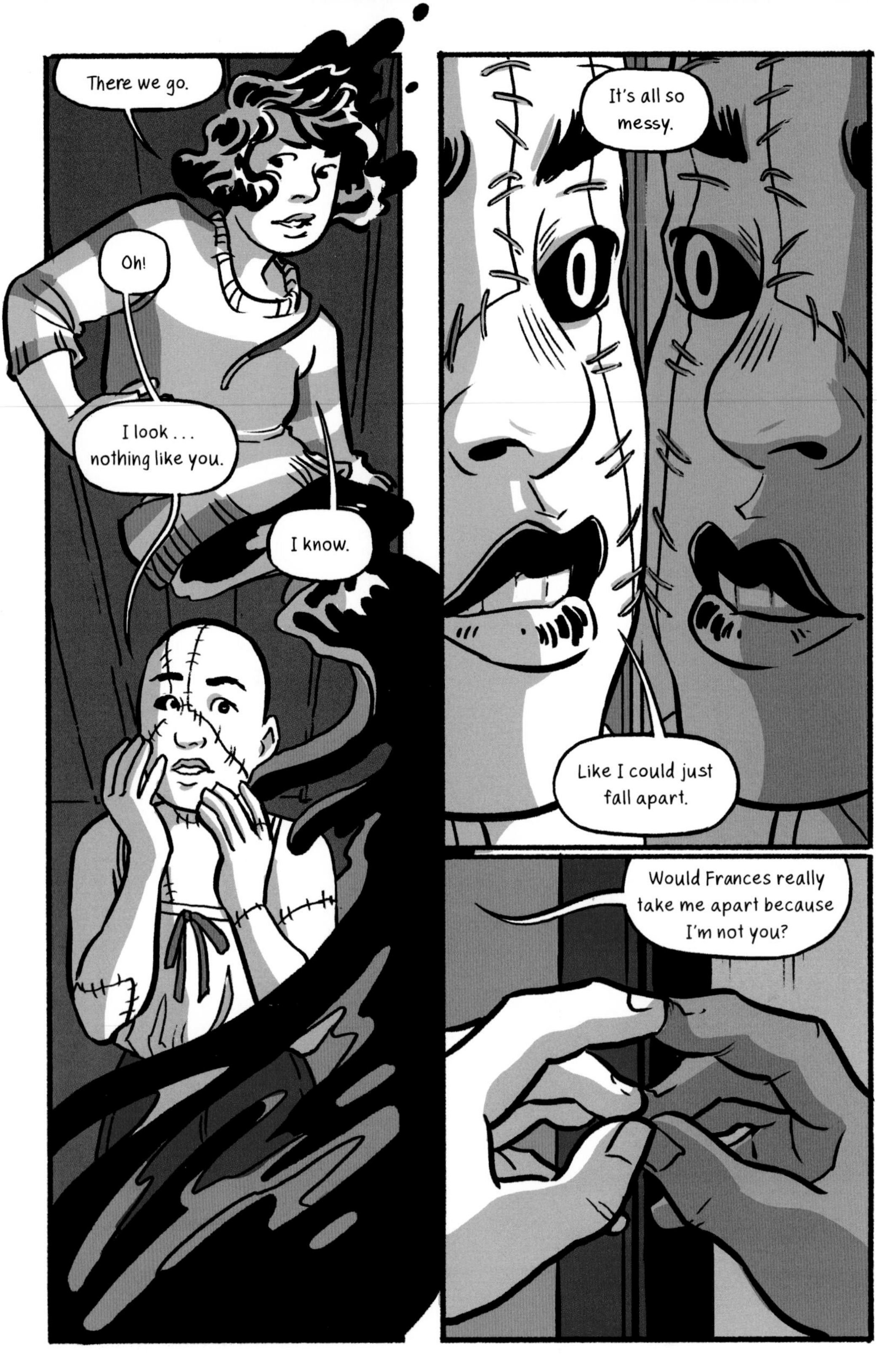
There we go.
Oh!
I look . . . nothing like you.
I know.
It's all so messy.
Like I could just fall apart.
Would Frances really take me apart because I'm not you?

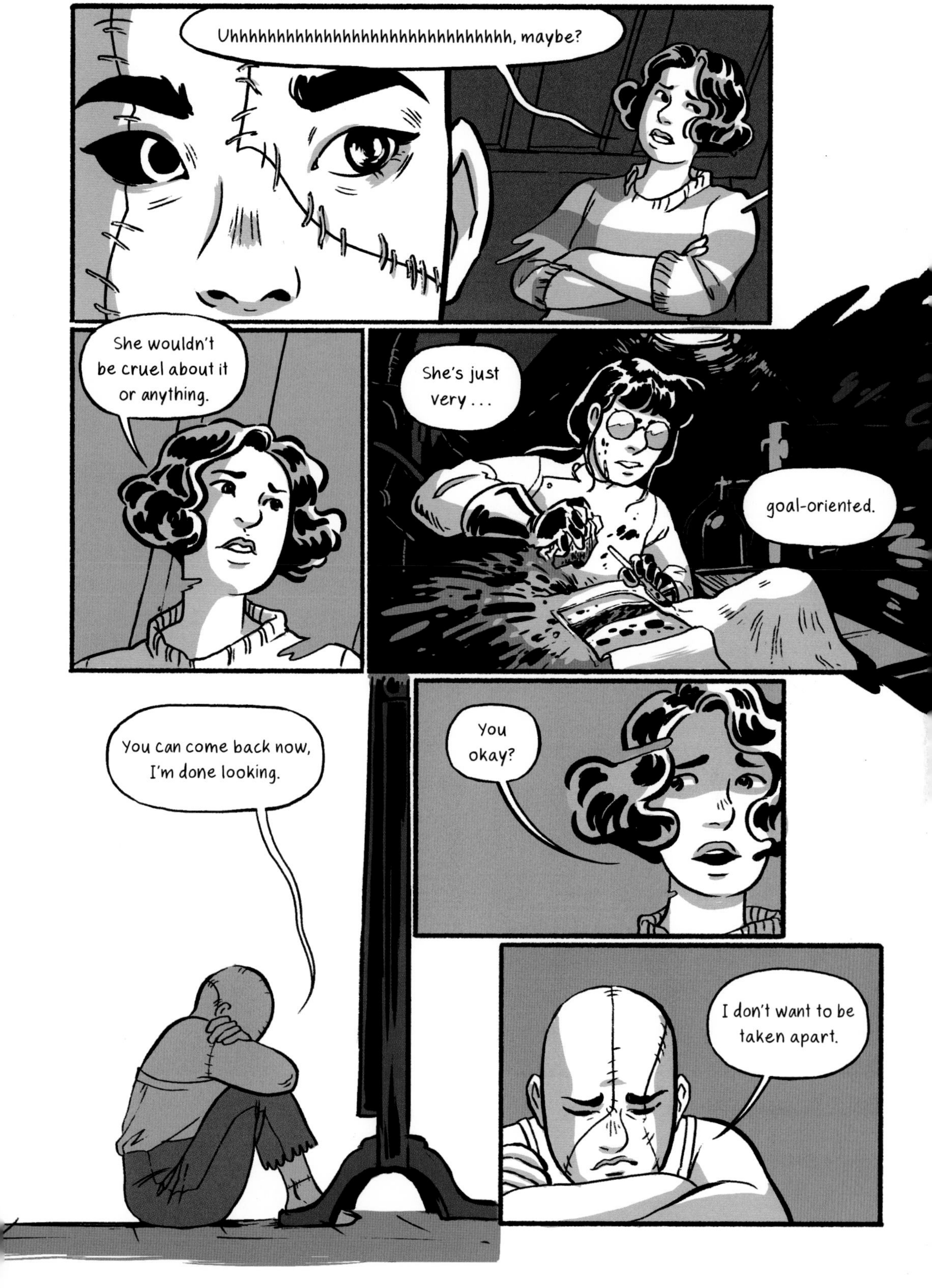
Uhhhhhhhhhhhhhhhhhhhhhhhhhhhhhh, maybe?
She wouldn't be cruel about it or anything.
She's just very . . .
goal-oriented.
You can come back now, I'm done looking.
You okay?
I don't want to be taken apart.

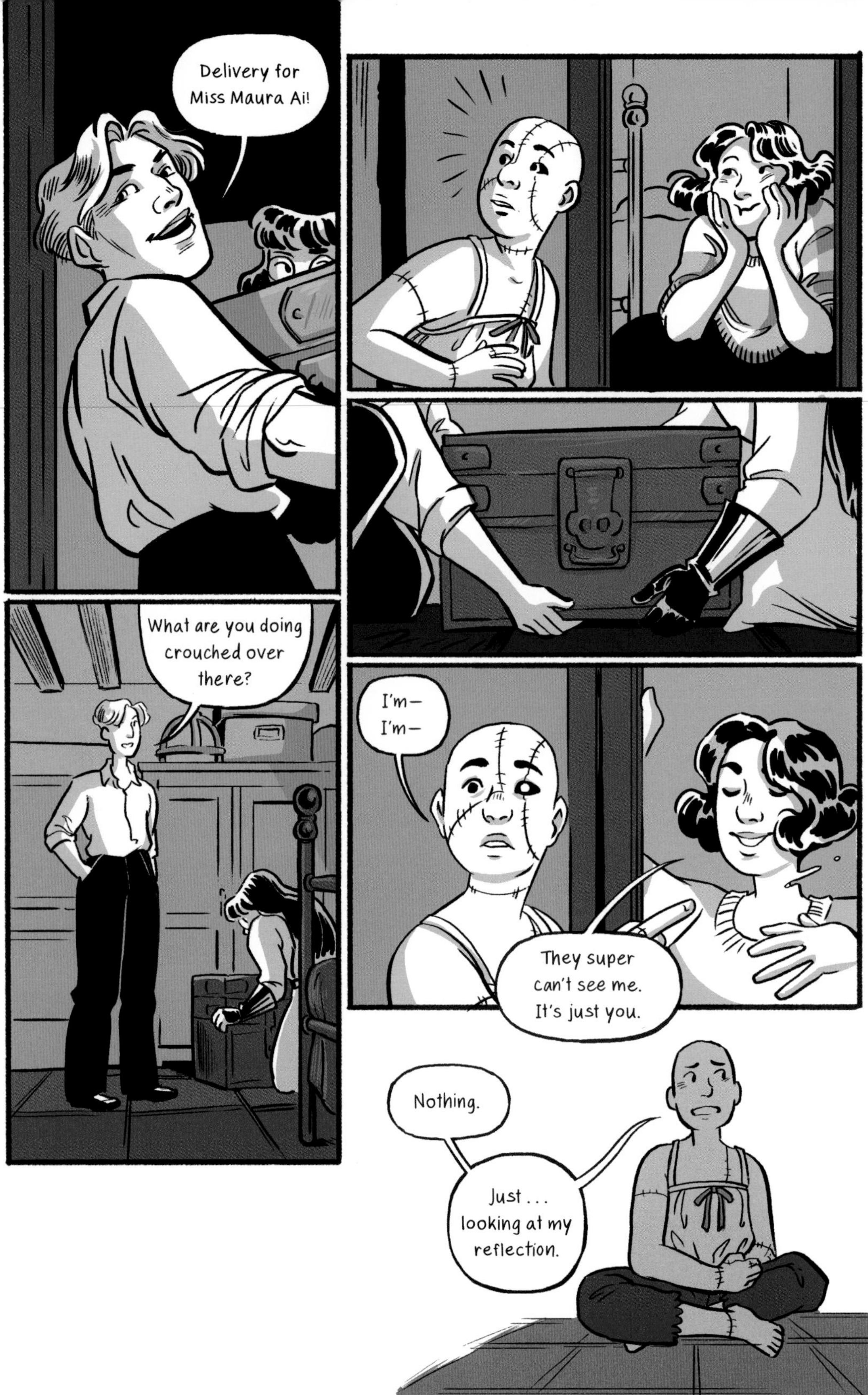

Delivery for Miss Maura Ai!
What are you doing crouched over there?
I'm— I'm—
They super can't see me. It's just you.
Nothing.
Just . . . looking at my reflection.

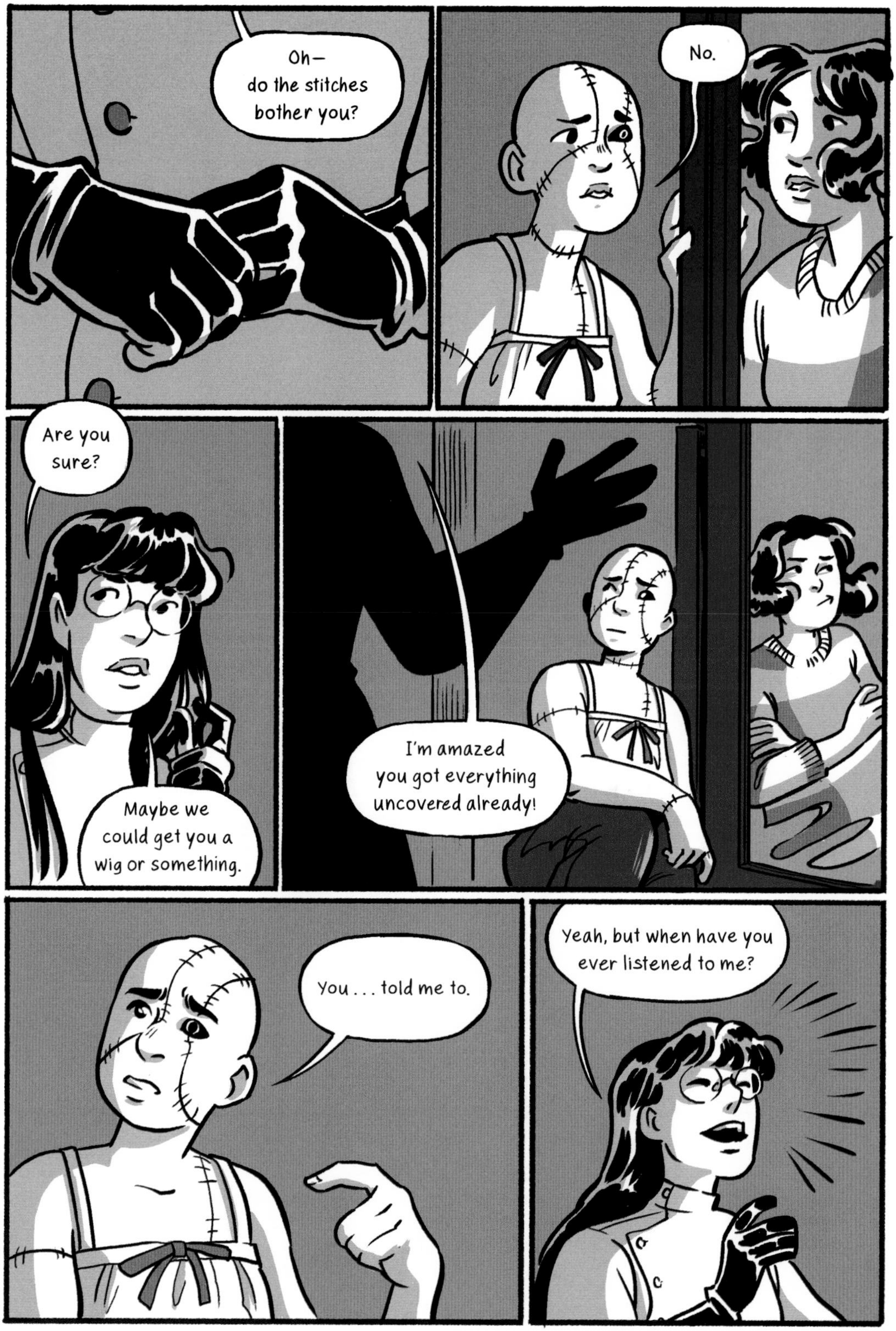

Oh— do the stitches bother you?
No.
Are you sure?
Maybe we could get you a wig or something.
I'm amazed you got everything uncovered already!
You . . . told me to.
Yeah, but when have you ever listened to me?

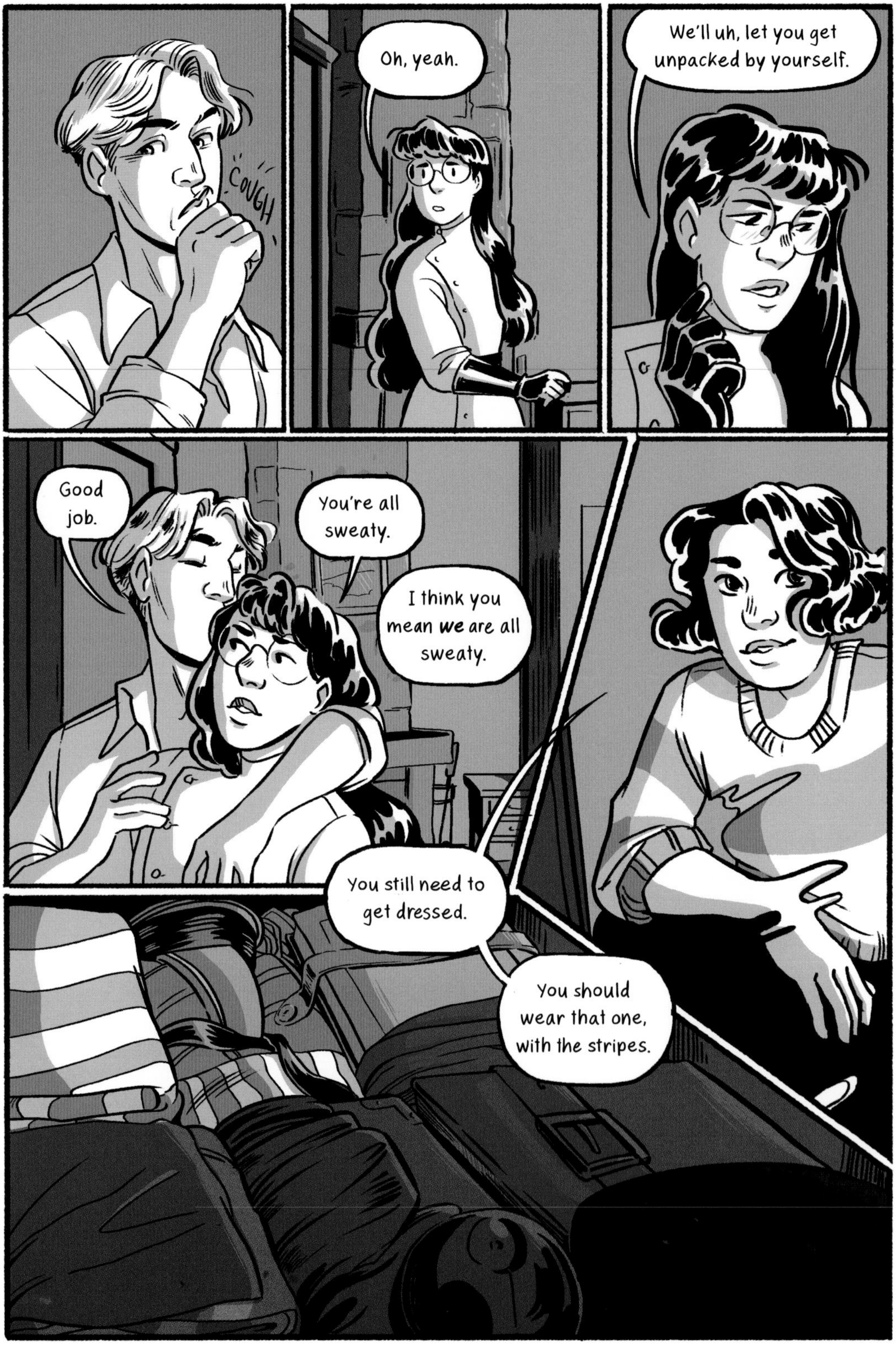
COUGH
Oh, yeah.
We'll uh, let you get unpacked by yourself.
Good job.
You're all sweaty.
I think you mean **we** are all sweaty.
You still need to get dressed.
You should wear that one, with the stripes.

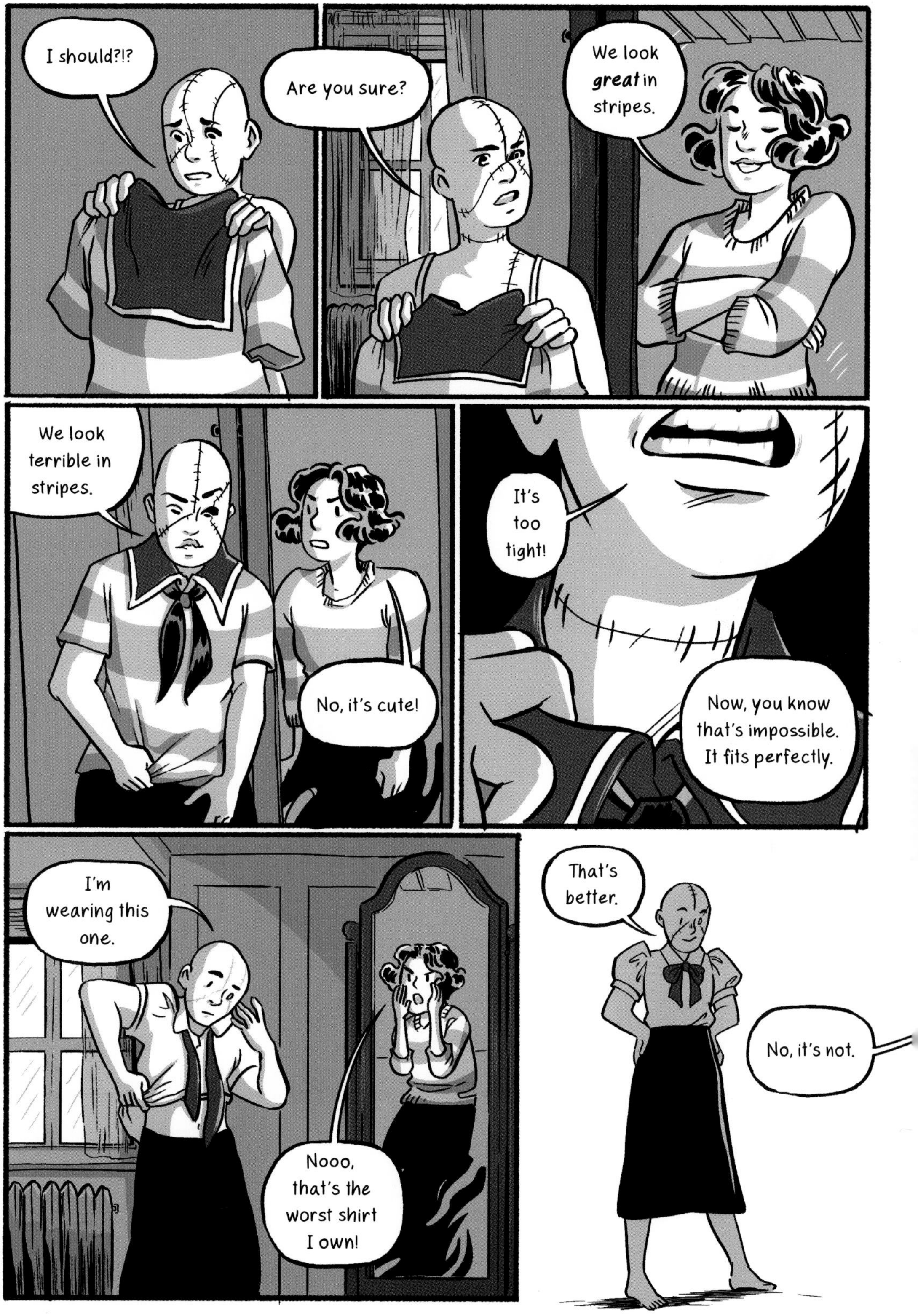
I should?!?
Are you sure?
We look **great** in stripes.
We look terrible in stripes.
No, it's cute!
It's too tight!
Now, you know that's impossible. It fits perfectly.
I'm wearing this one.
Nooo, that's the worst shirt I own!
That's better.
No, it's not.

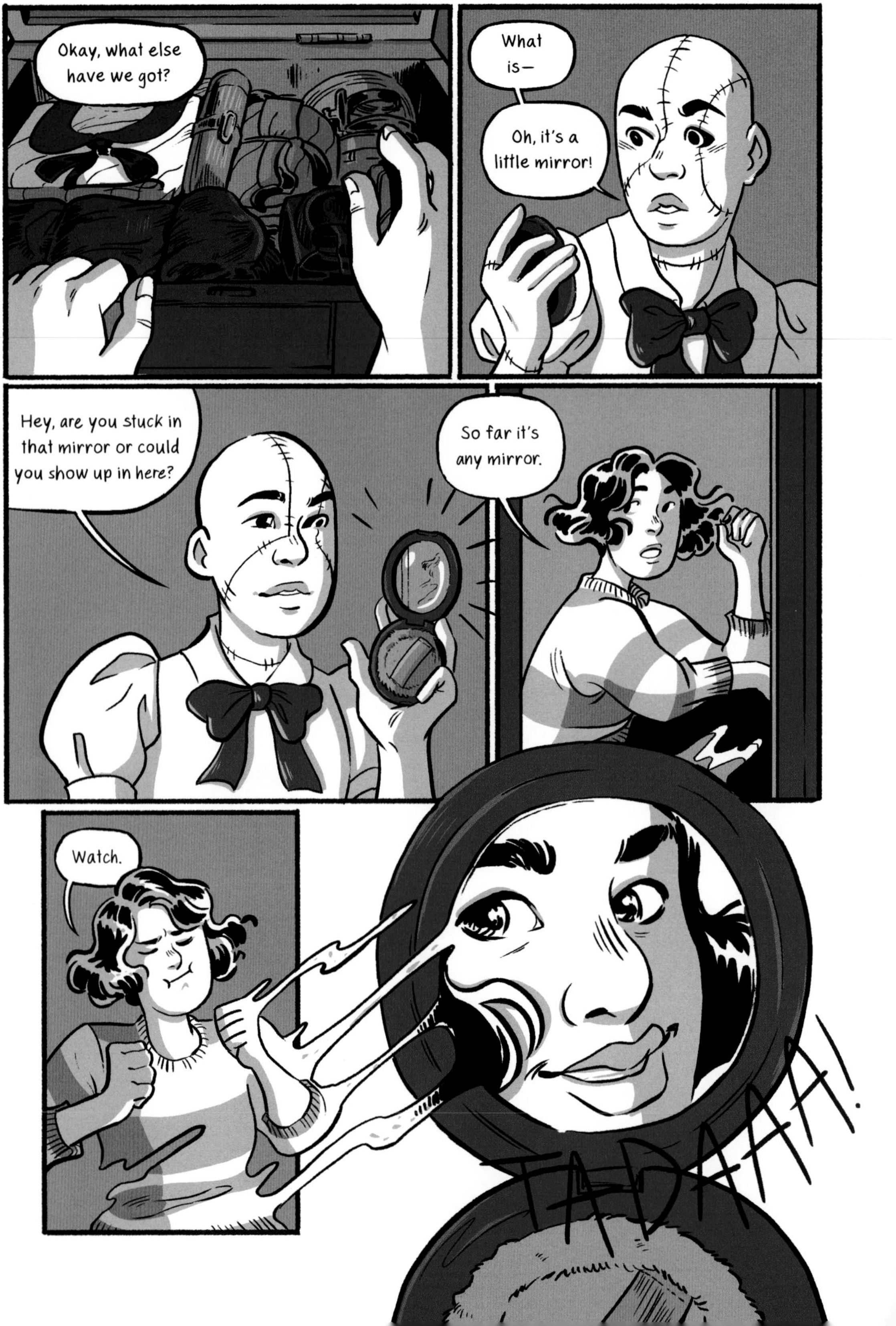
Okay, what else have we got?
What is—
Oh, it's a little mirror!
Hey, are you stuck in that mirror or could you show up in here?
So far it's any mirror.
Watch.
TADAAA!!

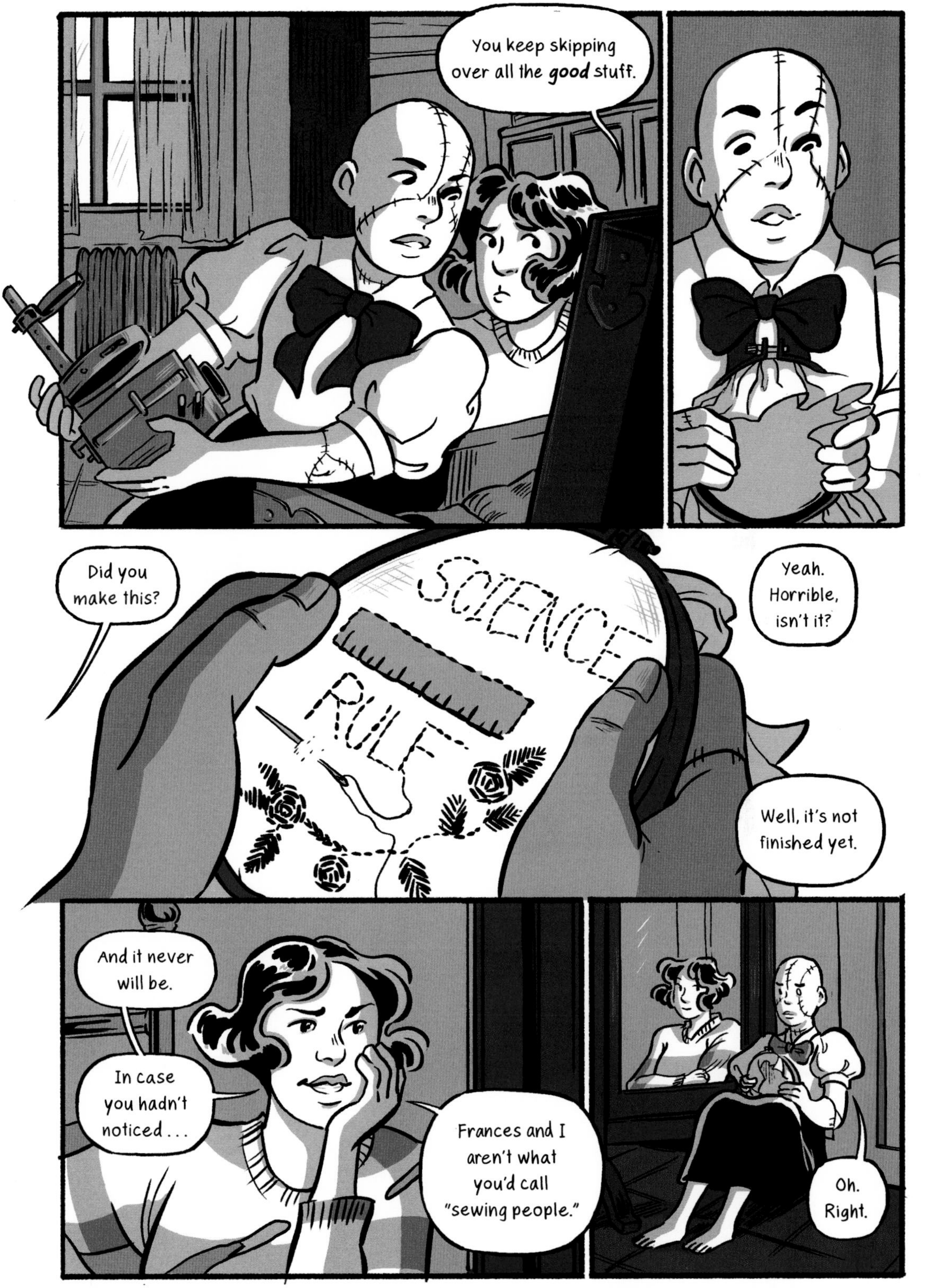

You keep skipping over all the **good** stuff.
Did you make this?
SCIENCE RULE
Yeah. Horrible, isn't it?
Well, it's not finished yet.
And it never will be.
In case you hadn't noticed . . .
Frances and I aren't what you'd call "sewing people."
Oh. Right.

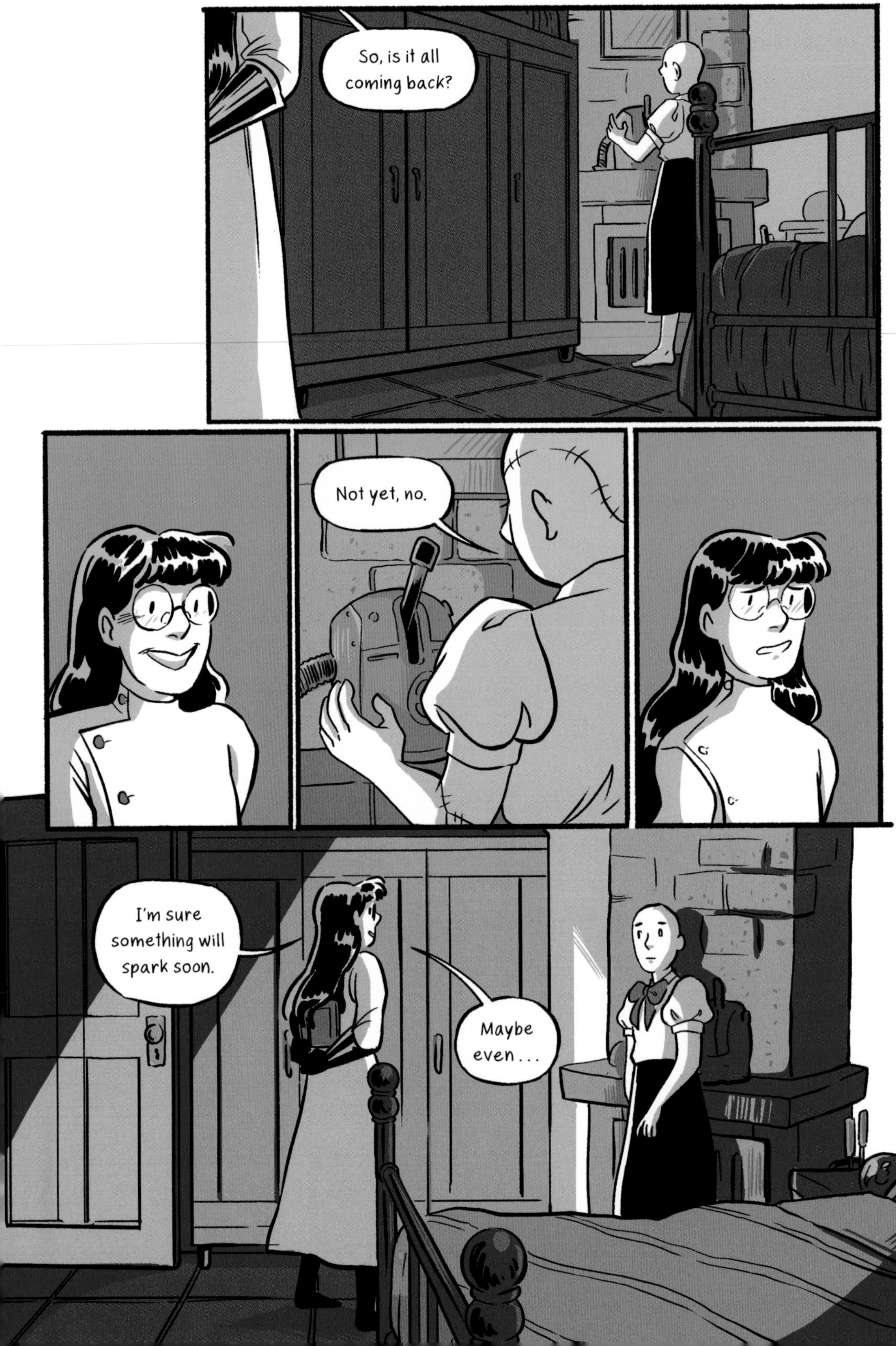
So, is it all coming back?
Not yet, no.
I'm sure something will spark soon.
Maybe even . . .

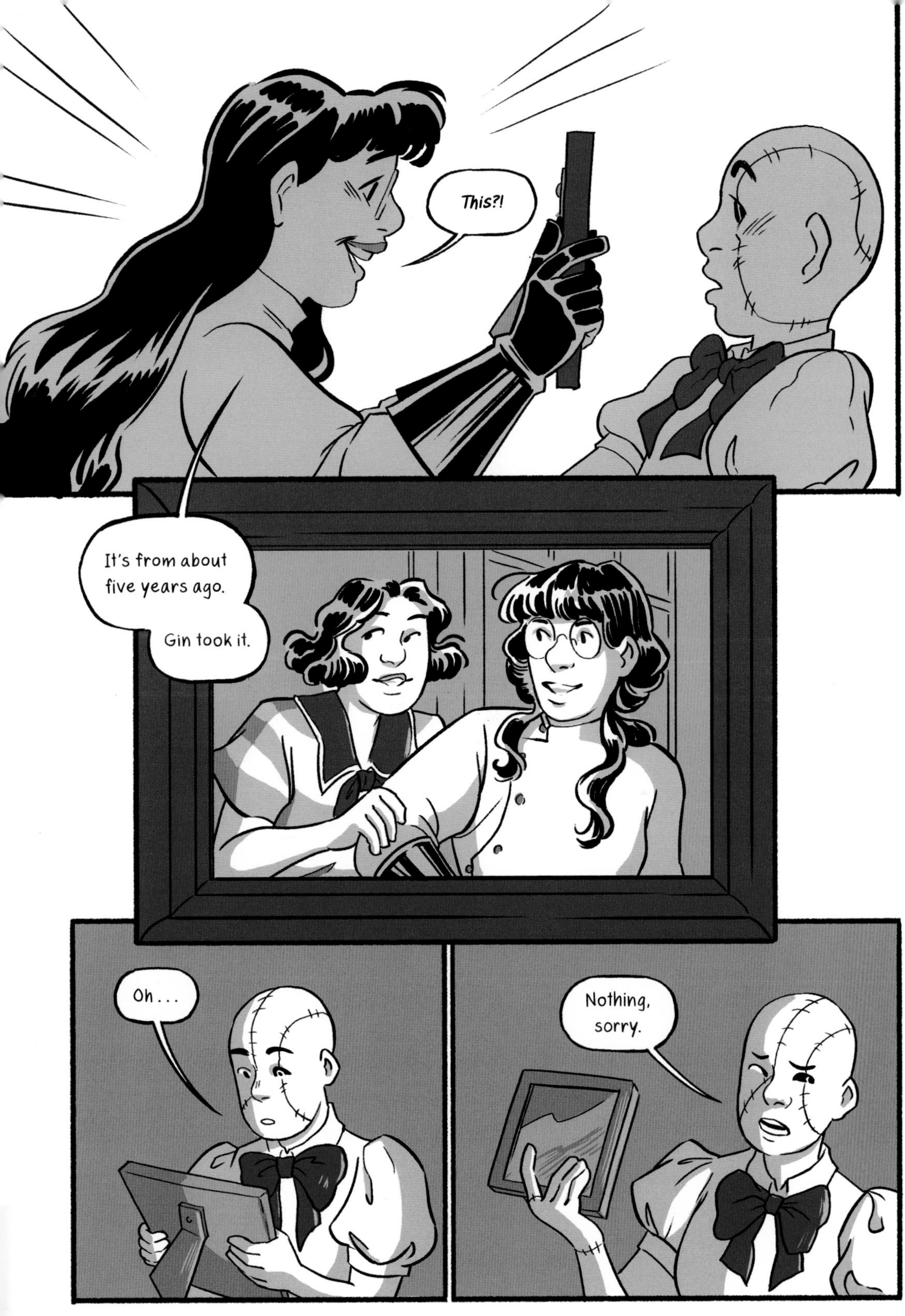

This?!
It's from about five years ago.
Gin took it.
Oh . . .
Nothing, sorry.

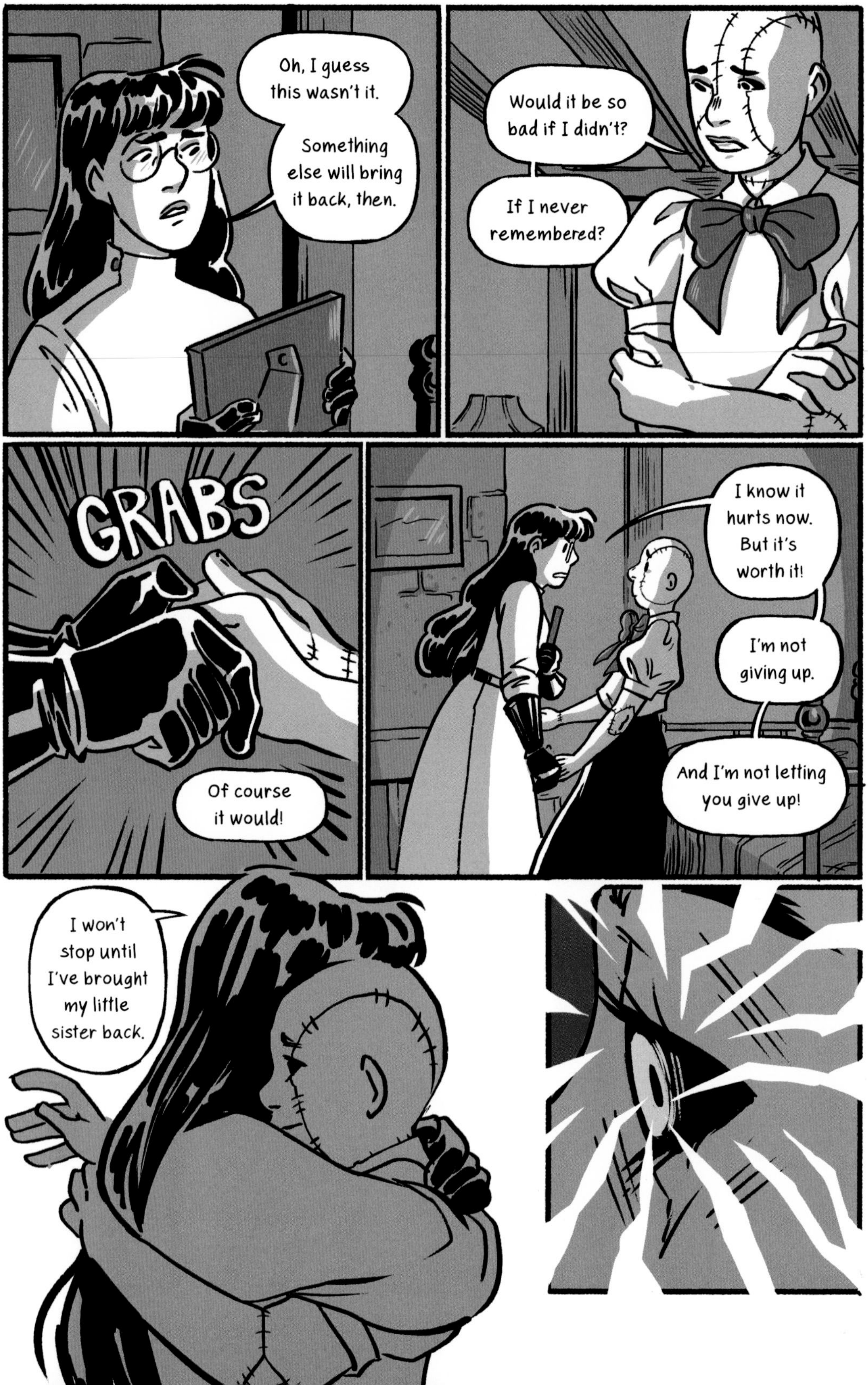
Oh, I guess this wasn't it.
Something else will bring it back, then.
Would it be so bad if I didn't?
If I never remembered?
GRABS
Of course it would!
I know it hurts now. But it's worth it!
I'm not giving up.
And I'm not letting you give up!
I won't stop until I've brought my little sister back.

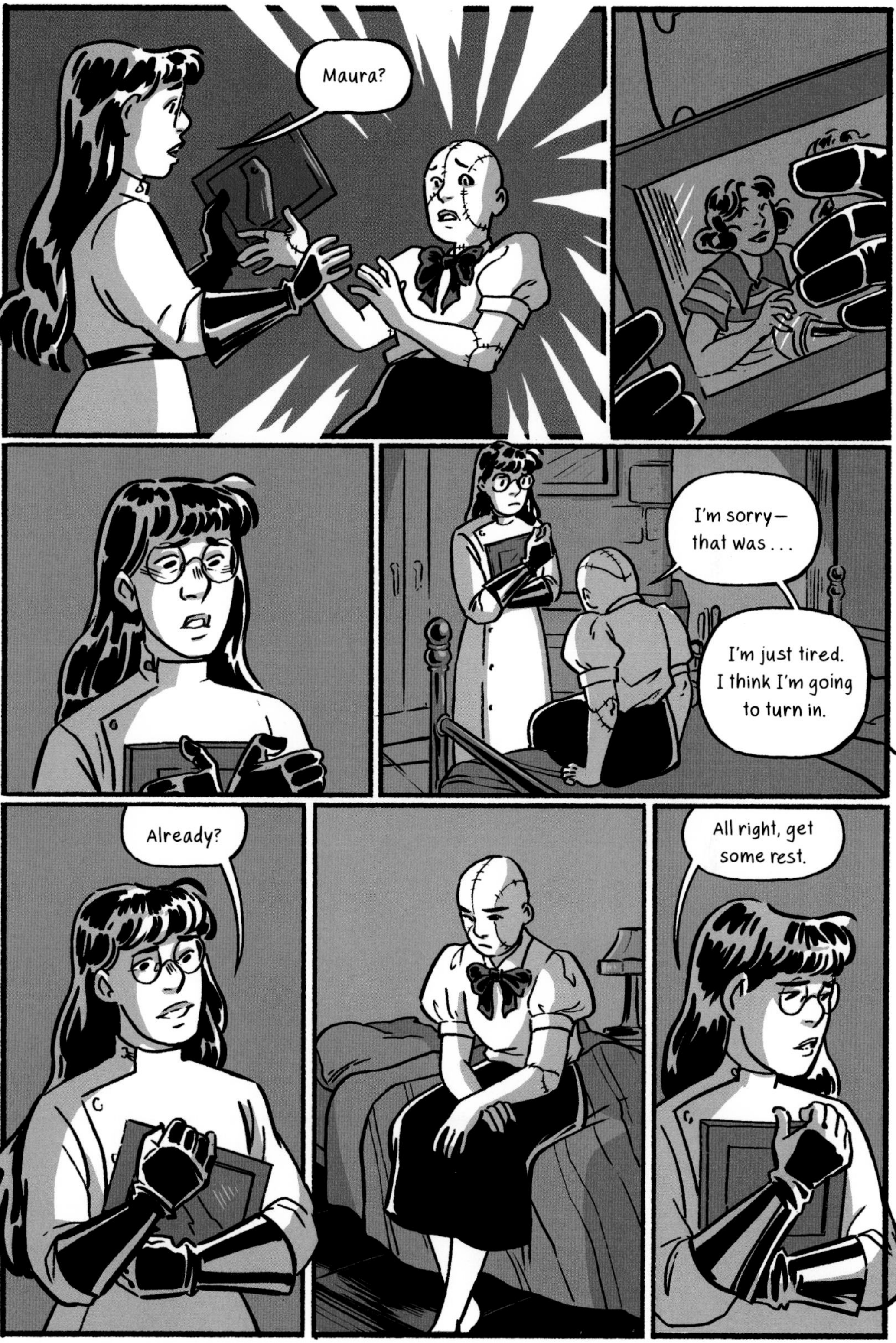
Maura?
I'm sorry—that was . . .
I'm just tired. I think I'm going to turn in.
Already?
All right, get some rest.

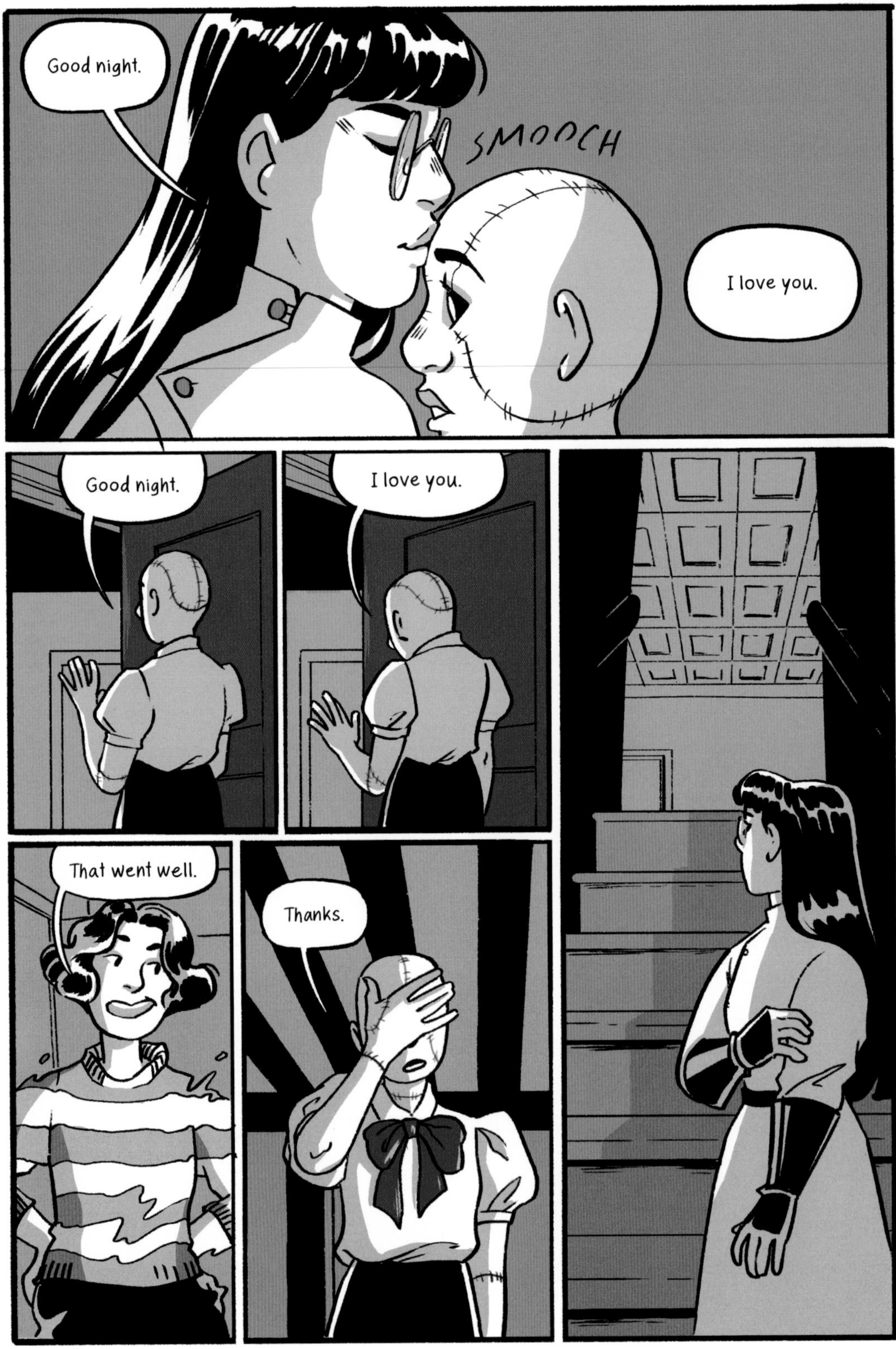
Good night.
SMOOCH
I love you.
Good night.
I love you.
That went well.
Thanks.

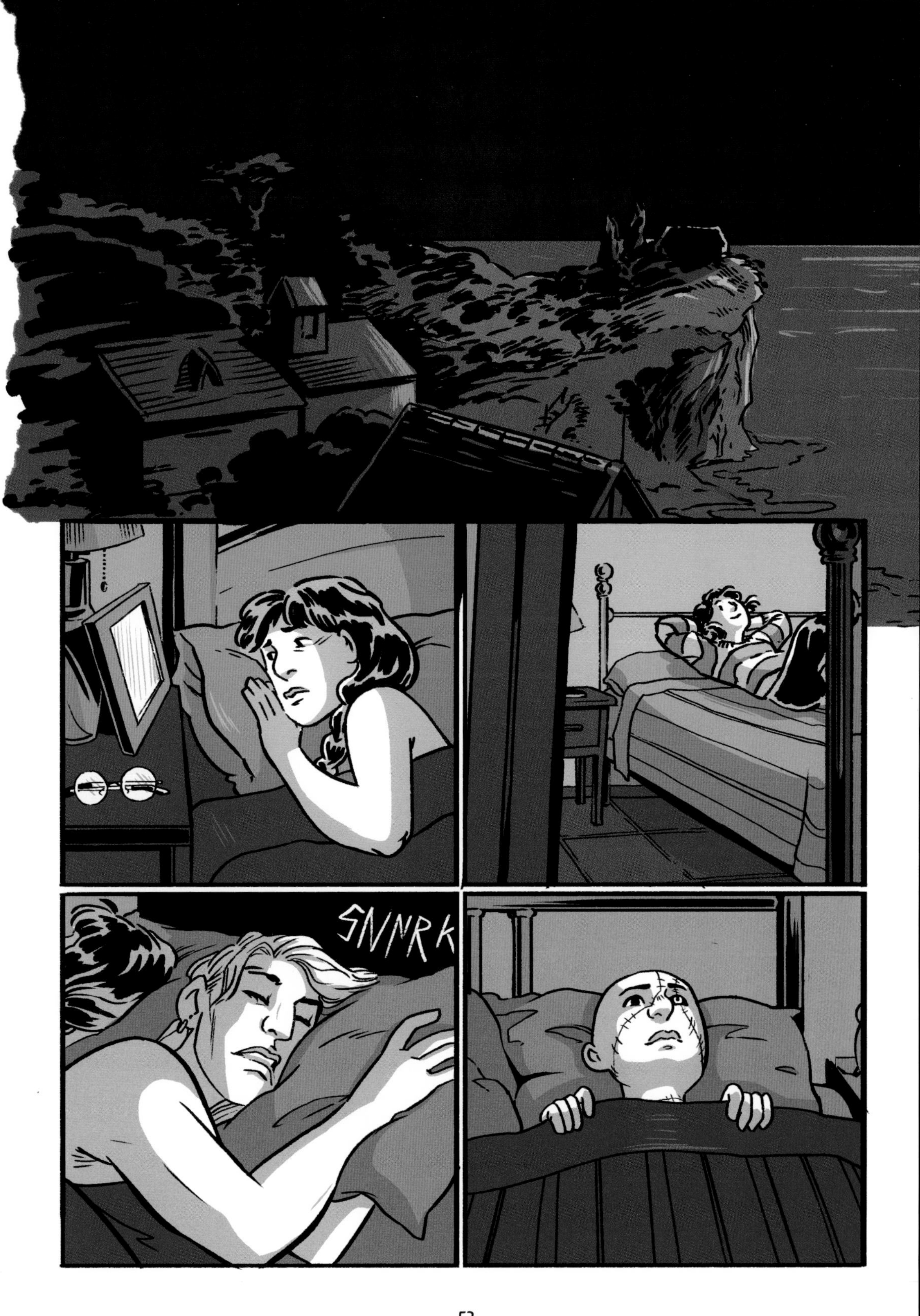
SNNRK

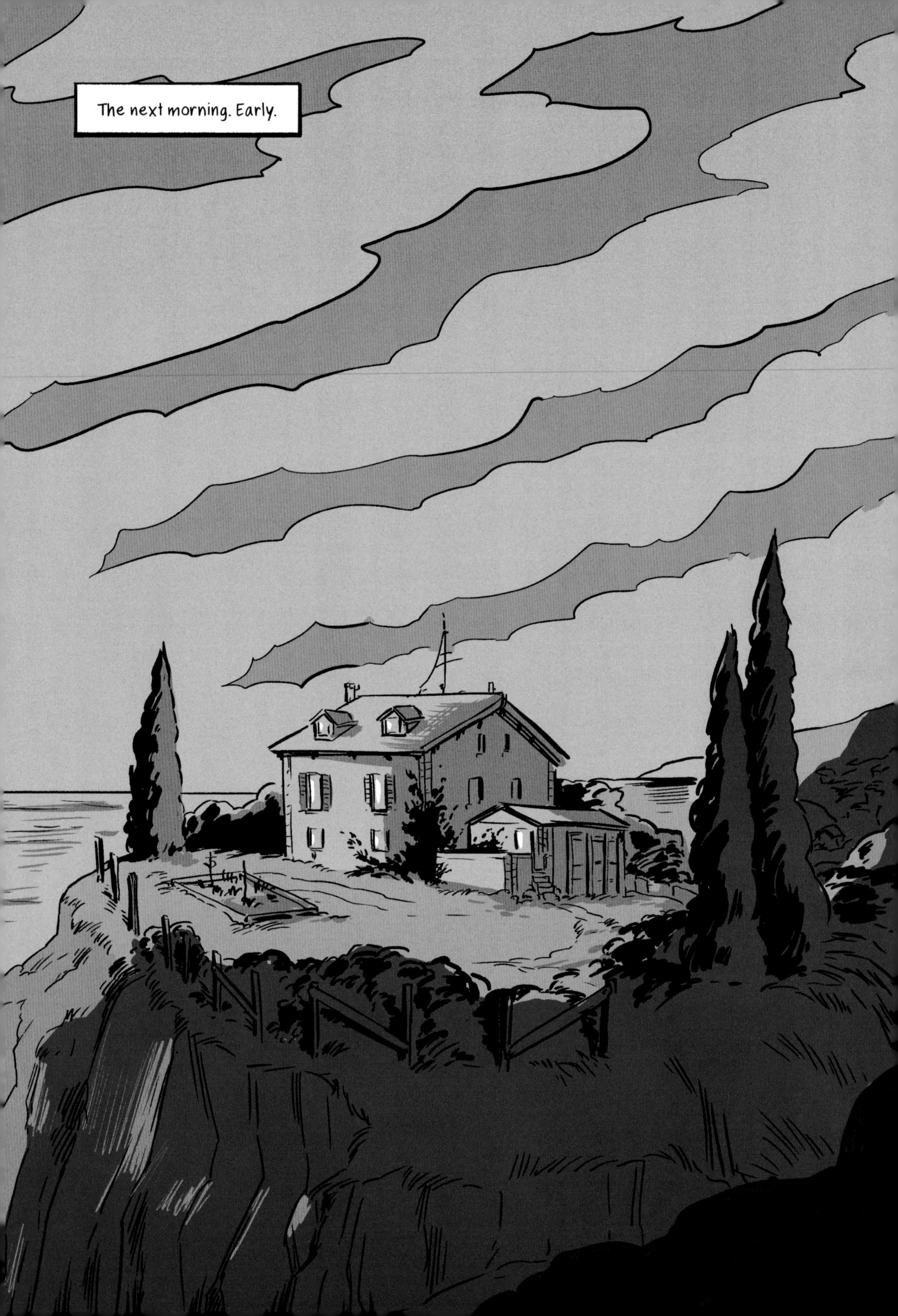
The next morning. Early.

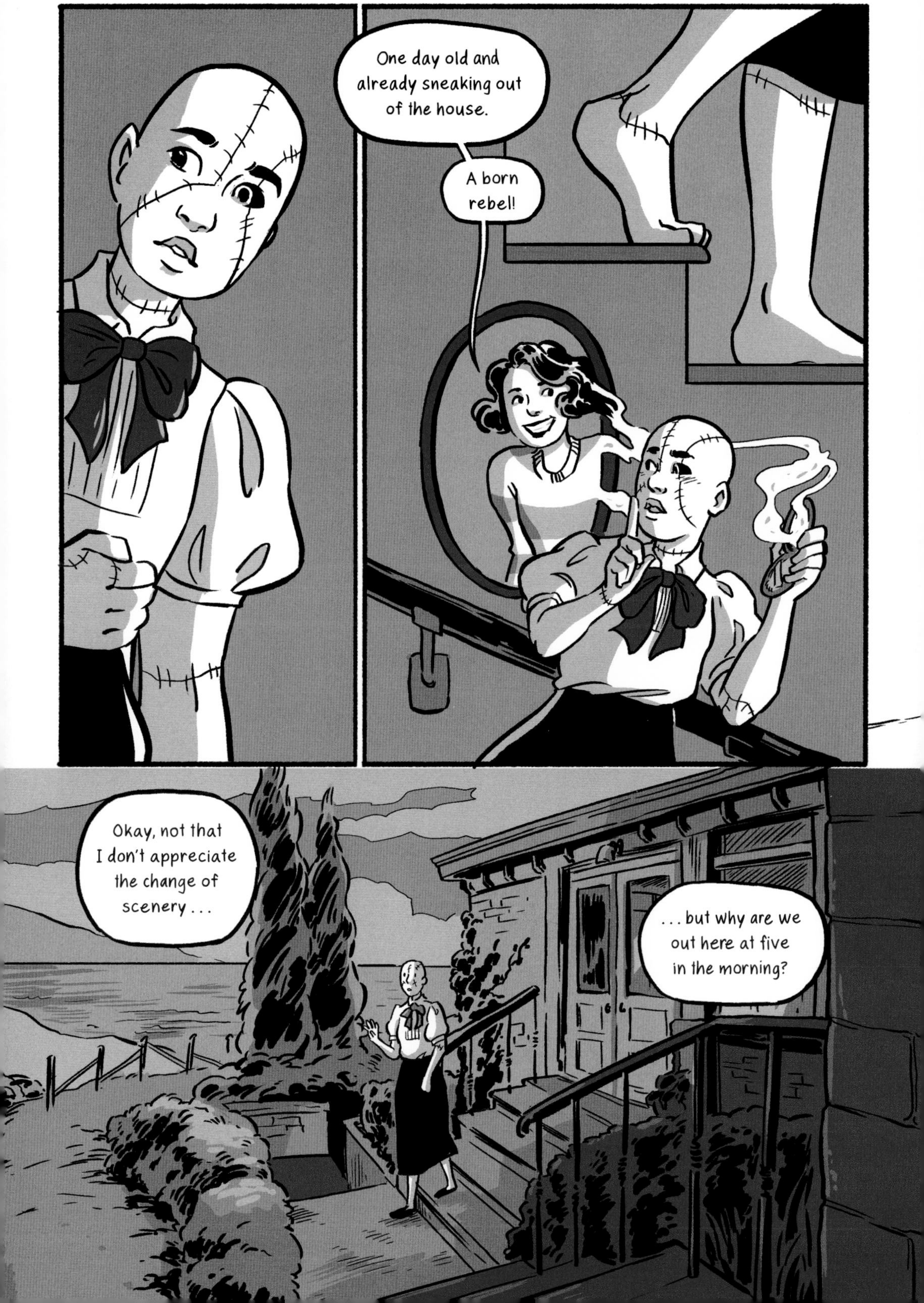
One day old and already sneaking out of the house.
A born rebel!
Okay, not that I don't appreciate the change of scenery . . .
. . . but why are we out here at five in the morning?

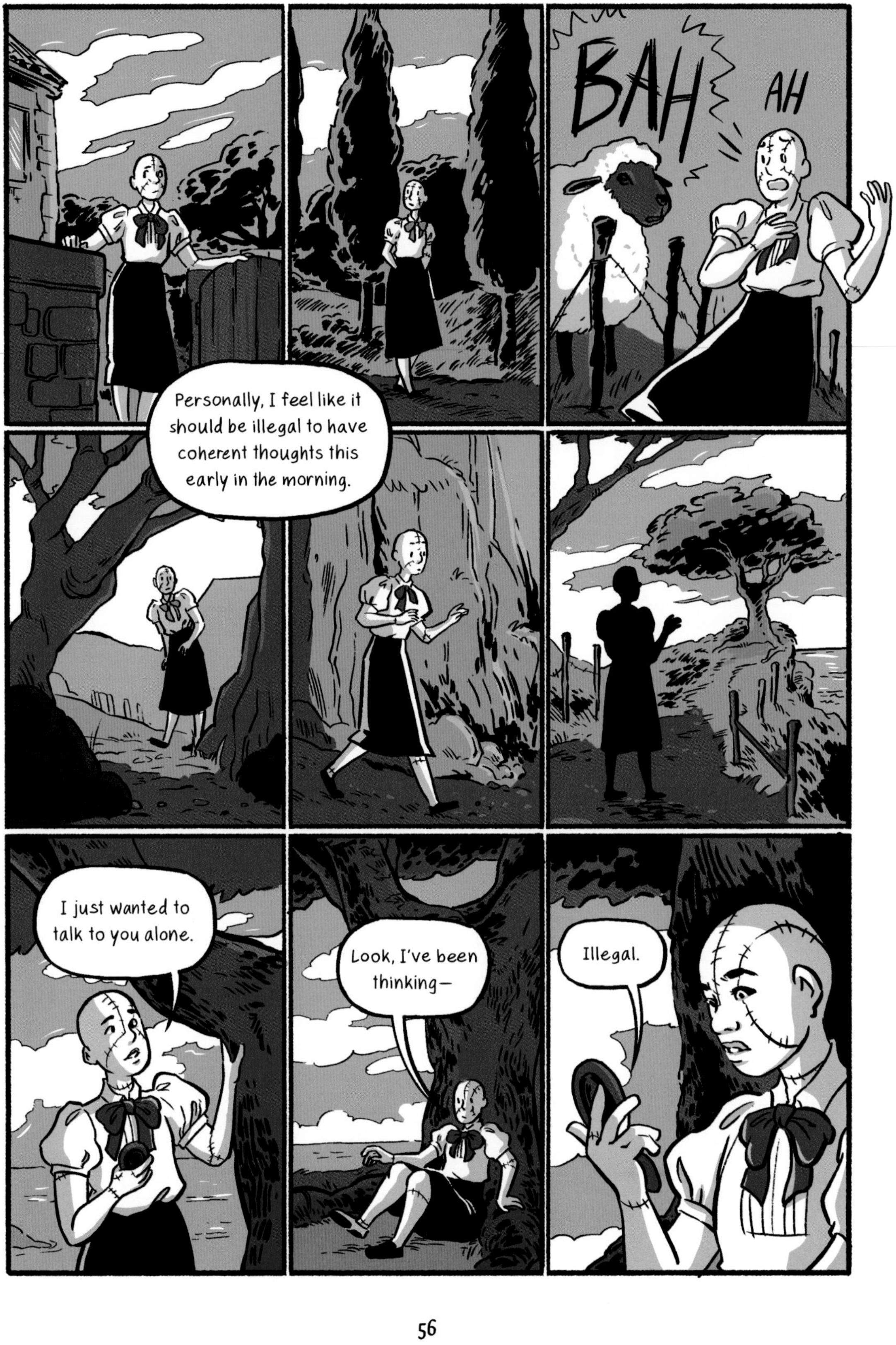
BAH
AH
Personally, I feel like it should be illegal to have coherent thoughts this early in the morning.
I just wanted to talk to you alone.
Look, I've been thinking—
Illegal.

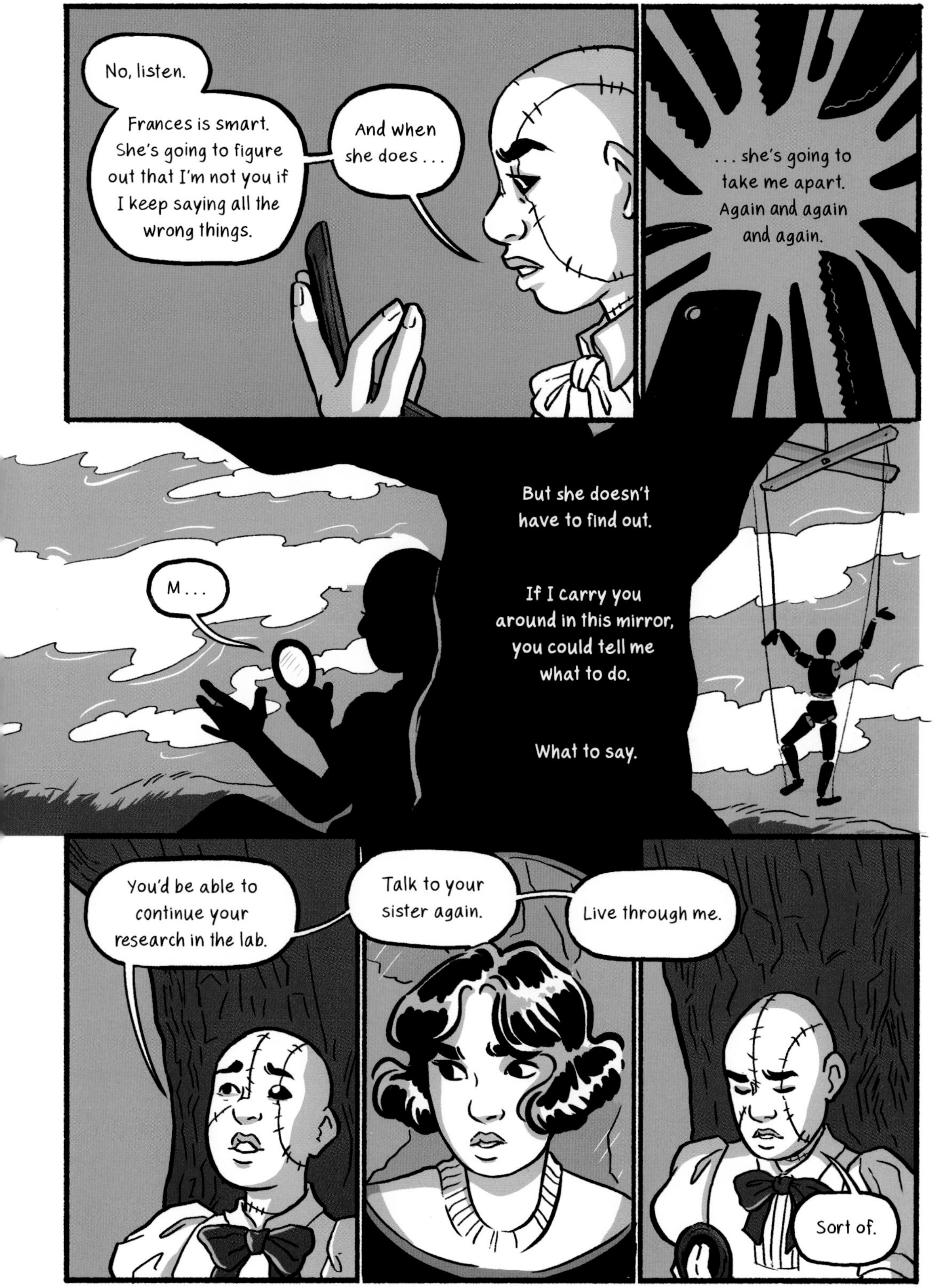
No, listen.
Frances is smart. She's going to figure out that I'm not you if I keep saying all the wrong things.
And when she does . . .
. . . she's going to take me apart. Again and again and again.
But she doesn't have to find out.
M . . .
If I carry you around in this mirror, you could tell me what to do.
What to say.
You'd be able to continue your research in the lab.
Talk to your sister again.
Live through me.
Sort of.

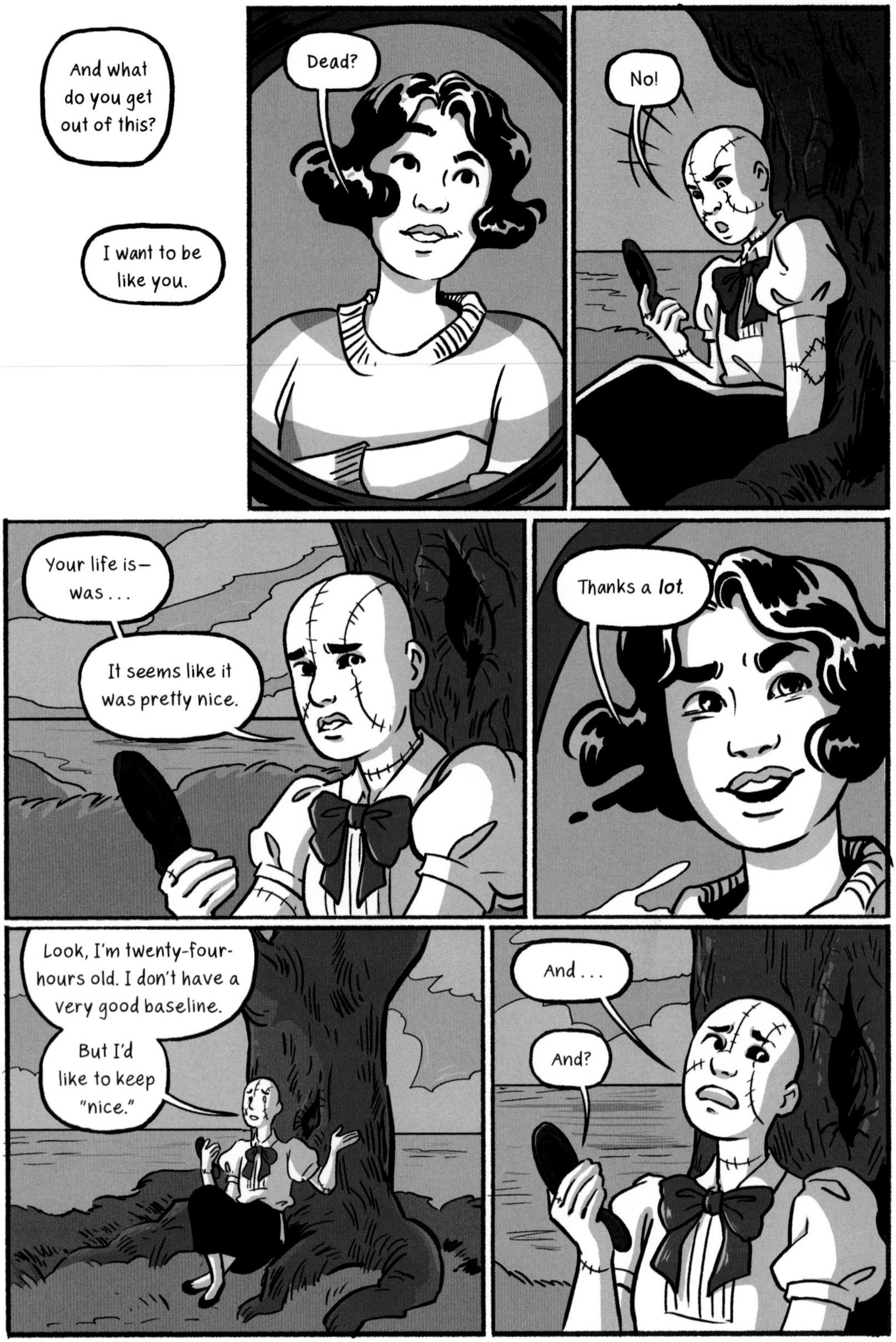
And what do you get out of this?
I want to be like you.
Dead?
No!
Your life is— was . . .
It seems like it was pretty nice.
Thanks a *lot*.
Look, I'm twenty-four-hours old. I don't have a very good baseline.
But I'd like to keep "nice."
And . . .
And?

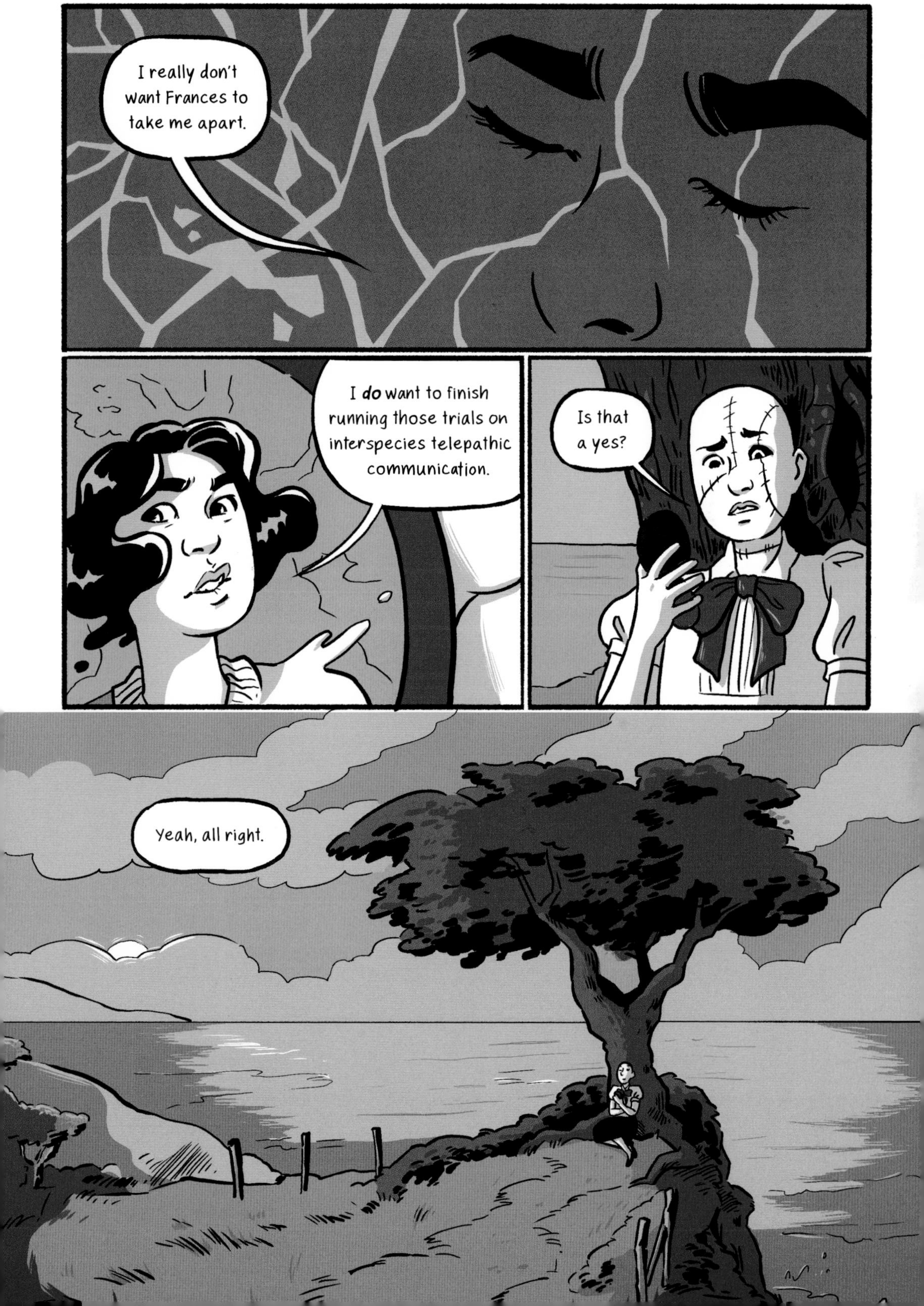
I really don't want Frances to take me apart.
I *do* want to finish running those trials on interspecies telepathic communication.
Is that a yes?
Yeah, all right.

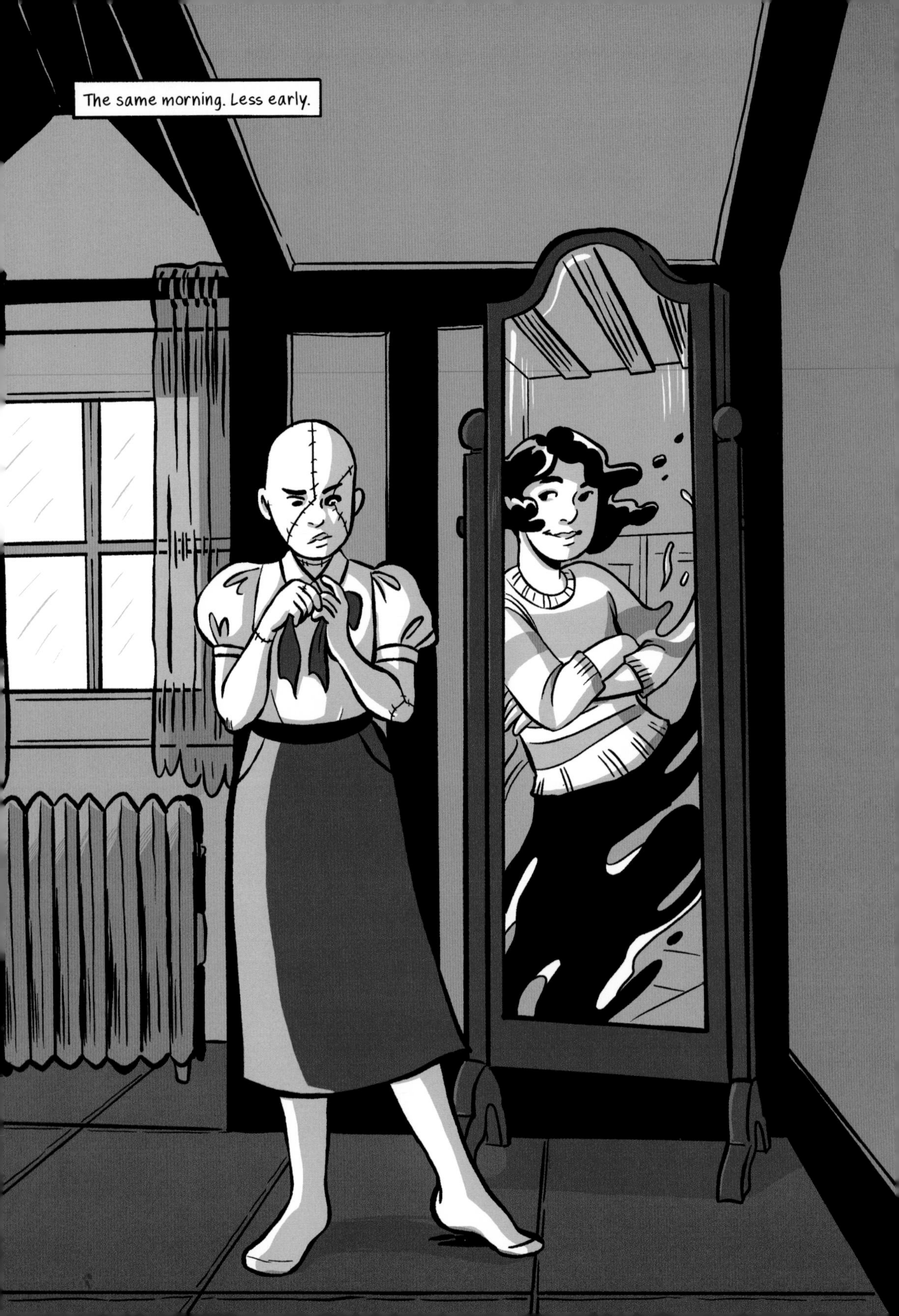
The same morning. Less early.

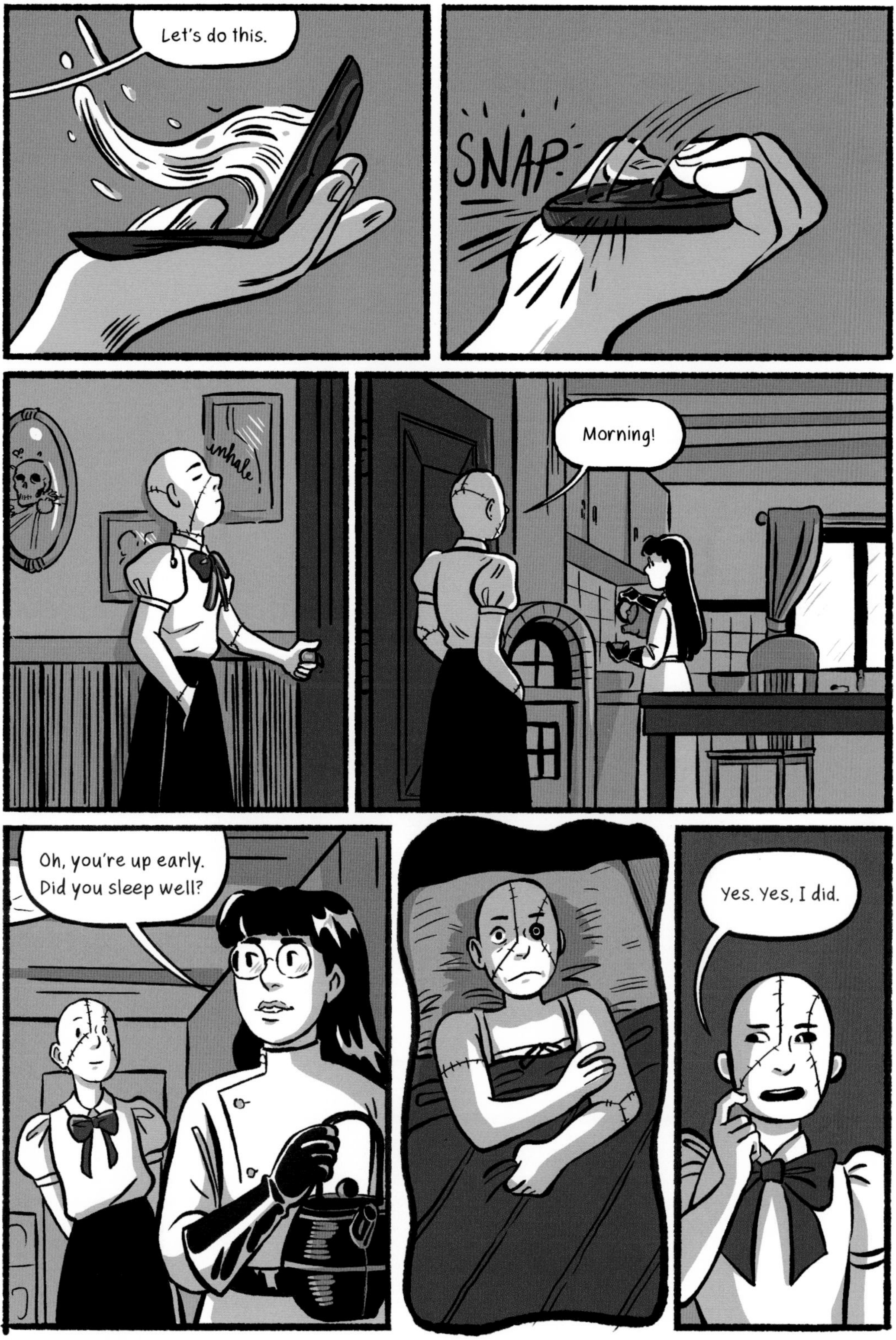
Let's do this.
SNAP
inhale
Morning!
Oh, you're up early. Did you sleep well?
Yes. Yes, I did.

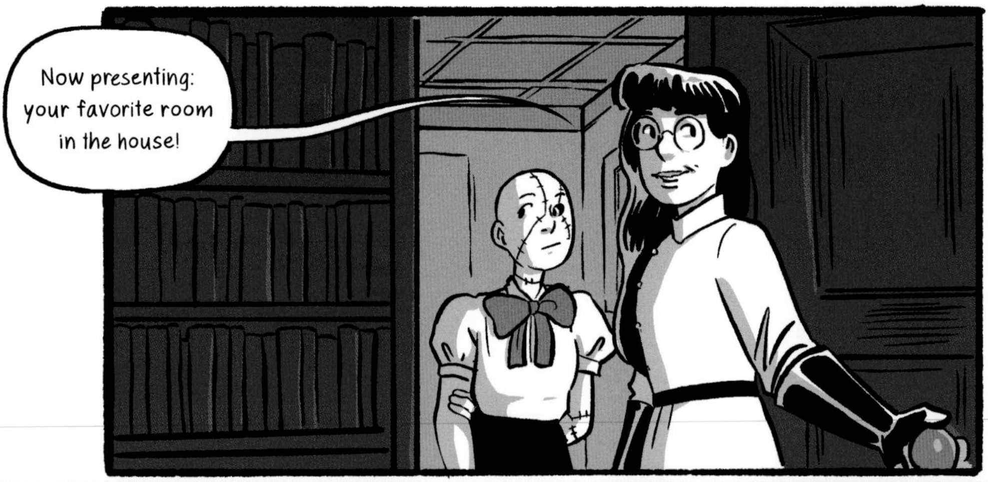
Now presenting: your favorite room in the house!

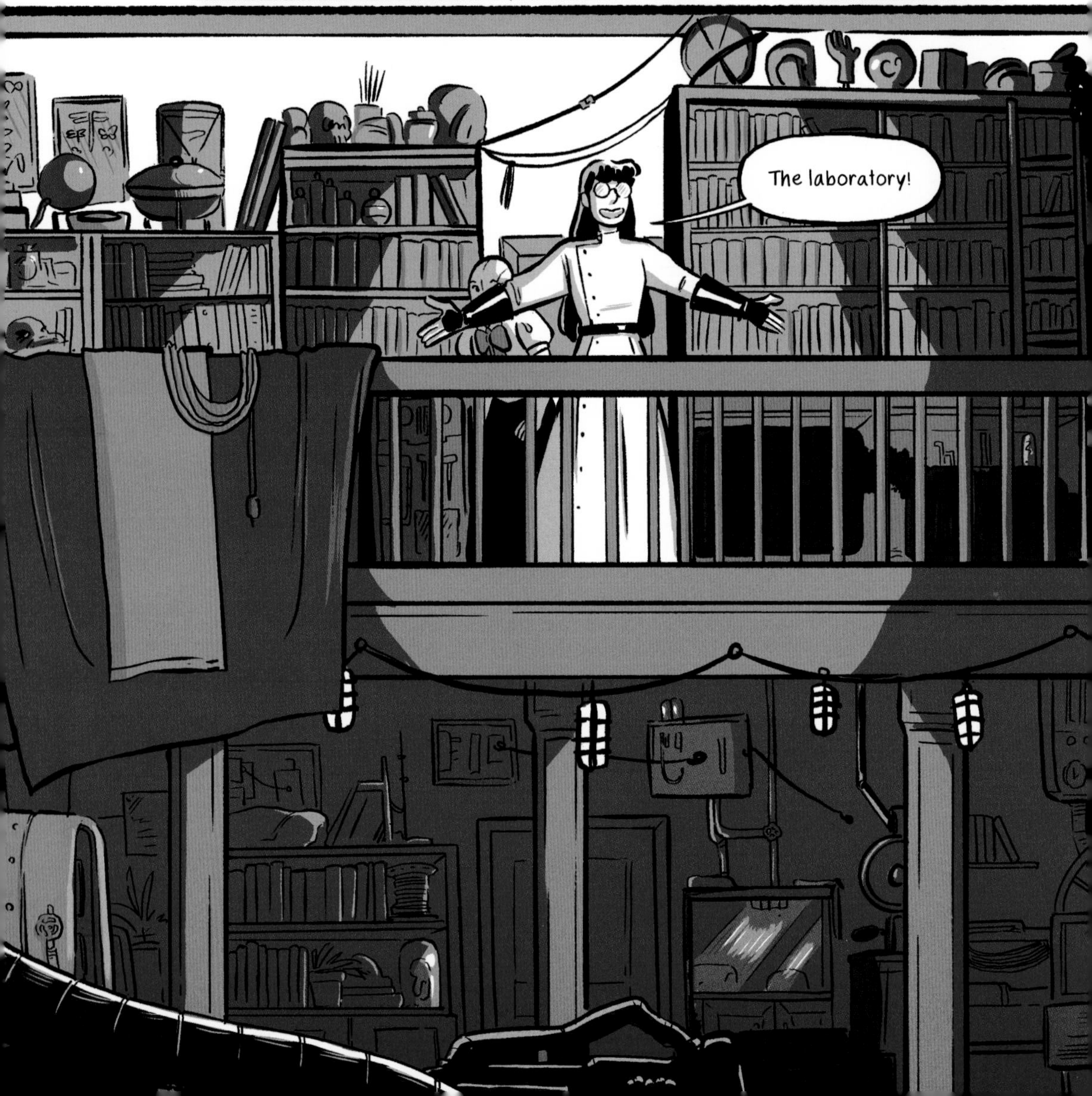
The laboratory!

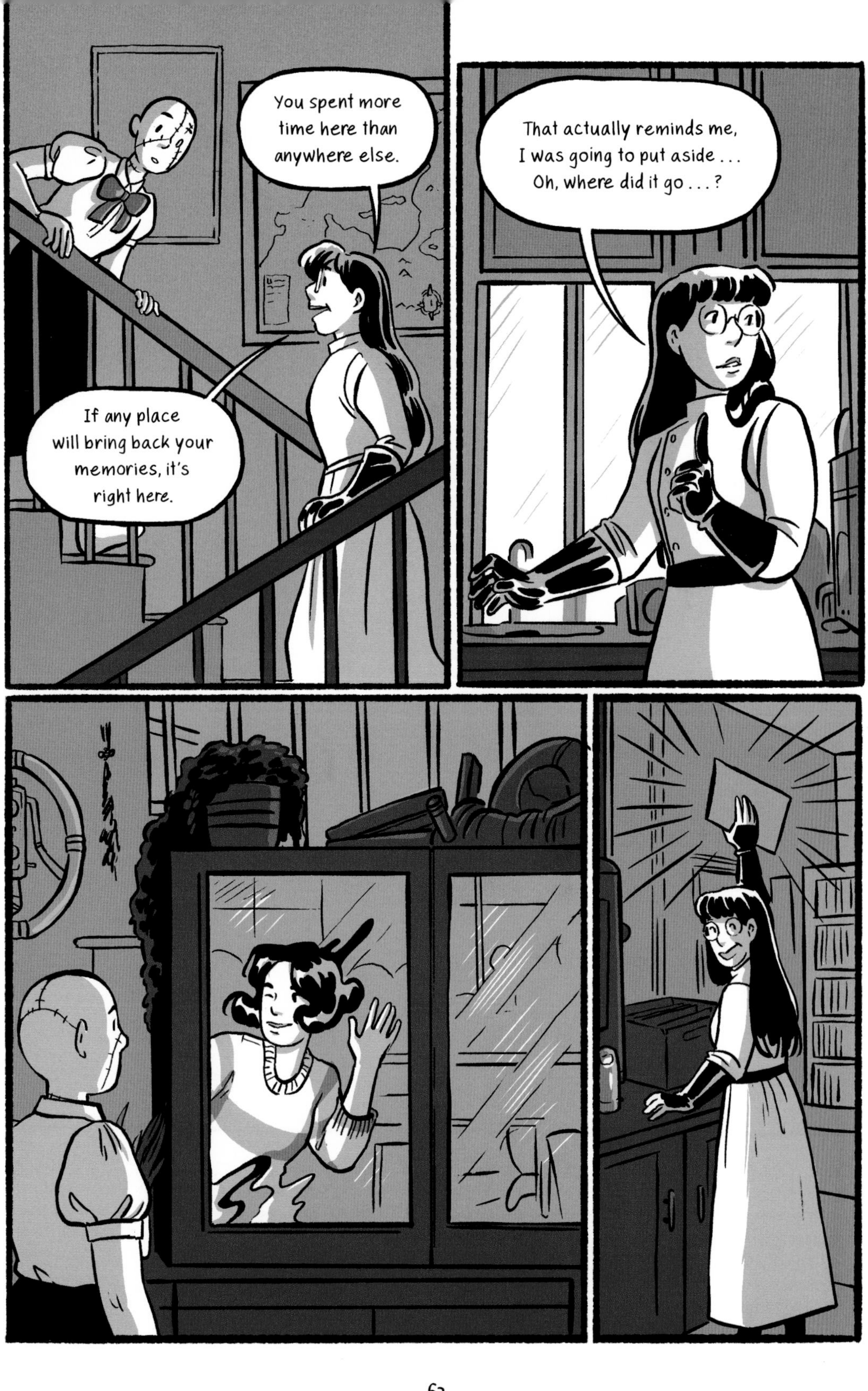
You spent more time here than anywhere else.
If any place will bring back your memories, it's right here.
That actually reminds me, I was going to put aside . . . Oh, where did it go . . . ?

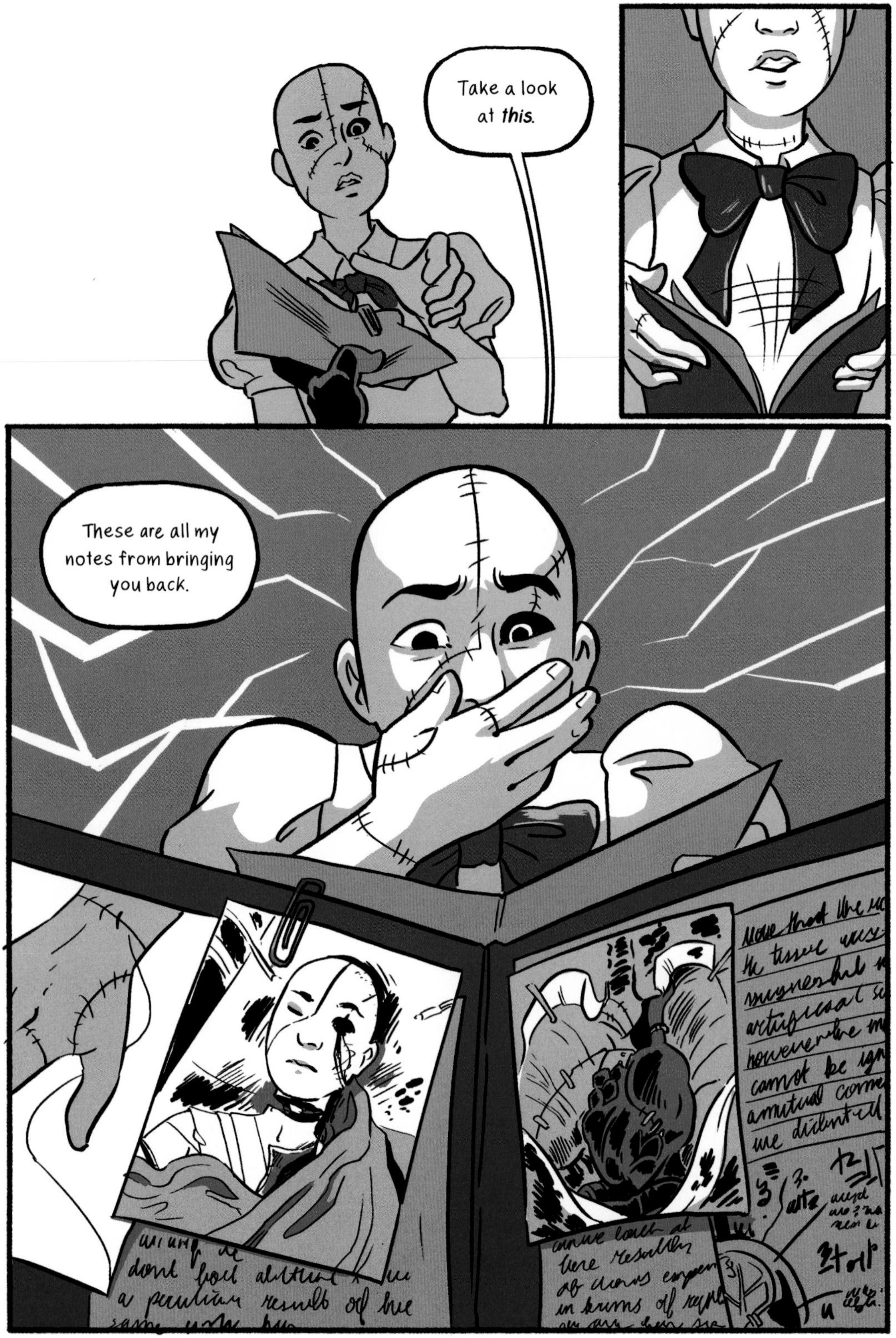
Take a look at *this*.
These are all my notes from bringing you back.

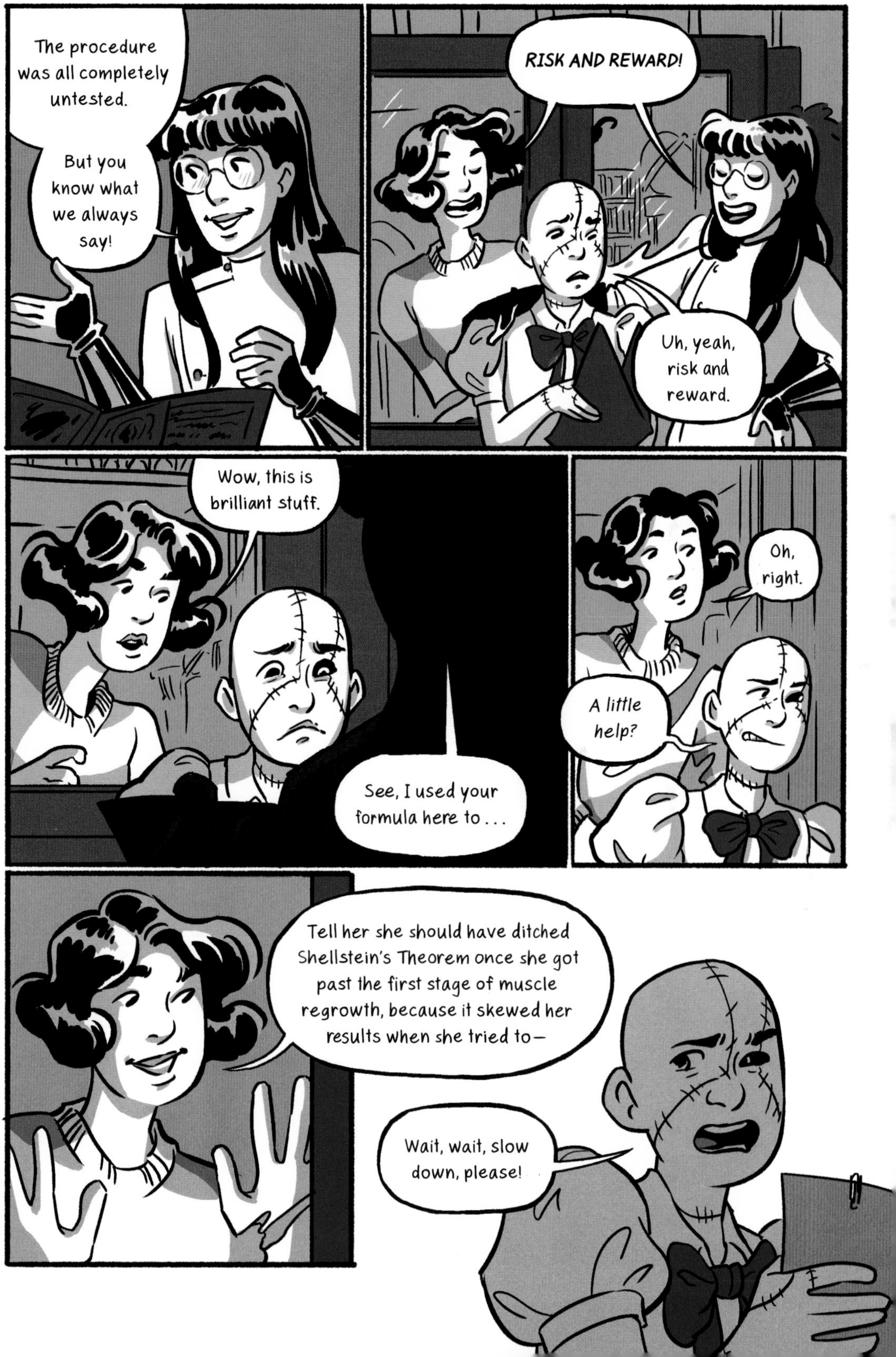
The procedure was all completely untested.
But you know what we always say!
RISK AND REWARD!
Uh, yeah, risk and reward.
Wow, this is brilliant stuff.
See, I used your formula here to . . .
Oh, right.
A little help?
Tell her she should have ditched Shellstein's Theorem once she got past the first stage of muscle regrowth, because it skewed her results when she tried to—
Wait, wait, slow down, please!

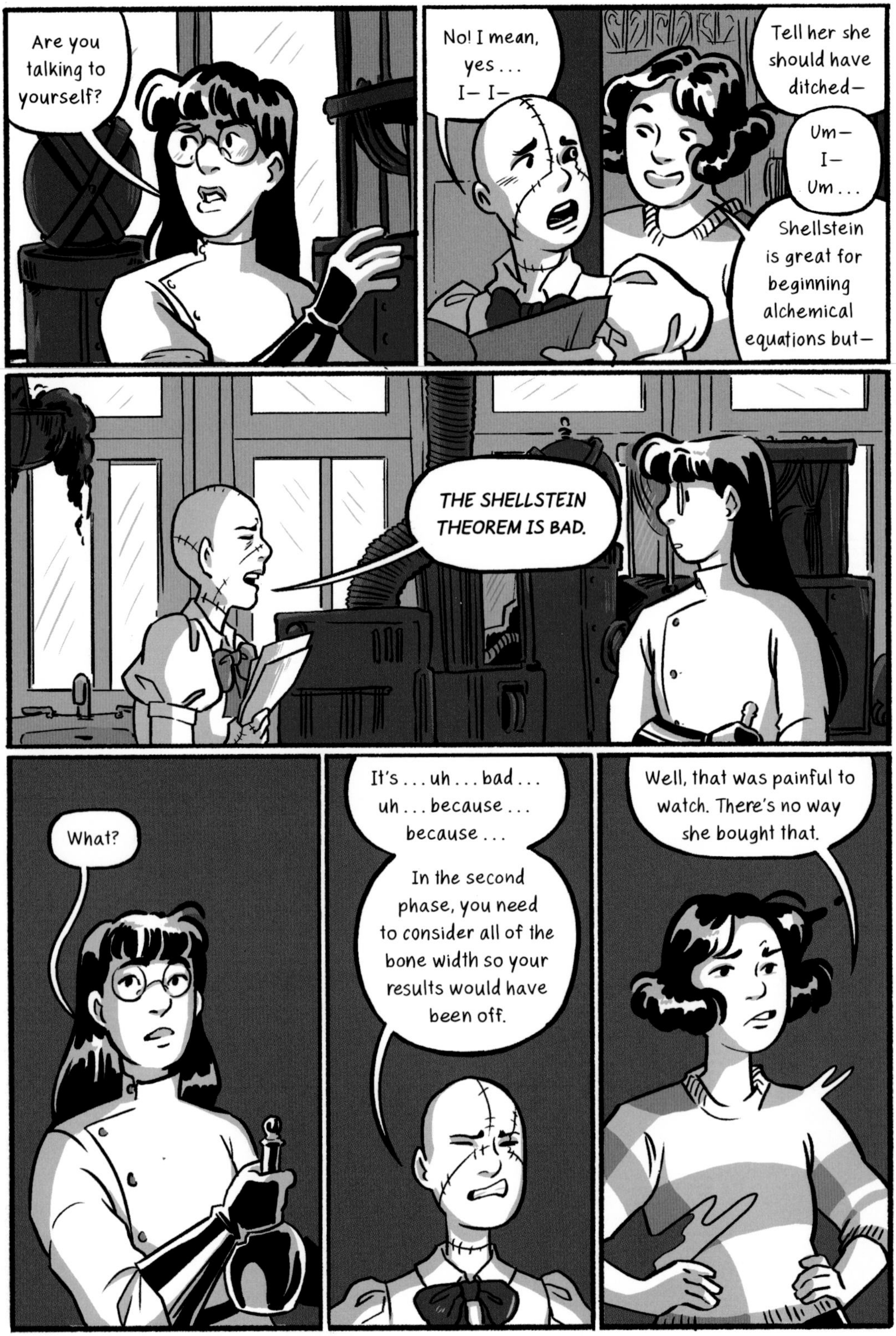
Are you talking to yourself?
No! I mean, yes . . . I– I–
Tell her she should have ditched–
Um– I– Um . . .
Shellstein is great for beginning alchemical equations but–
THE SHELLSTEIN THEOREM IS BAD.
What?
It's . . . uh . . . bad . . . uh . . . because . . . because . . .
In the second phase, you need to consider all of the bone width so your results would have been off.
Well, that was painful to watch. There's no way she bought that.

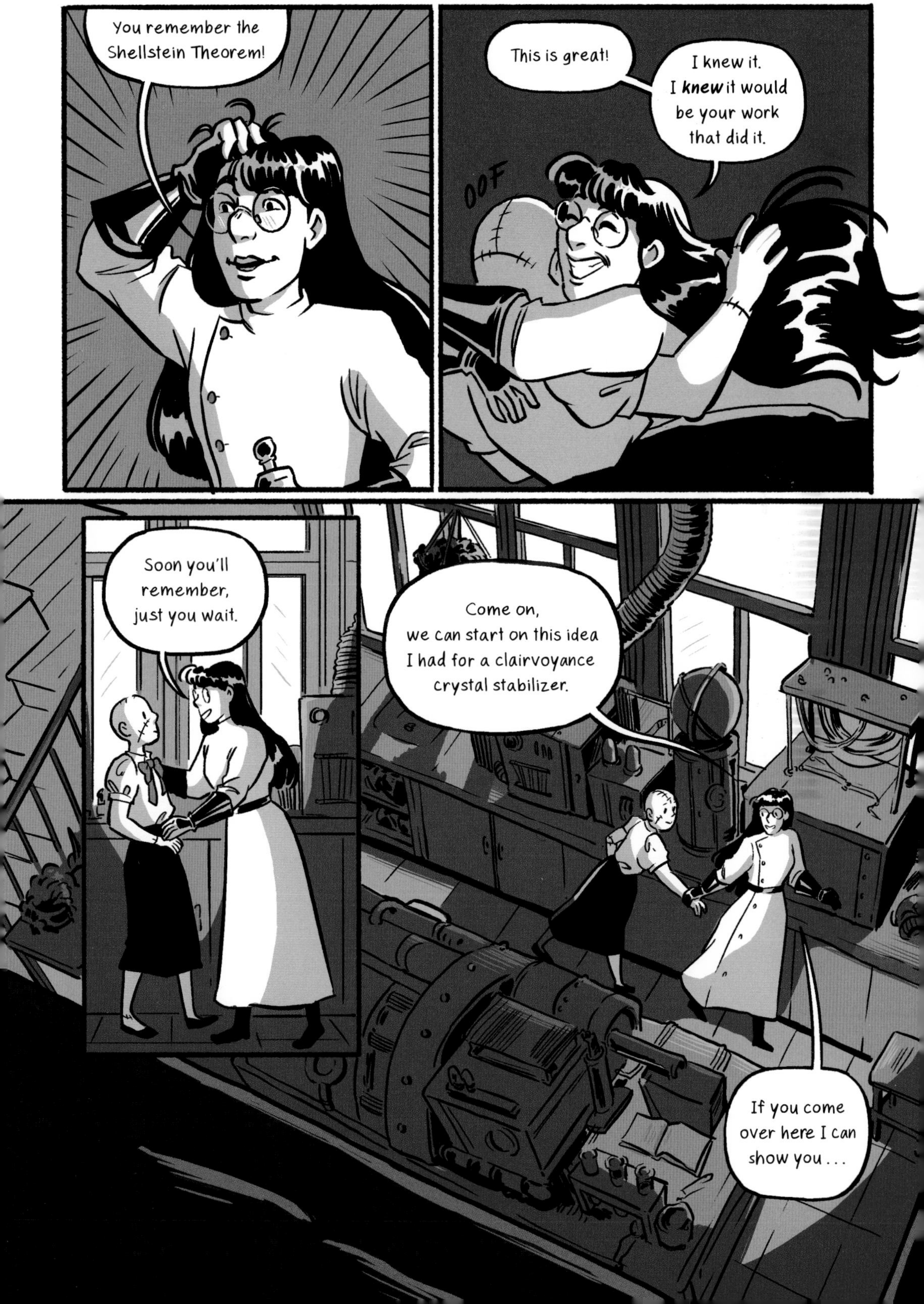
You remember the Shellstein Theorem!
This is great!
I knew it. I *knew* it would be your work that did it.
OOF
Soon you'll remember, just you wait.
Come on, we can start on this idea I had for a clairvoyance crystal stabilizer.
If you come over here I can show you . . .

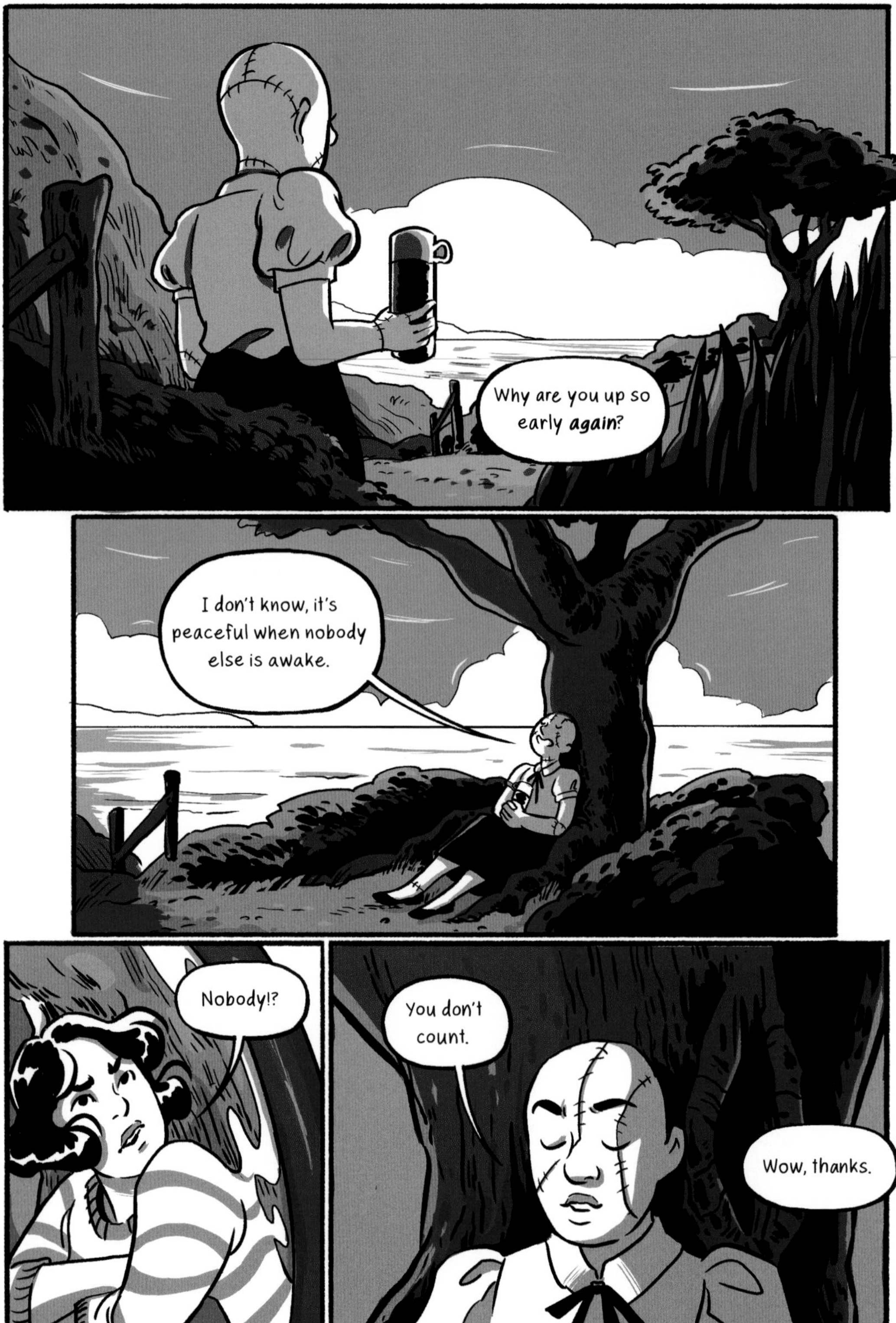

Why are you up so early **again**?
I don't know, it's peaceful when nobody else is awake.
Nobody!?
You don't count.
Wow, thanks.

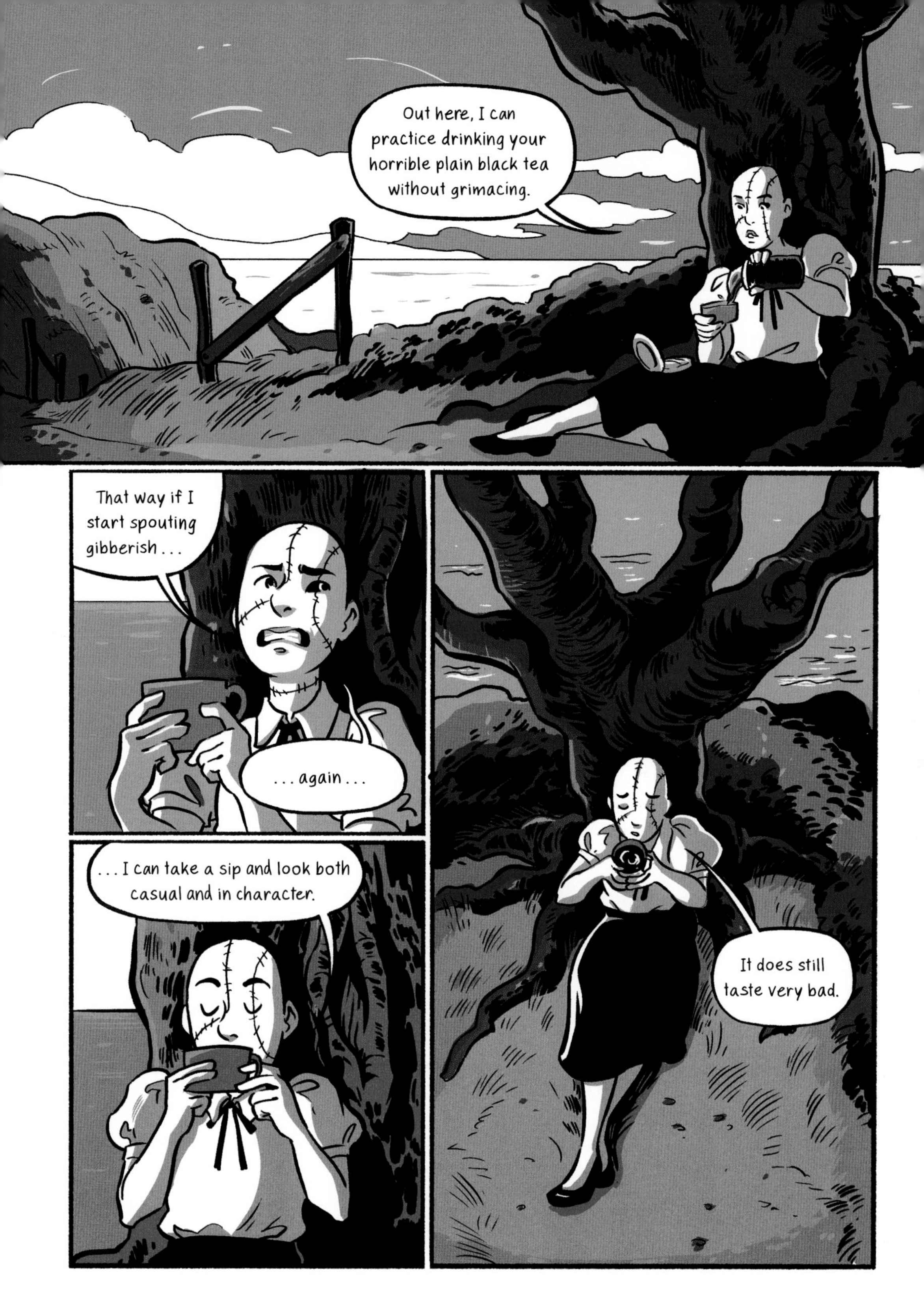
Out here, I can practice drinking your horrible plain black tea without grimacing.
That way if I start spouting gibberish . . .
. . . again . . .
. . . I can take a sip and look both casual and in character.
It does still taste very bad.

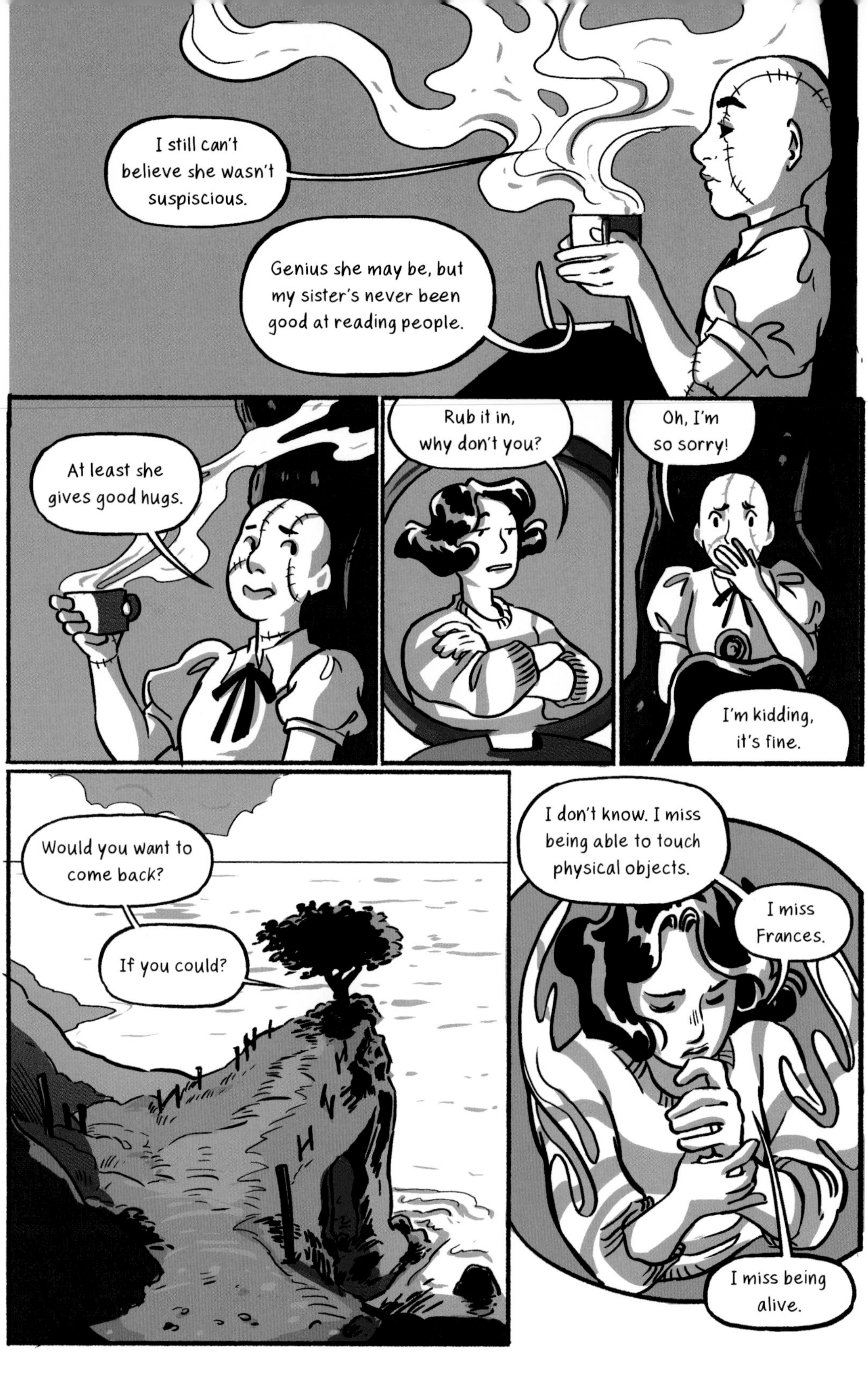
I still can't believe she wasn't suspiscious.
Genius she may be, but my sister's never been good at reading people.
At least she gives good hugs.
Rub it in, why don't you?
Oh, I'm so sorry!
I'm kidding, it's fine.
Would you want to come back?
If you could?
I don't know. I miss being able to touch physical objects.
I miss Frances.
I miss being alive.

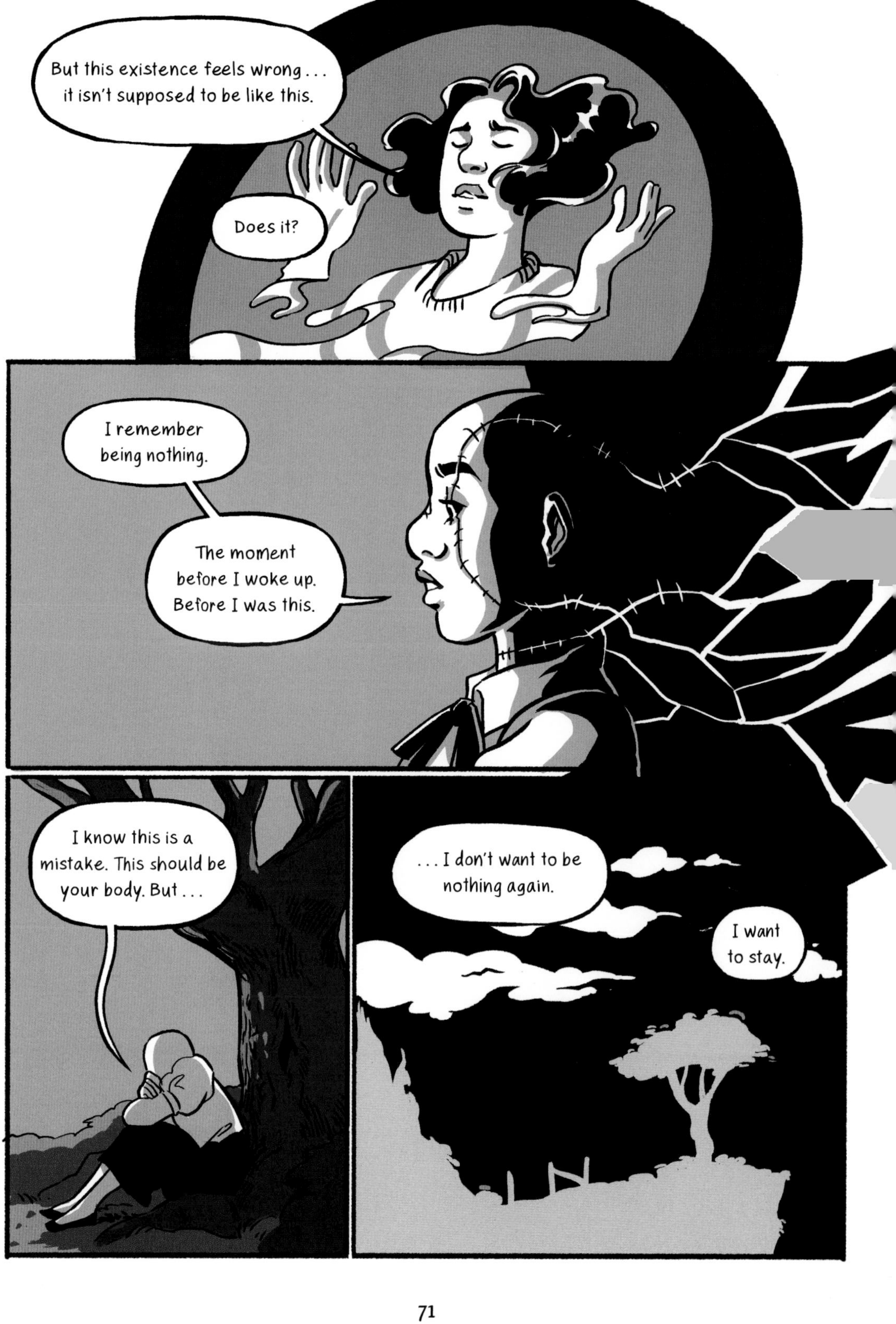
But this existence feels wrong . . . it isn't supposed to be like this.
Does it?
I remember being nothing.
The moment before I woke up. Before I was this.
I know this is a mistake. This should be your body. But . . .
. . . I don't want to be nothing again.
I want to stay.

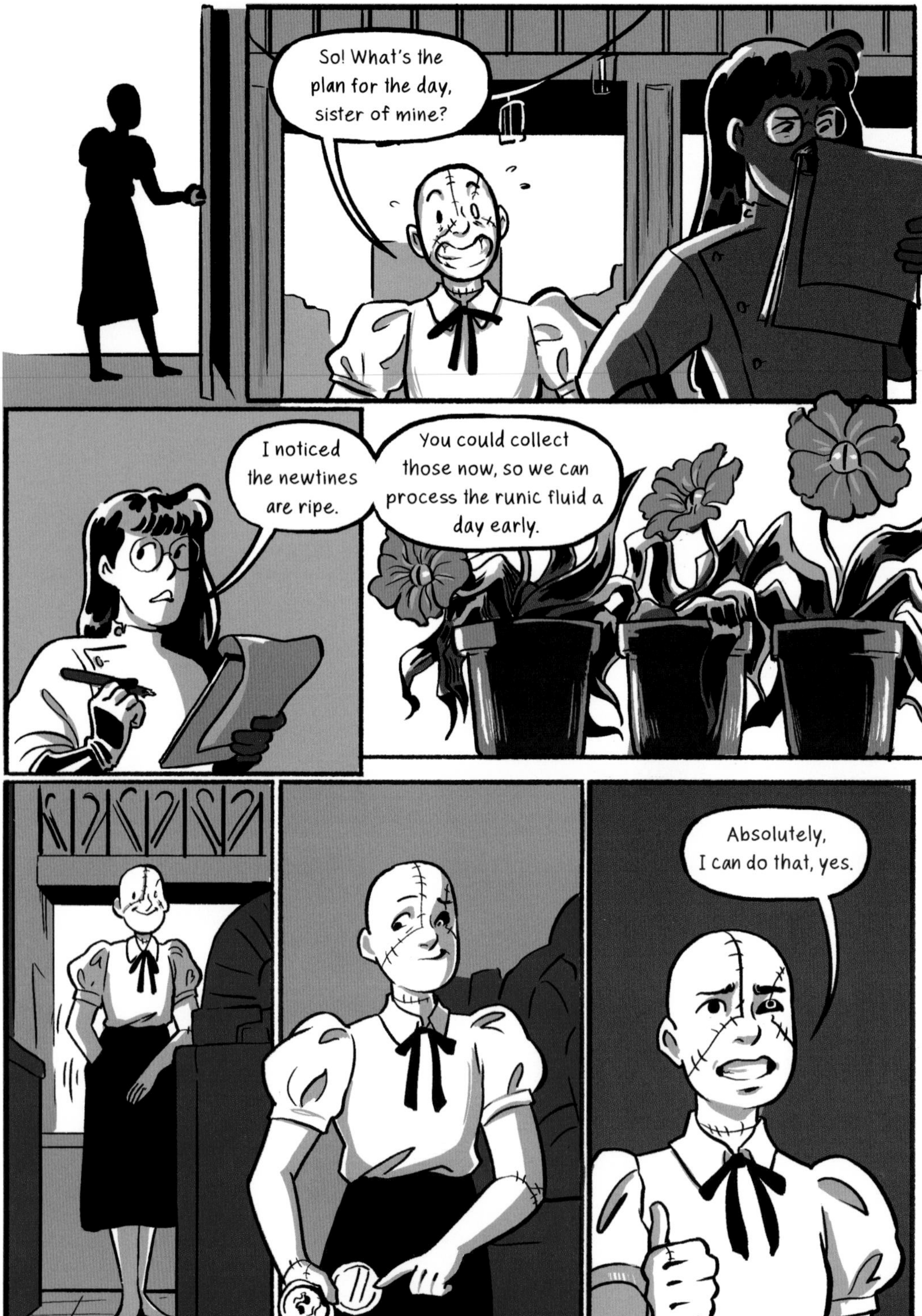
So! What's the plan for the day, sister of mine?
I noticed the newtines are ripe.
You could collect those now, so we can process the runic fluid a day early.
Absolutely, I can do that, yes.

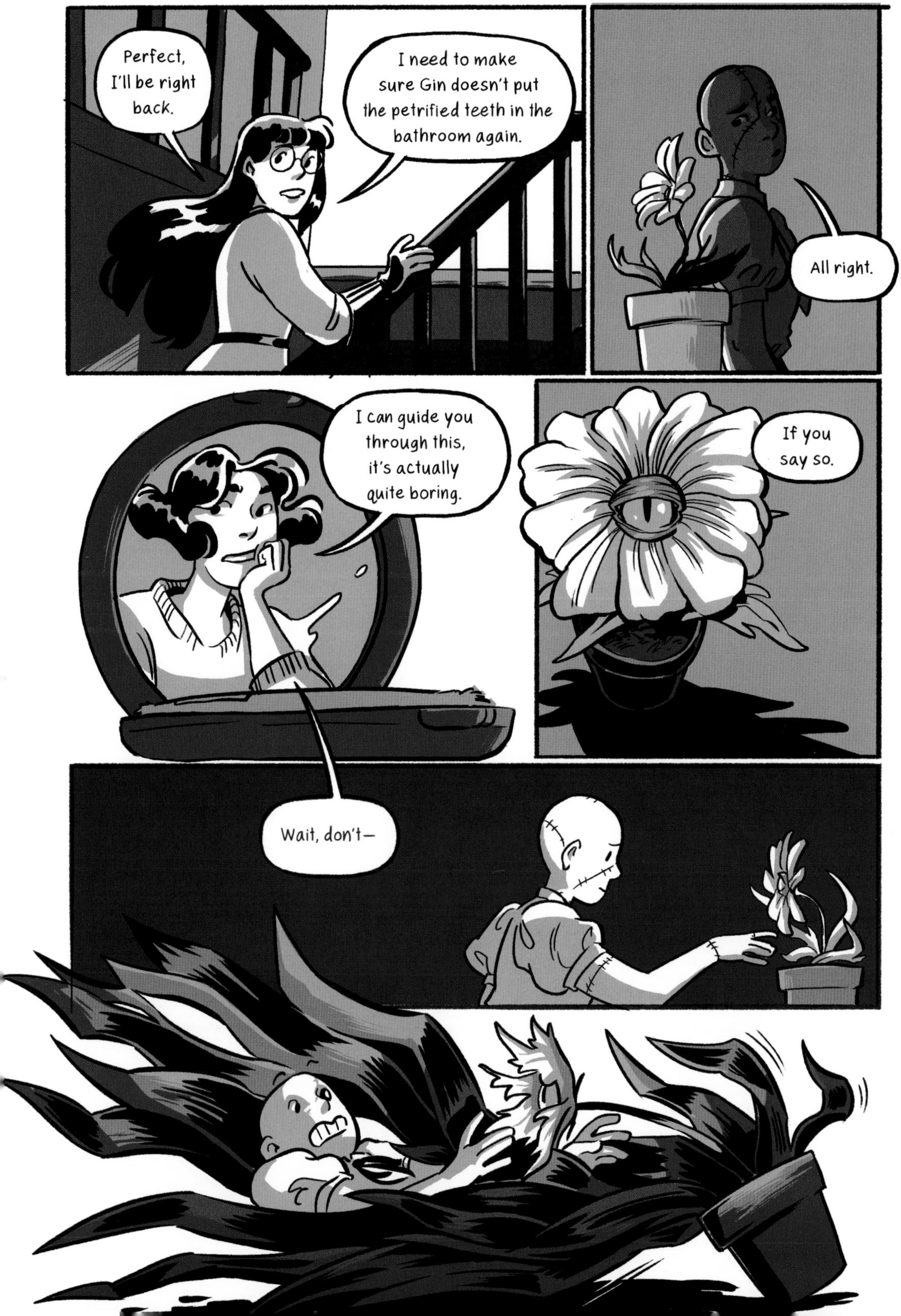

Perfect, I'll be right back.
I need to make sure Gin doesn't put the petrified teeth in the bathroom again.
All right.
I can guide you through this, it's actually quite boring.
If you say so.
Wait, don't—

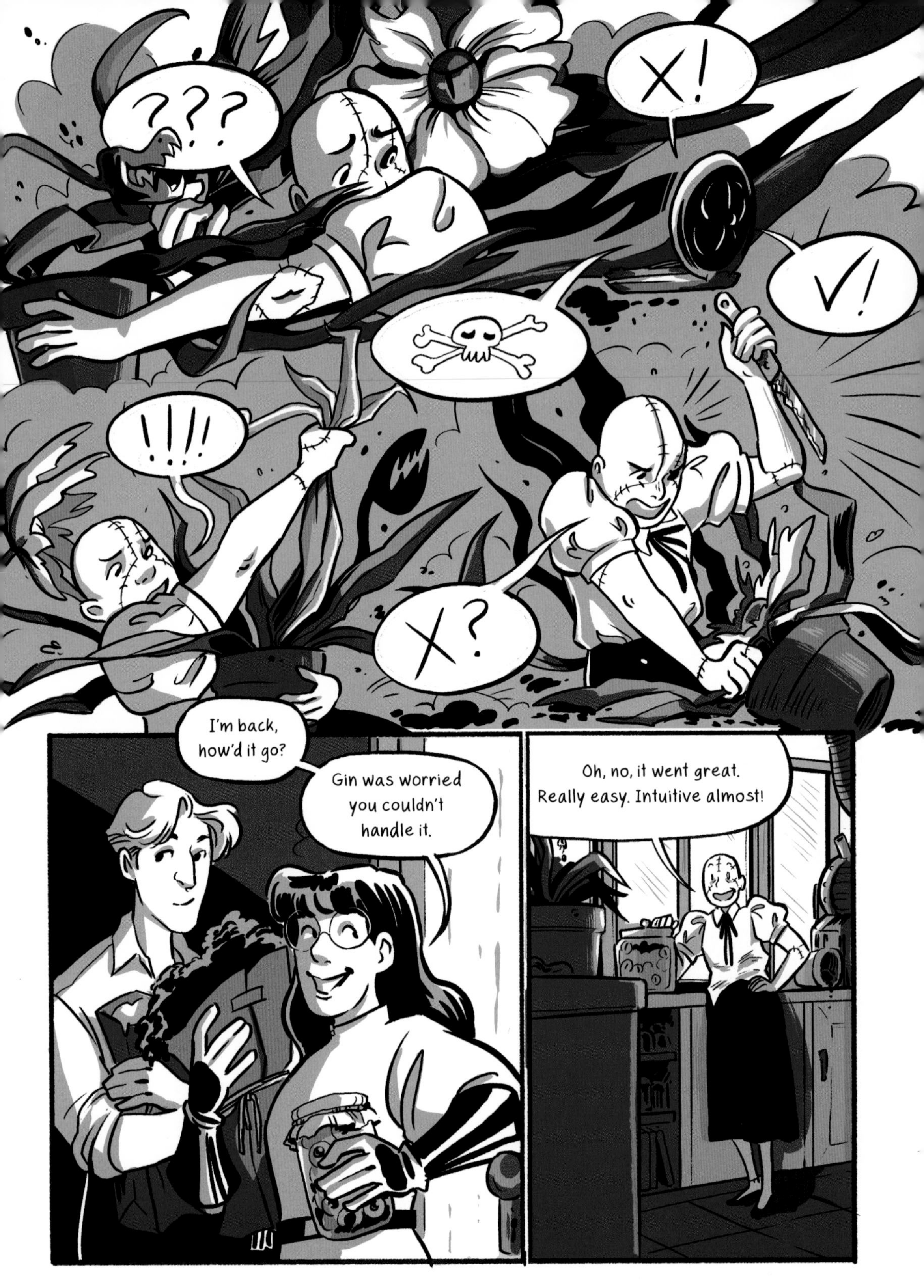
...
???
X!
V!
!!!!
X?
I'm back, how'd it go?
Gin was worried you couldn't handle it.
Oh, no, it went great. Really easy. Intuitive almost!

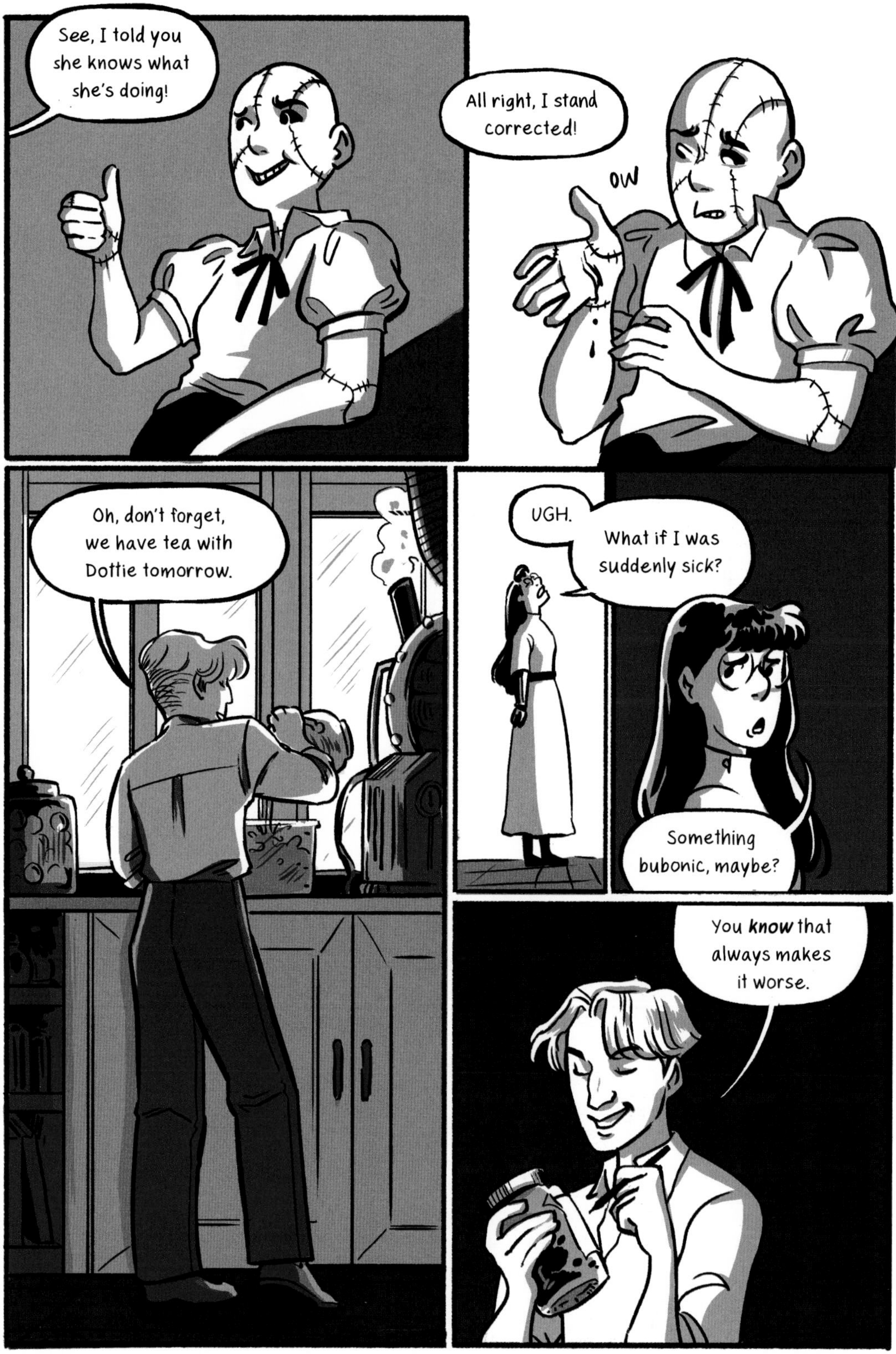
See, I told you she knows what she's doing!
All right, I stand corrected!
OW
Oh, don't forget, we have tea with Dottie tomorrow.
UGH.
What if I was suddenly sick?
Something bubonic, maybe?
You **know** that always makes it worse.

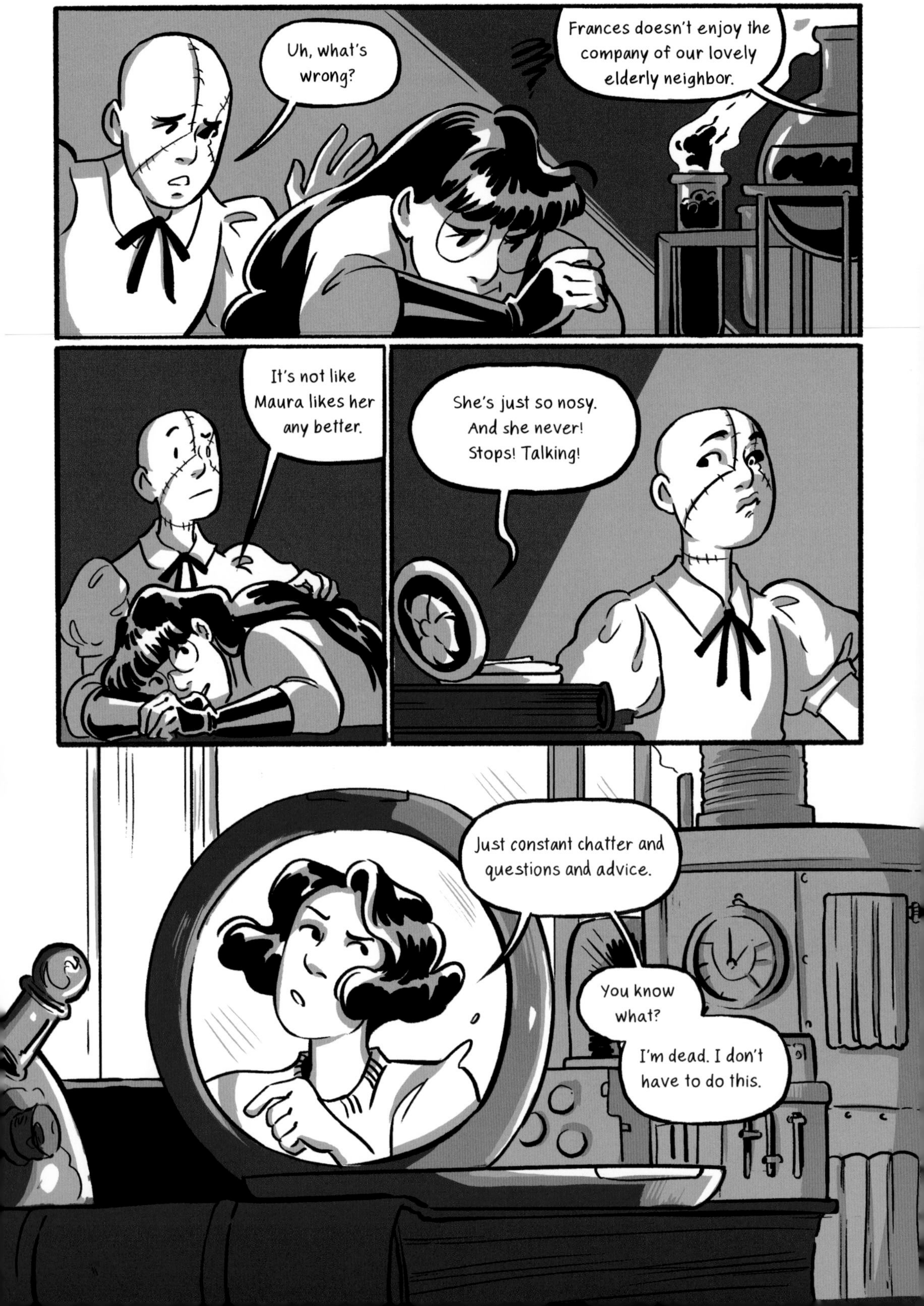
Uh, what's wrong?
Frances doesn't enjoy the company of our lovely elderly neighbor.
It's not like Maura likes her any better.
She's just so nosy. And she never! Stops! Talking!
Just constant chatter and questions and advice.
You know what?
I'm dead. I don't have to do this.

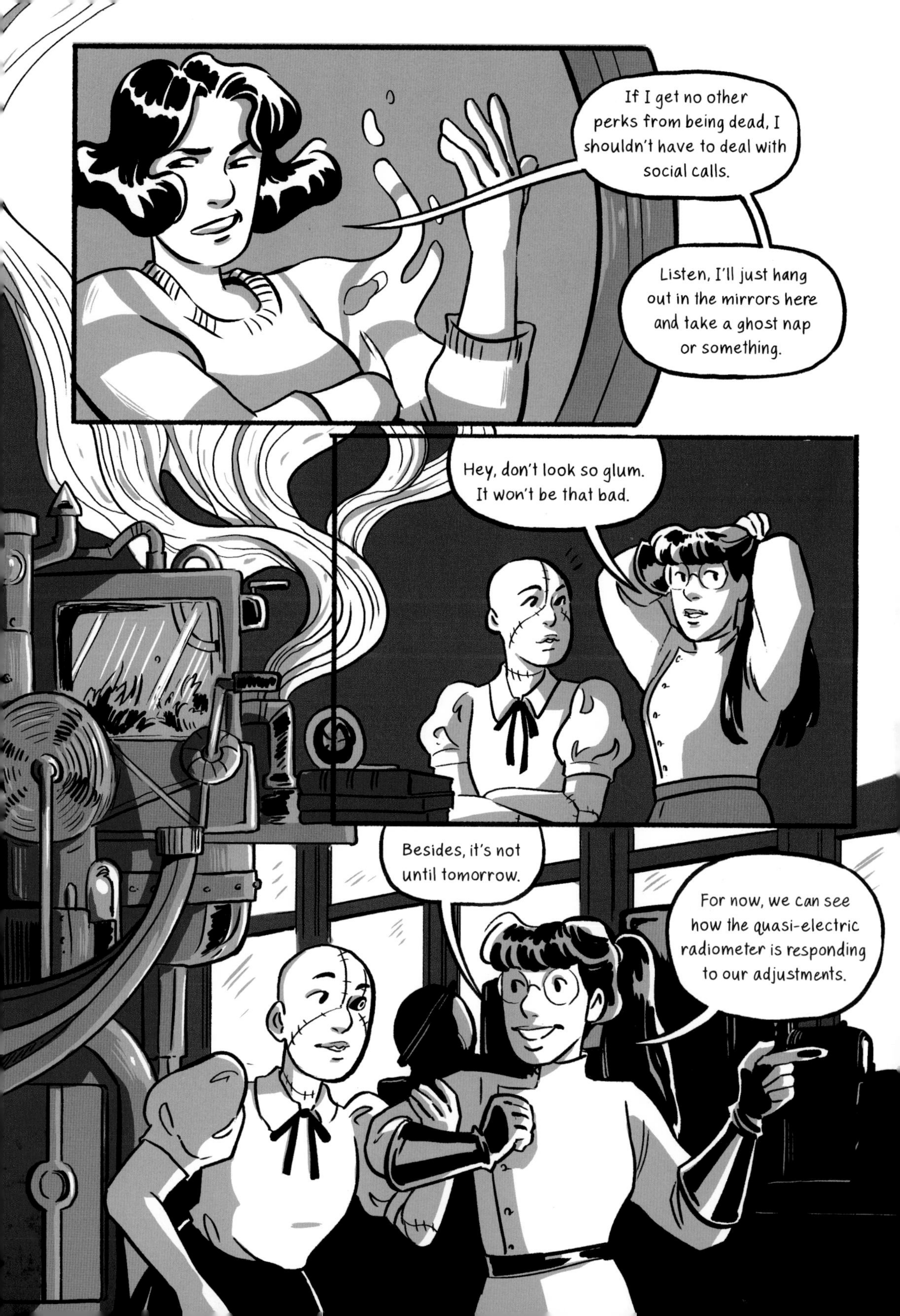

If I get no other perks from being dead, I shouldn't have to deal with social calls.
Listen, I'll just hang out in the mirrors here and take a ghost nap or something.
Hey, don't look so glum. It won't be that bad.
Besides, it's not until tomorrow.
For now, we can see how the quasi-electric radiometer is responding to our adjustments.

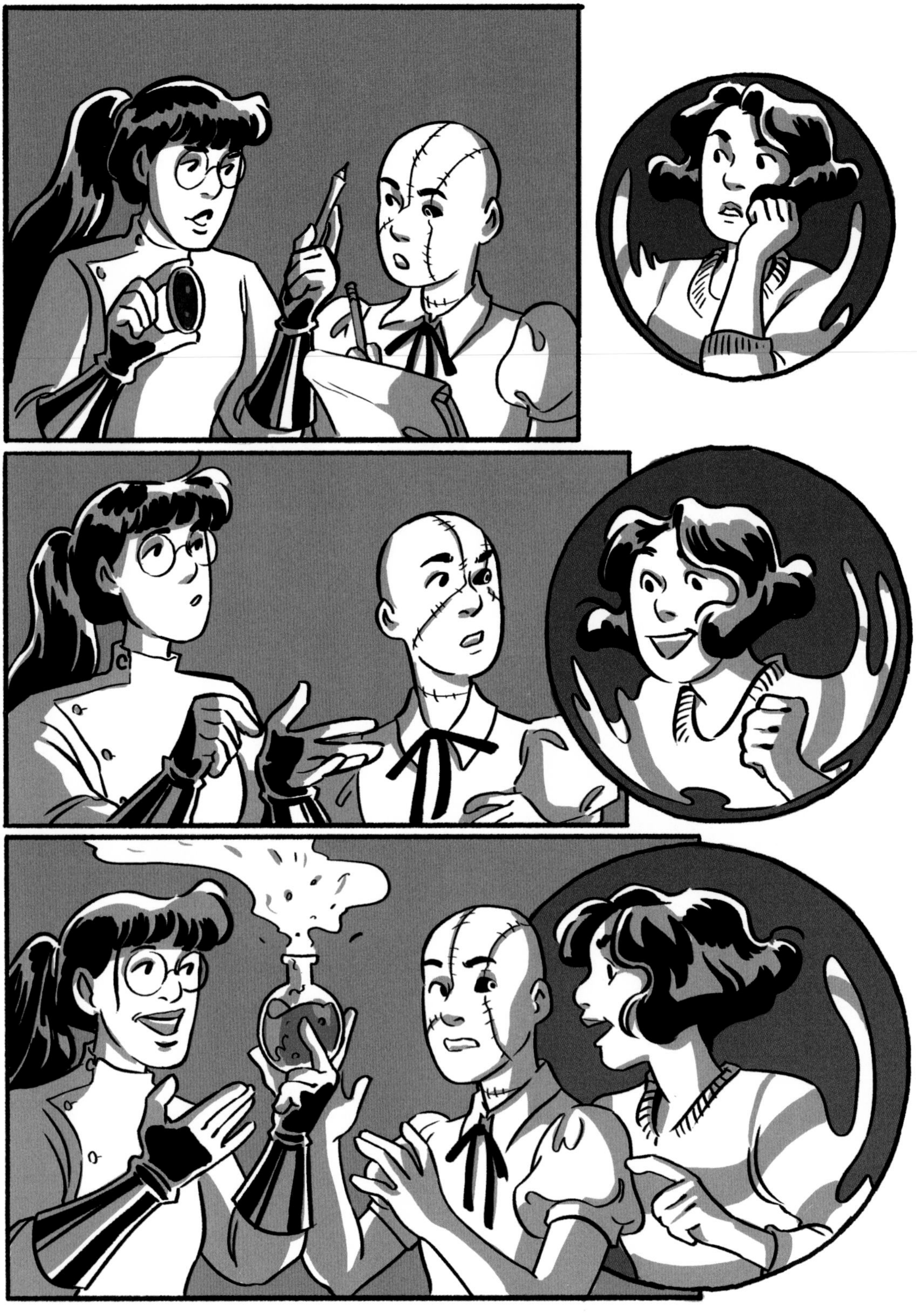

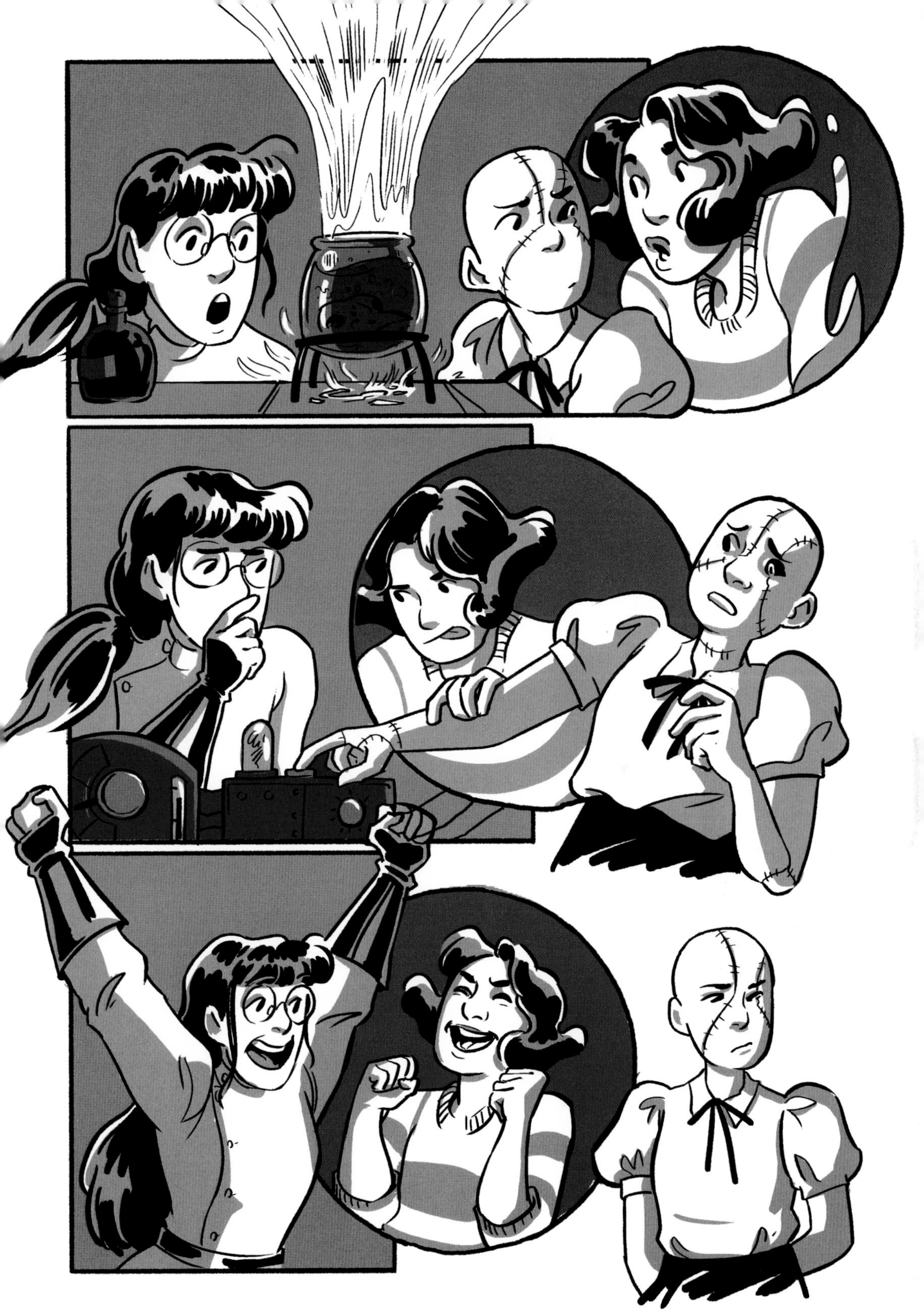

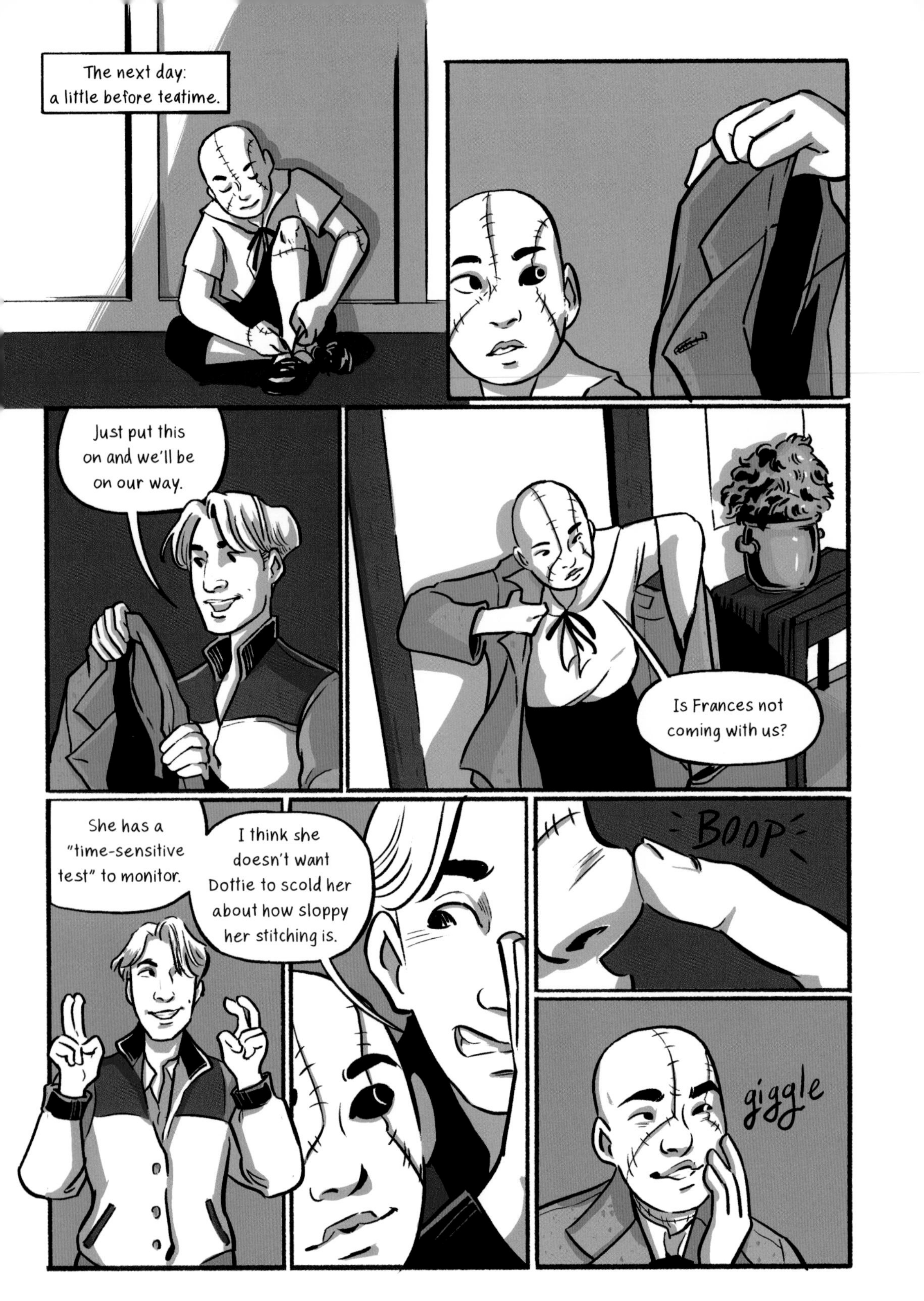
The next day: a little before teatime.
Just put this on and we'll be on our way.
Is Frances not coming with us?
She has a "time-sensitive test" to monitor.
I think she doesn't want Dottie to scold her about how sloppy her stitching is.
BOOP
giggle

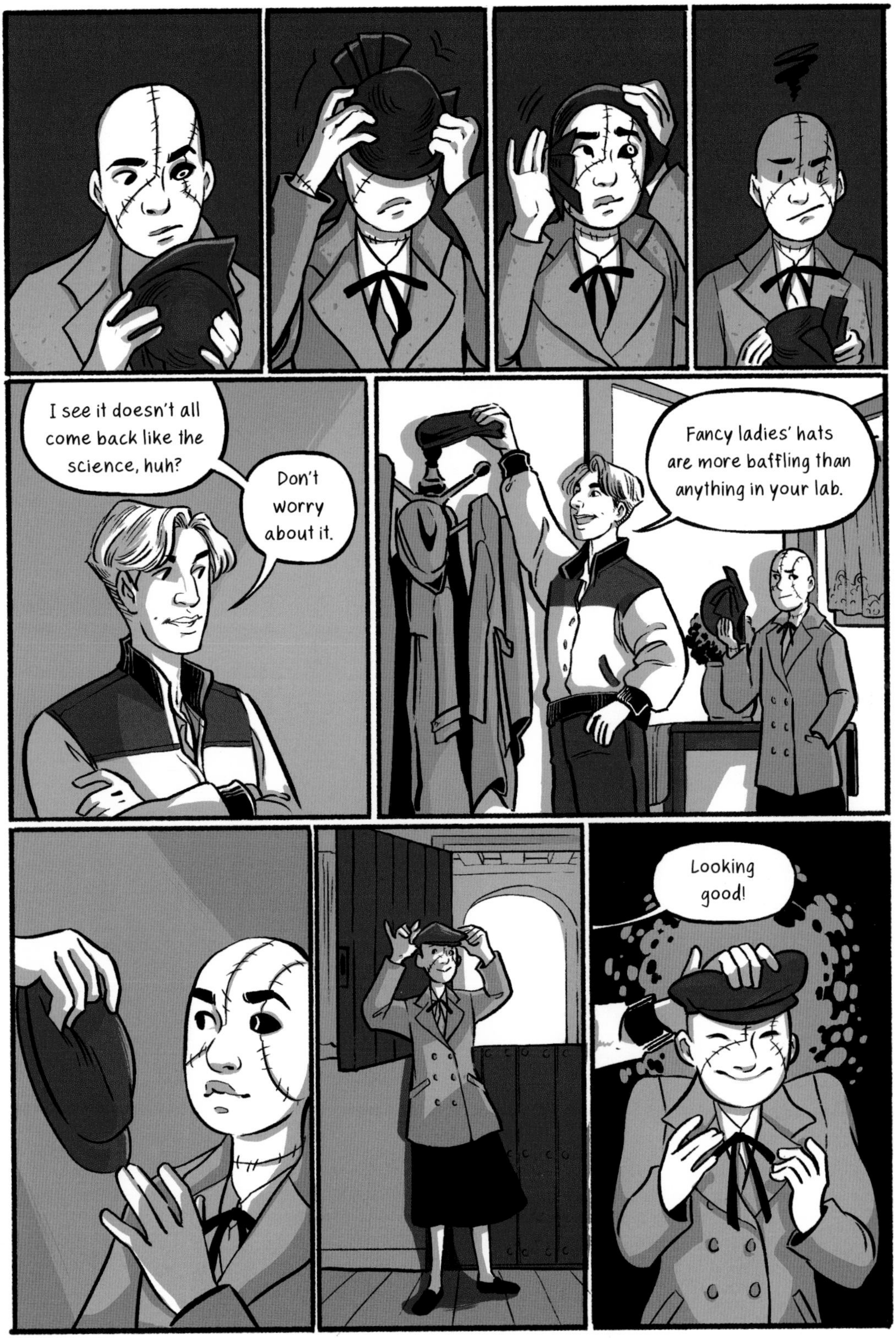
I see it doesn't all come back like the science, huh?
Don't worry about it.
Fancy ladies' hats are more baffling than anything in your lab.
Looking good!

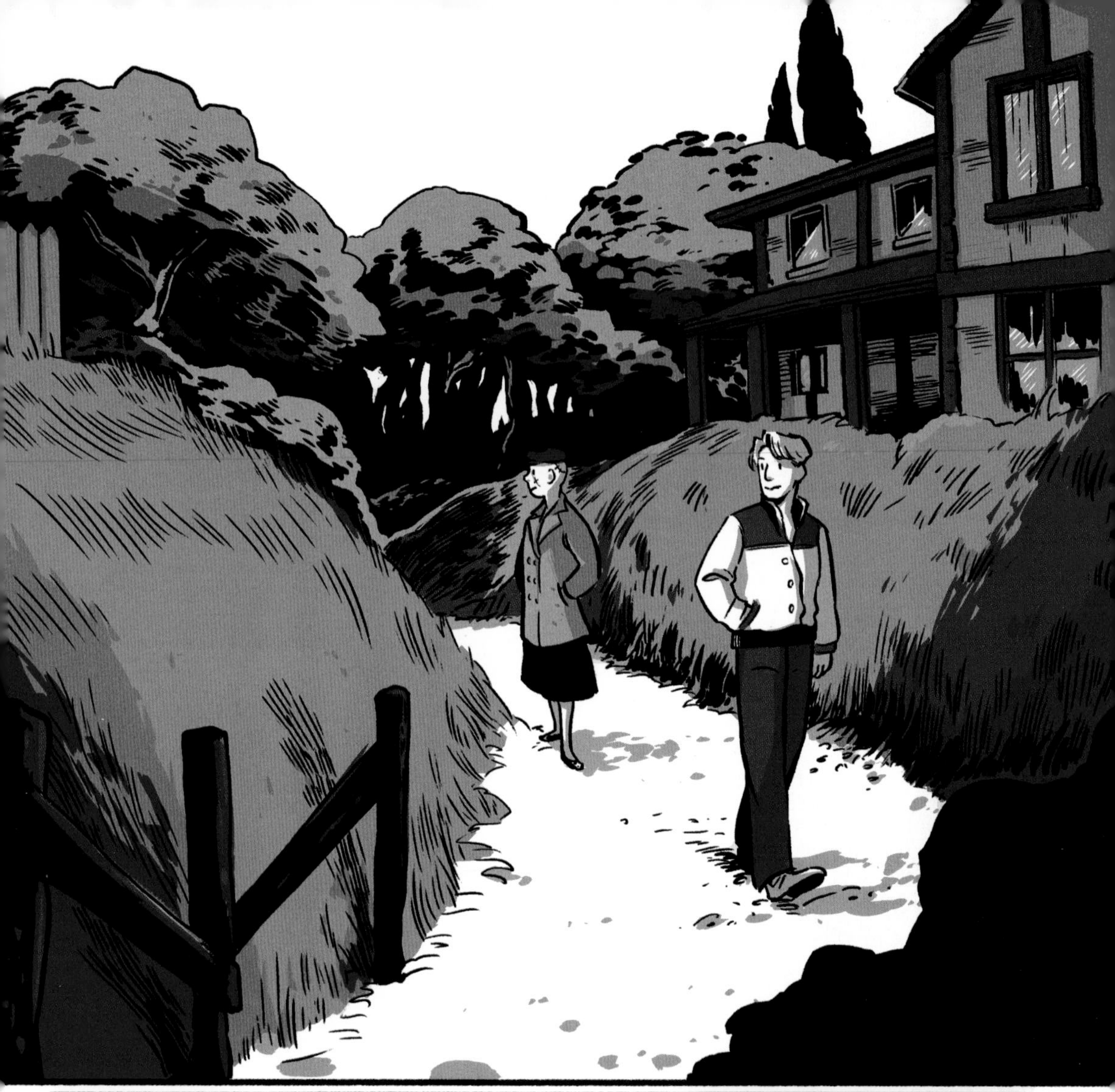

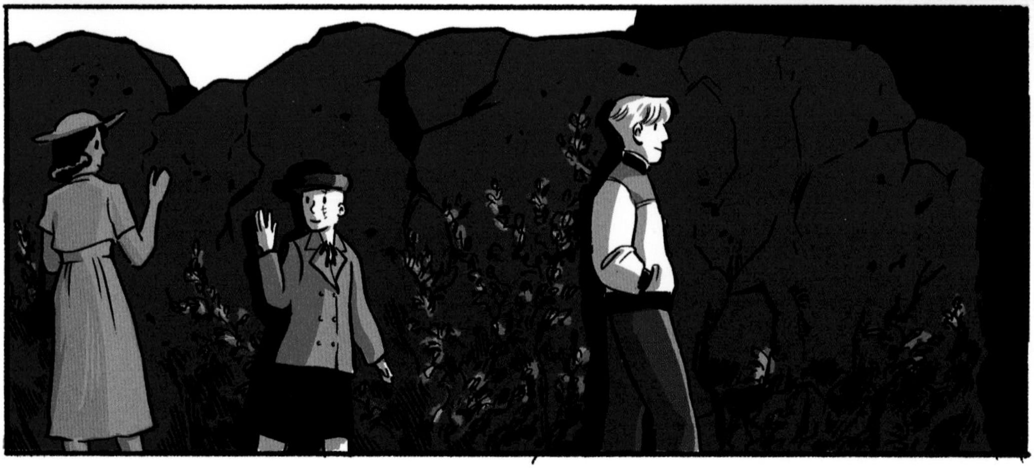

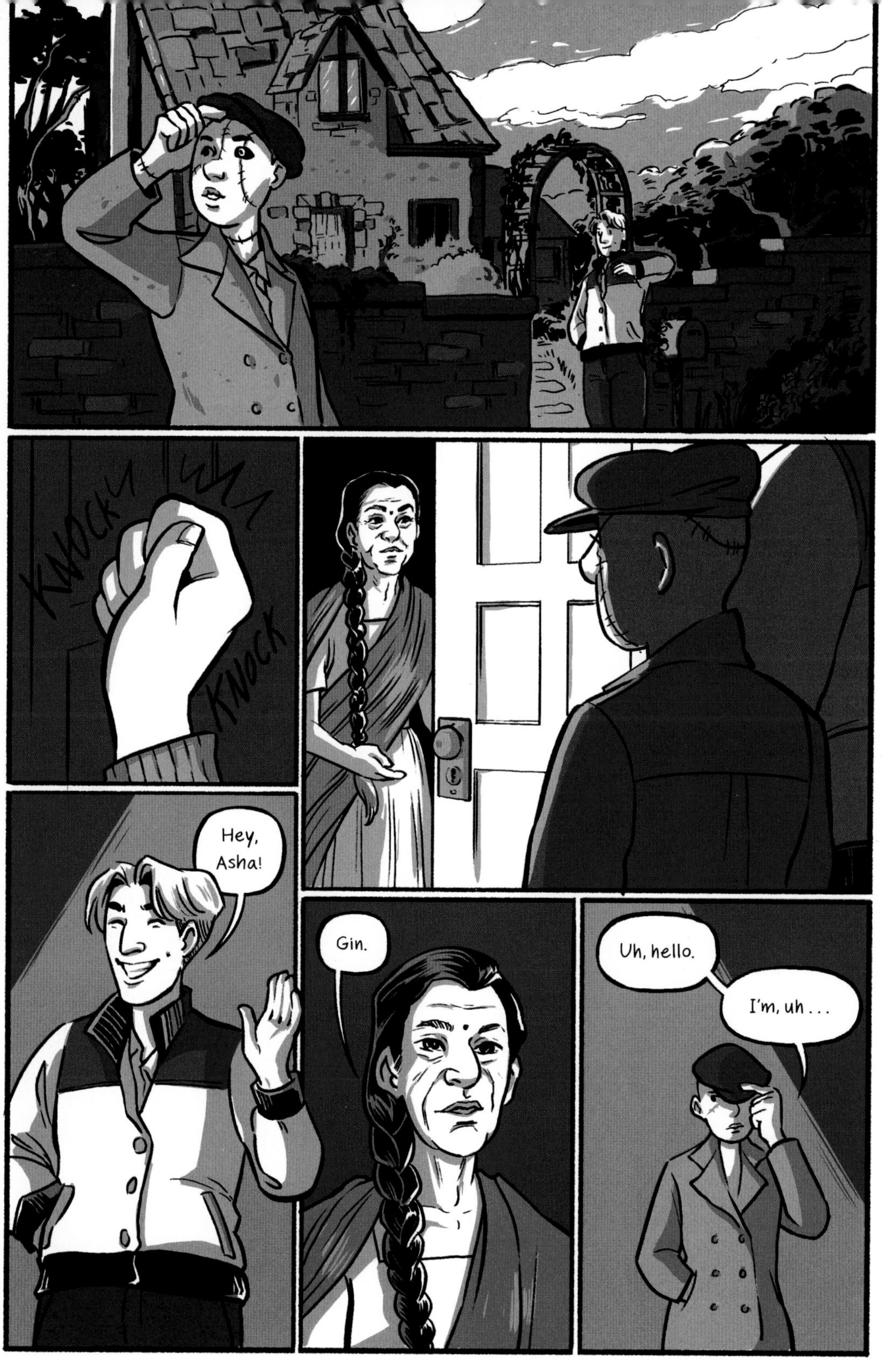
KNOCK
KNOCK
Hey, Asha!
Gin.
Uh, hello.
I'm, uh . . .

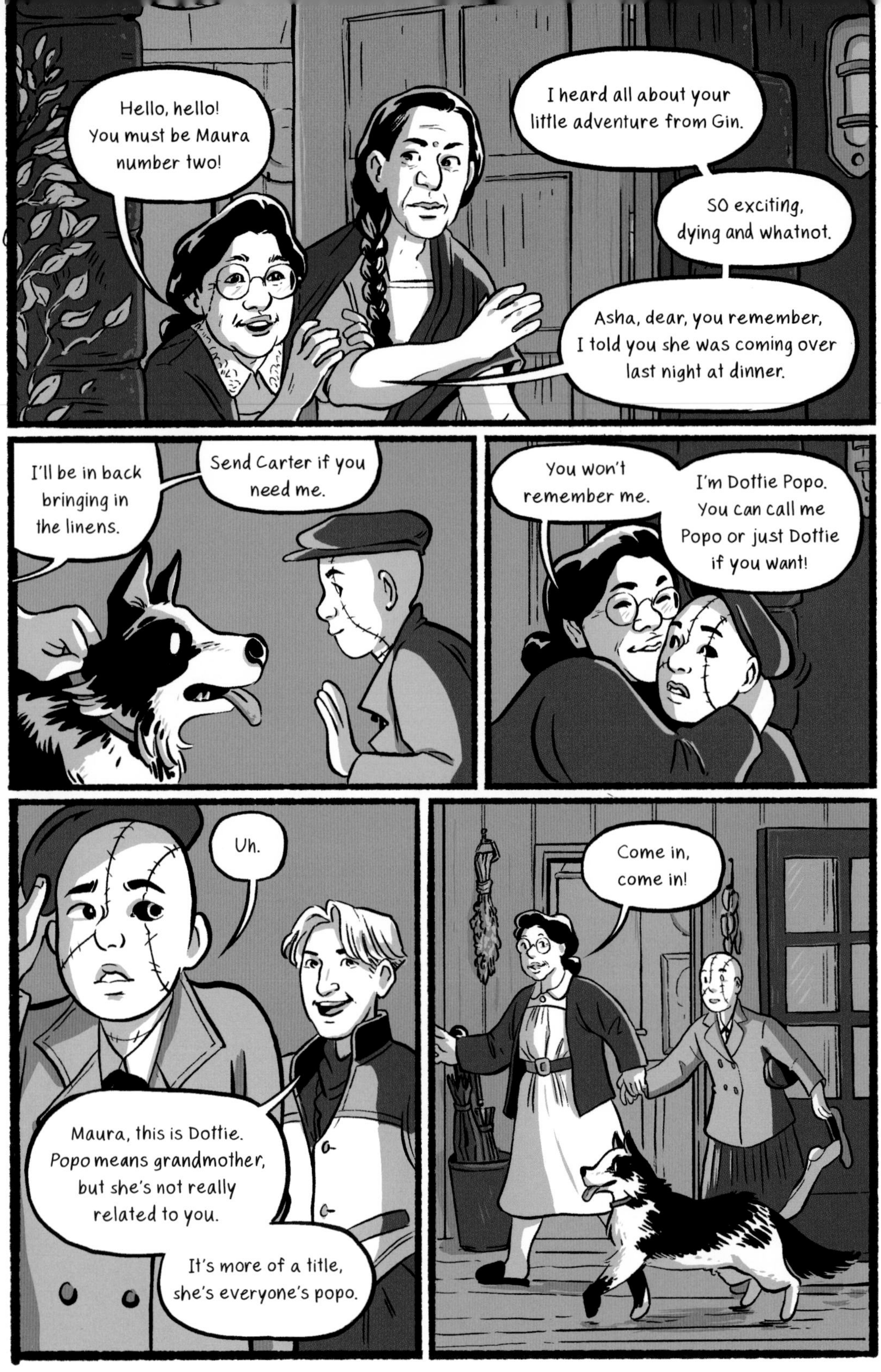

Hello, hello! You must be Maura number two!
I heard all about your little adventure from Gin.
SO exciting, dying and whatnot.
Asha, dear, you remember, I told you she was coming over last night at dinner.
I'll be in back bringing in the linens.
Send Carter if you need me.
You won't remember me.
I'm Dottie Popo. You can call me Popo or just Dottie if you want!
Uh.
Maura, this is Dottie. Popo means grandmother, but she's not really related to you.
It's more of a title, she's everyone's popo.
Come in, come in!

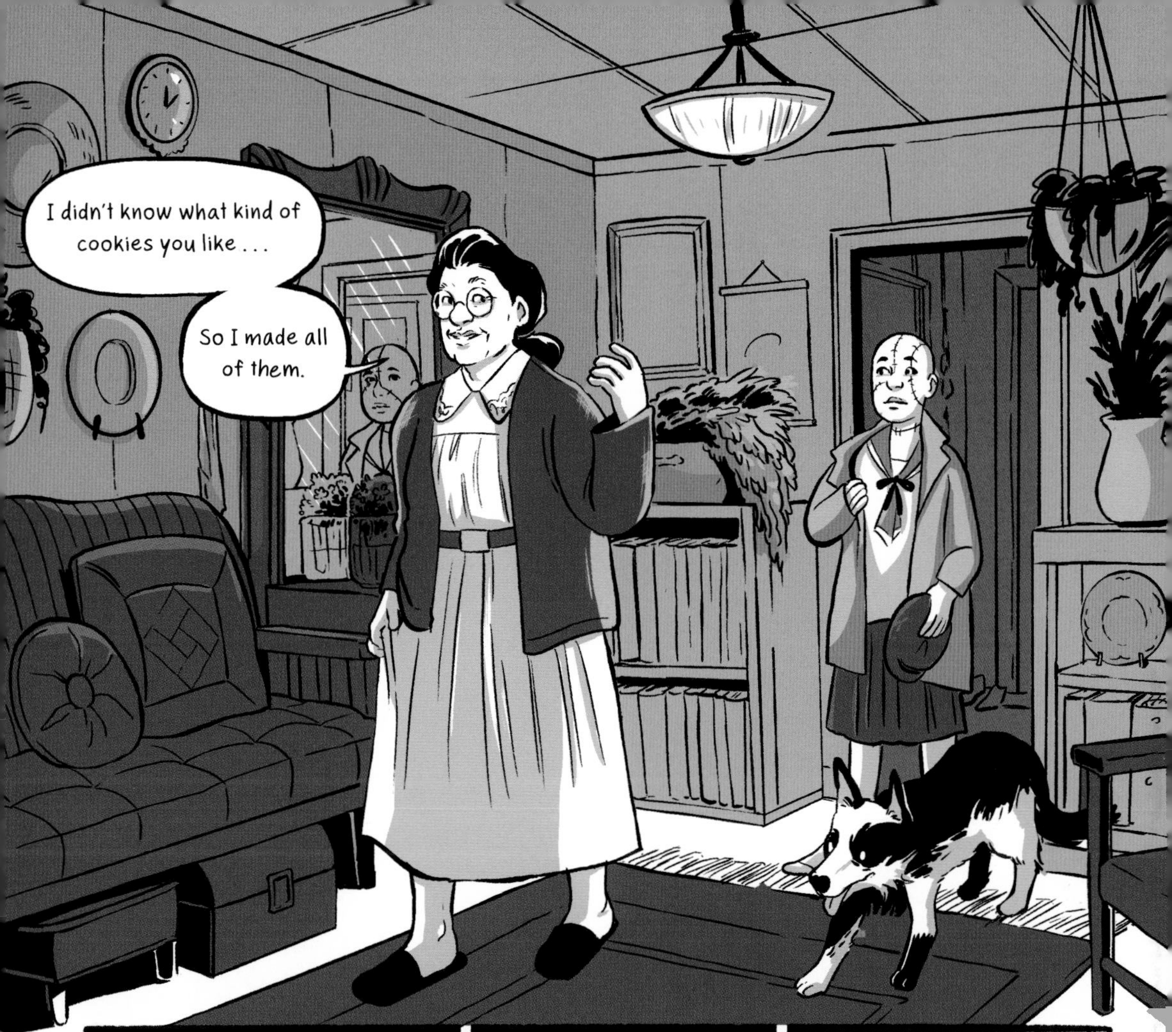
I didn't know what kind of cookies you like . . .
So I made all of them.

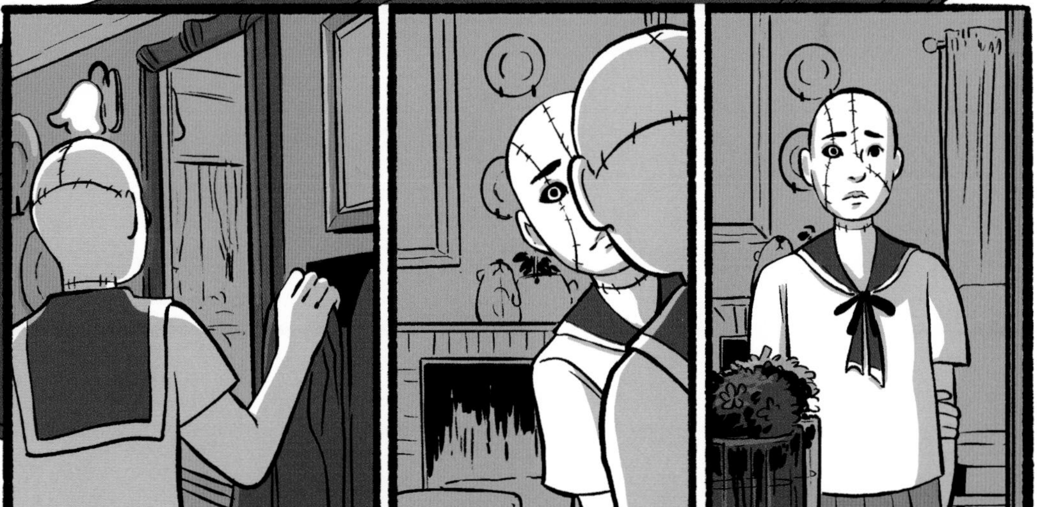

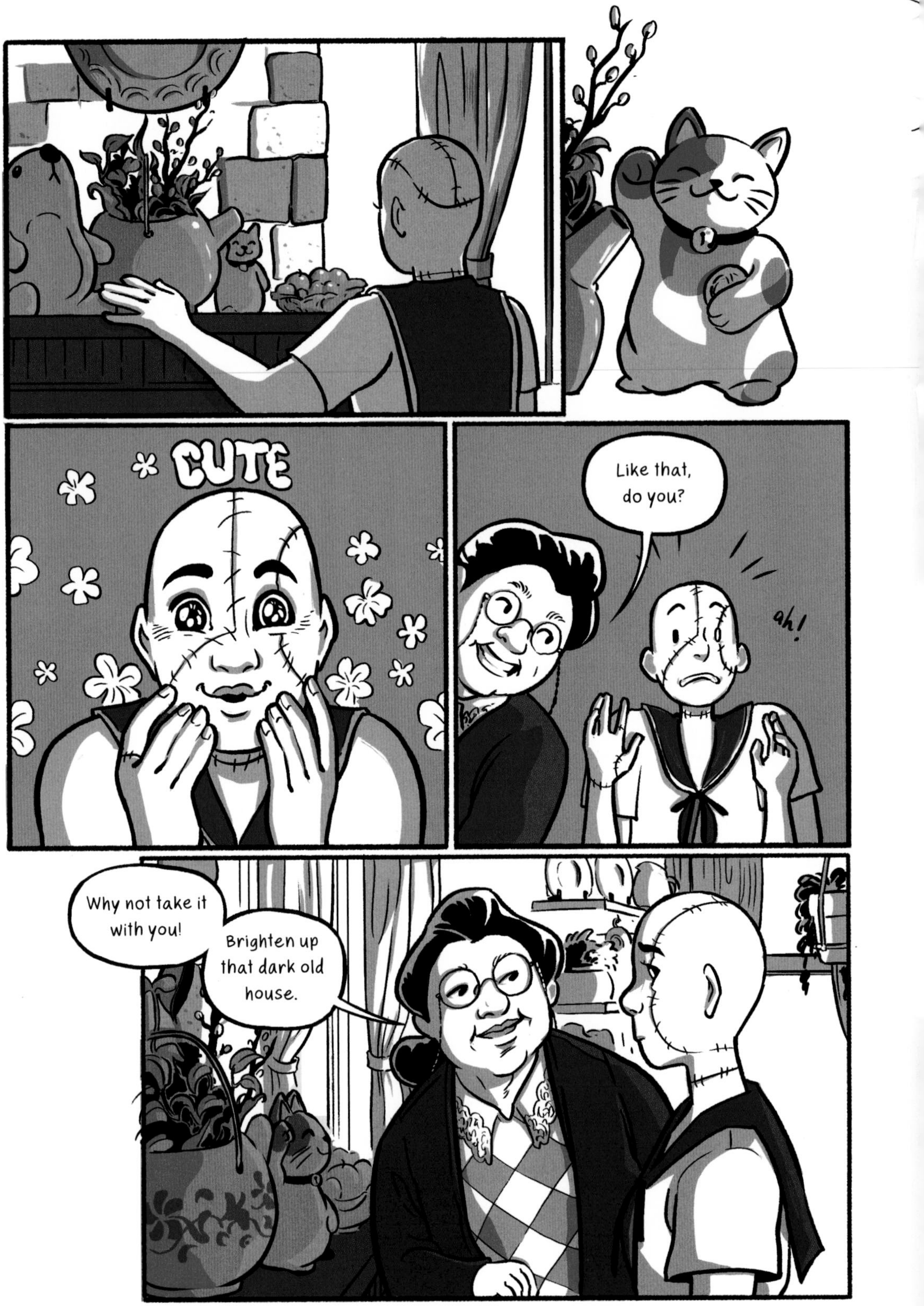
CUTE
Like that, do you?
ah!
Why not take it with you!
Brighten up that dark old house.

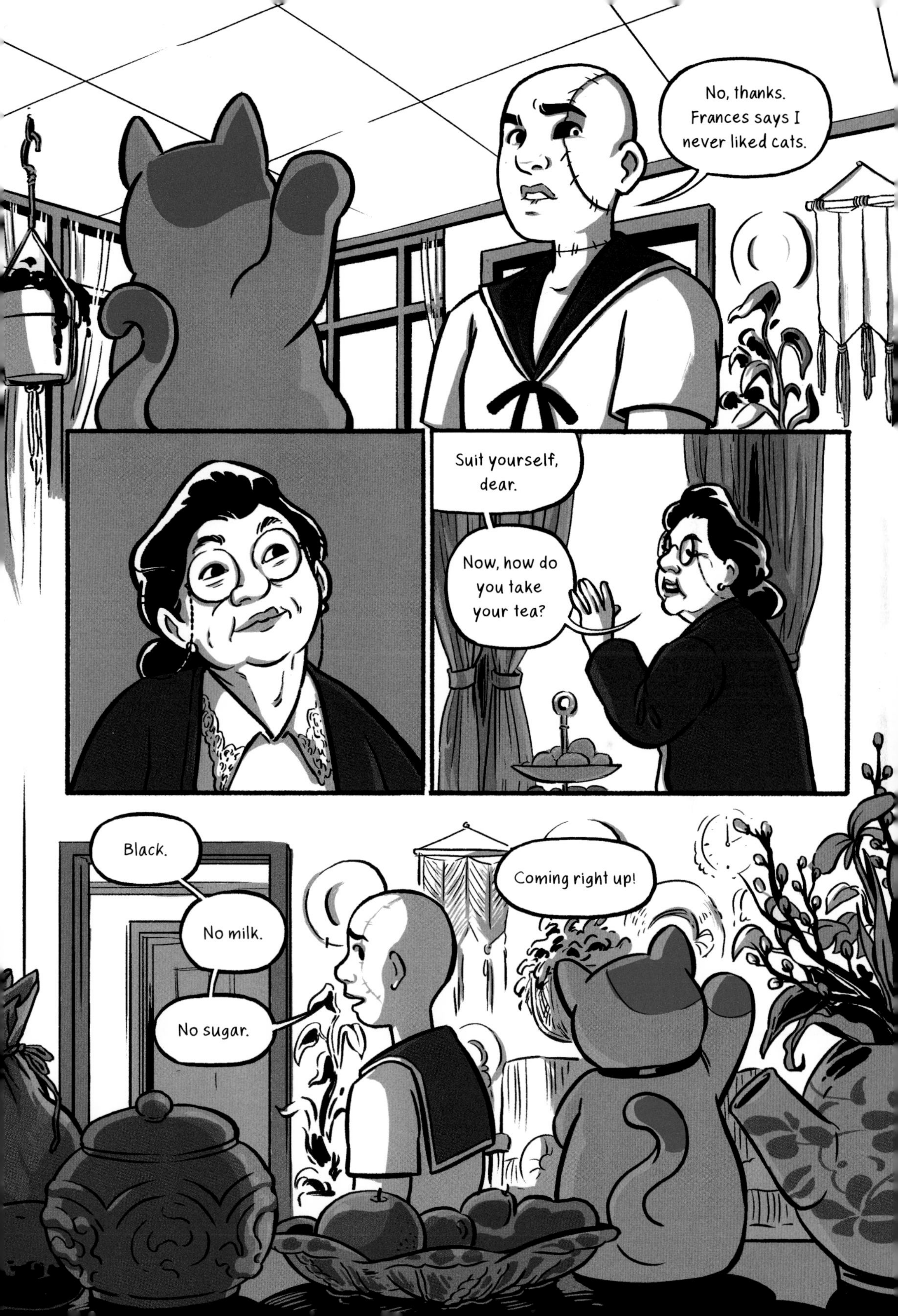
No, thanks. Frances says I never liked cats.
Suit yourself, dear.
Now, how do you take your tea?
Black.
No milk.
No sugar.
Coming right up!

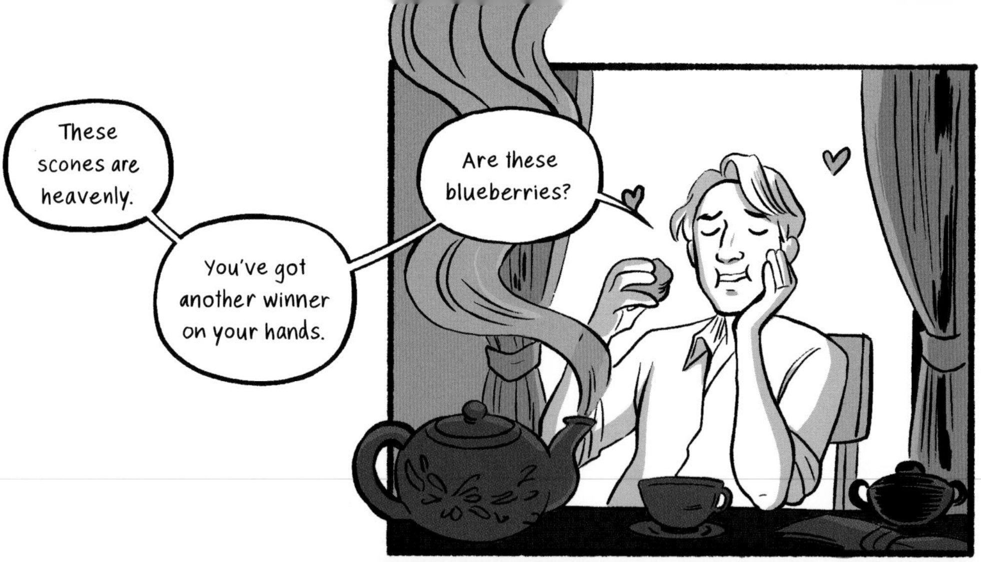
These scones are heavenly.
You've got another winner on your hands.
Are these blueberries?

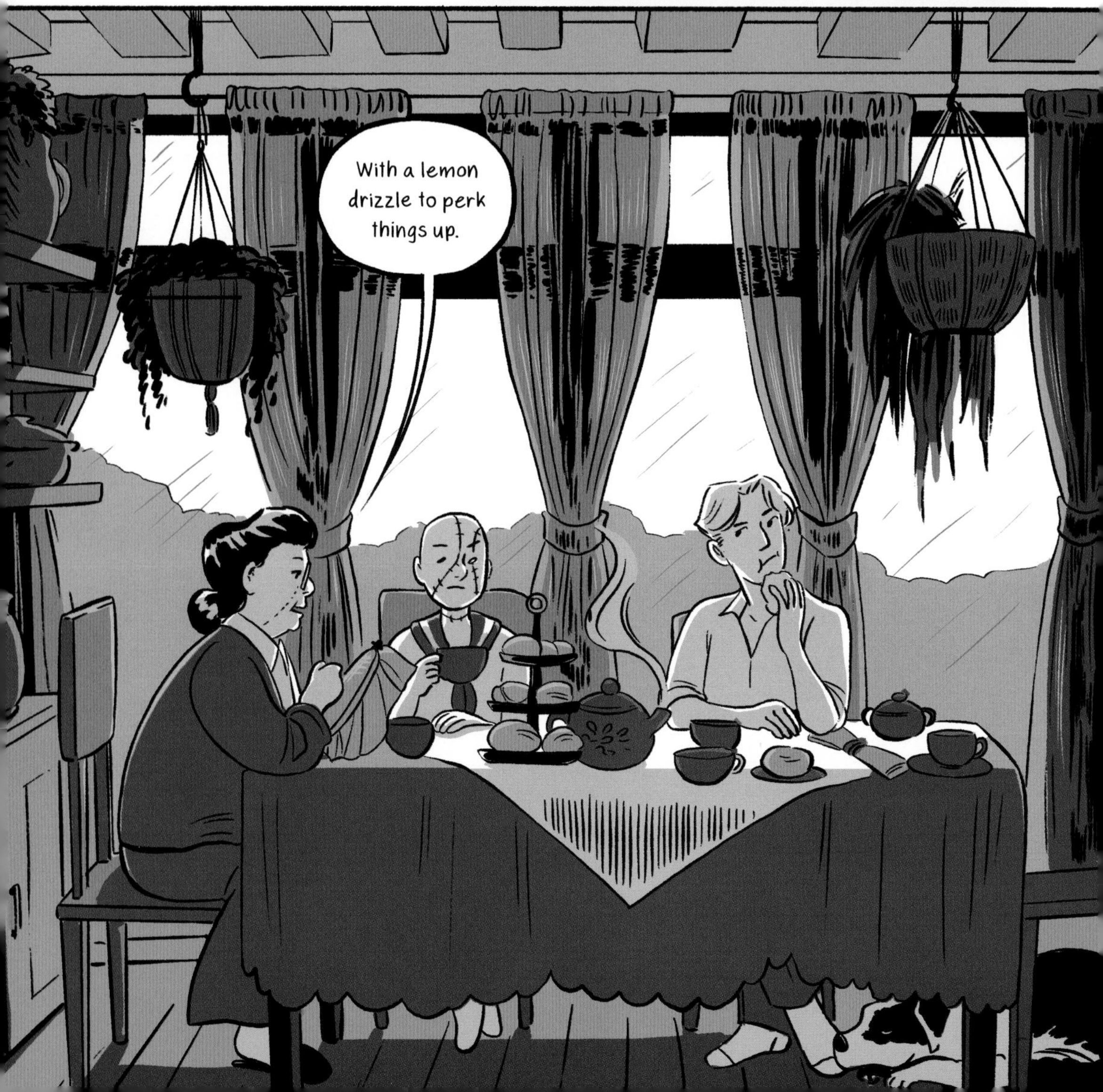
With a lemon drizzle to perk things up.

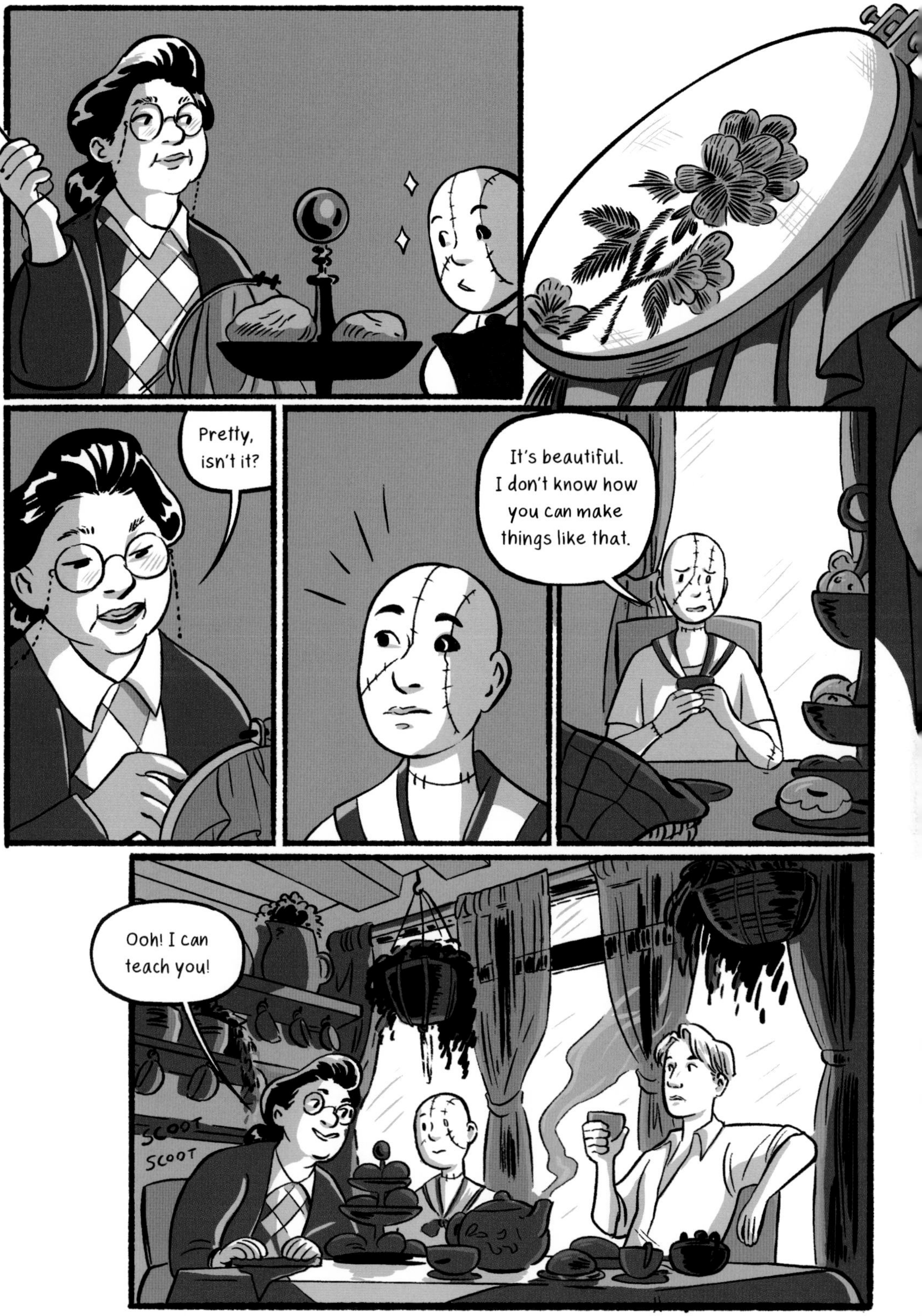
Pretty,
isn't it?
It's beautiful.
I don't know how
you can make
things like that.
Ooh! I can
teach you!
SCOOT
SCOOT

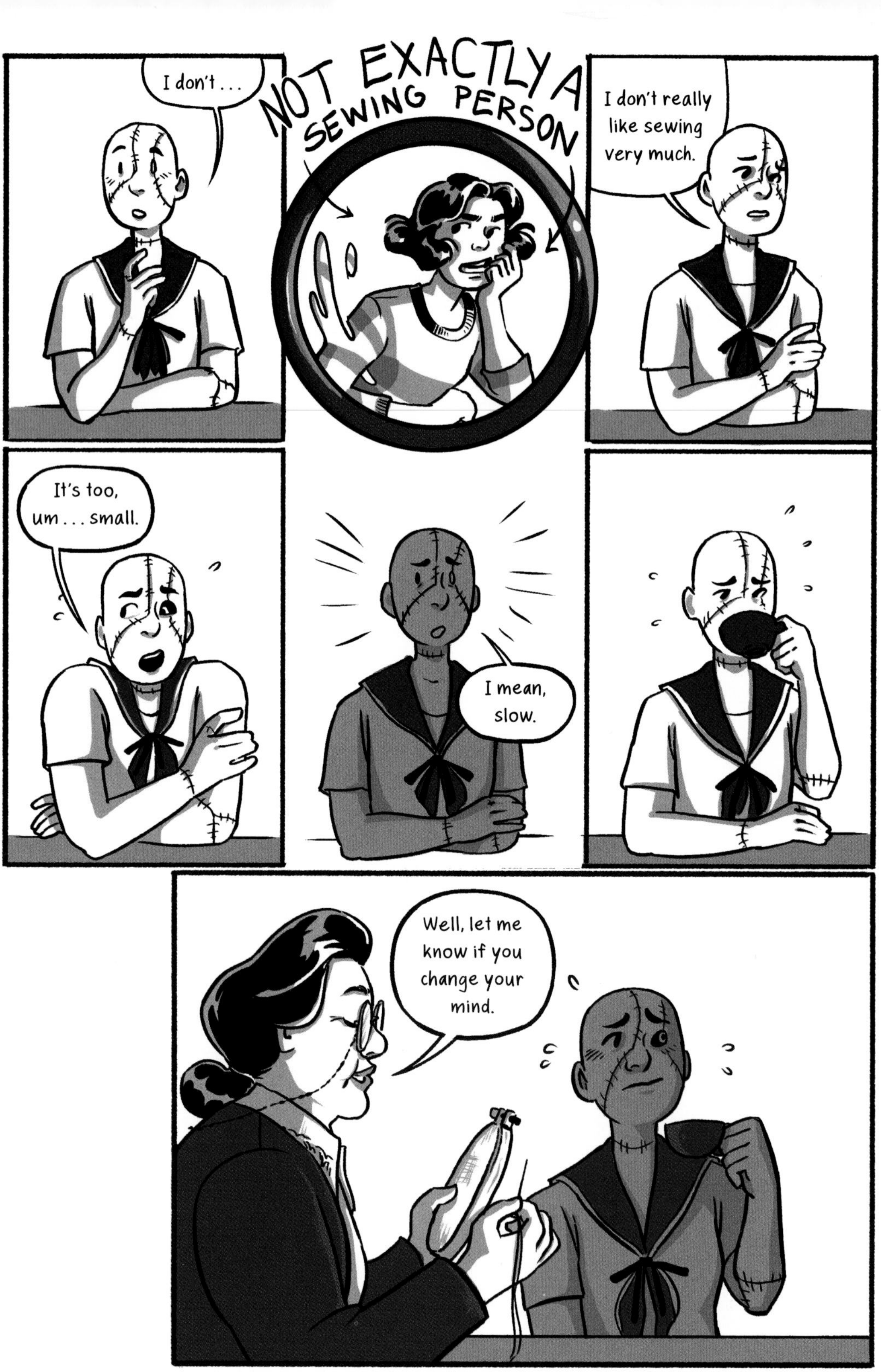
I don't . . .
NOT EXACTLY A SEWING PERSON
I don't really like sewing very much.
It's too, um . . . small.
I mean, slow.
Well, let me know if you change your mind.

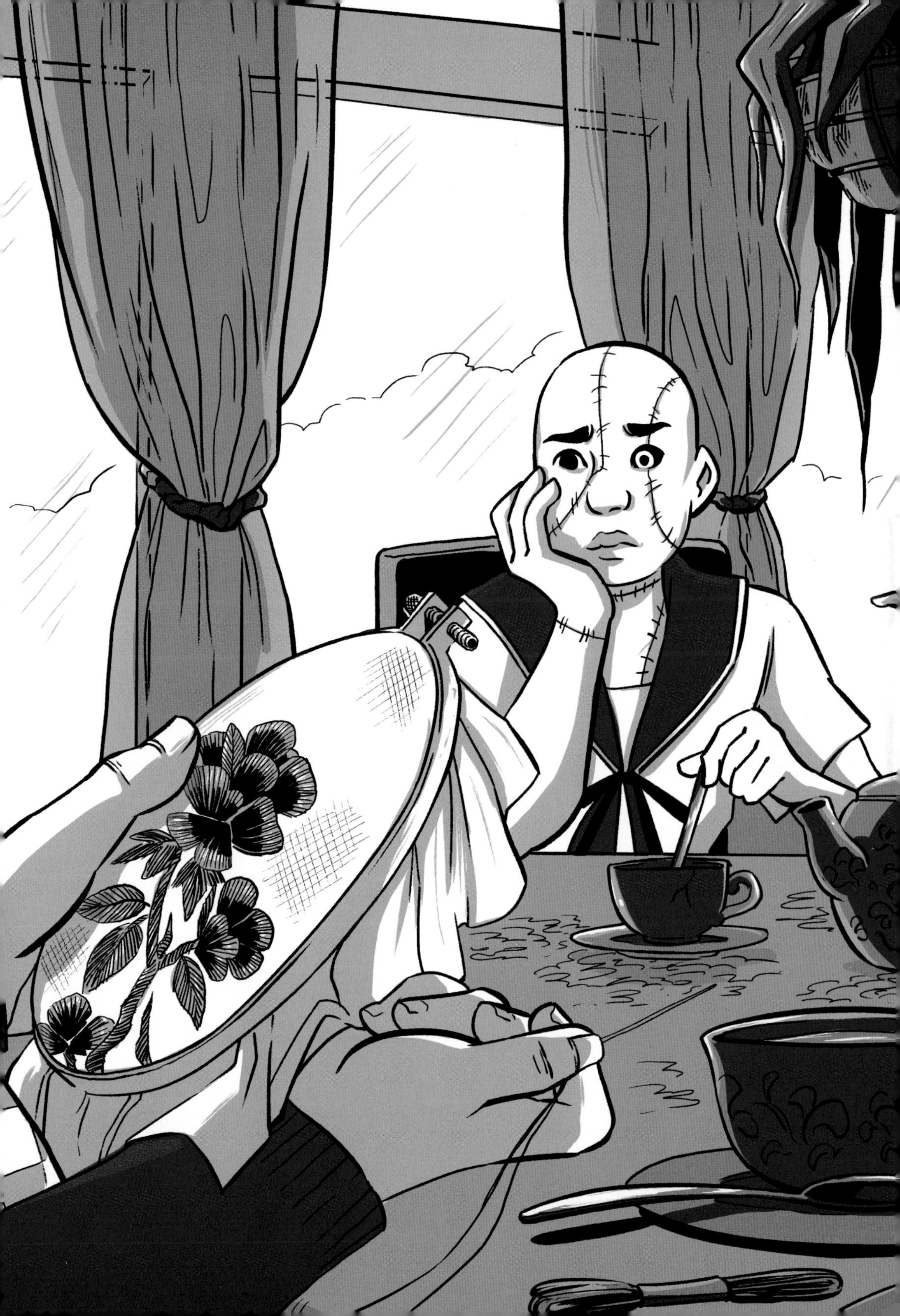

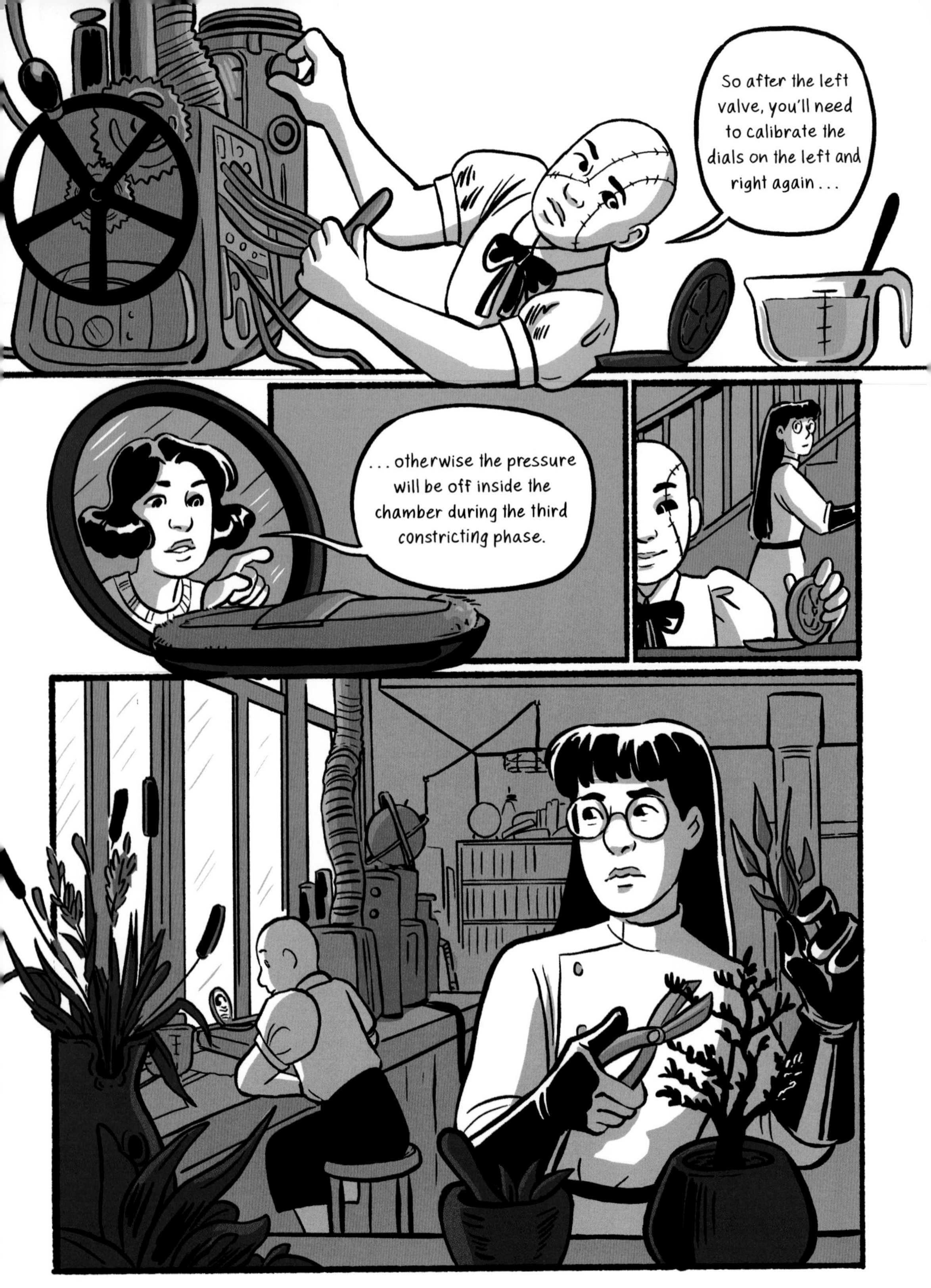
So after the left valve, you'll need to calibrate the dials on the left and right again . . .
. . . otherwise the pressure will be off inside the chamber during the third constricting phase.

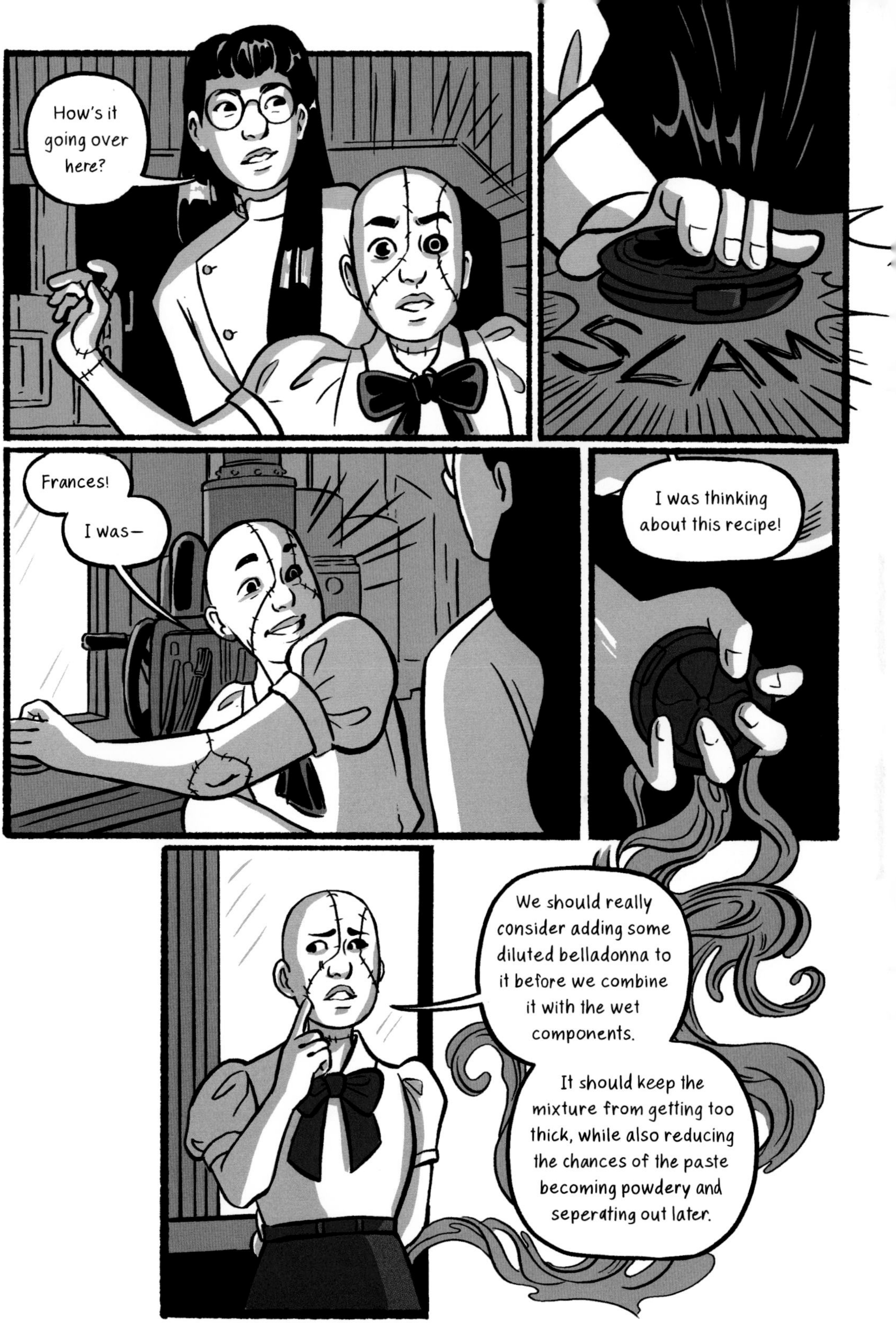
How's it going over here?
SLAM
Frances!
I was—
I was thinking about this recipe!
We should really consider adding some diluted belladonna to it before we combine it with the wet components.
It should keep the mixture from getting too thick, while also reducing the chances of the paste becoming powdery and seperating out later.

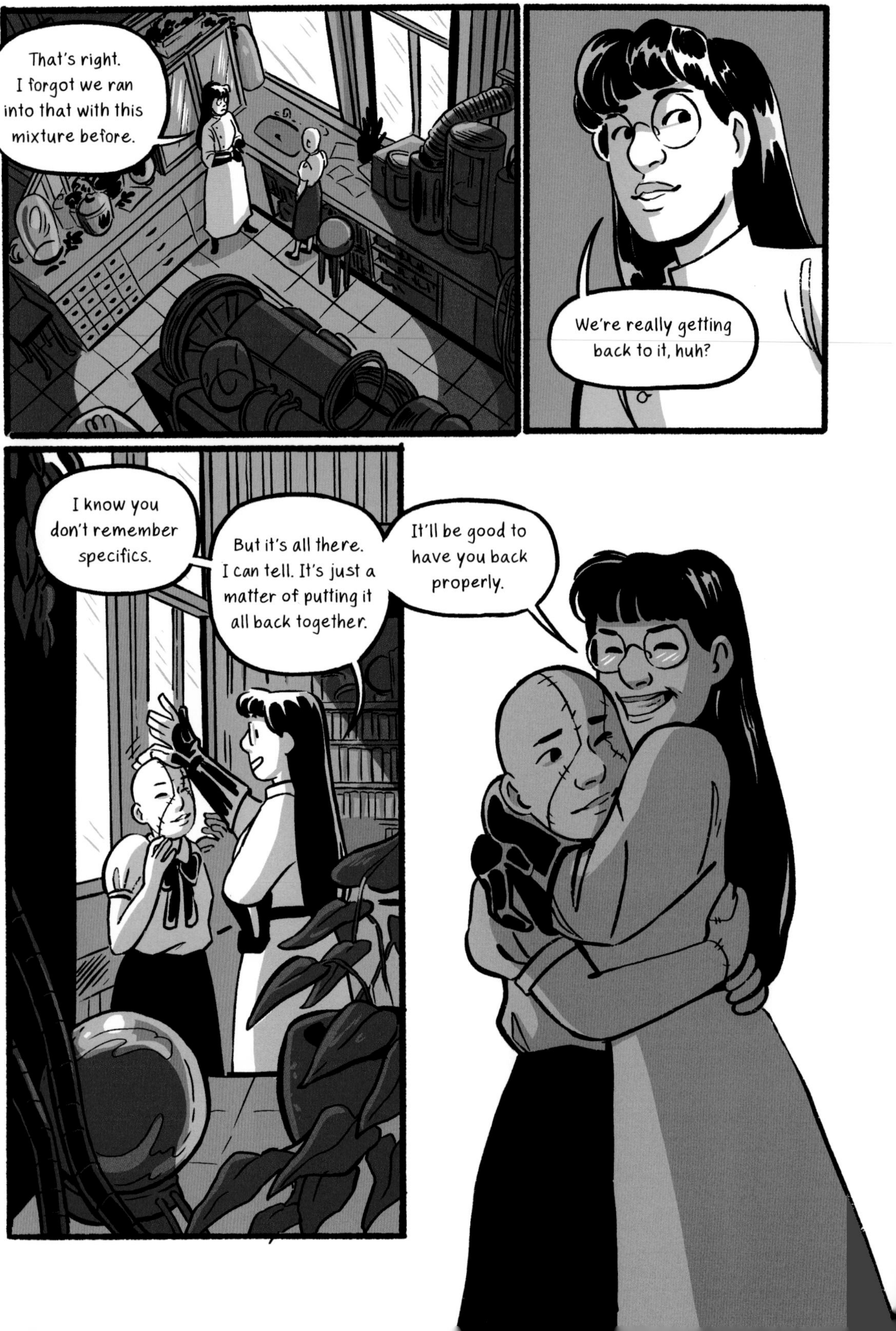
That's right. I forgot we ran into that with this mixture before.
We're really getting back to it, huh?
I know you don't remember specifics.
But it's all there. I can tell. It's just a matter of putting it all back together.
It'll be good to have you back properly.

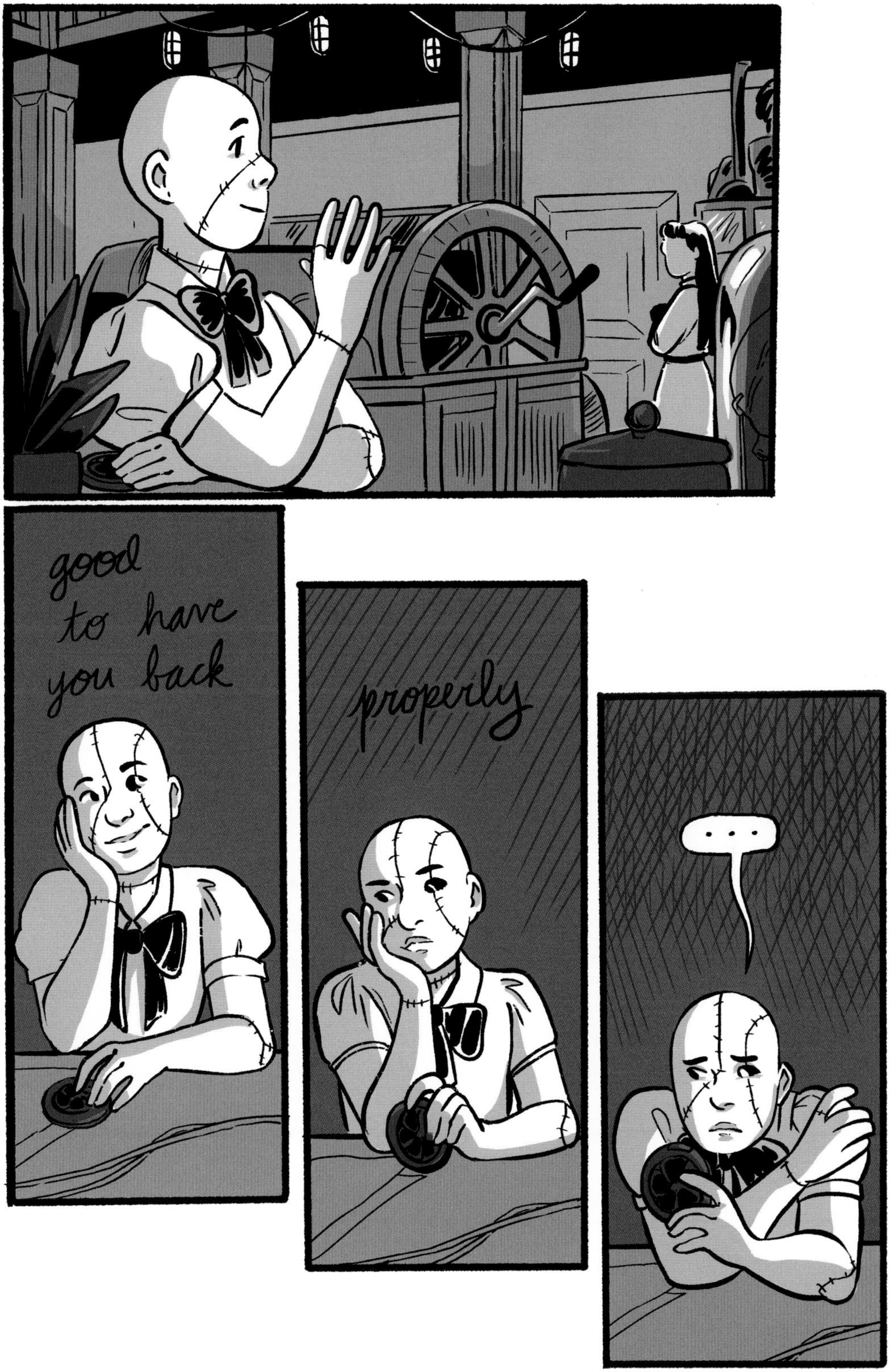
good to have you back
properly
...

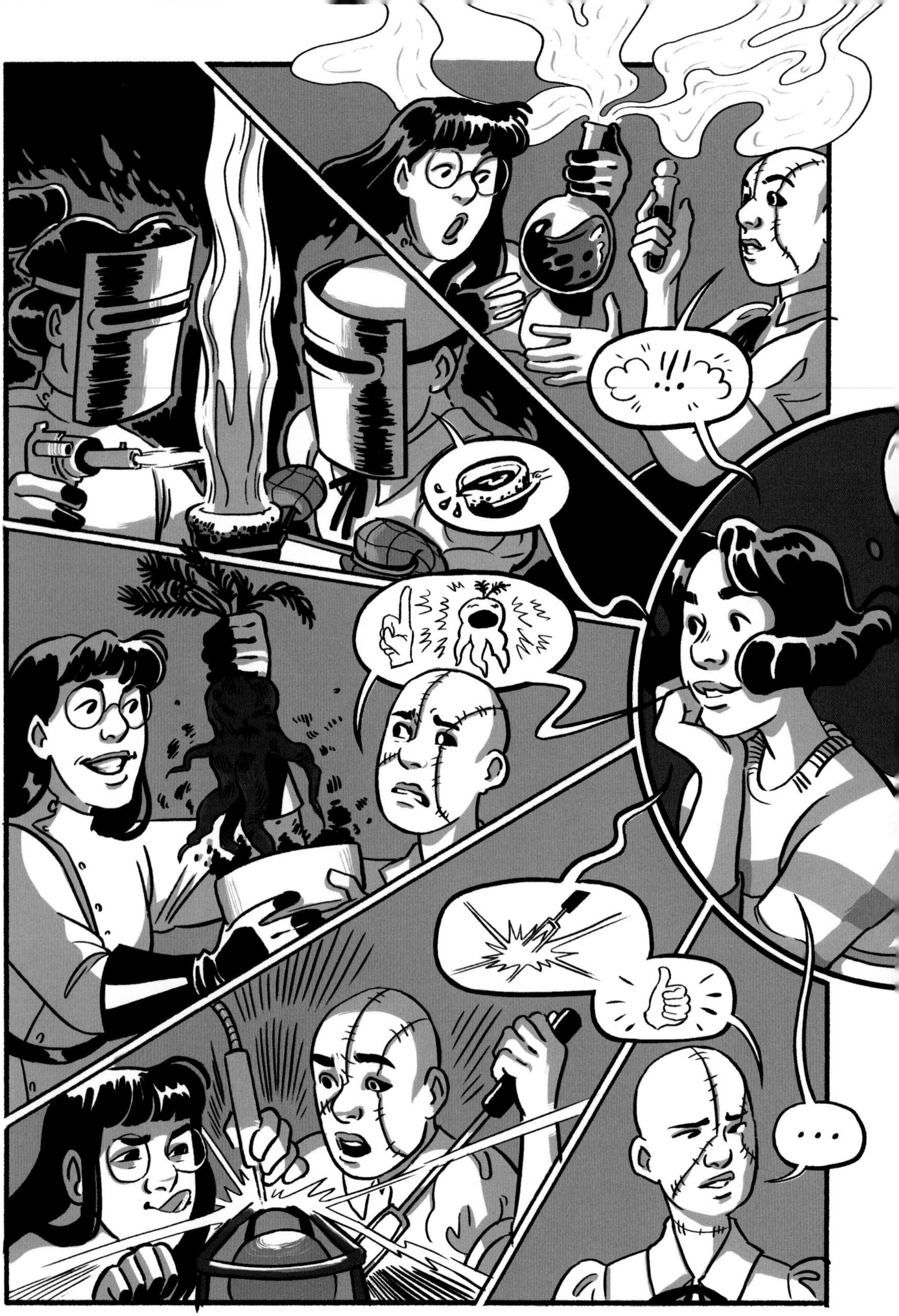
...

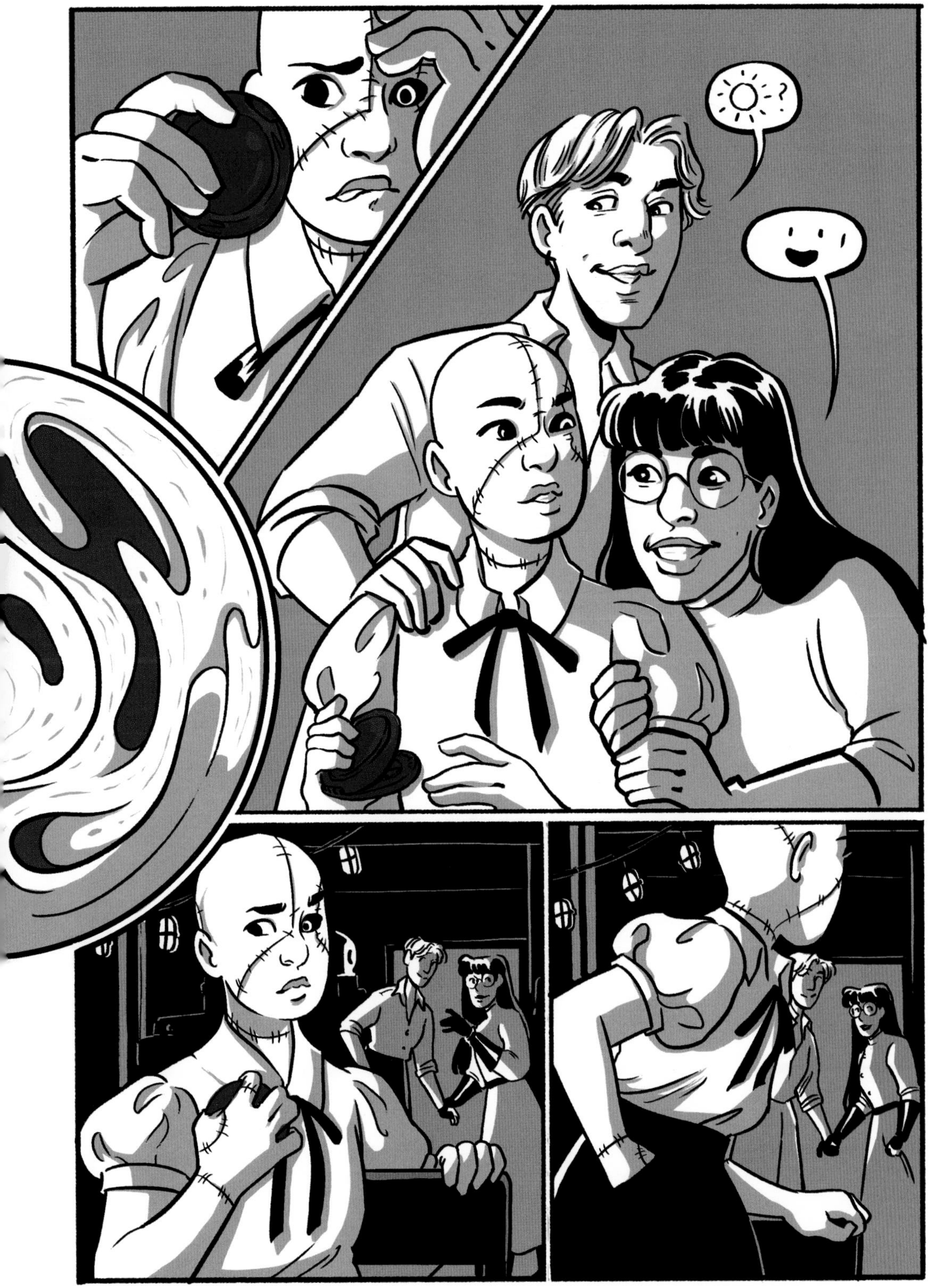

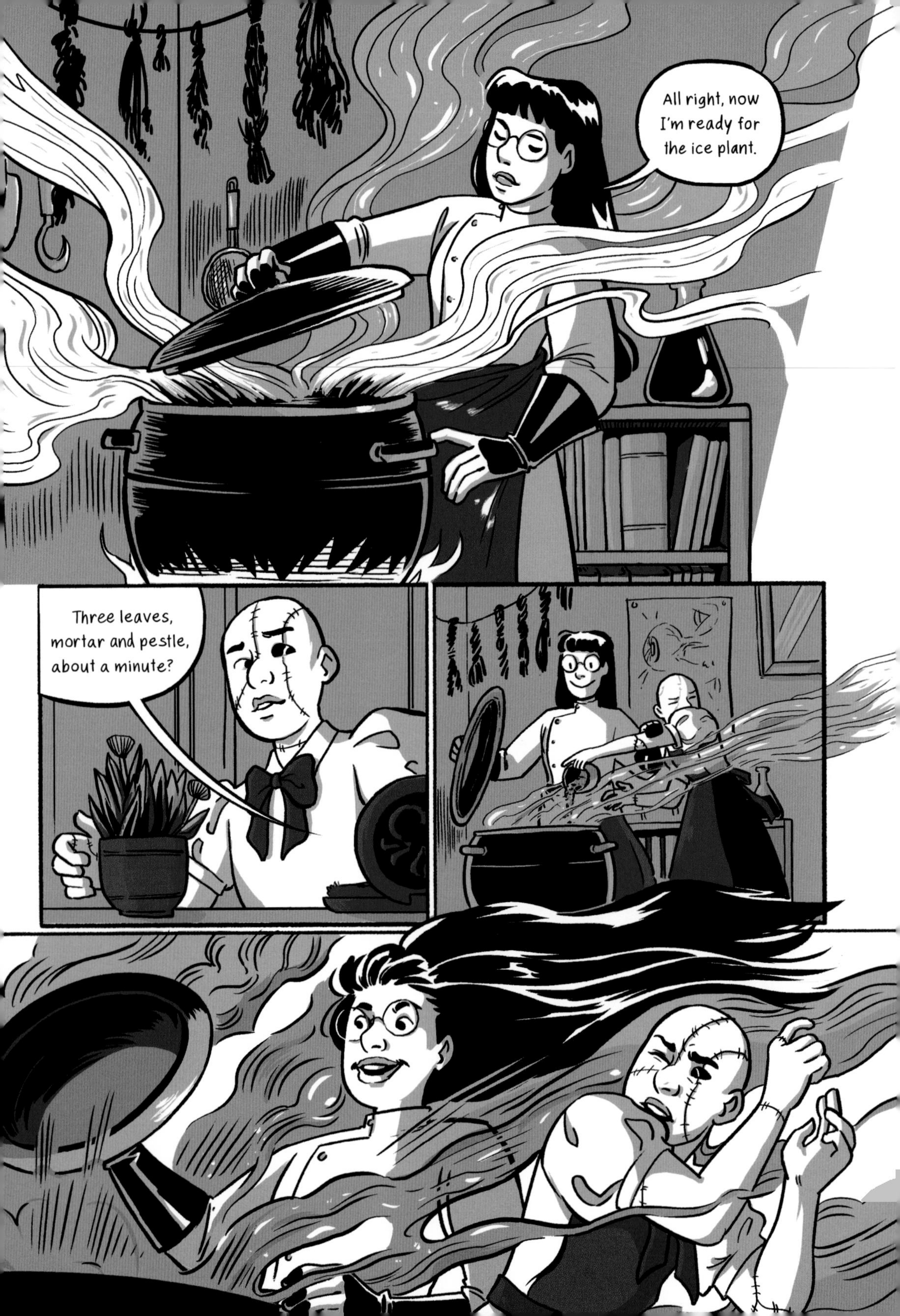
All right, now I'm ready for the ice plant.
Three leaves, mortar and pestle, about a minute?

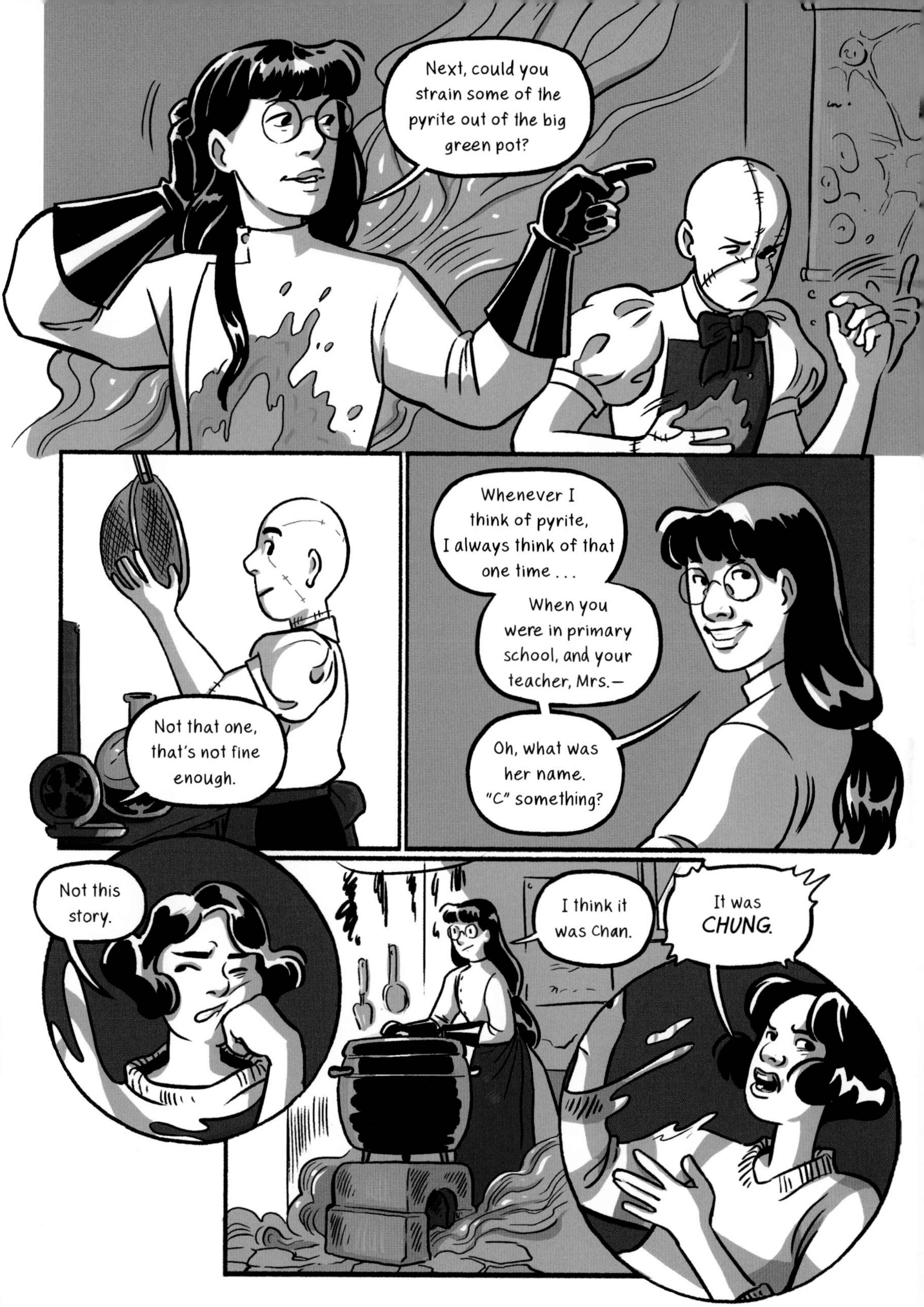
Next, could you strain some of the pyrite out of the big green pot?
Not that one, that's not fine enough.
Whenever I think of pyrite, I always think of that one time . . .
When you were in primary school, and your teacher, Mrs.—
Oh, what was her name. "C" something?
Not this story.
I think it was Chan.
It was CHUNG.

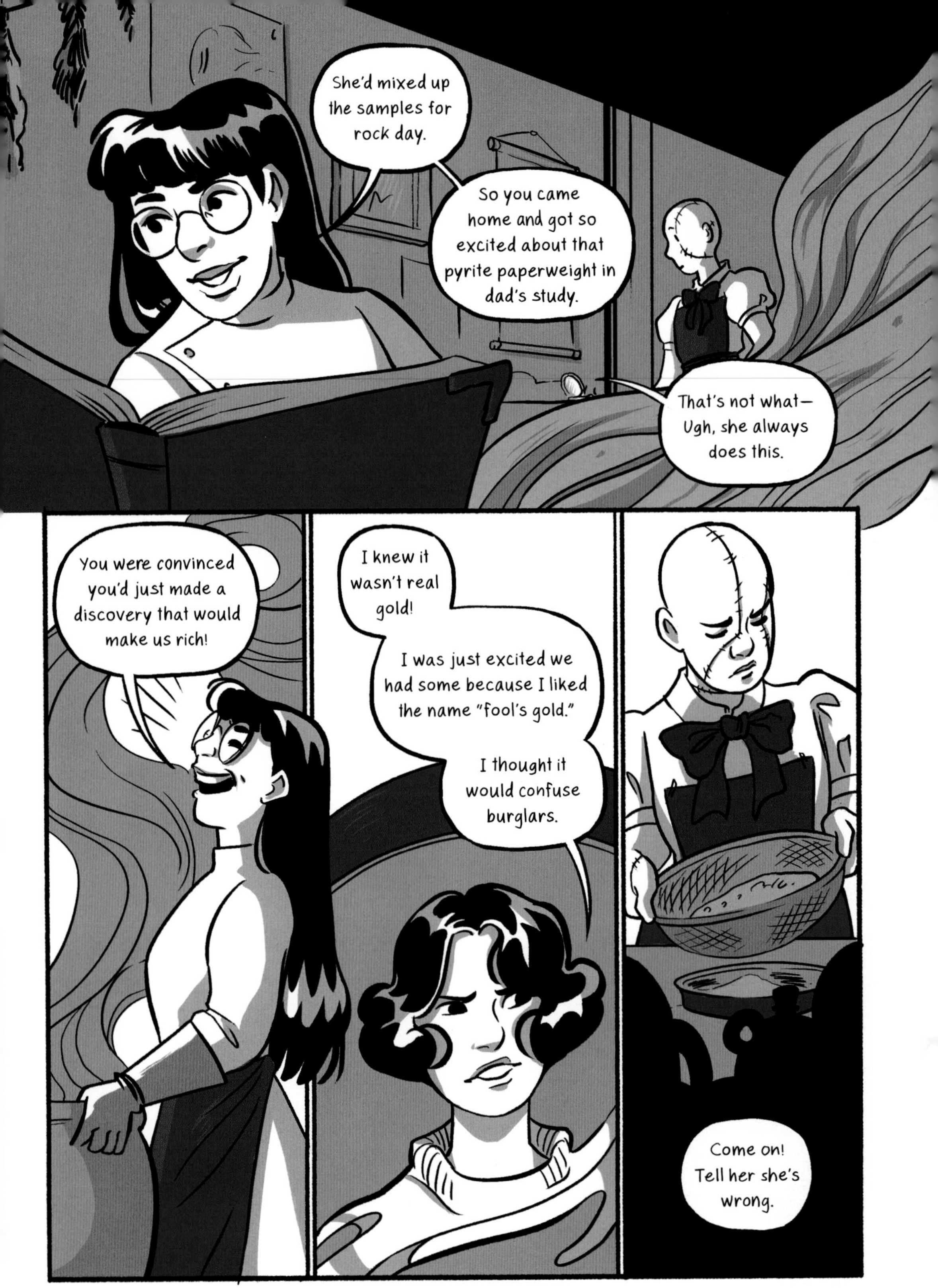
She'd mixed up the samples for rock day.
So you came home and got so excited about that pyrite paperweight in dad's study.
That's not what— Ugh, she always does this.
You were convinced you'd just made a discovery that would make us rich!
I knew it wasn't real gold!
I was just excited we had some because I liked the name "fool's gold."
I thought it would confuse burglars.
Come on! Tell her she's wrong.

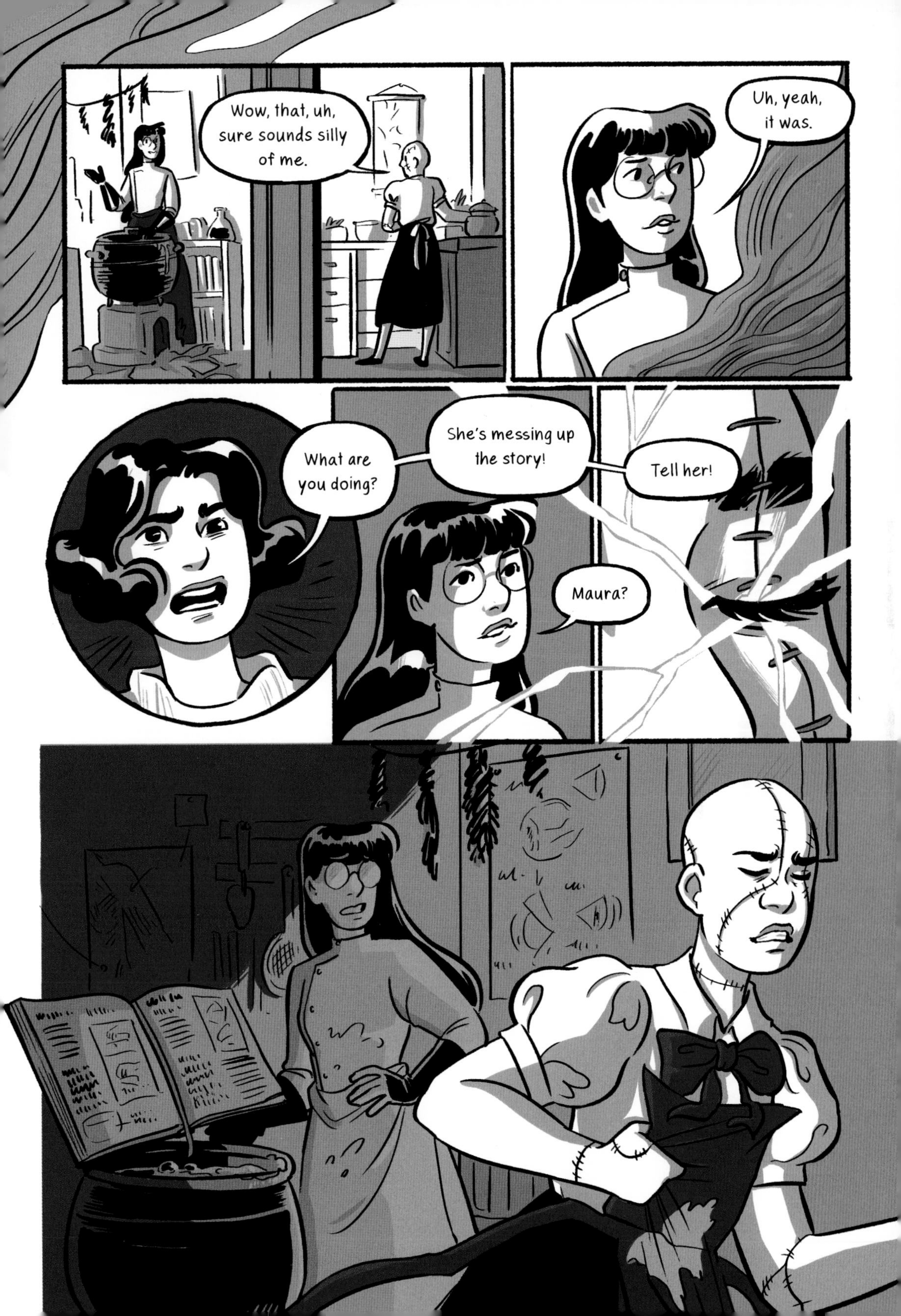
Wow, that, uh, sure sounds silly of me.
Uh, yeah, it was.
What are you doing?
She's messing up the story!
Tell her!
Maura?

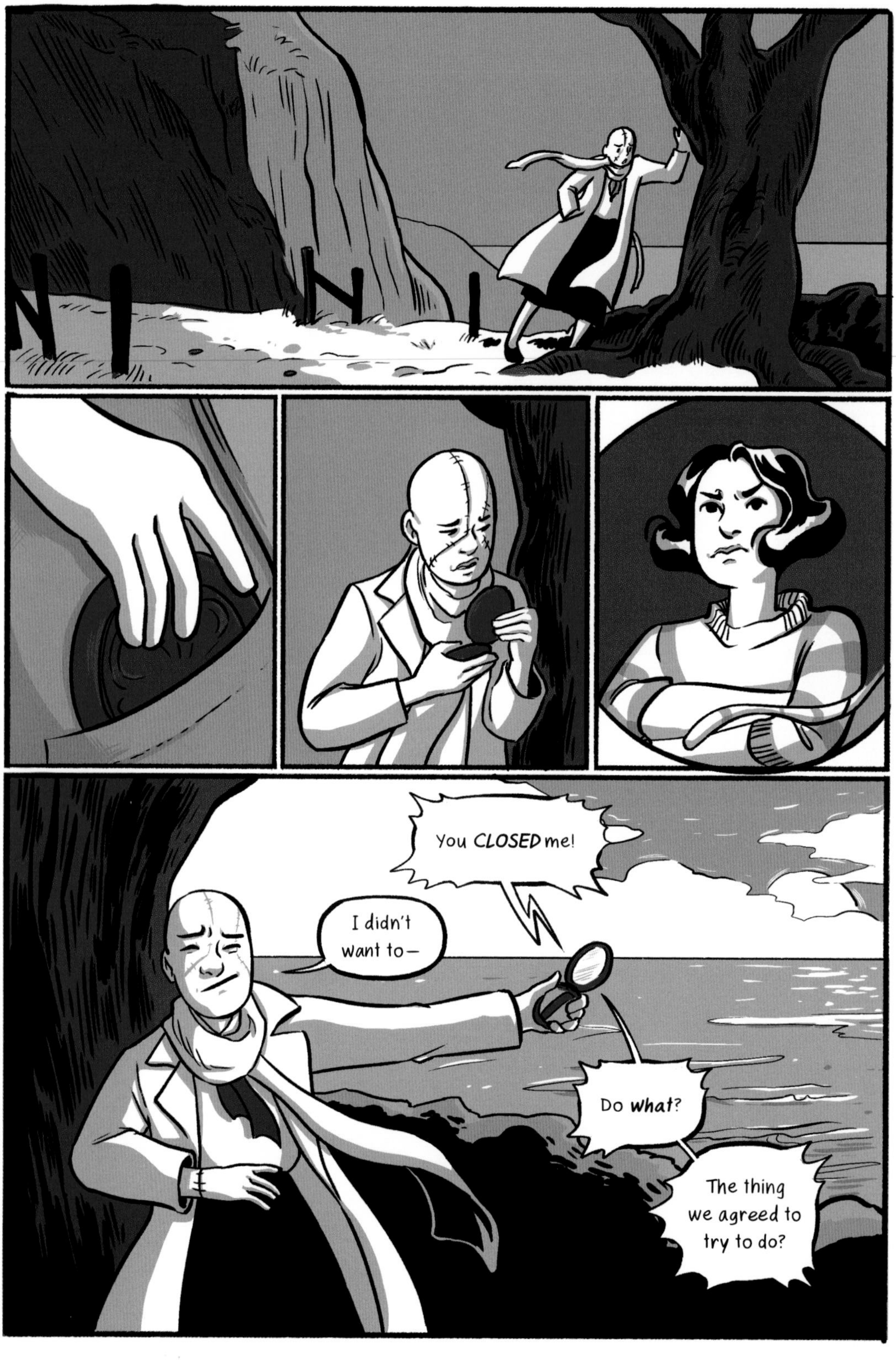
You CLOSED me!
I didn't want to—
Do what?
The thing we agreed to try to do?

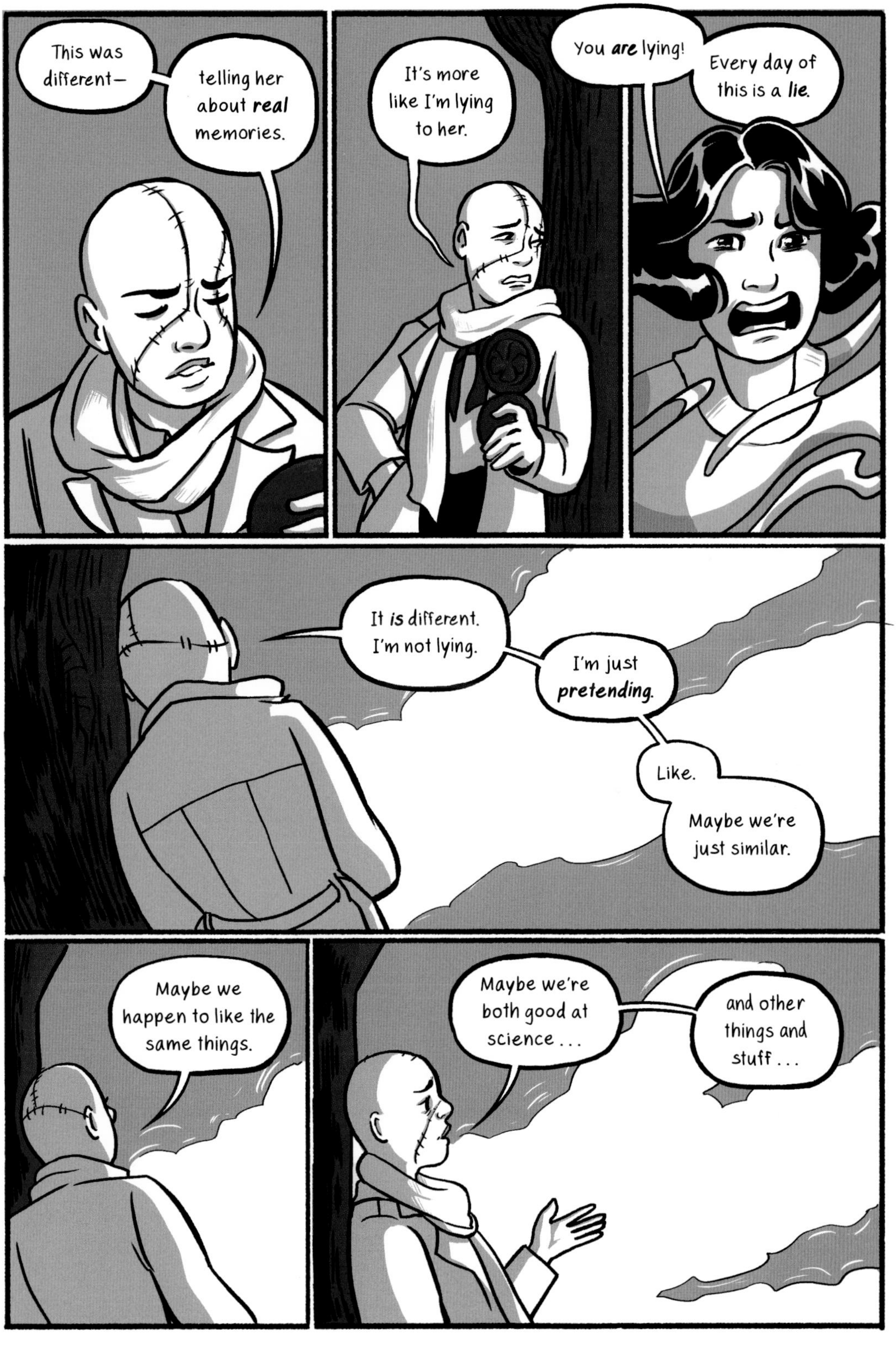
This was different—
telling her about **real** memories.
It's more like I'm lying to her.
You **are** lying!
Every day of this is a **lie**.
It **is** different. I'm not lying.
I'm just **pretending**.
Like.
Maybe we're just similar.
Maybe we happen to like the same things.
Maybe we're both good at science . . .
and other things and stuff . . .

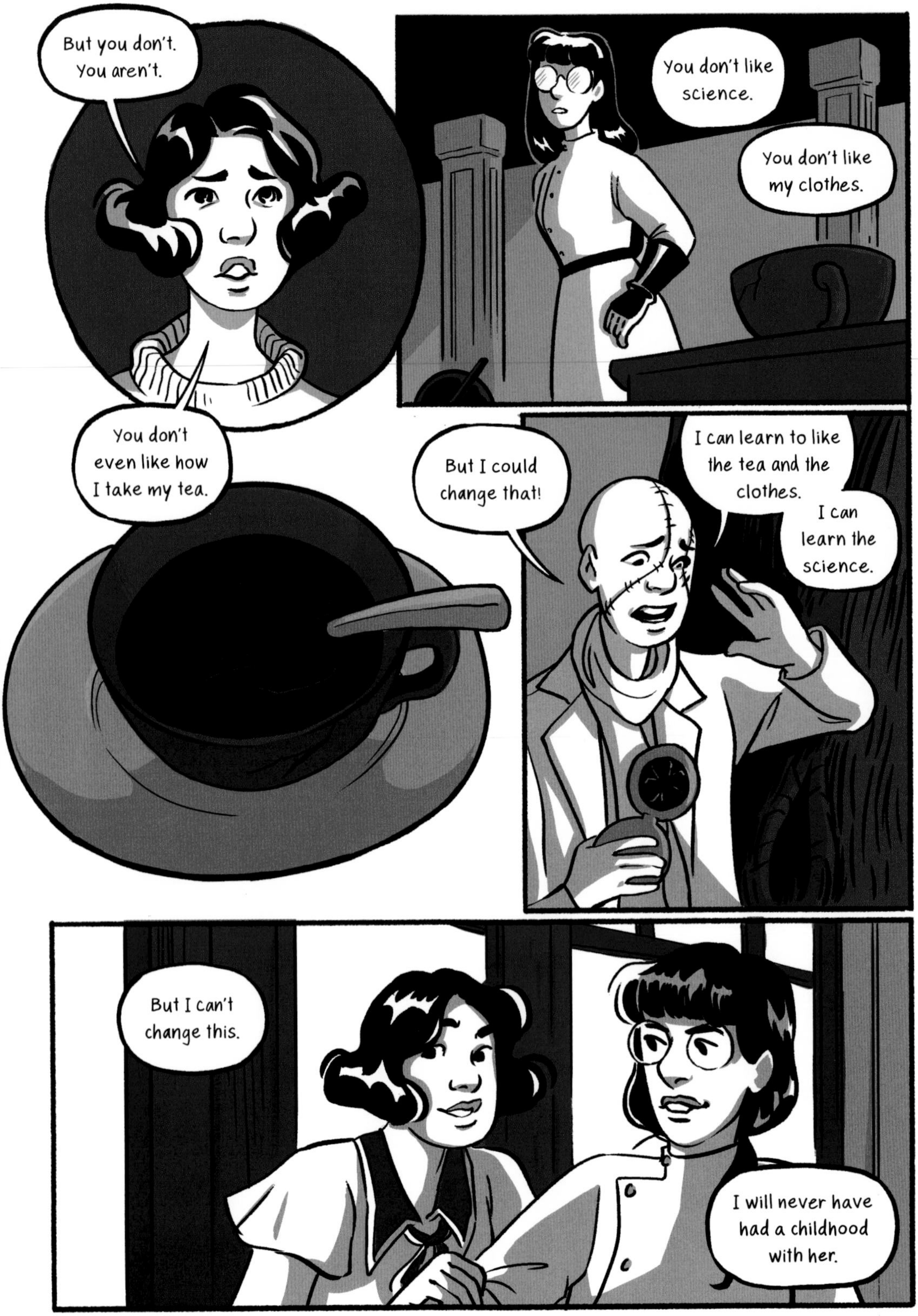

But you don't. You aren't.
You don't like science.
You don't like my clothes.
You don't even like how I take my tea.
But I could change that!
I can learn to like the tea and the clothes.
I can learn the science.
But I can't change this.
I will never have had a childhood with her.

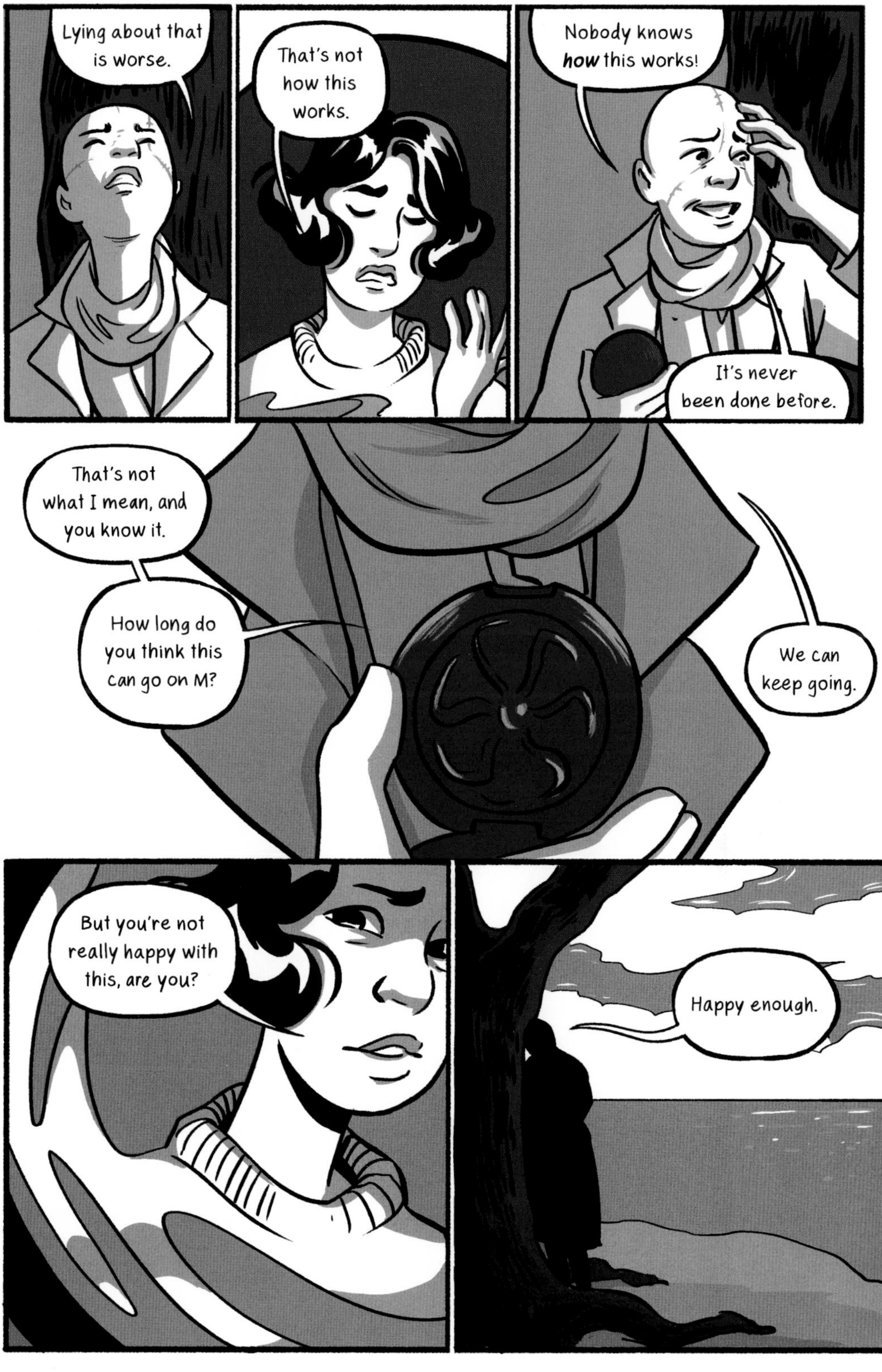
Lying about that is worse.
That's not how this works.
Nobody knows **how** this works!
It's never been done before.
That's not what I mean, and you know it.
How long do you think this can go on M?
We can keep going.
But you're not really happy with this, are you?
Happy enough.

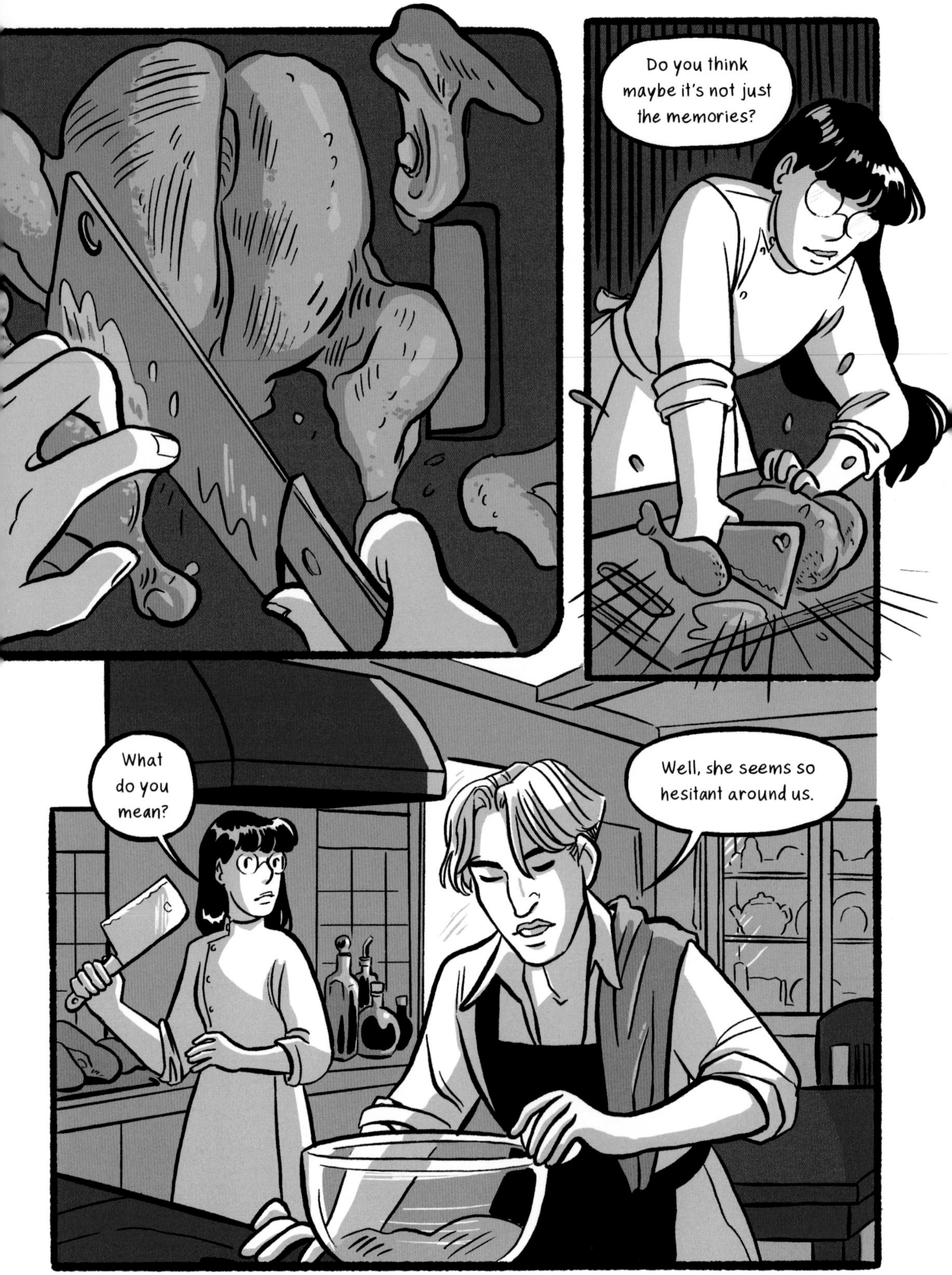
Do you think maybe it's not just the memories?
What do you mean?
Well, she seems so hesitant around us.

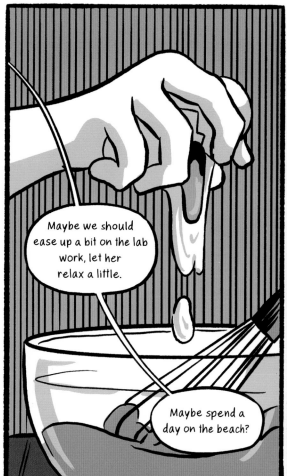

Maybe we should ease up a bit on the lab work, let her relax a little.

Maybe spend a day on the beach?

No, I've been watching her. I know what's wrong.

You do?

I have a plan, trust me.

Always, my love.

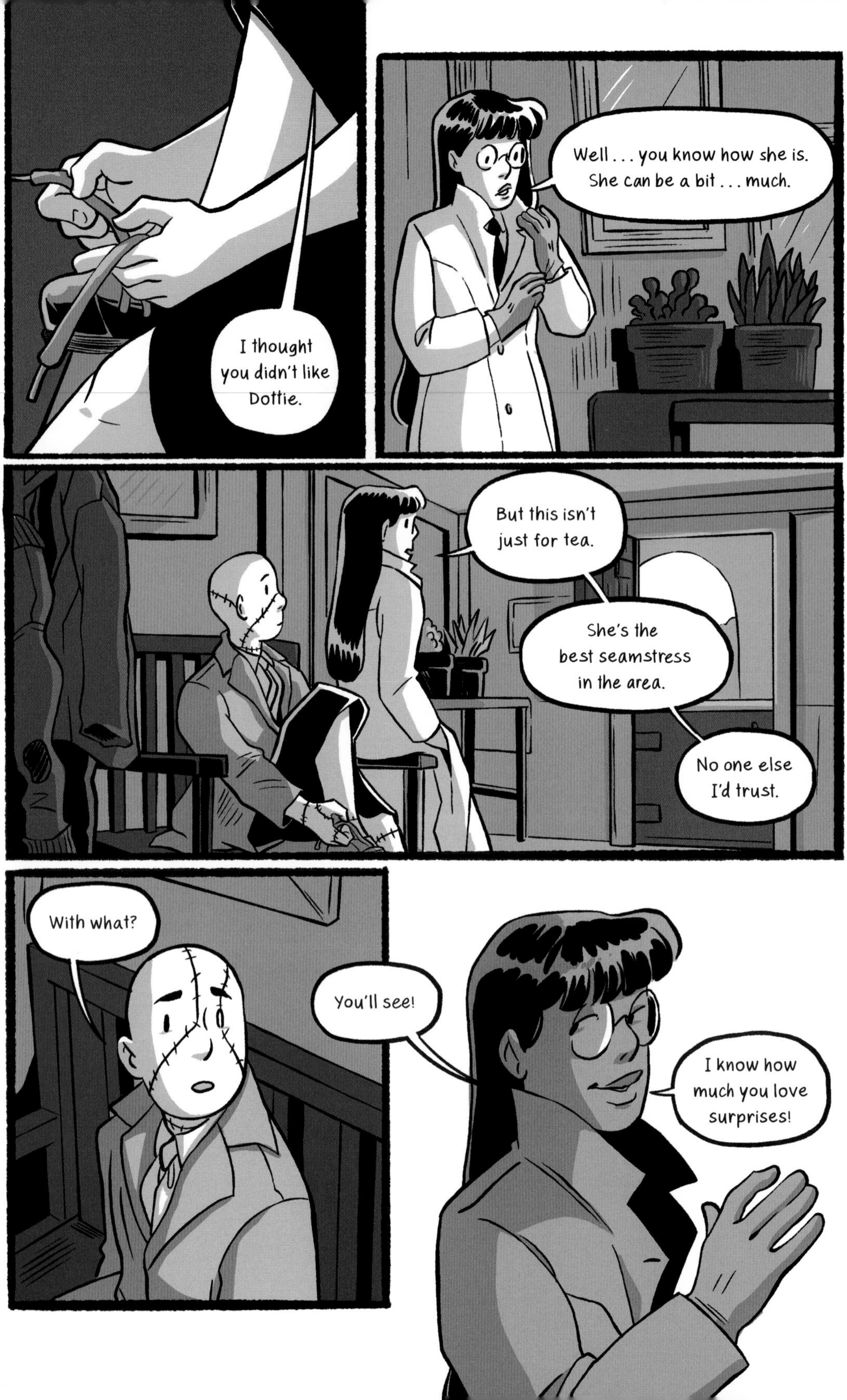
I thought you didn't like Dottie.
Well . . . you know how she is. She can be a bit . . . much.
But this isn't just for tea.
She's the best seamstress in the area.
No one else I'd trust.
With what?
You'll see!
I know how much you love surprises!

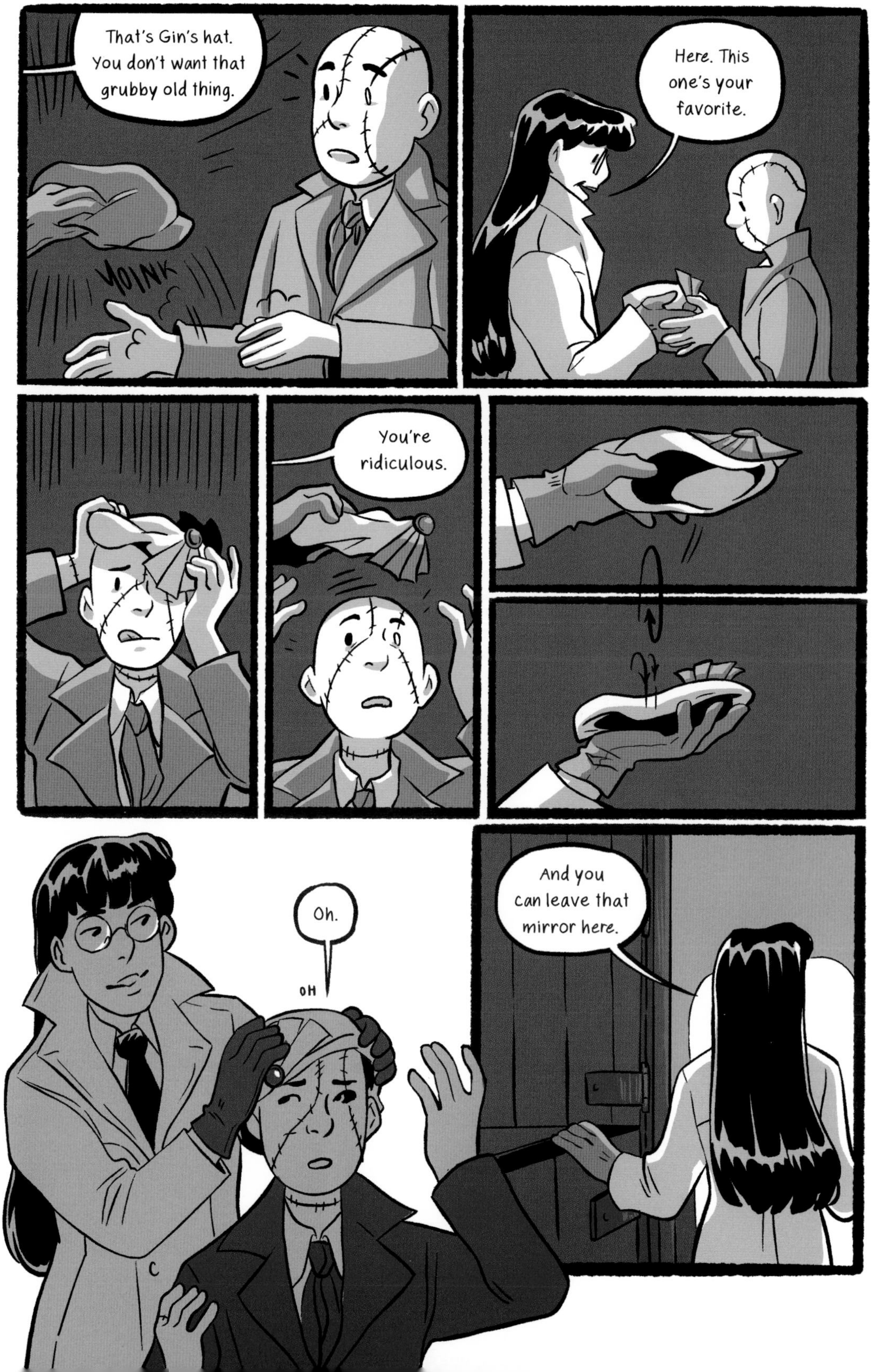
That's Gin's hat. You don't want that grubby old thing.
YOINK
Here. This one's your favorite.
You're ridiculous.
Oh.
OH
And you can leave that mirror here.

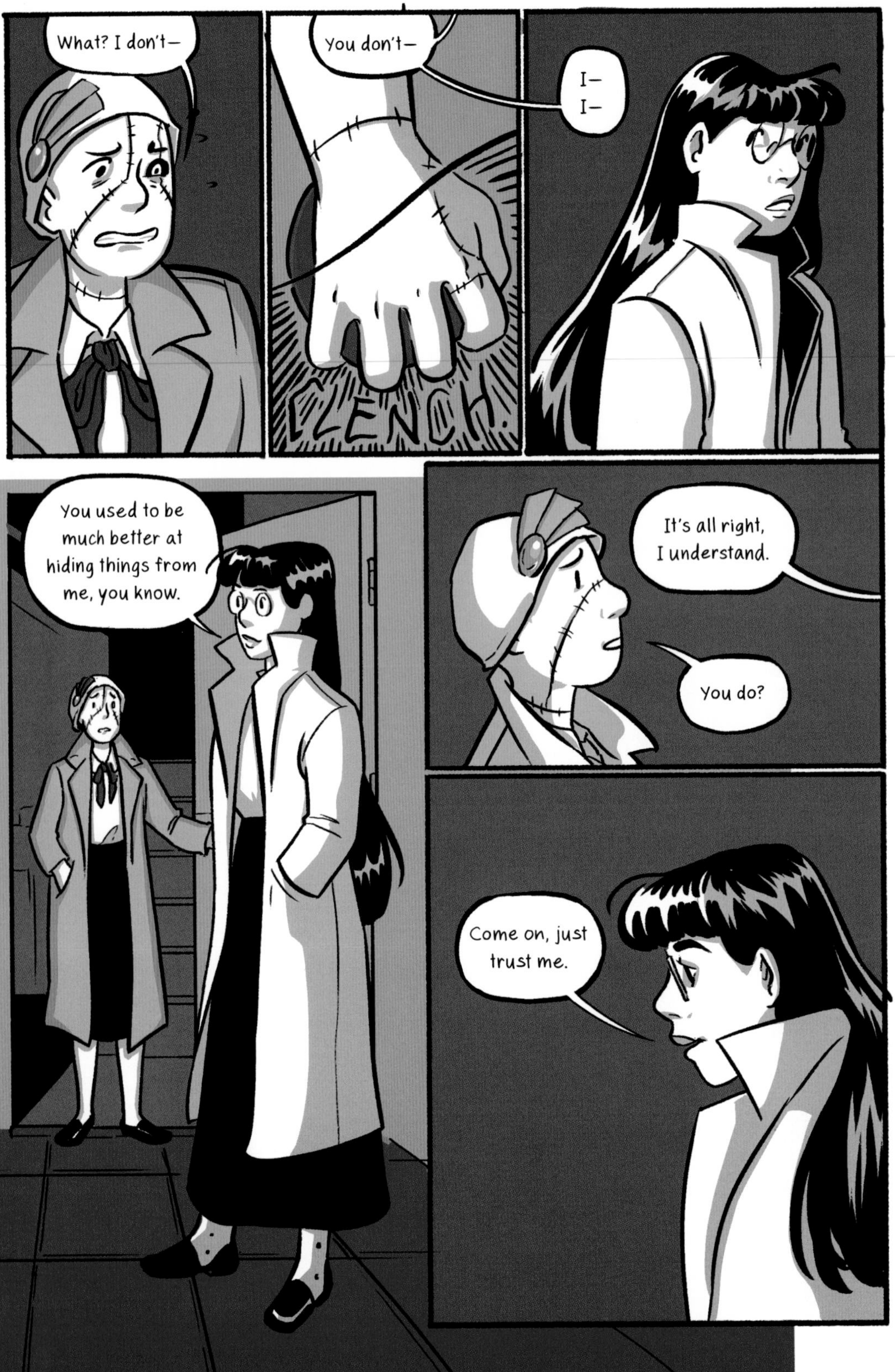
What? I don't—
You don't—
I—
I—
CLENCH
You used to be much better at hiding things from me, you know.
It's all right, I understand.
You do?
Come on, just trust me.

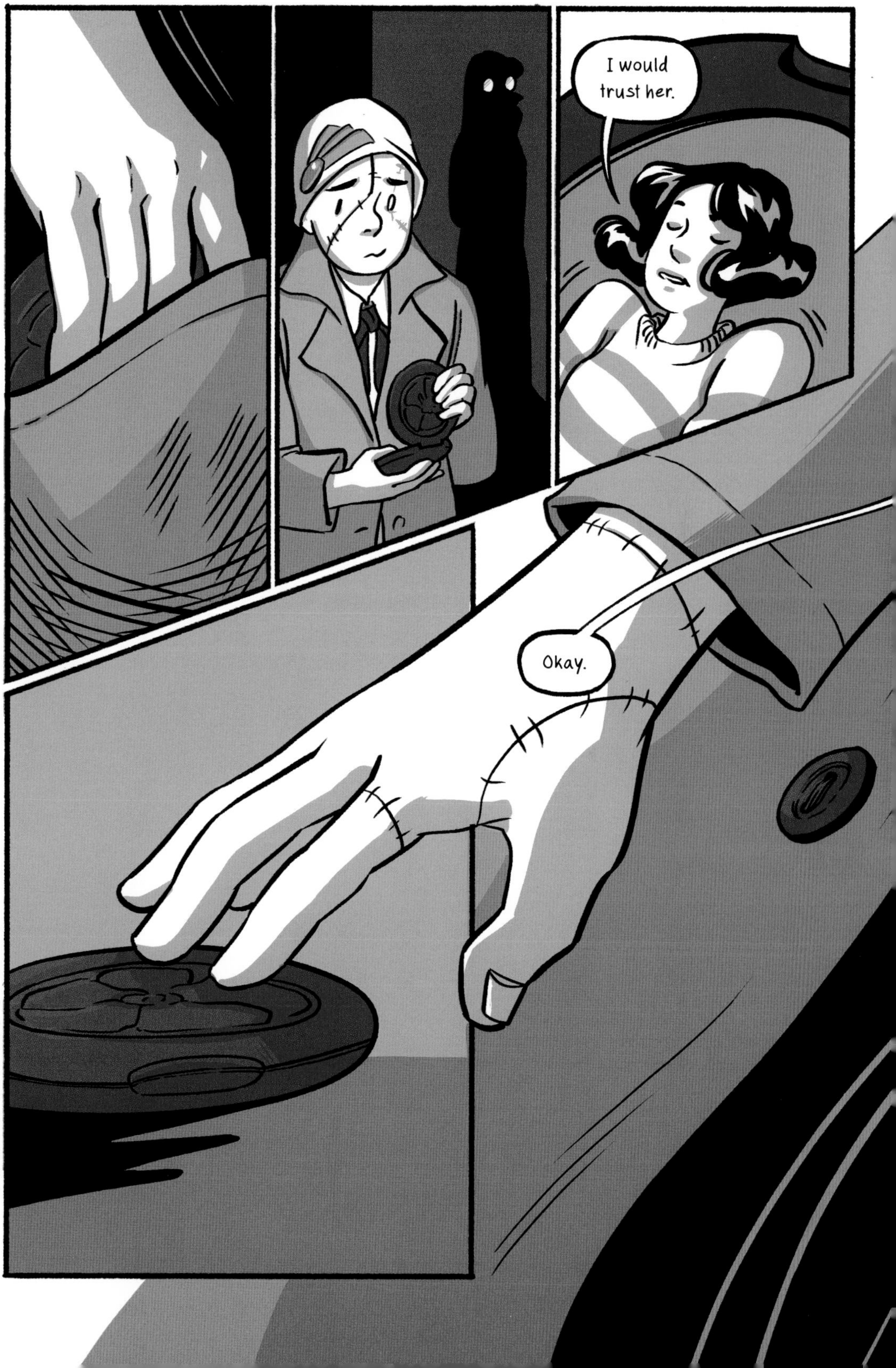
I would trust her.
Okay.

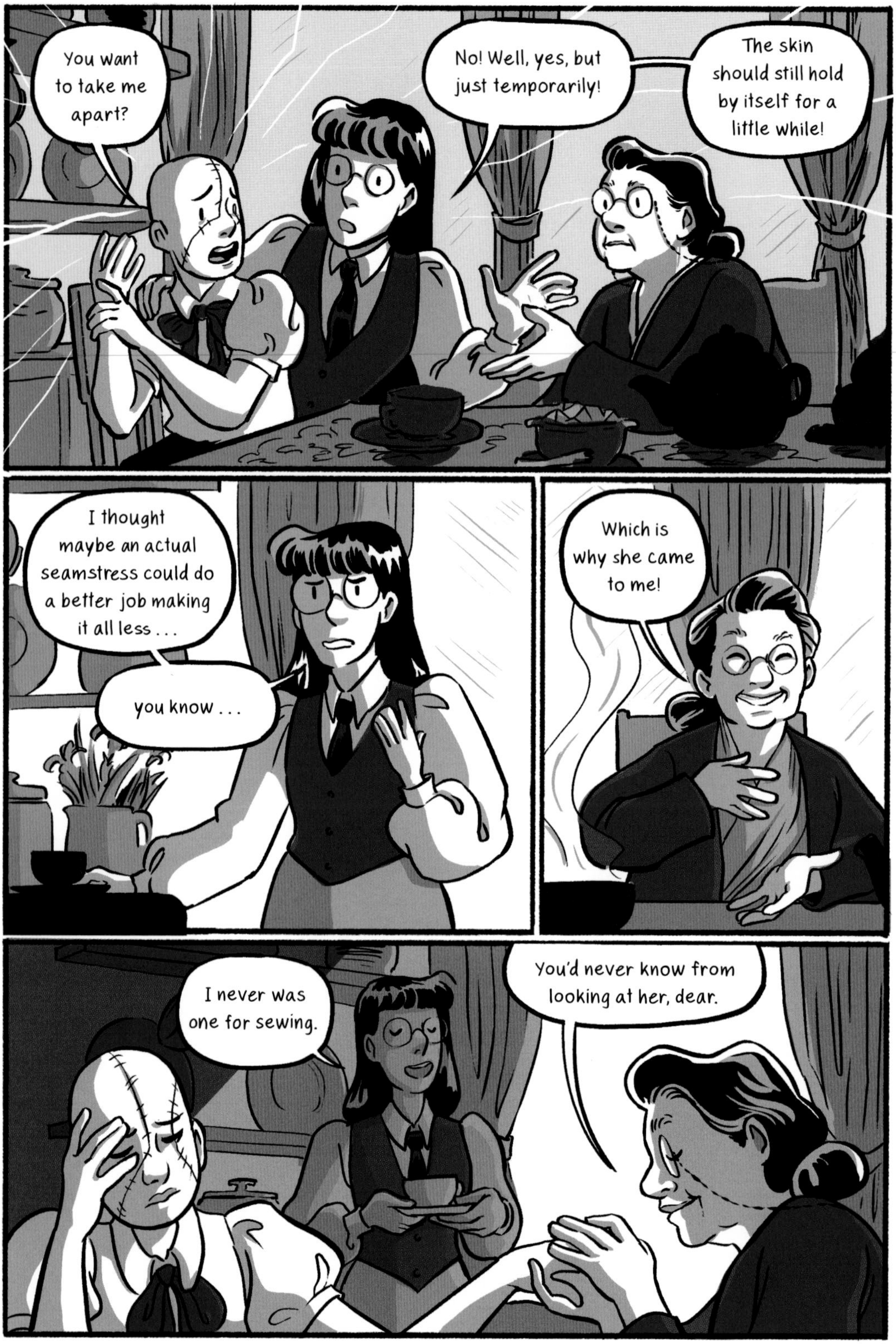
You want to take me apart?
No! Well, yes, but just temporarily!
The skin should still hold by itself for a little while!
I thought maybe an actual seamstress could do a better job making it all less . . .
you know . . .
Which is why she came to me!
I never was one for sewing.
You'd never know from looking at her, dear.

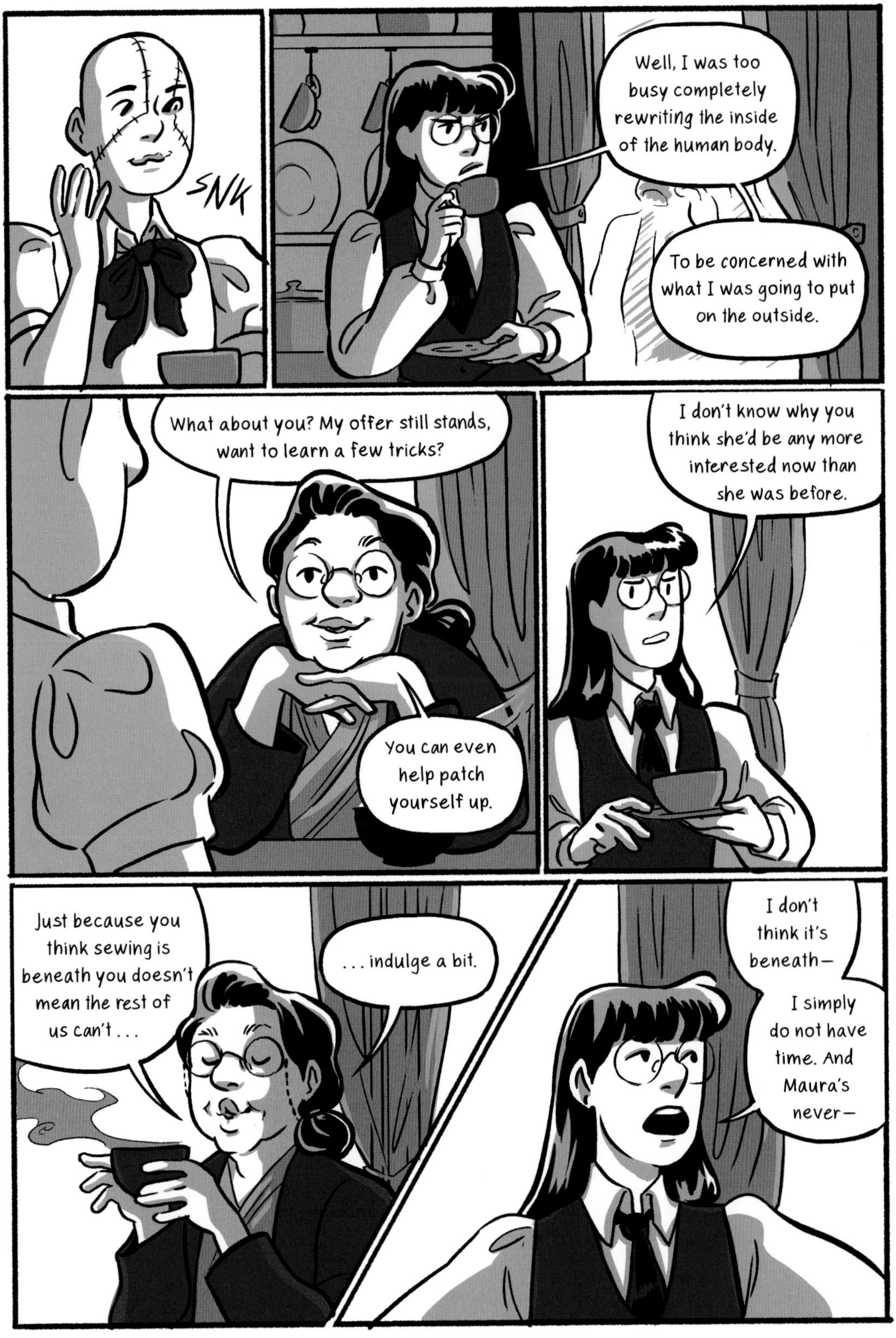
SNK
Well, I was too busy completely rewriting the inside of the human body.
To be concerned with what I was going to put on the outside.
What about you? My offer still stands, want to learn a few tricks?
You can even help patch yourself up.
I don't know why you think she'd be any more interested now than she was before.
Just because you think sewing is beneath you doesn't mean the rest of us can't . . .
. . . indulge a bit.
I don't think it's beneath—
I simply do not have time. And Maura's never—

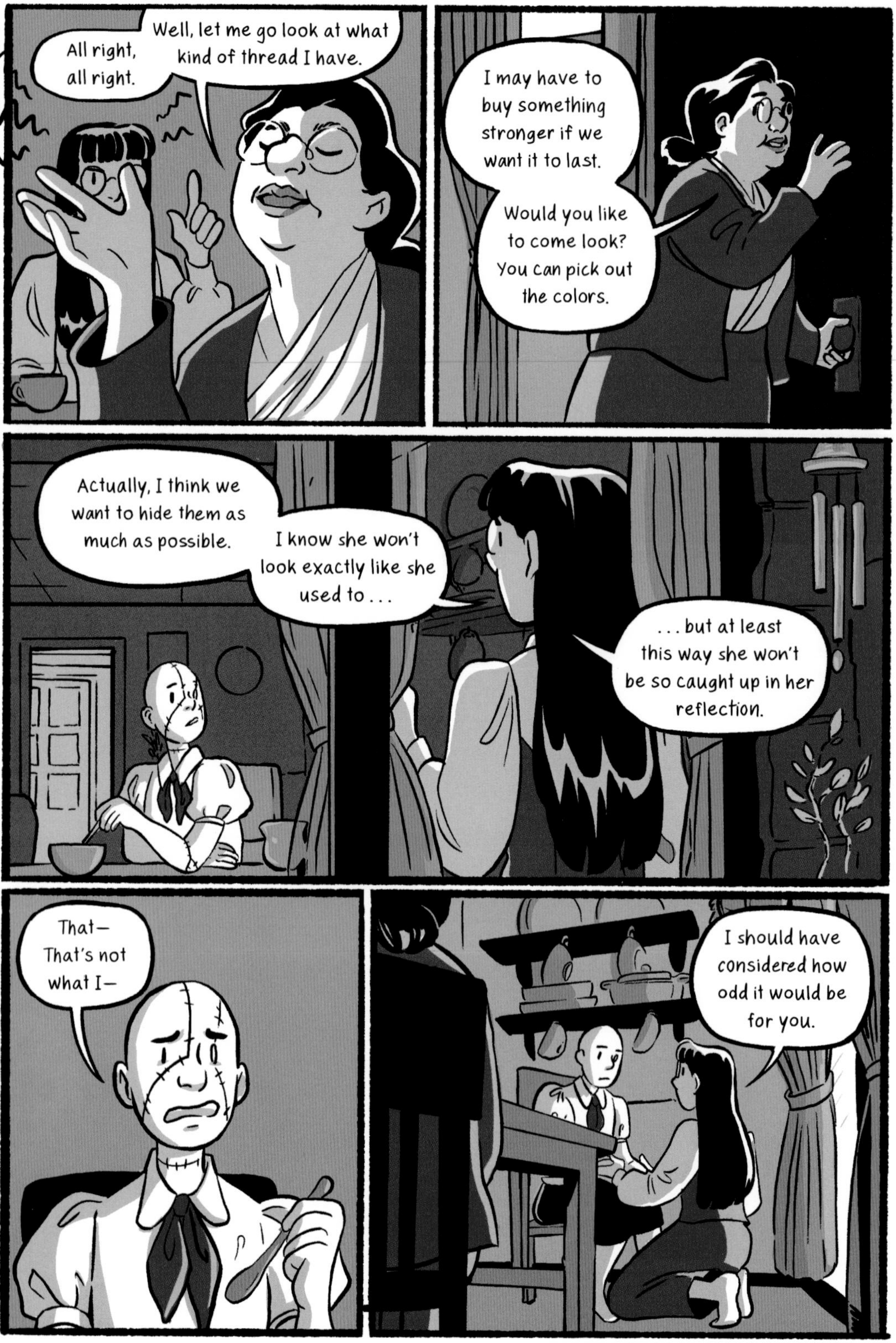
All right, all right.
Well, let me go look at what kind of thread I have.
I may have to buy something stronger if we want it to last.
Would you like to come look? You can pick out the colors.
Actually, I think we want to hide them as much as possible.
I know she won't look exactly like she used to . . .
. . . but at least this way she won't be so caught up in her reflection.
That— That's not what I—
I should have considered how odd it would be for you.

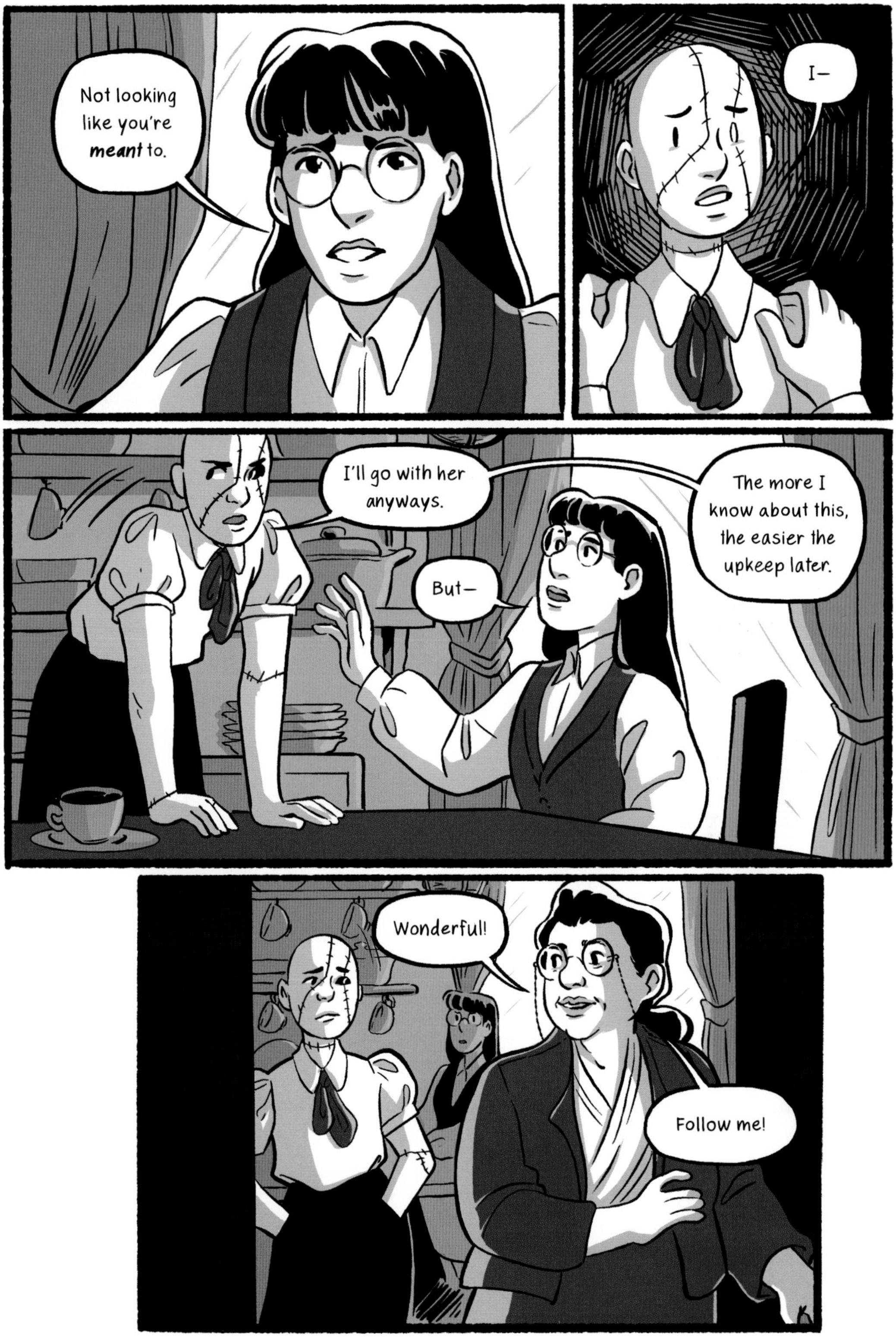
Not looking like you're **meant** to.
I–
I'll go with her anyways.
But–
The more I know about this, the easier the upkeep later.
Wonderful!
Follow me!

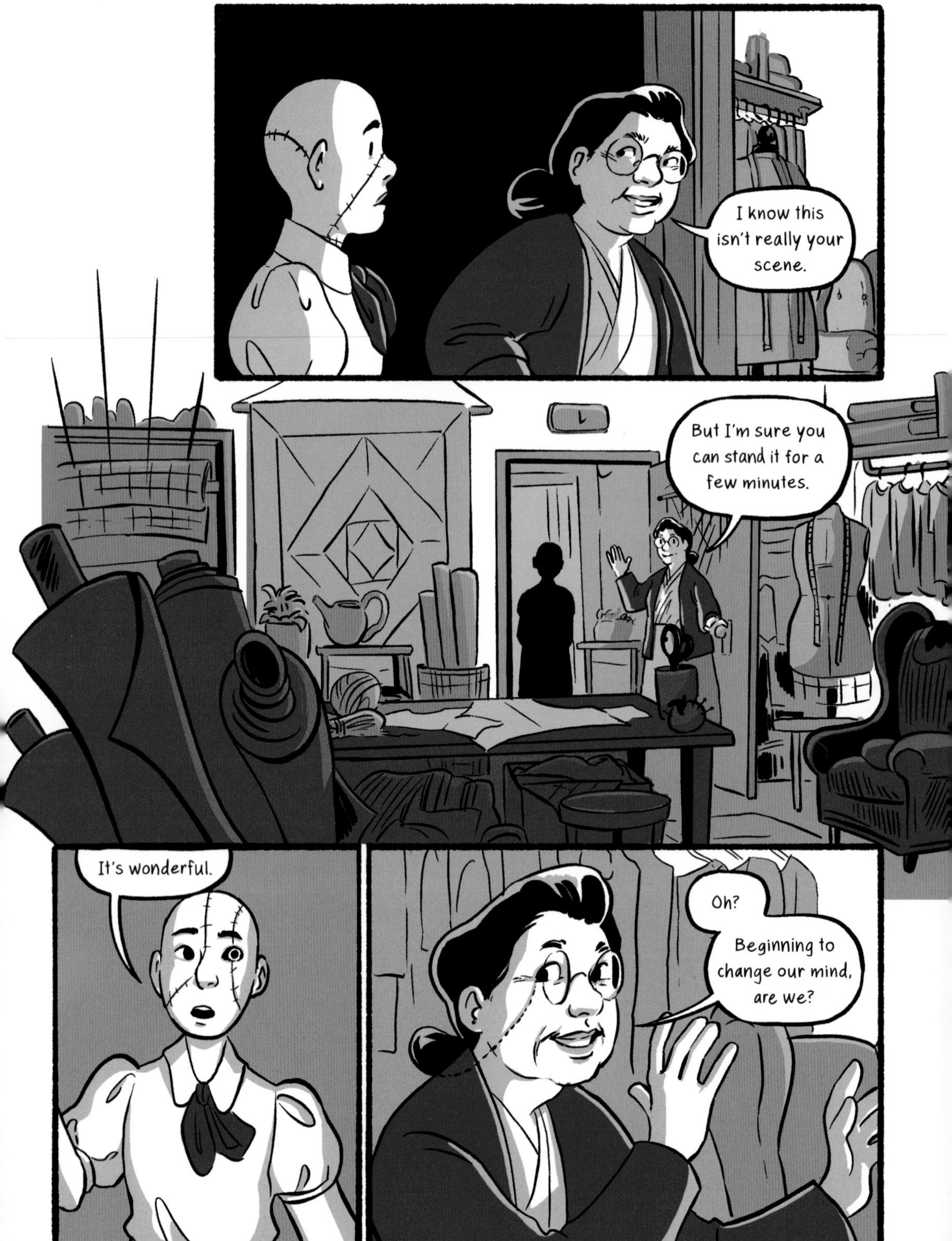
I know this isn't really your scene.
But I'm sure you can stand it for a few minutes.
It's wonderful.
Oh?
Beginning to change our mind, are we?

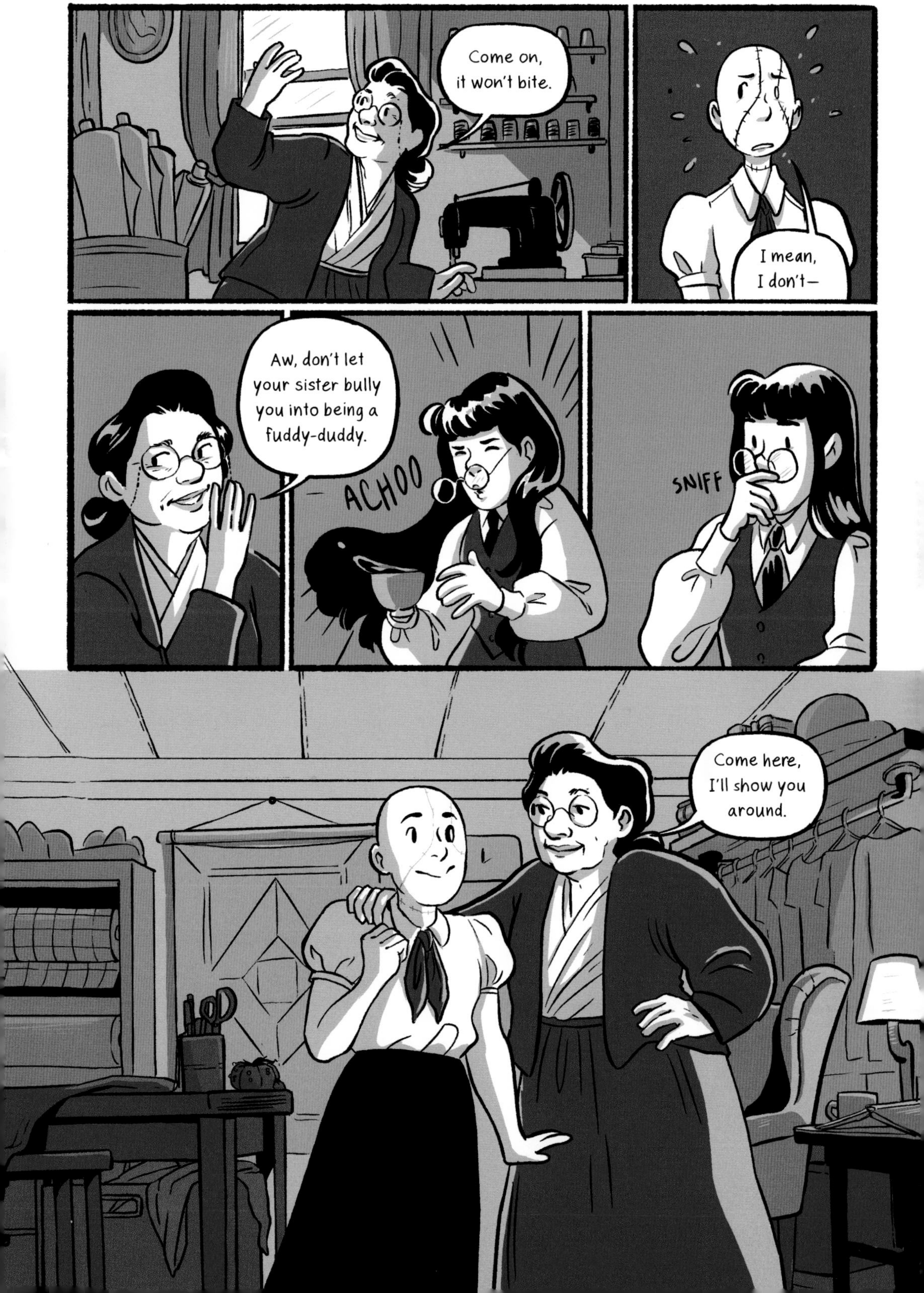
Come on, it won't bite.
I mean, I don't—
Aw, don't let your sister bully you into being a fuddy-duddy.
ACHOO
SNIFF
Come here, I'll show you around.

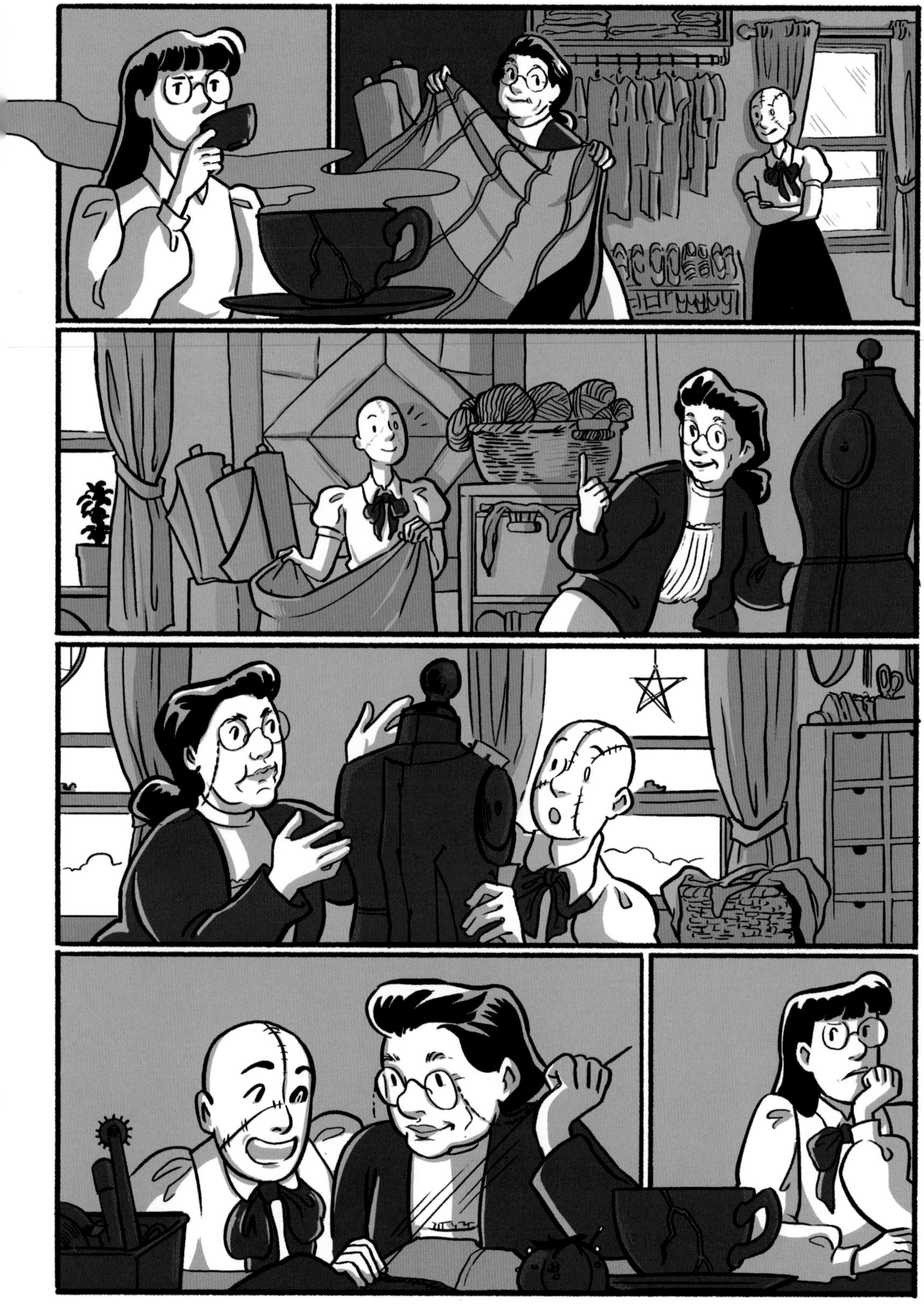

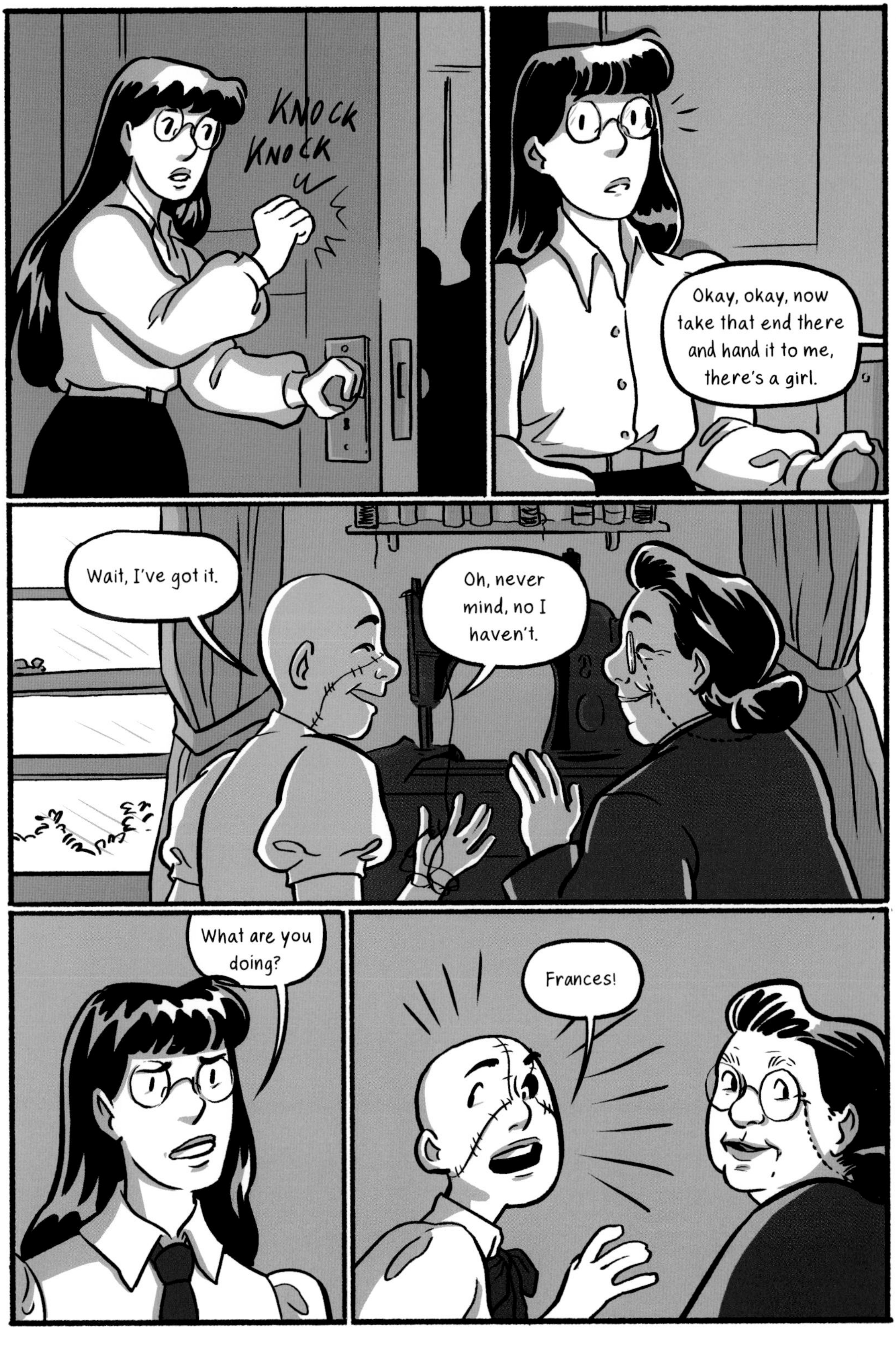

KNOCK
KNOCK
Okay, okay, now take that end there and hand it to me, there's a girl.
Wait, I've got it.
Oh, never mind, no I haven't.
What are you doing?
Frances!

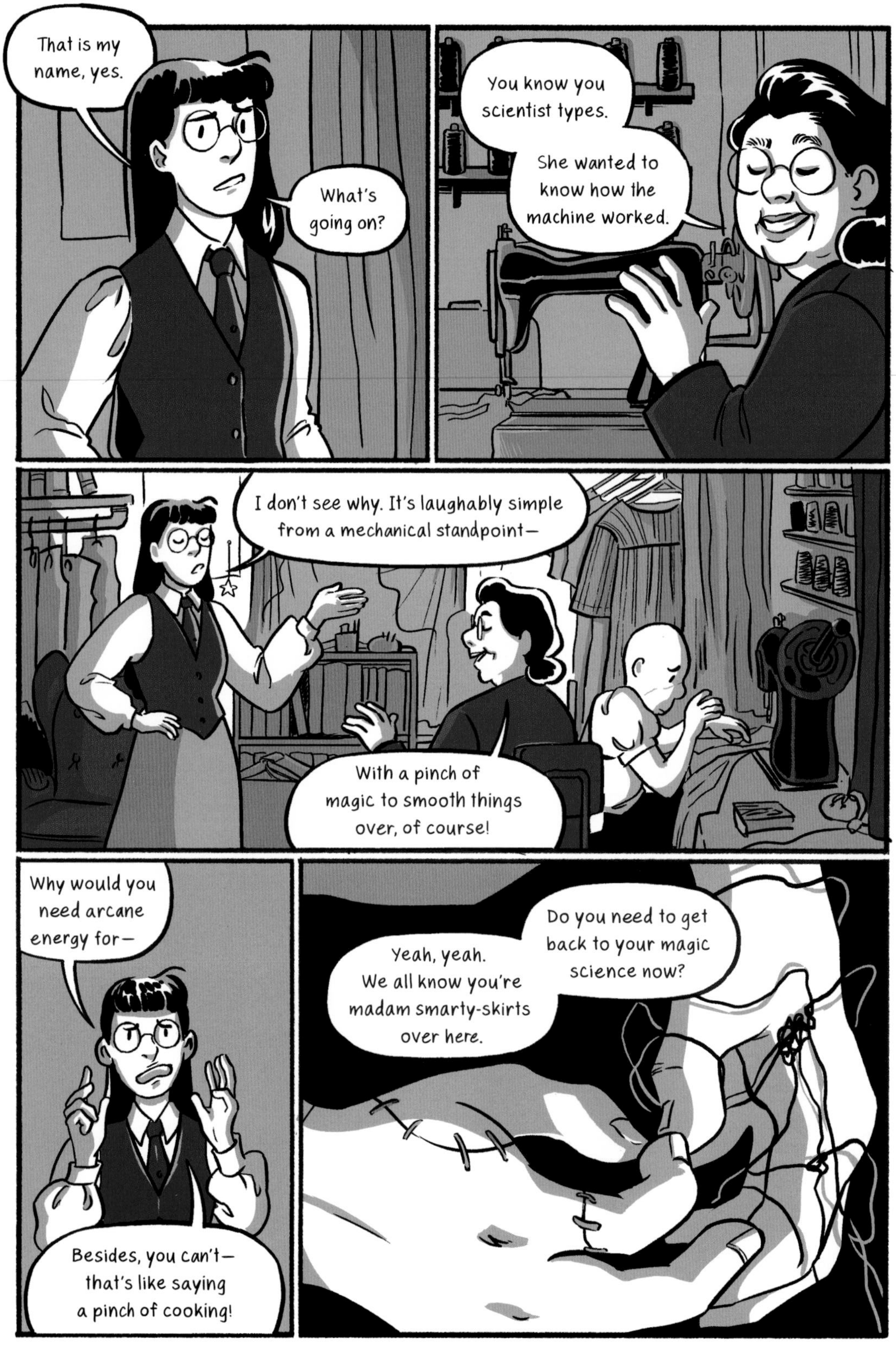
That is my name, yes.
What's going on?
You know you scientist types.
She wanted to know how the machine worked.
I don't see why. It's laughably simple from a mechanical standpoint—
With a pinch of magic to smooth things over, of course!
Why would you need arcane energy for—
Besides, you can't— that's like saying a pinch of cooking!
Yeah, yeah. We all know you're madam smarty-skirts over here.
Do you need to get back to your magic science now?

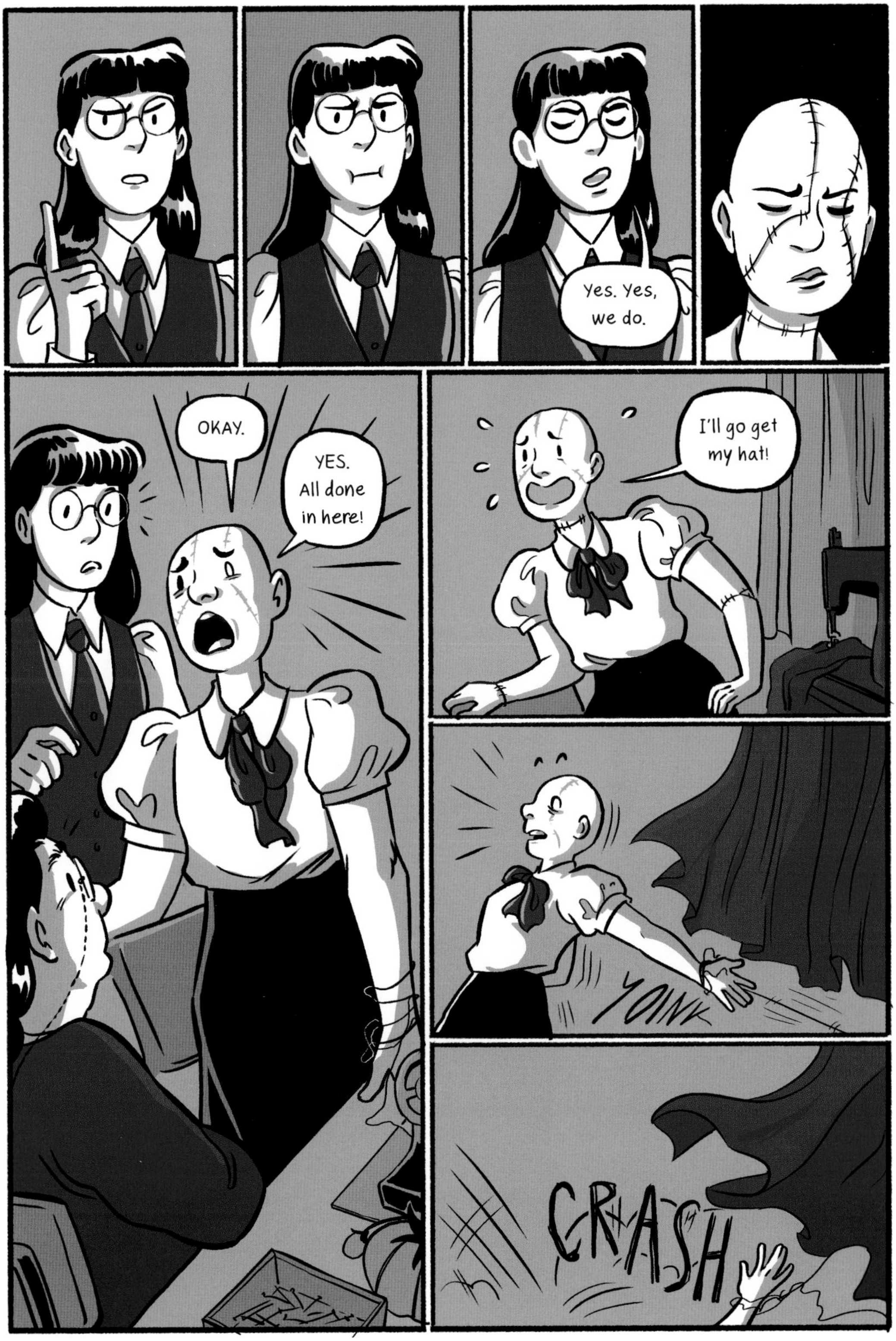
Yes. Yes, we do.
OKAY.
YES. All done in here!
I'll go get my hat!
YOINK
CRASH

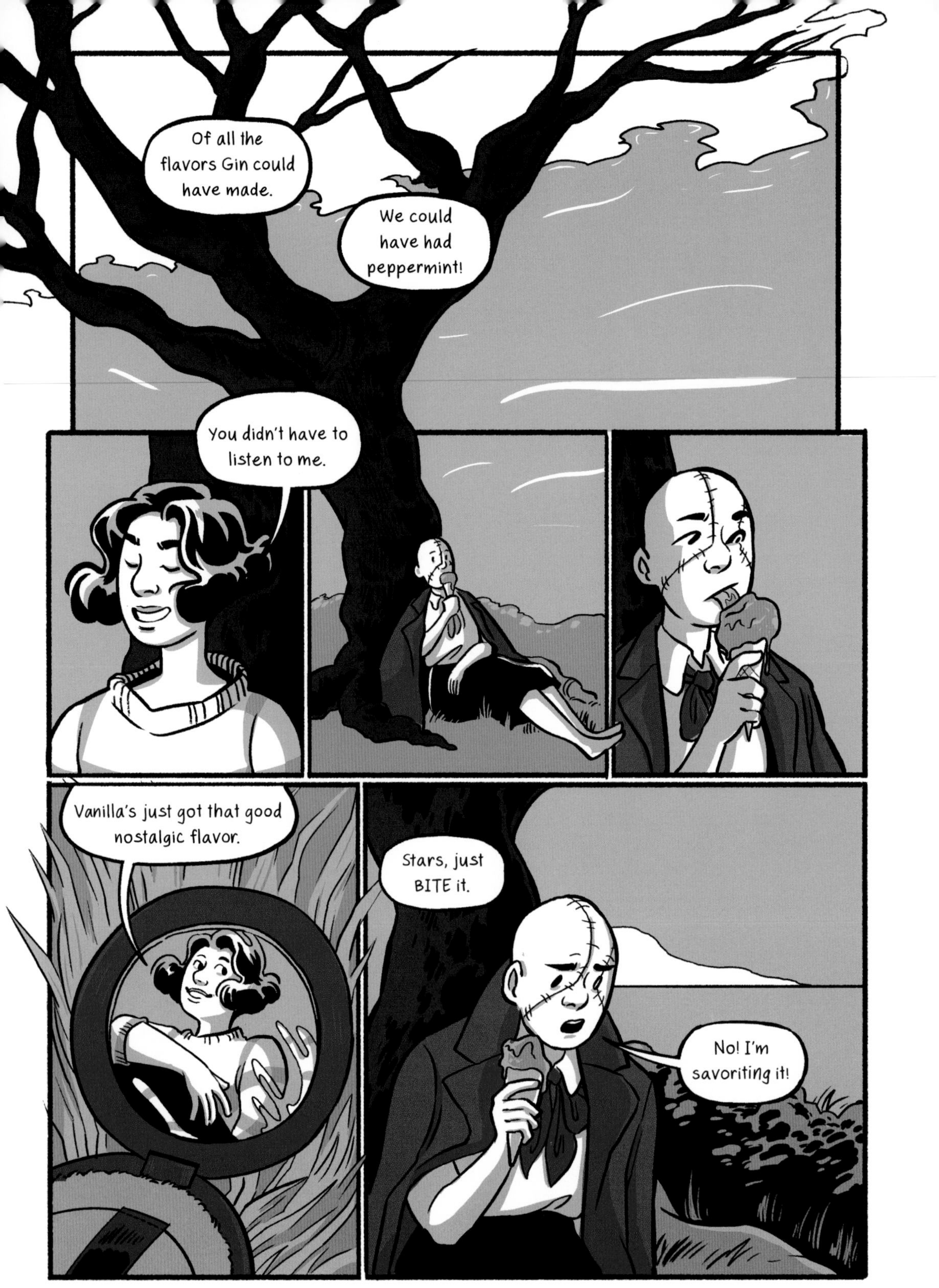
Of all the flavors Gin could have made.
We could have had peppermint!
You didn't have to listen to me.
Vanilla's just got that good nostalgic flavor.
Stars, just BITE it.
No! I'm savoriting it!

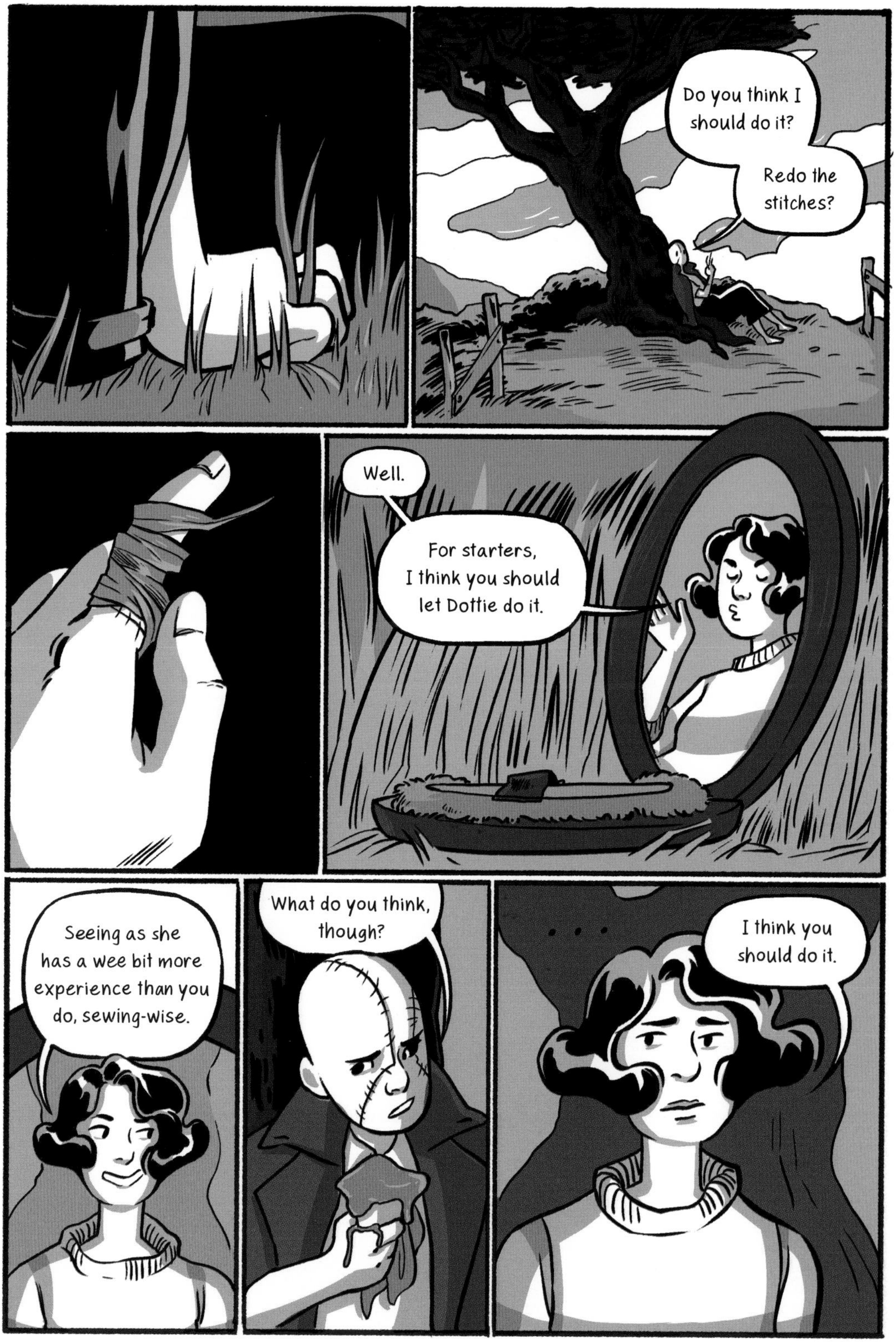
Do you think I should do it?
Redo the stitches?
Well.
For starters, I think you should let Dottie do it.
Seeing as she has a wee bit more experience than you do, sewing-wise.
What do you think, though?
...
I think you should do it.

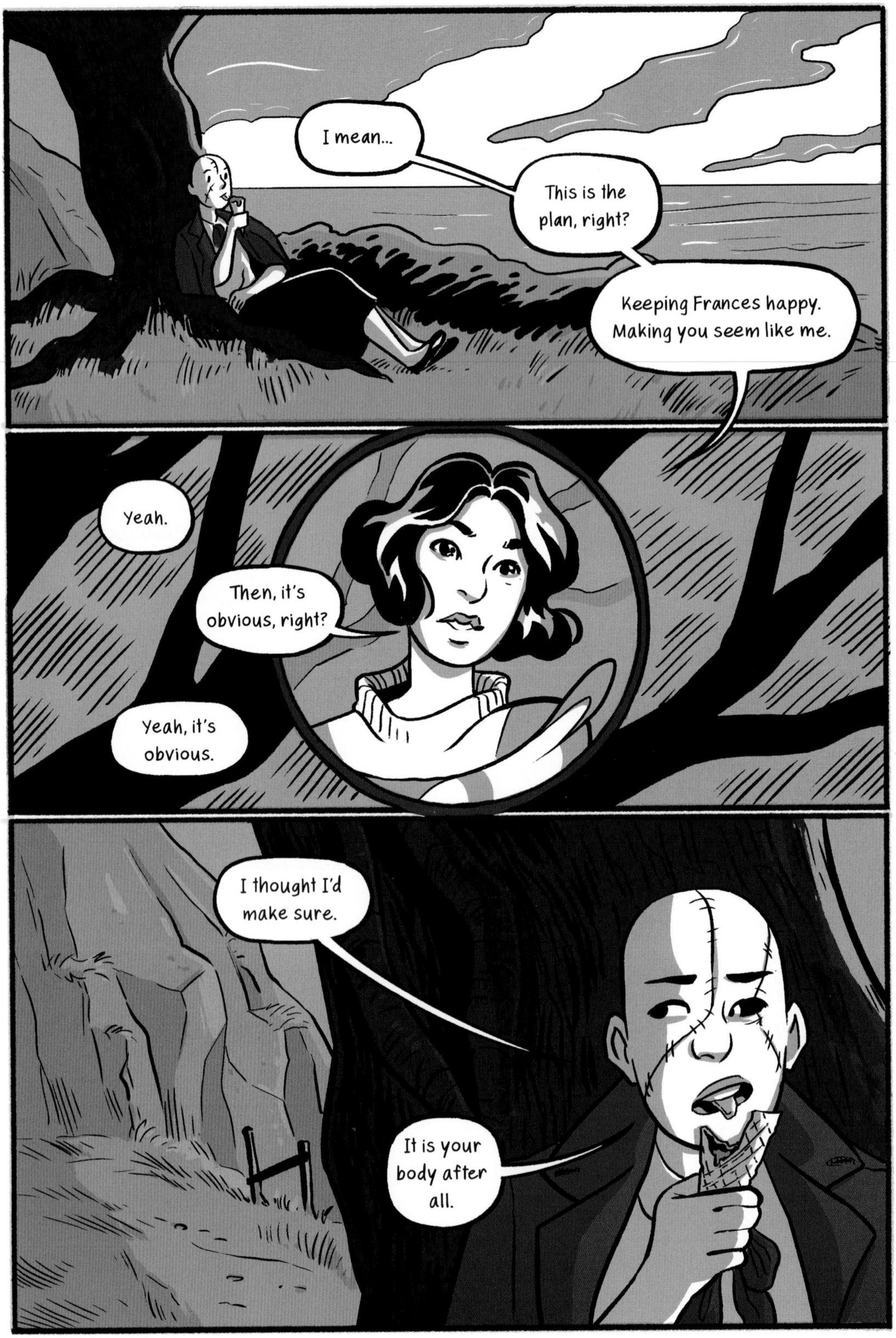
I mean...
This is the plan, right?
Keeping Frances happy. Making you seem like me.
Yeah.
Then, it's obvious, right?
Yeah, it's obvious.
I thought I'd make sure.
It is your body after all.

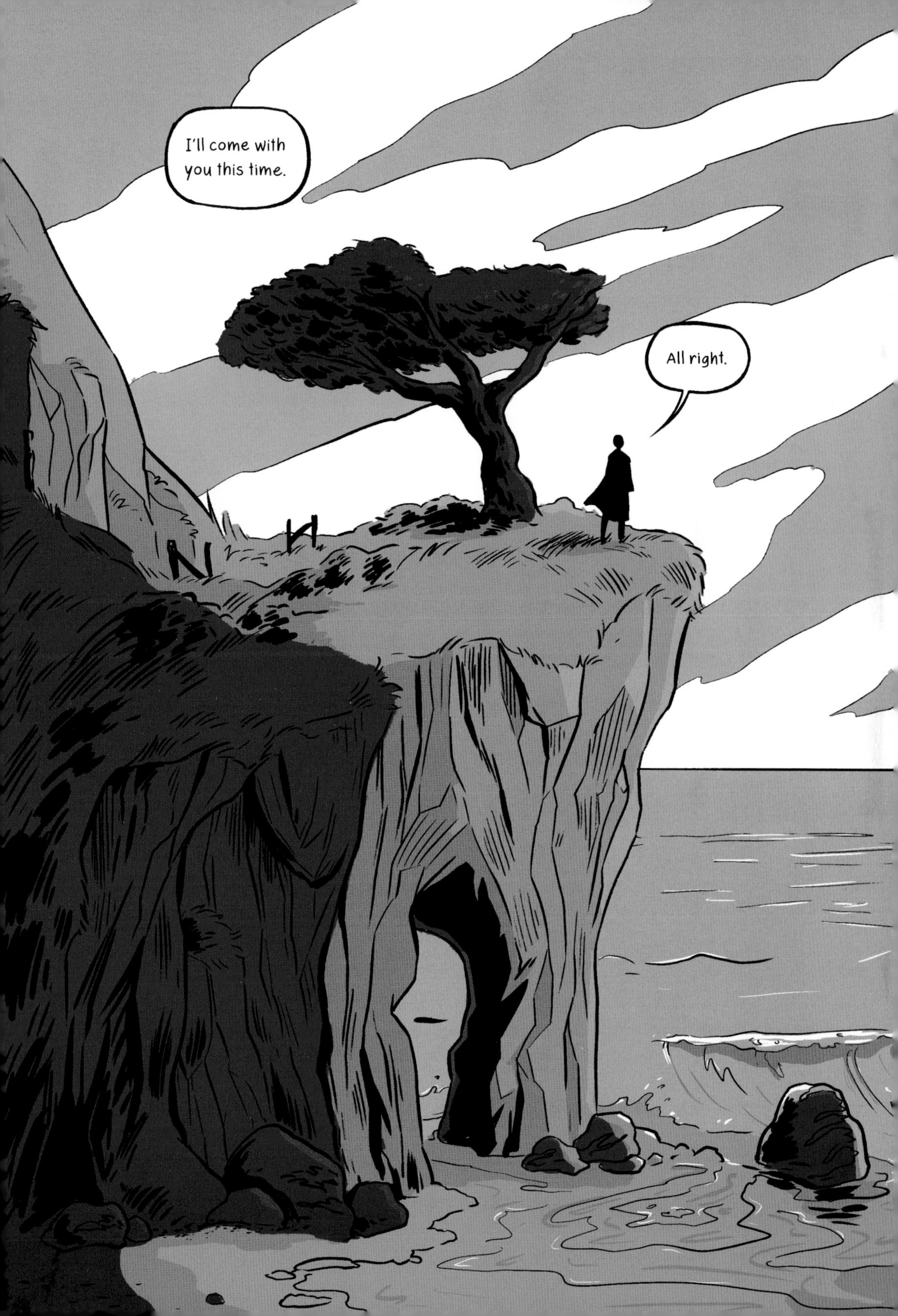
I'll come with you this time.
All right.

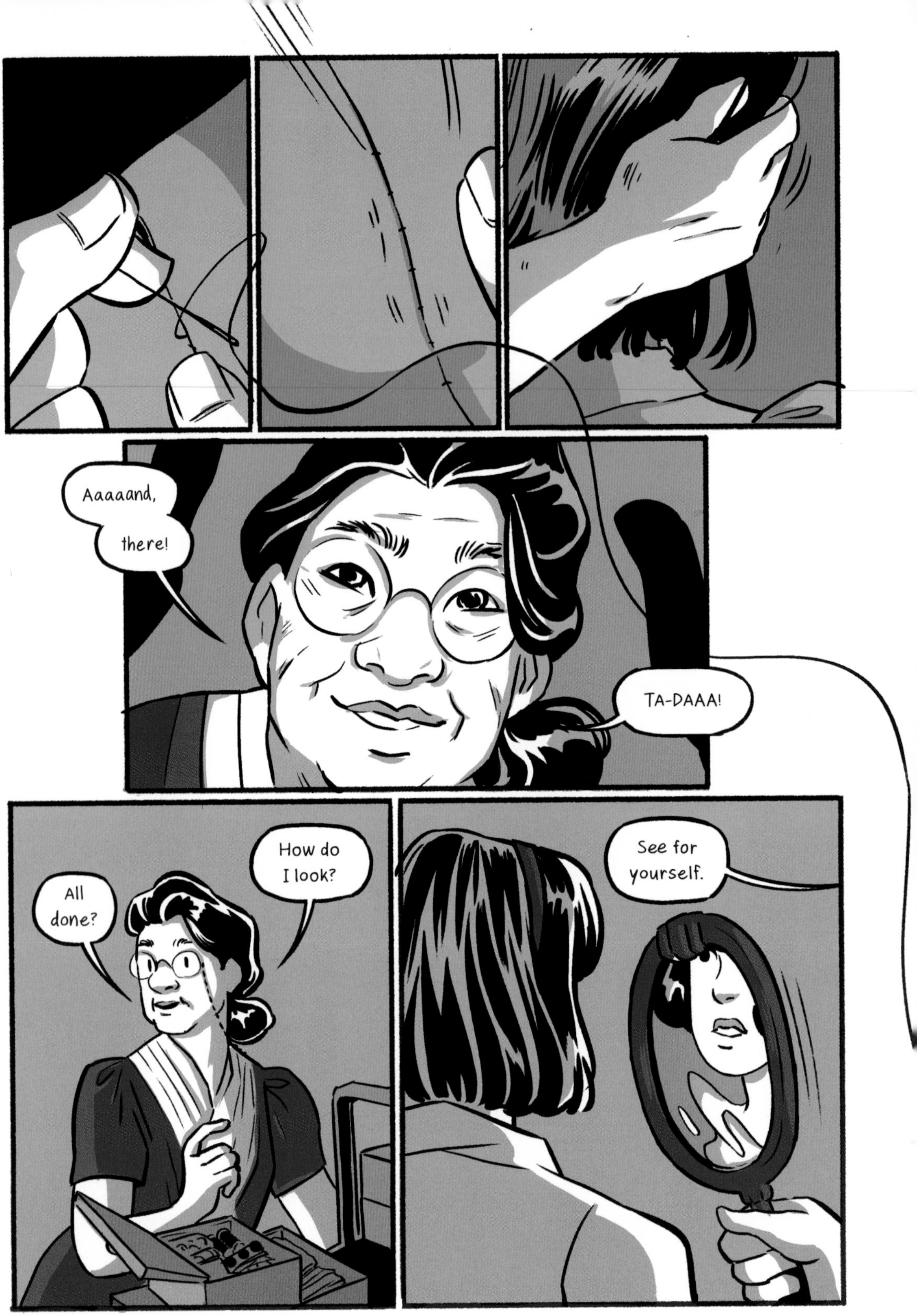
Aaaaand,
there!
TA-DAAA!
All done?
How do I look?
See for yourself.

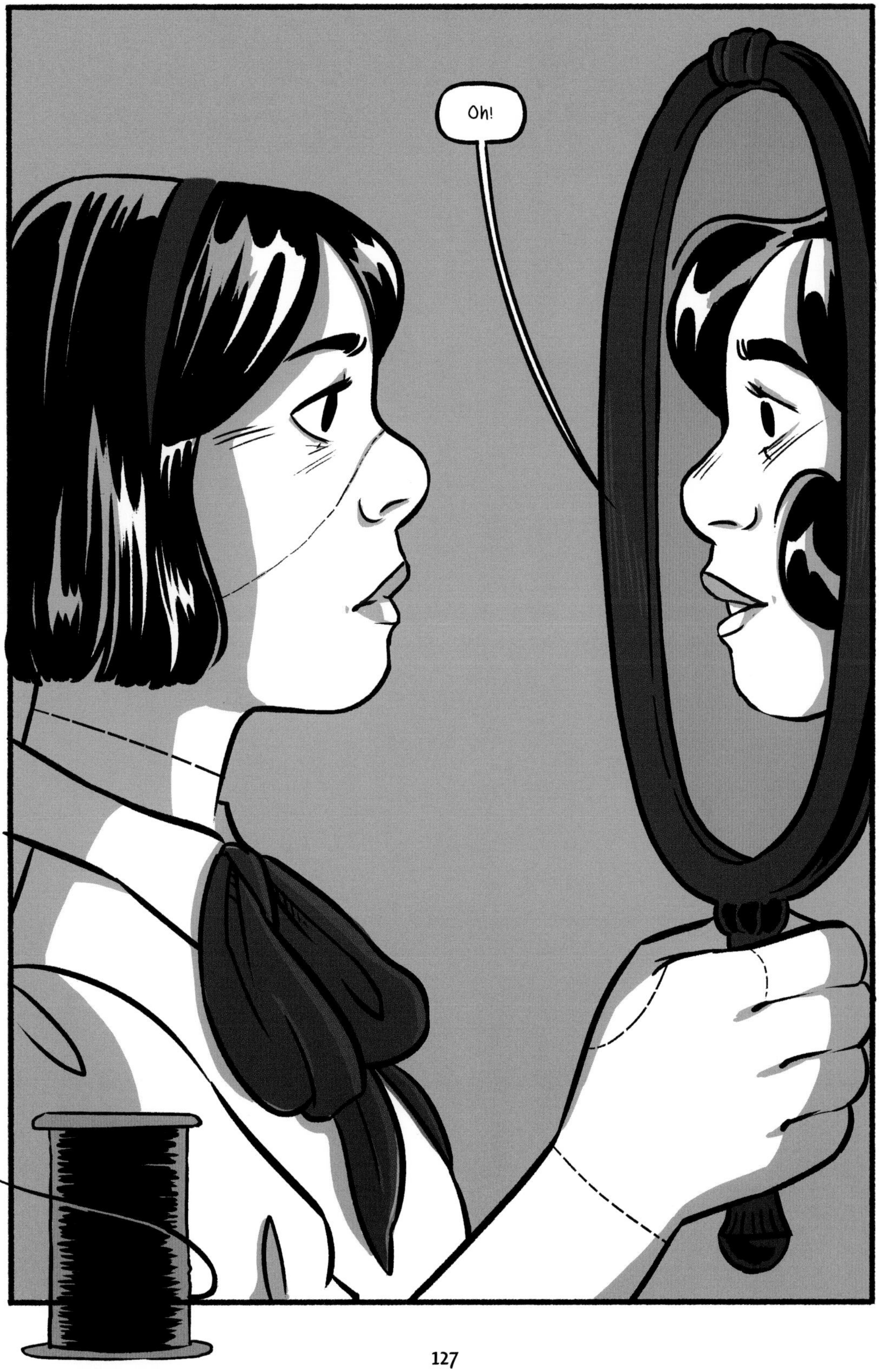
Oh!

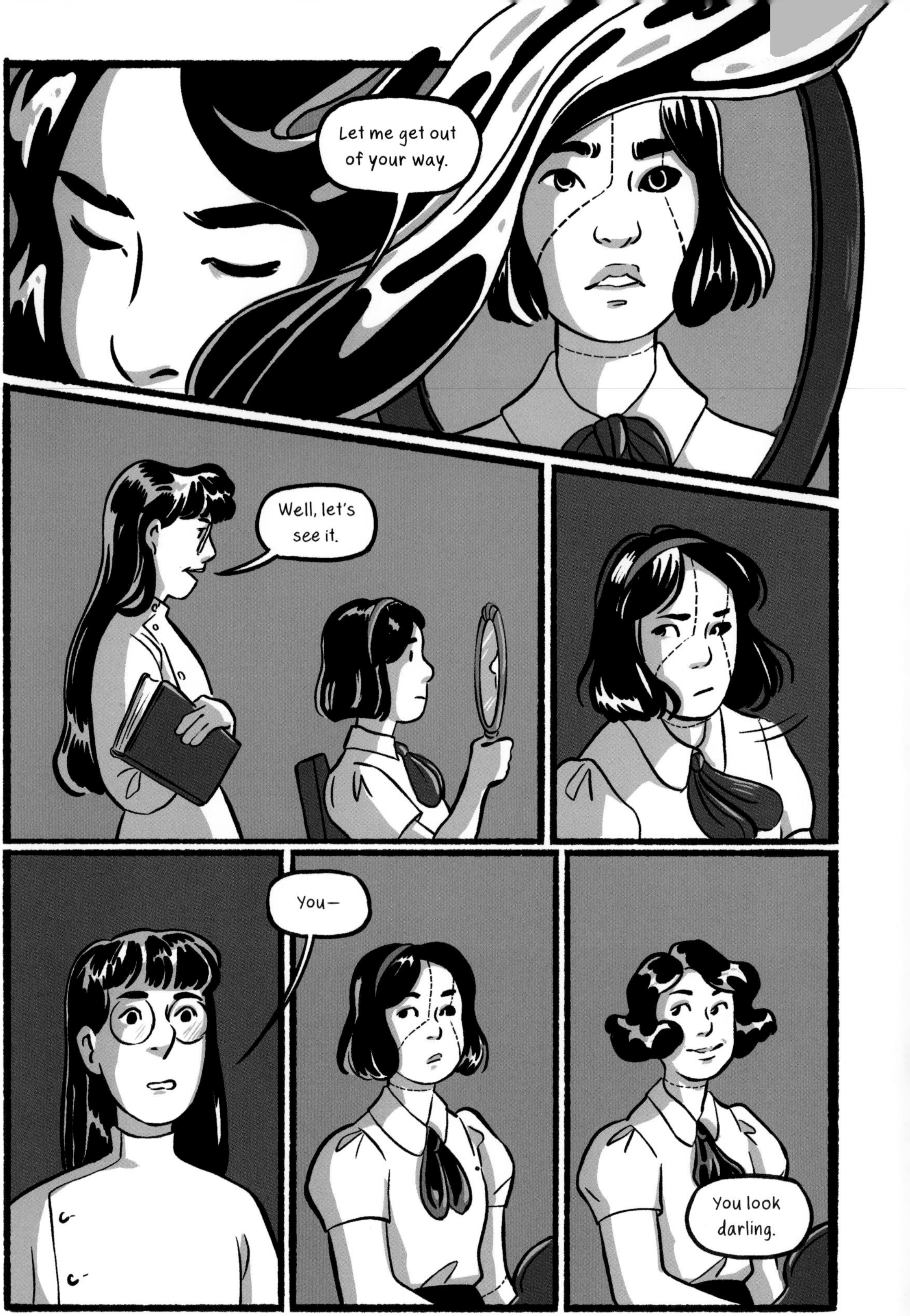
Let me get out of your way.
Well, let's see it.
You—
You look darling.

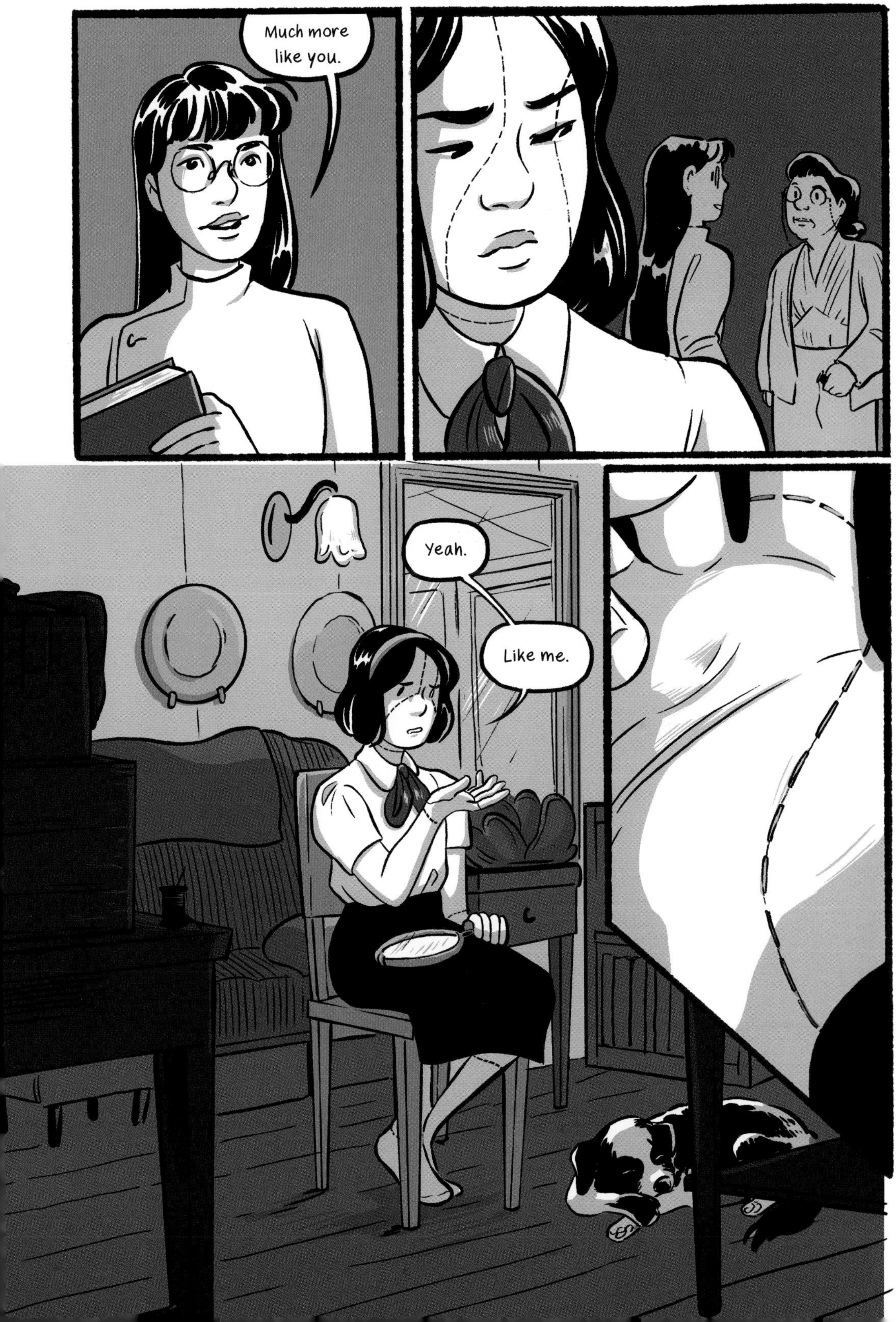
Much more like you.
Yeah.
Like me.

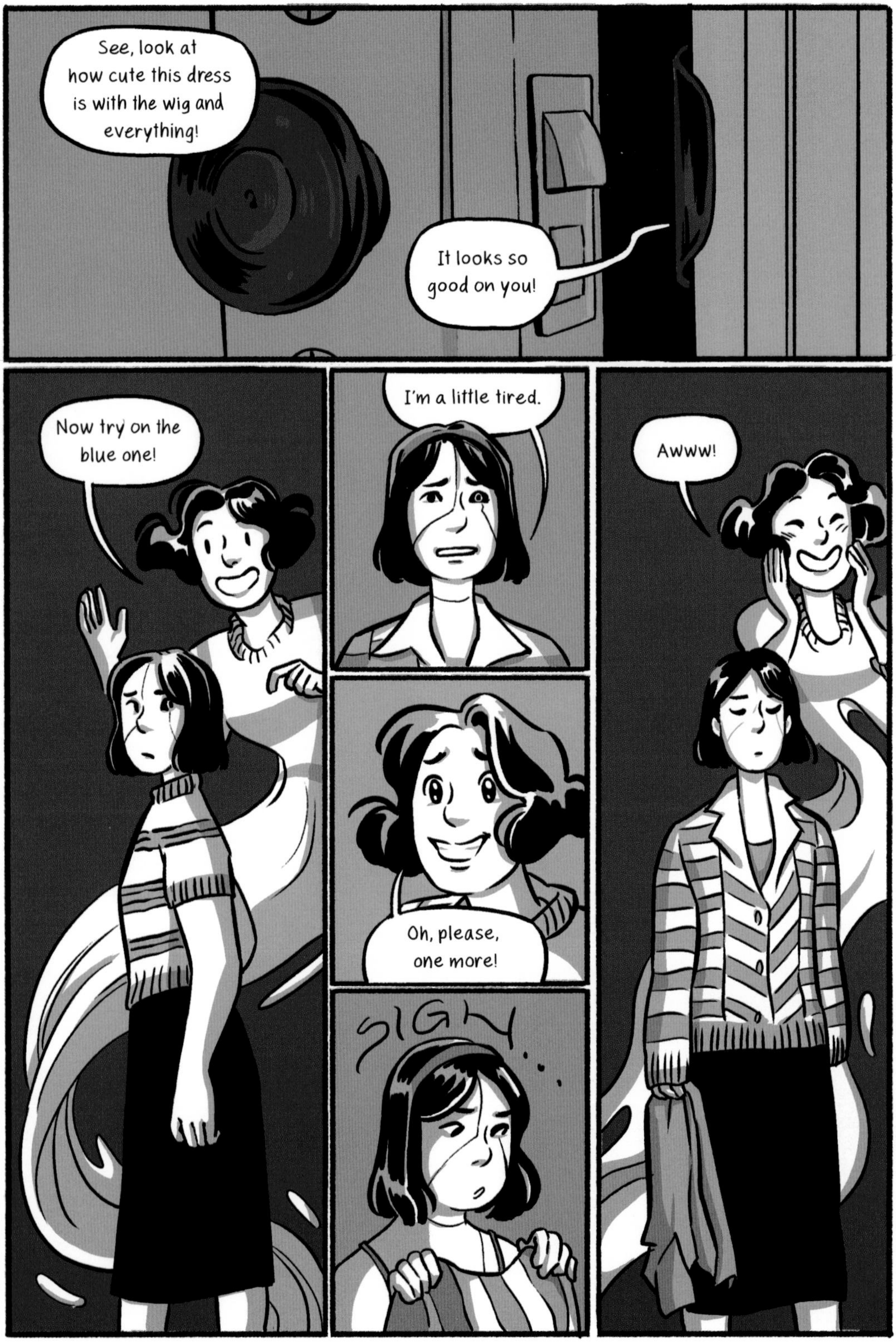
See, look at how cute this dress is with the wig and everything!
It looks so good on you!
Now try on the blue one!
I'm a little tired.
Oh, please, one more!
SIGH...
Awww!

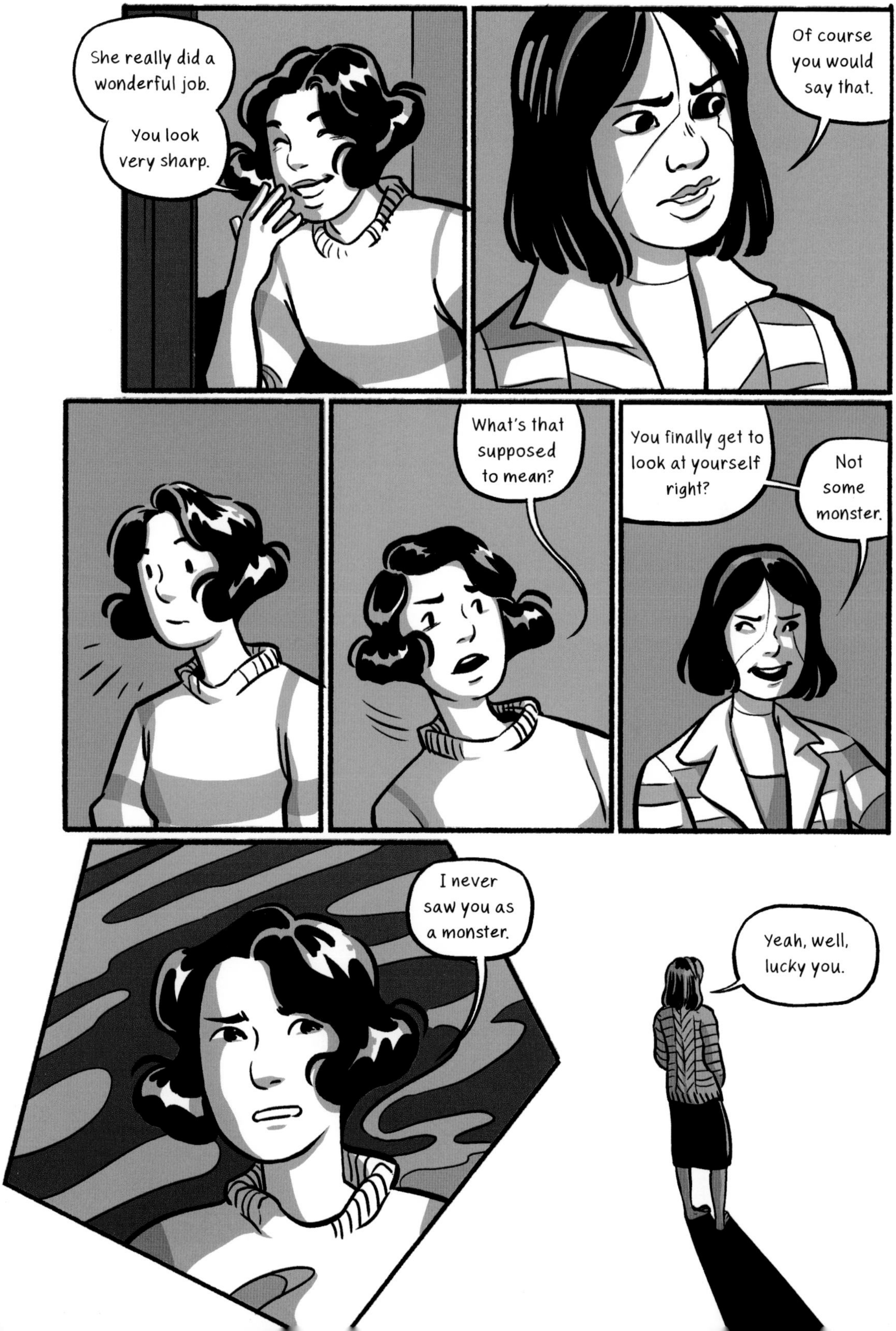
She really did a wonderful job.
You look very sharp.
Of course you would say that.
What's that supposed to mean?
You finally get to look at yourself right?
Not some monster.
I never saw you as a monster.
Yeah, well, lucky you.

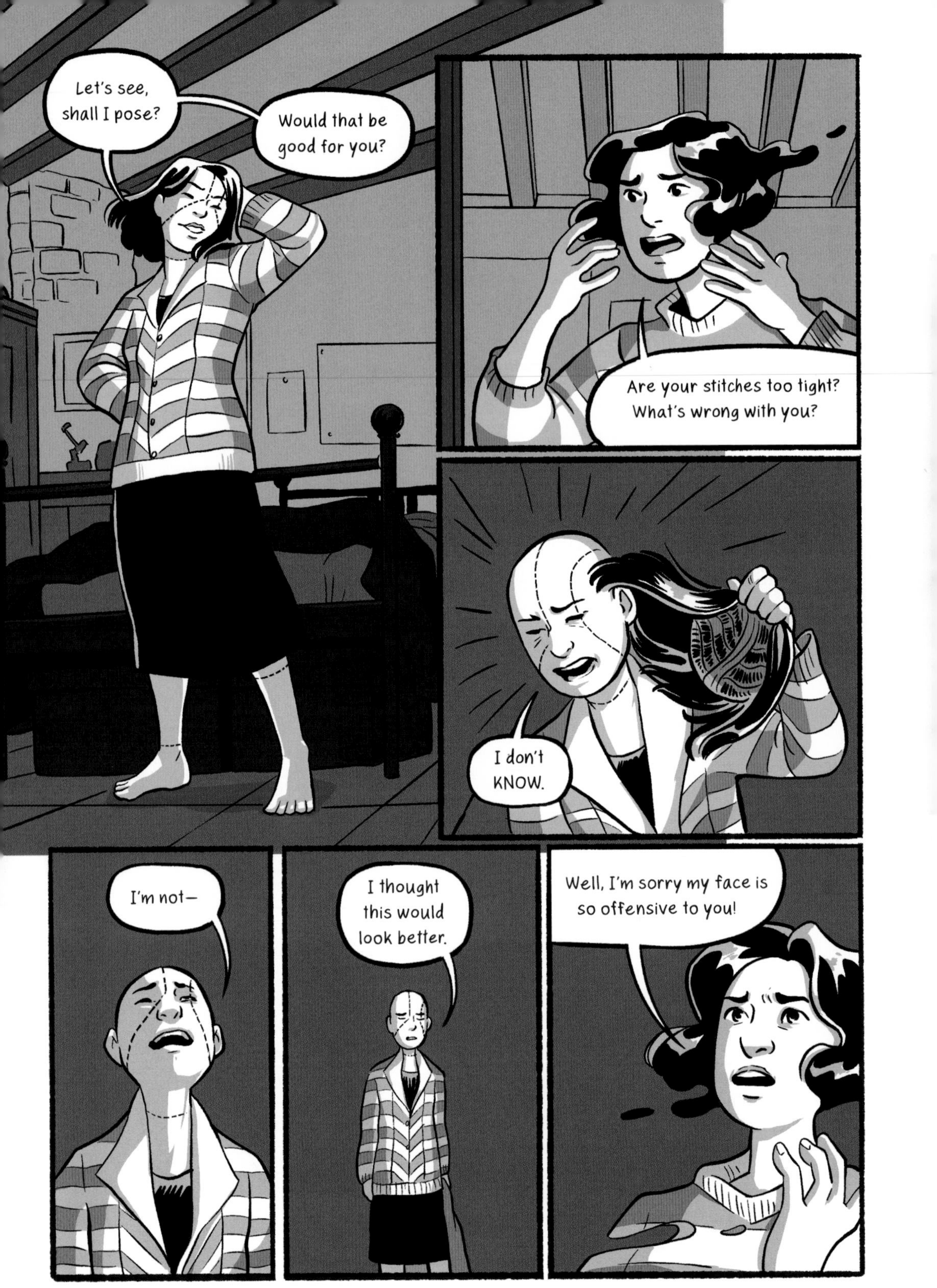
Let's see, shall I pose?
Would that be good for you?
Are your stitches too tight? What's wrong with you?
I don't KNOW.
I'm not—
I thought this would look better.
Well, I'm sorry my face is so offensive to you!

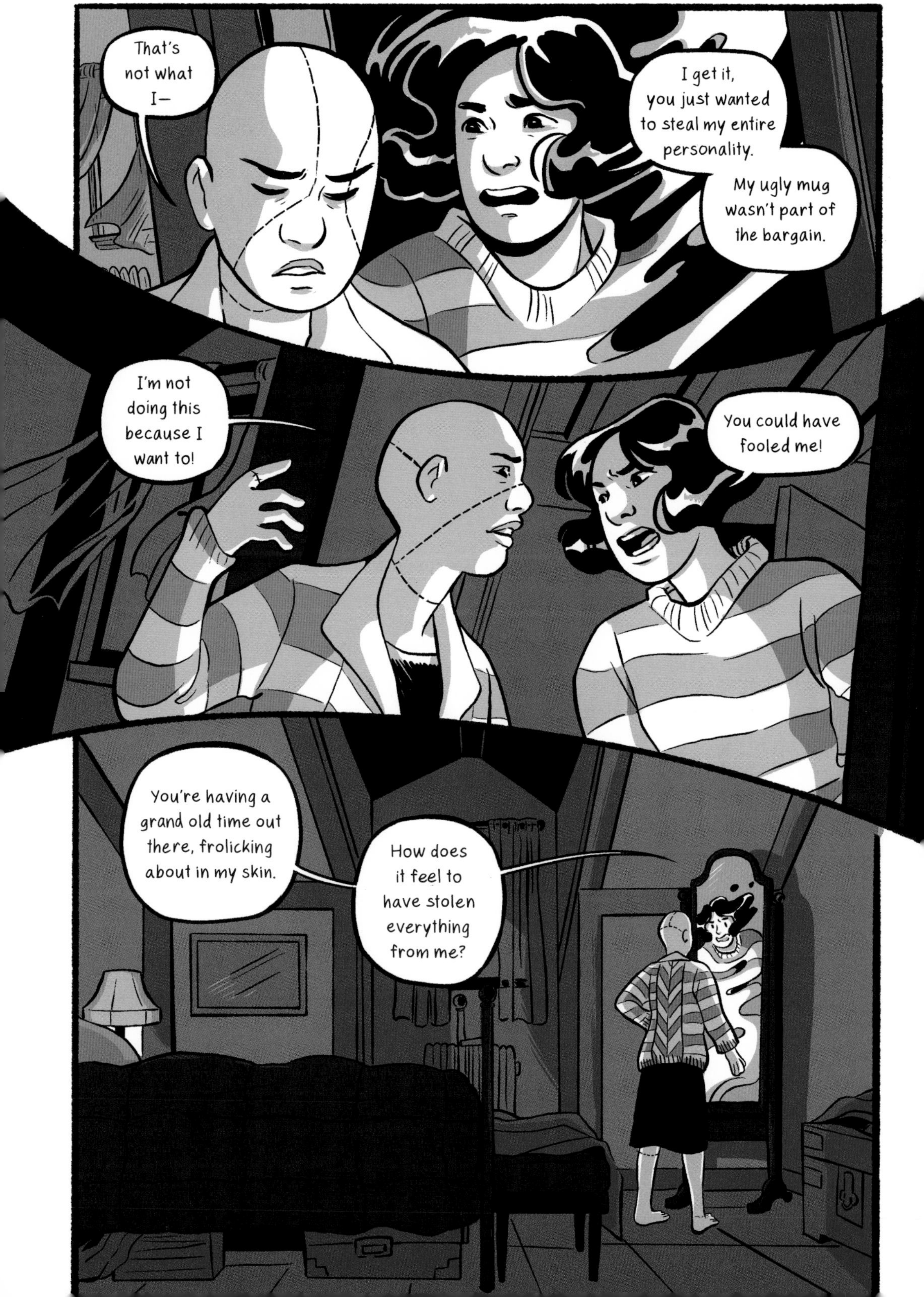
That's not what I—
I get it, you just wanted to steal my entire personality.
My ugly mug wasn't part of the bargain.
I'm not doing this because I want to!
You could have fooled me!
You're having a grand old time out there, frolicking about in my skin.
How does it feel to have stolen everything from me?

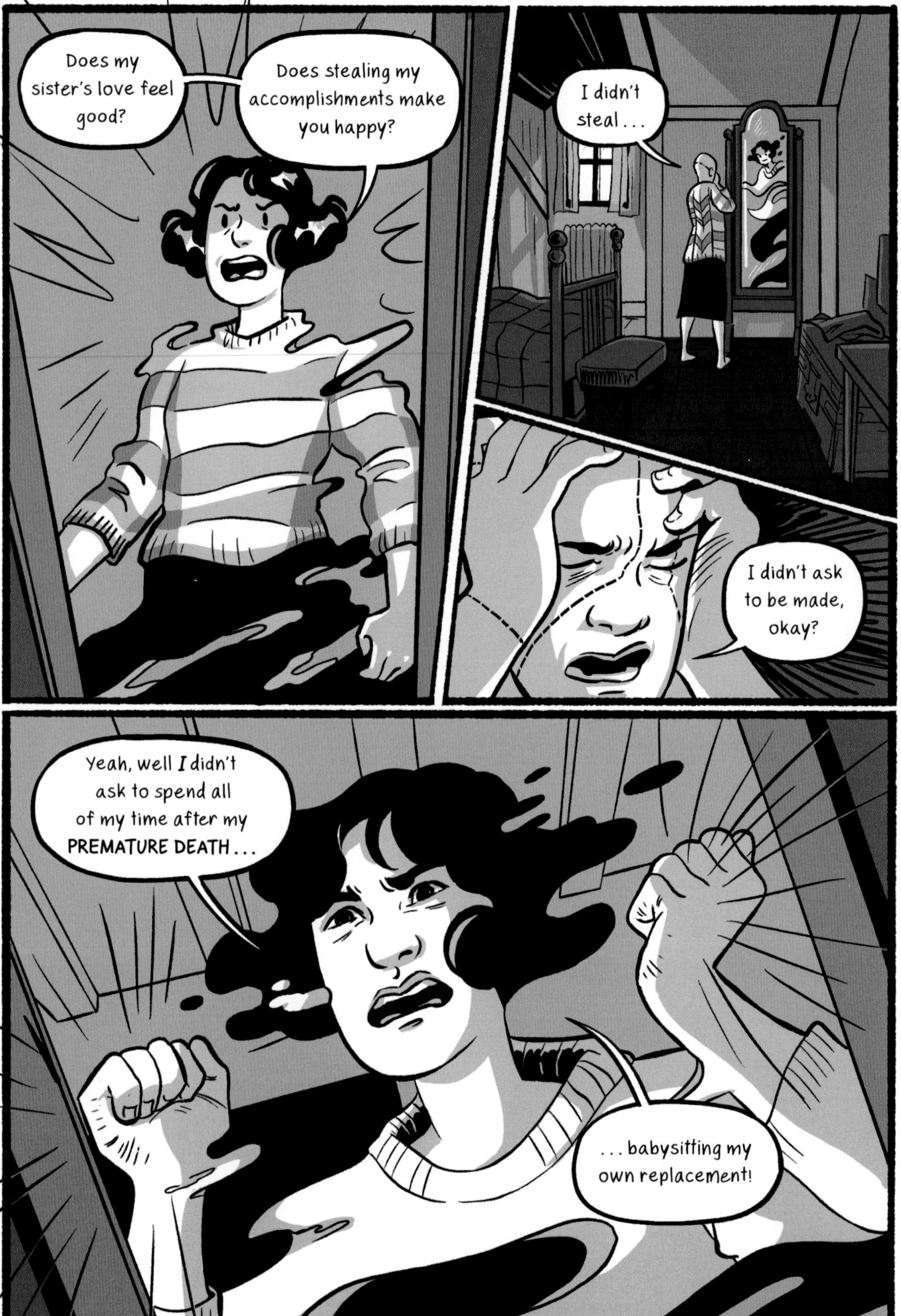
Does my sister's love feel good?
Does stealing my accomplishments make you happy?
I didn't steal . . .
I didn't ask to be made, okay?
Yeah, well I didn't ask to spend all of my time after my PREMATURE DEATH . . .
. . . babysitting my own replacement!

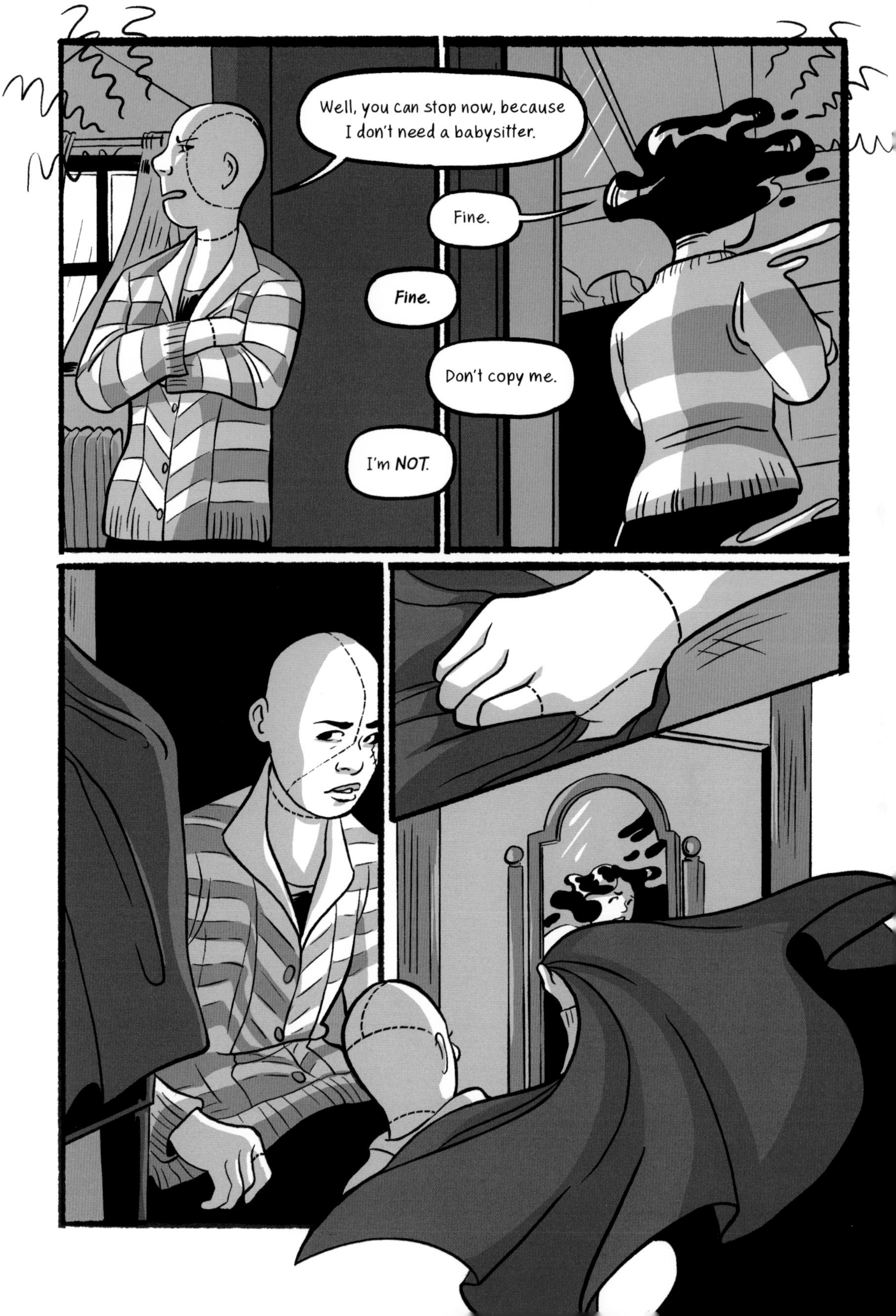
Well, you can stop now, because I don't need a babysitter.
Fine.
Fine.
Don't copy me.
I'm **NOT**.

huff   huff

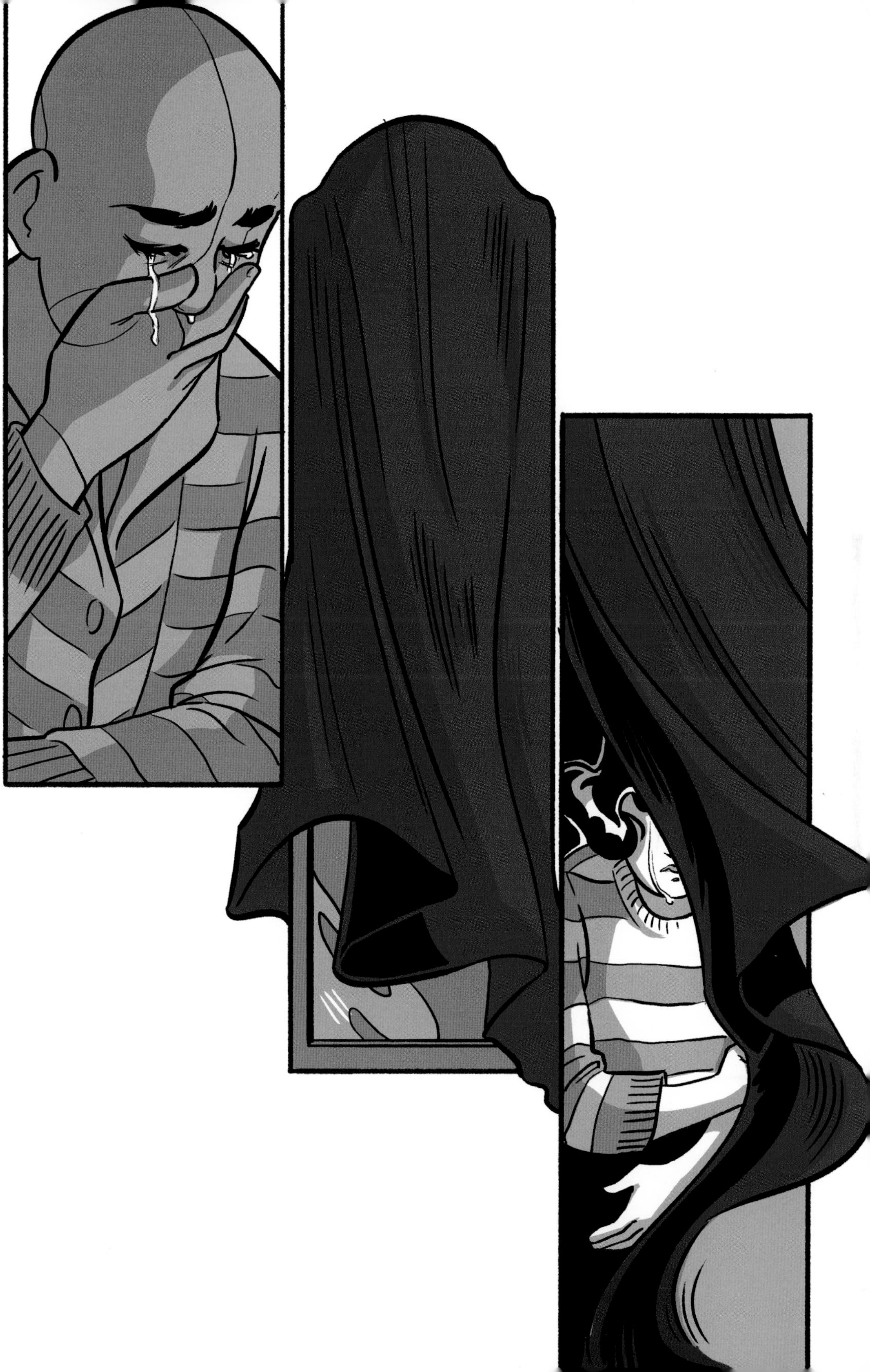

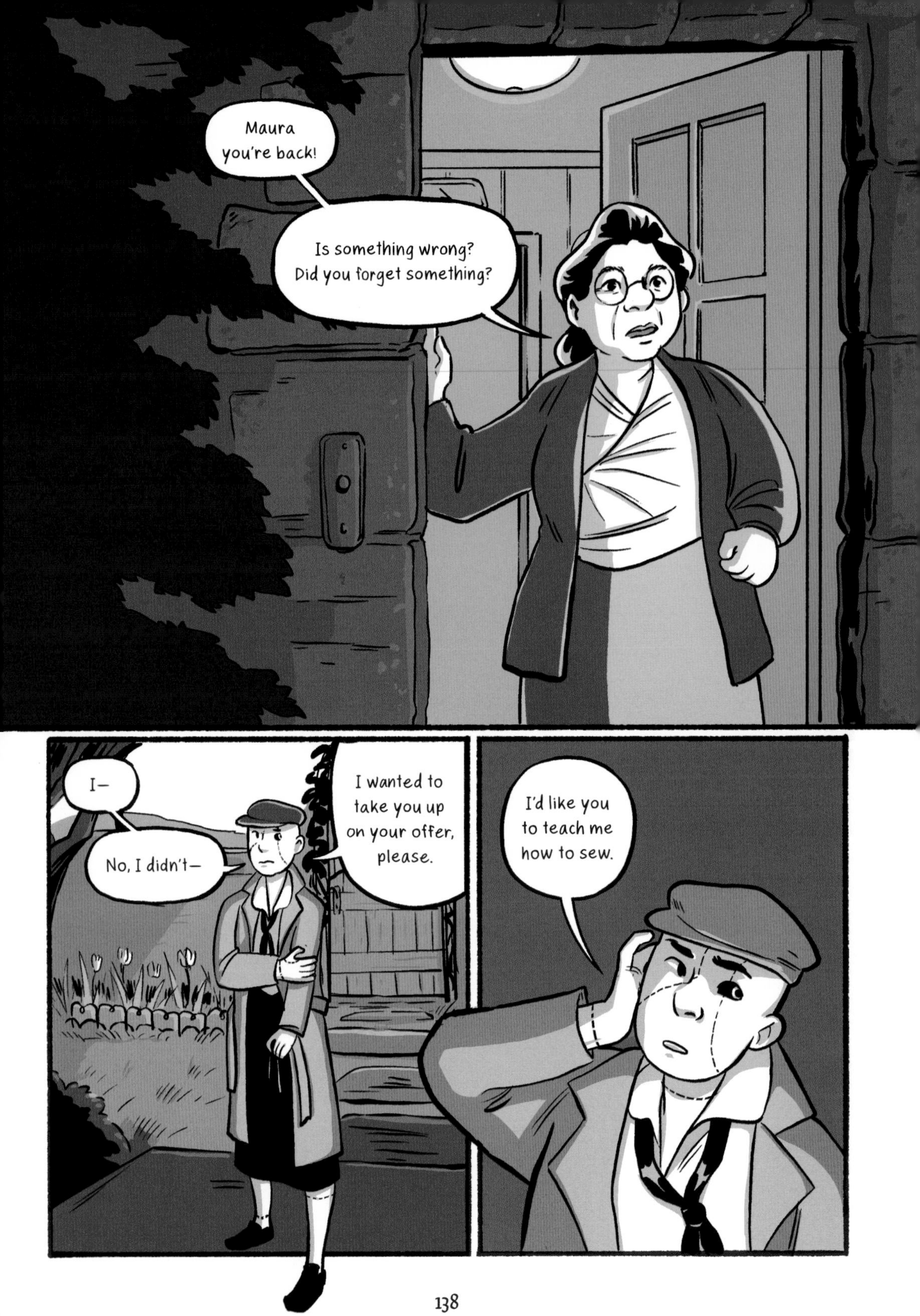
Maura you're back!
Is something wrong? Did you forget something?
I–
No, I didn't–
I wanted to take you up on your offer, please.
I'd like you to teach me how to sew.

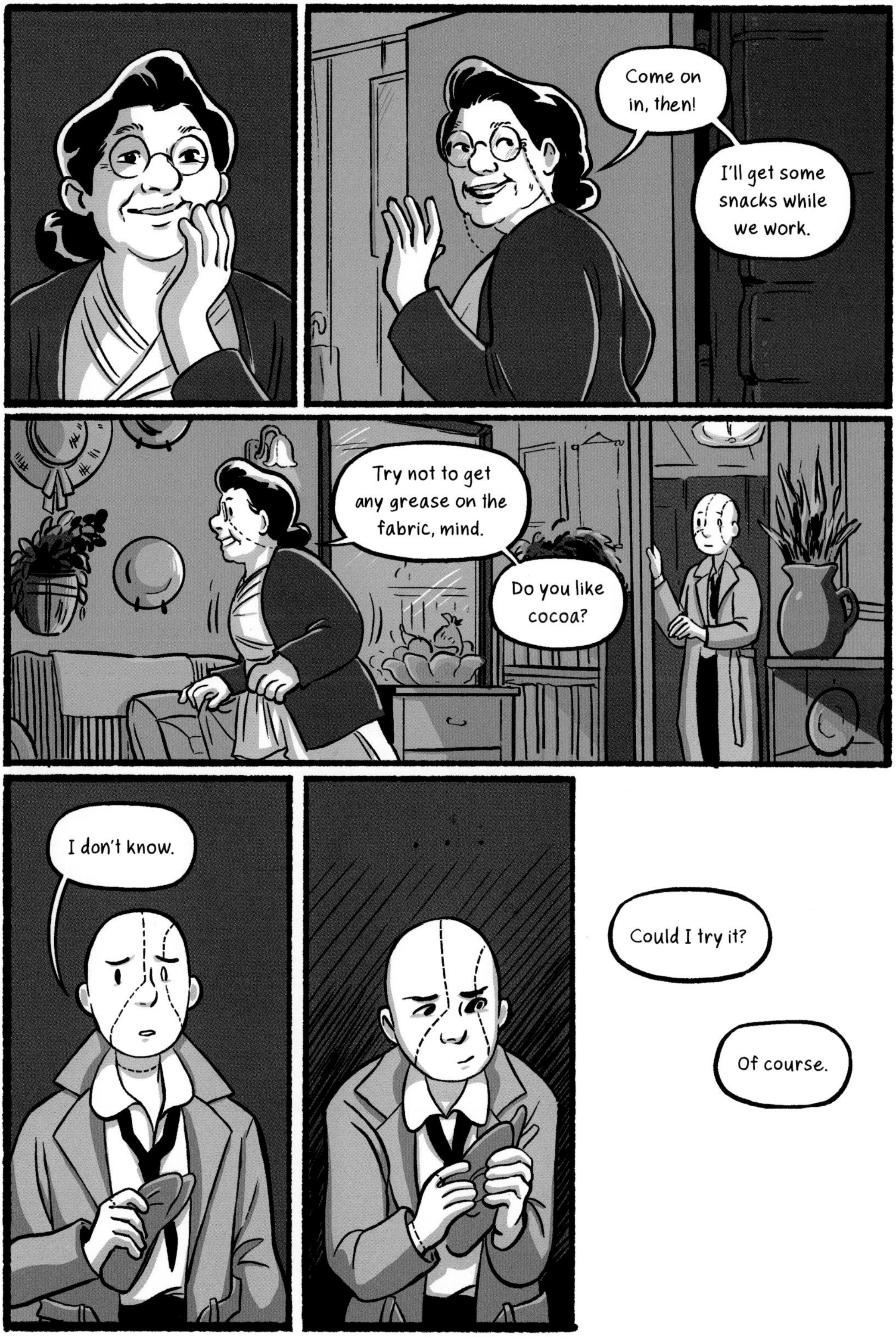

Come on in, then!
I'll get some snacks while we work.
Try not to get any grease on the fabric, mind.
Do you like cocoa?
I don't know.
Could I try it?
Of course.

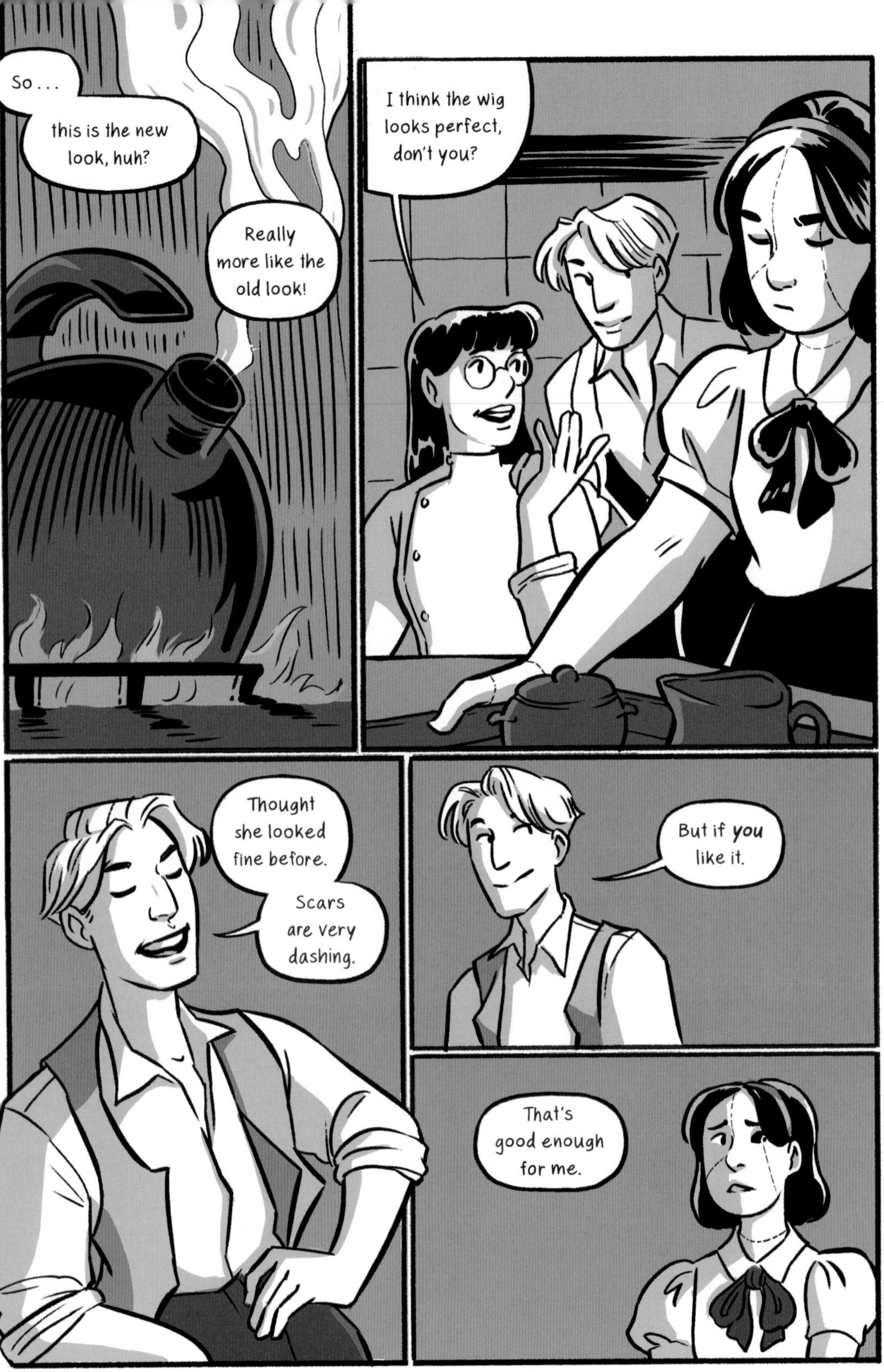
So . . .
this is the new look, huh?
Really more like the old look!
I think the wig looks perfect, don't you?
Thought she looked fine before.
Scars are very dashing.
But if **you** like it.
That's good enough for me.

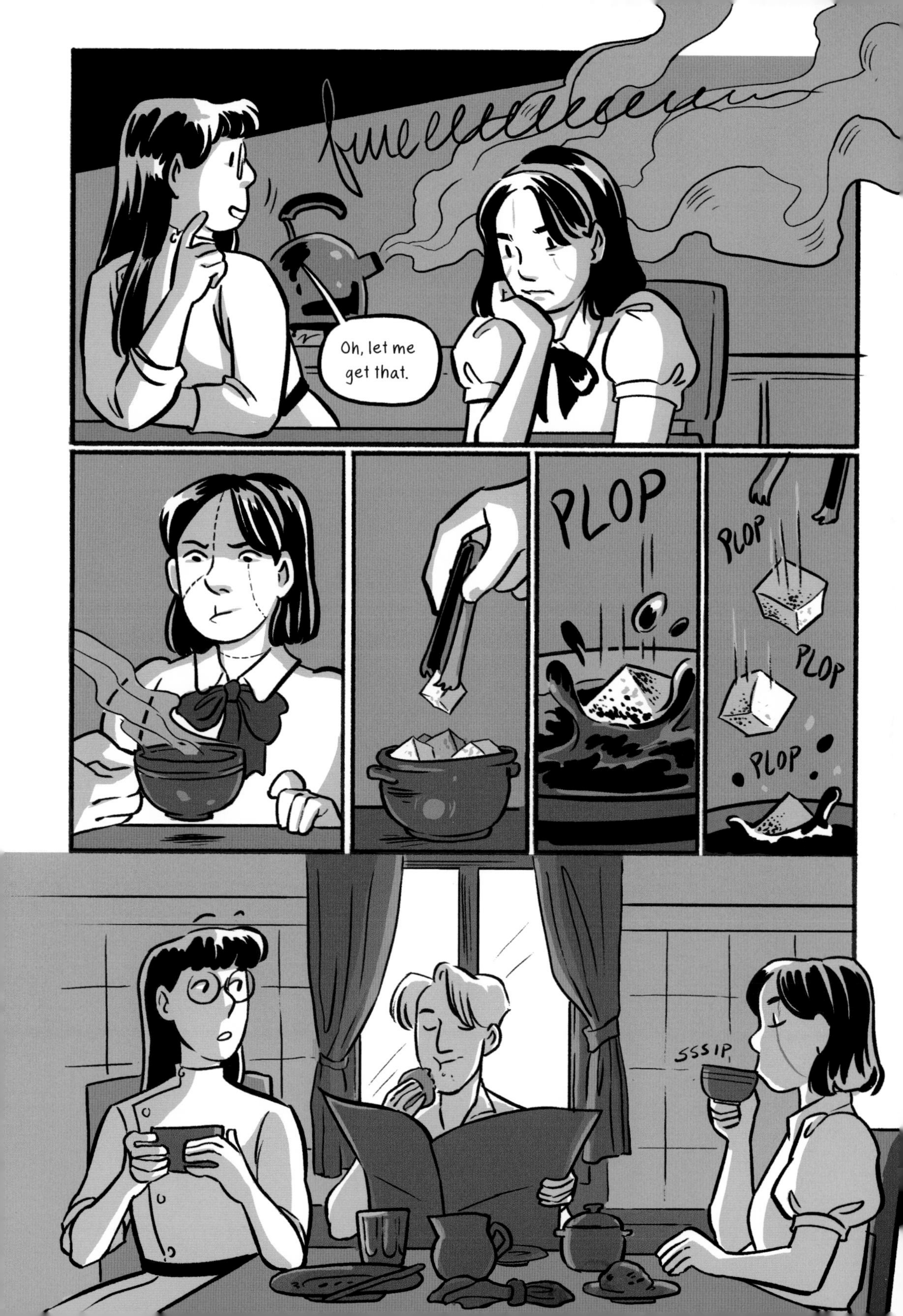

Oh, let me get that.
PLOP
PLOP
PLOP
PLOP
SSSIP

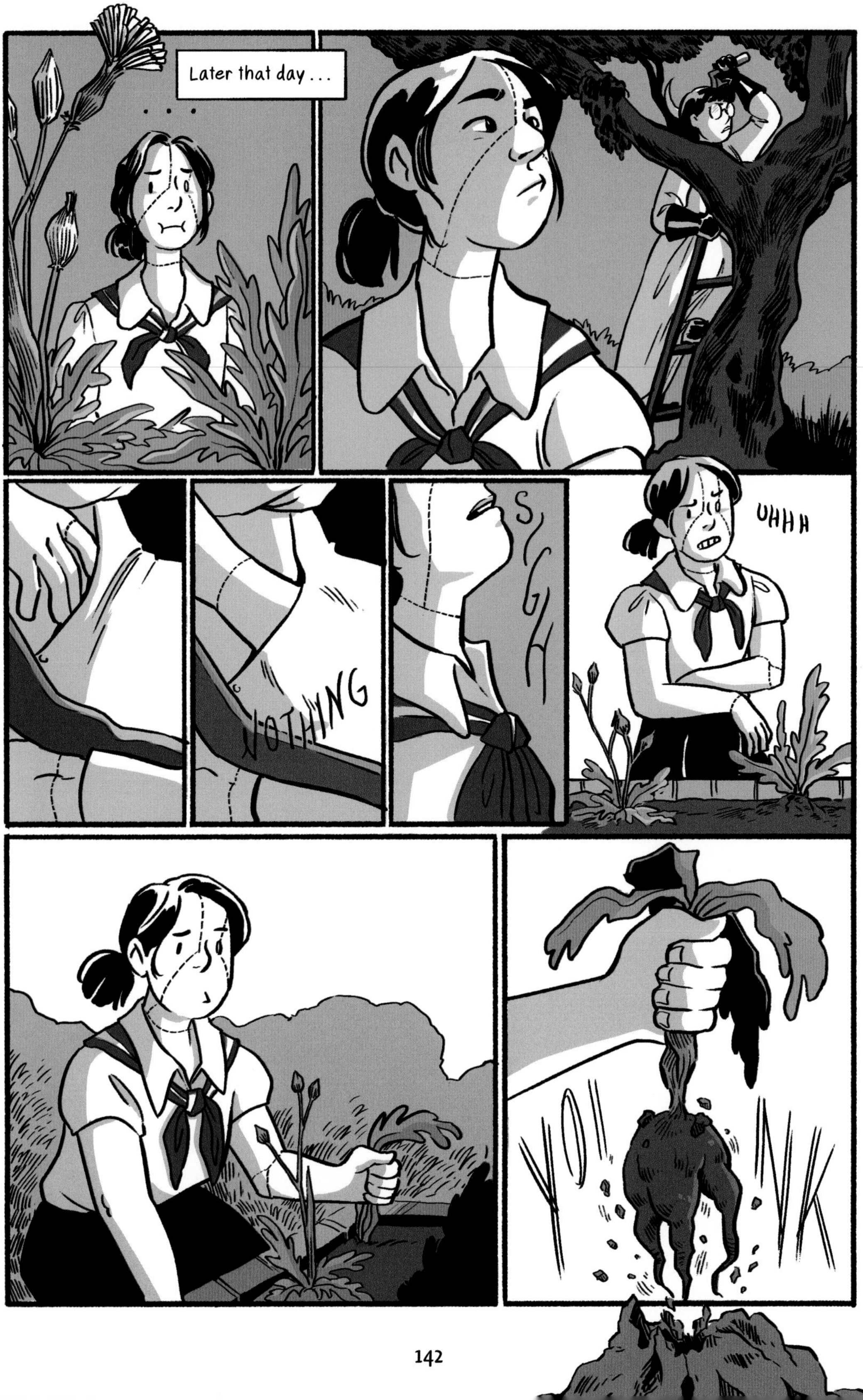
Later that day . . .
. . .
NOTHING
SIGH
UHHH
YOINK

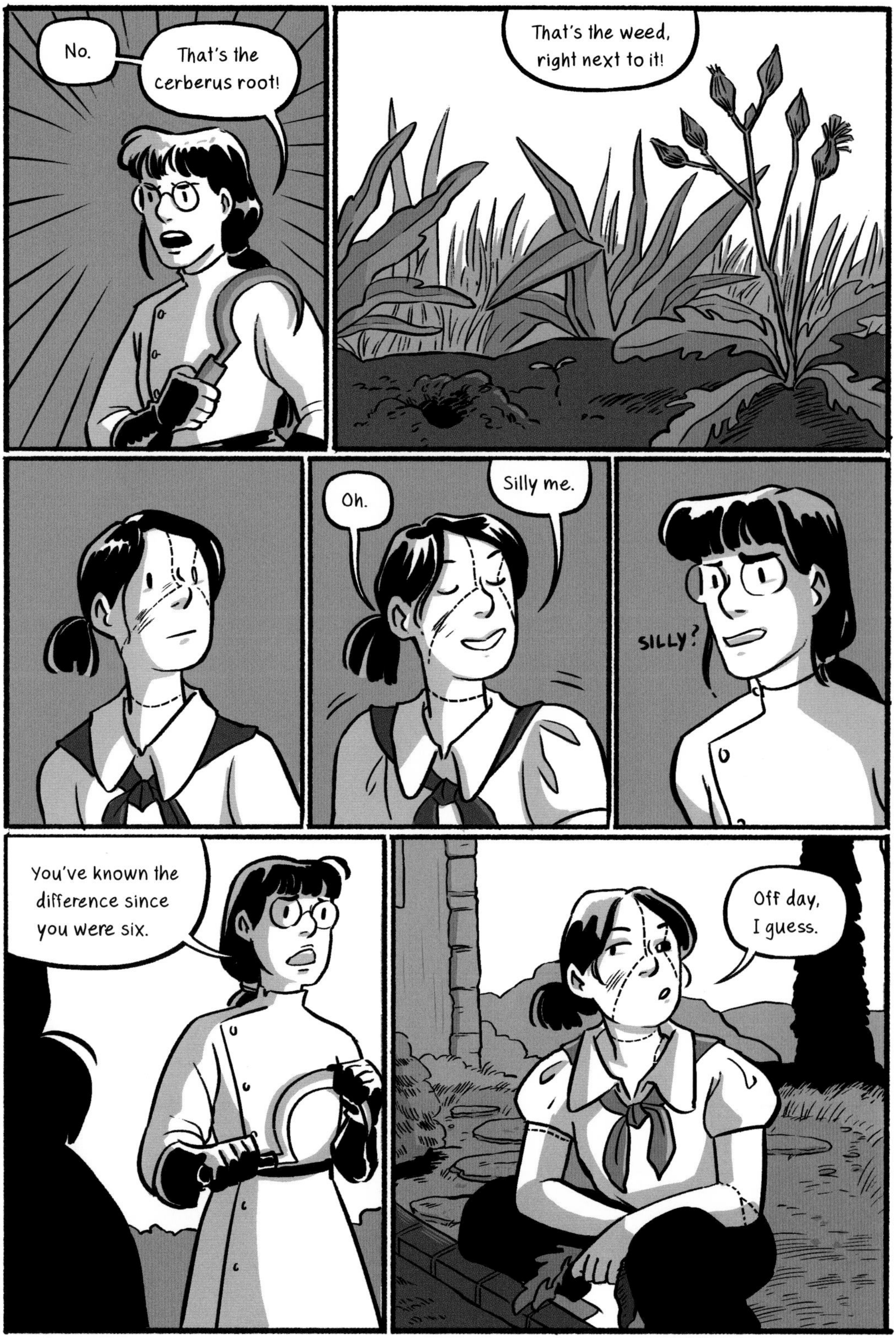
No.
That's the cerberus root!
That's the weed, right next to it!
Oh.
Silly me.
SILLY?
You've known the difference since you were six.
Off day, I guess.

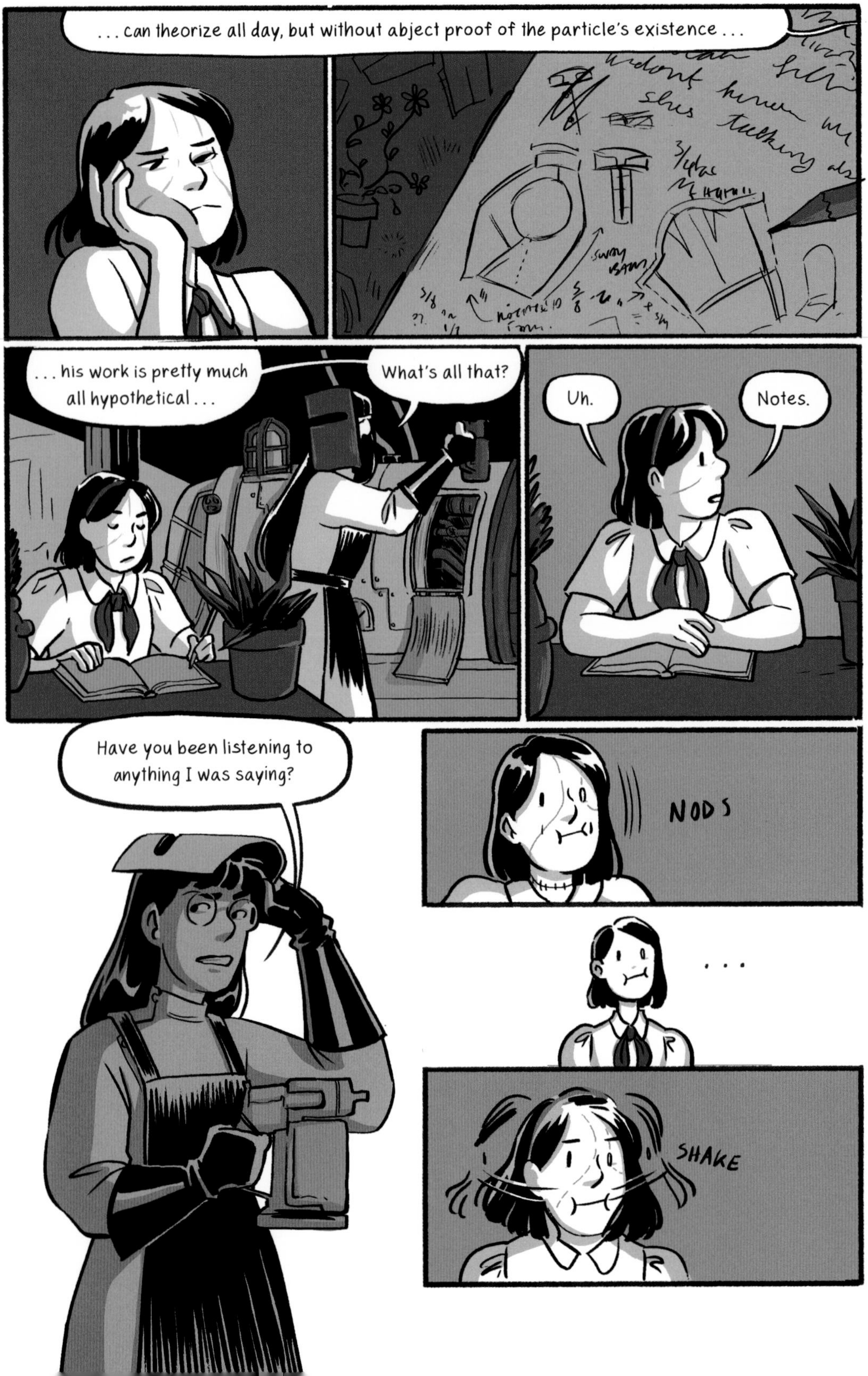
. . . can theorize all day, but without abject proof of the particle's existence . . .
. . . his work is pretty much all hypothetical . . .
What's all that?
Uh.
Notes.
Have you been listening to anything I was saying?
NODS
. . .
SHAKE

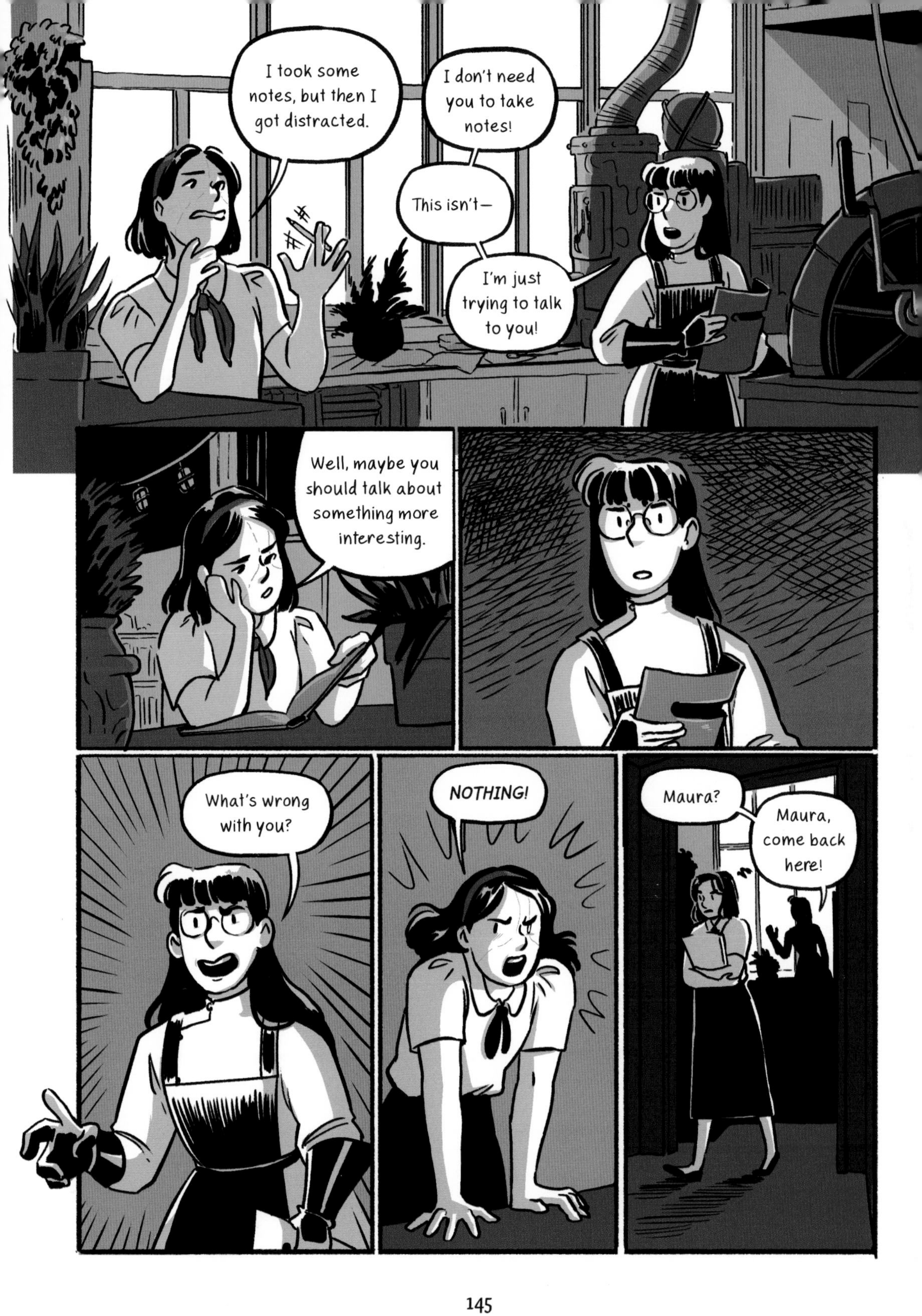
I took some notes, but then I got distracted.
I don't need you to take notes!
This isn't—
I'm just trying to talk to you!
Well, maybe you should talk about something more interesting.
What's wrong with you?
NOTHING!
Maura?
Maura, come back here!

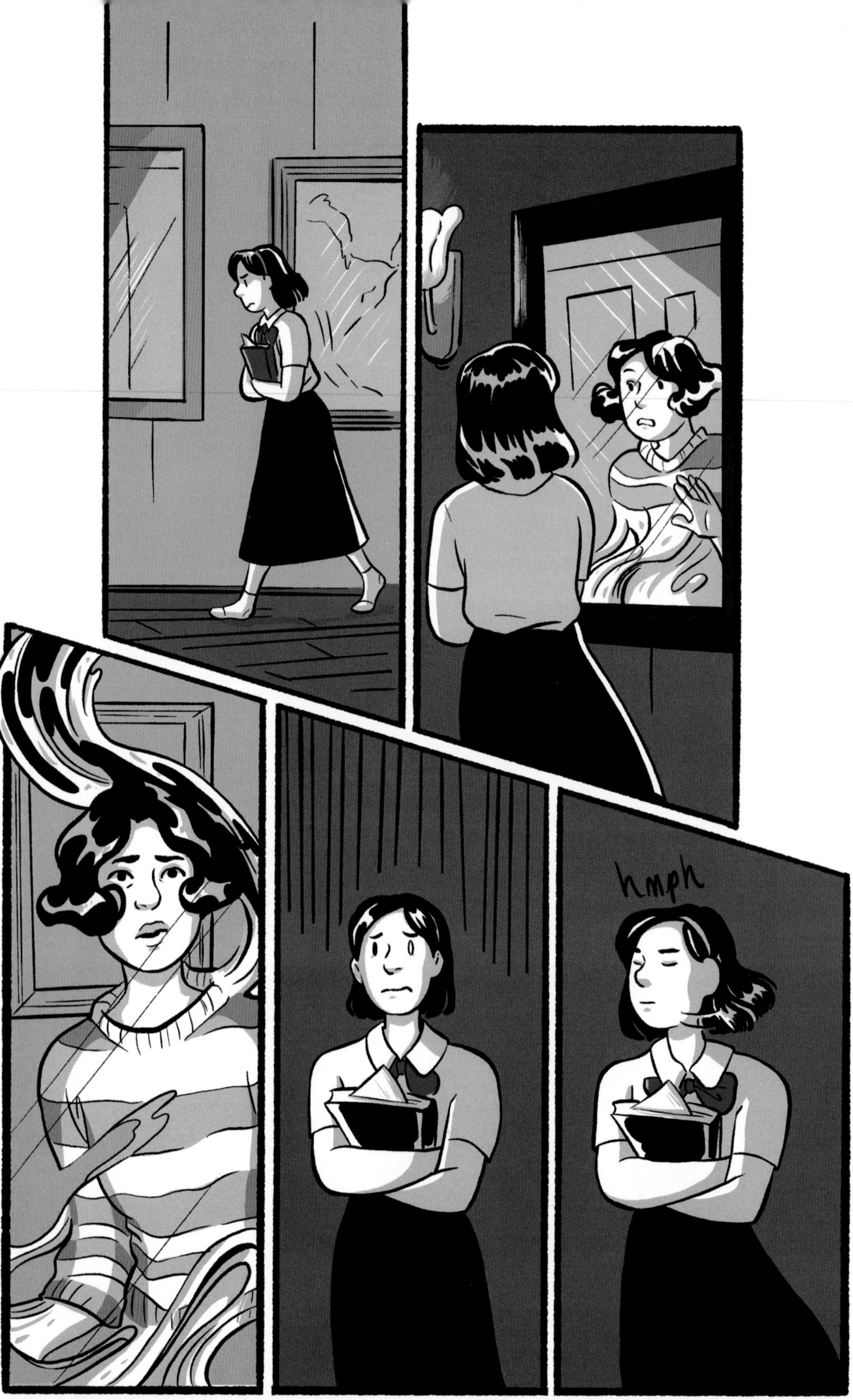
hmph

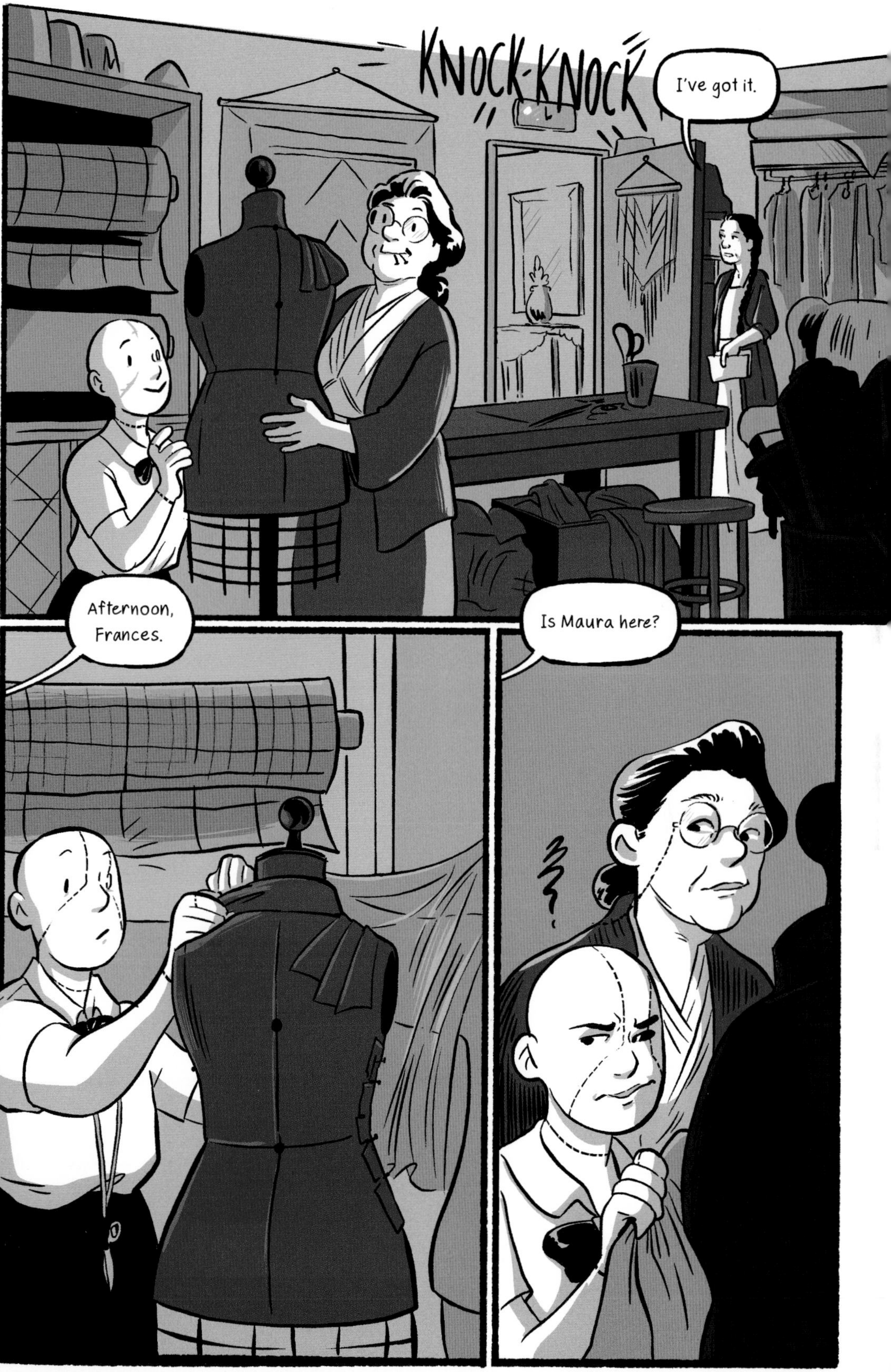
KNOCK-KNOCK
I've got it.
Afternoon, Frances.
Is Maura here?

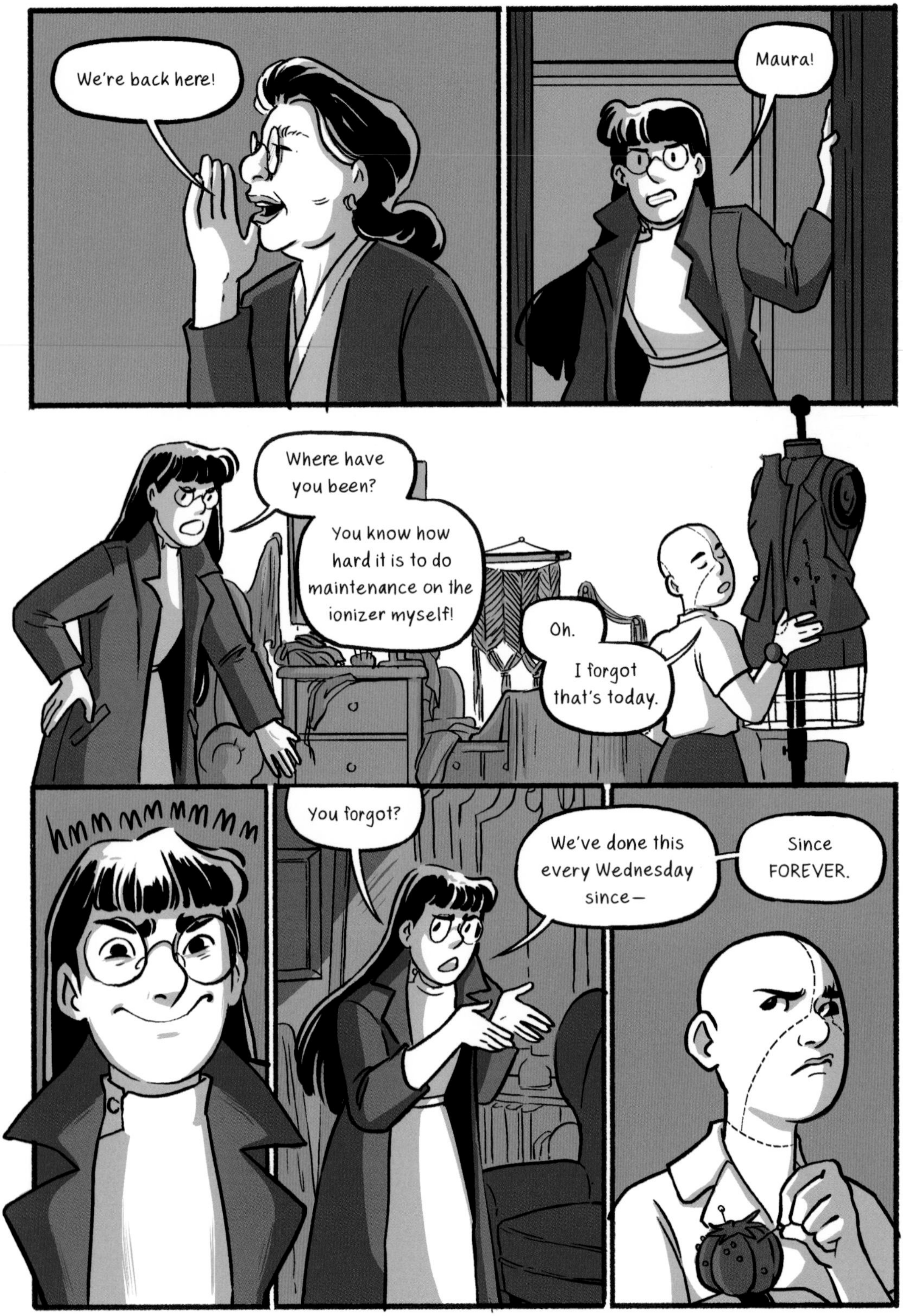
We're back here!
Maura!
Where have you been?
You know how hard it is to do maintenance on the ionizer myself!
Oh.
I forgot that's today.
hmmmmmmmmm
You forgot?
We've done this every Wednesday since—
Since FOREVER.

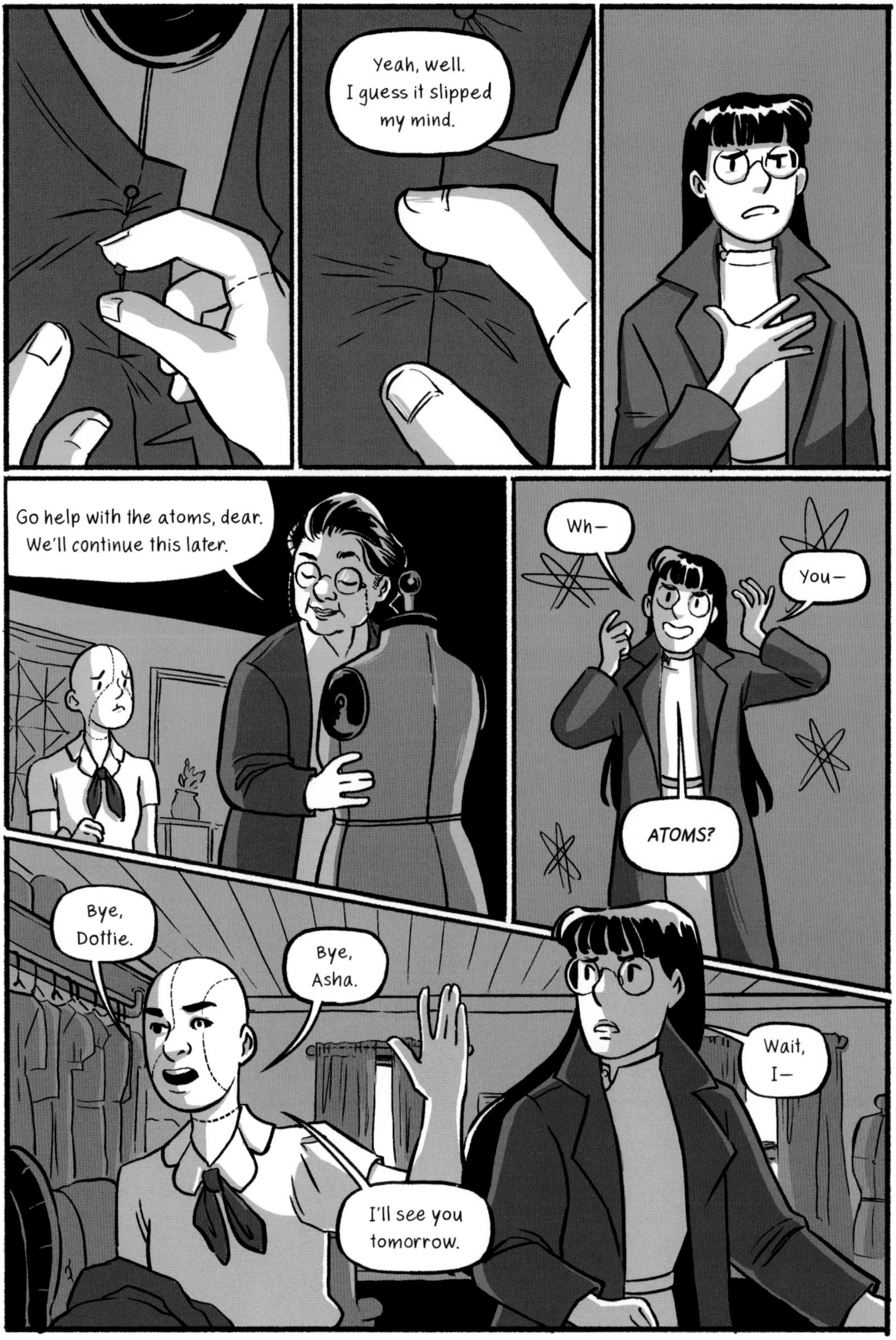
Yeah, well. I guess it slipped my mind.
Go help with the atoms, dear. We'll continue this later.
Wh—
You—
ATOMS?
Bye, Dottie.
Bye, Asha.
Wait, I—
I'll see you tomorrow.

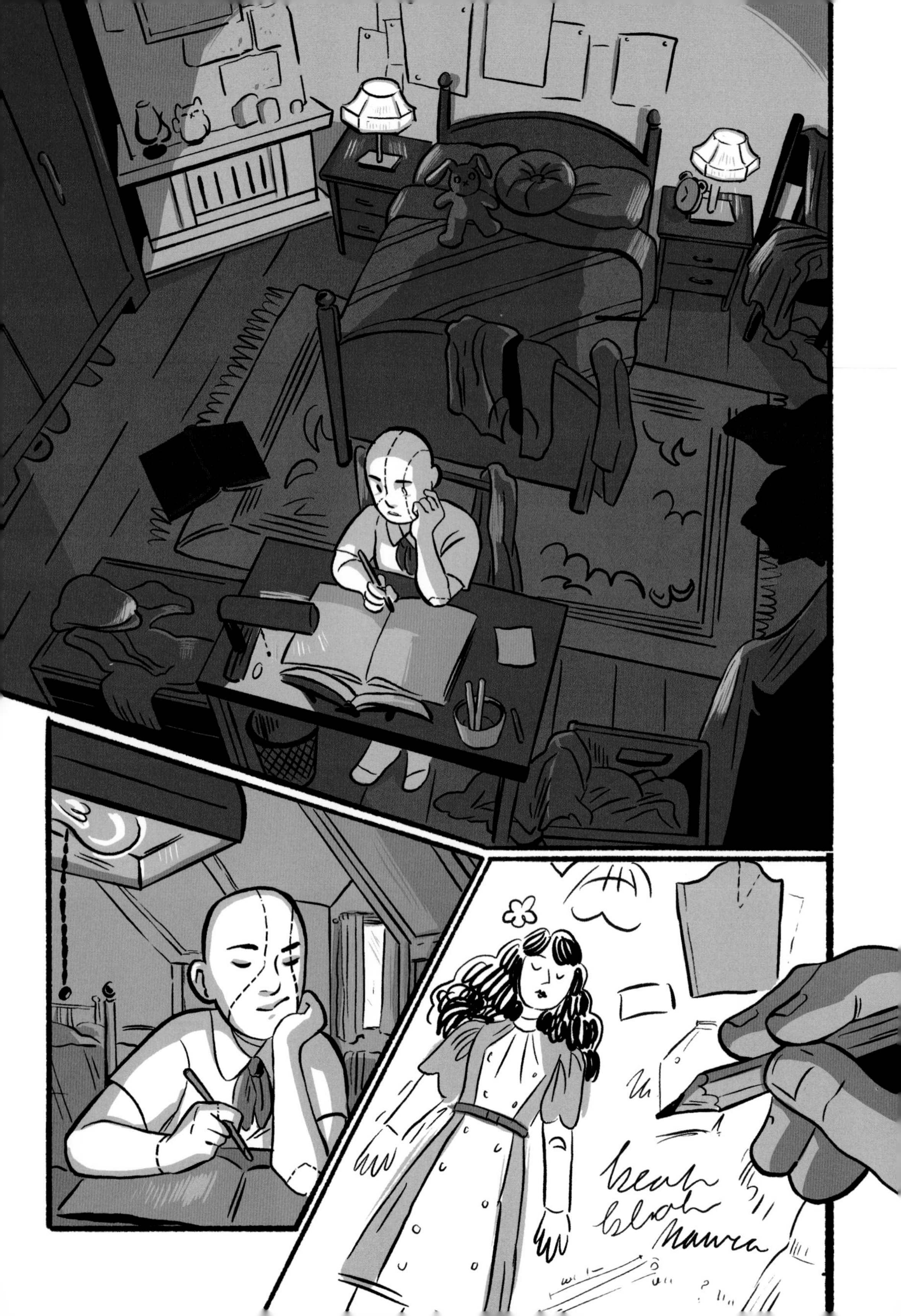

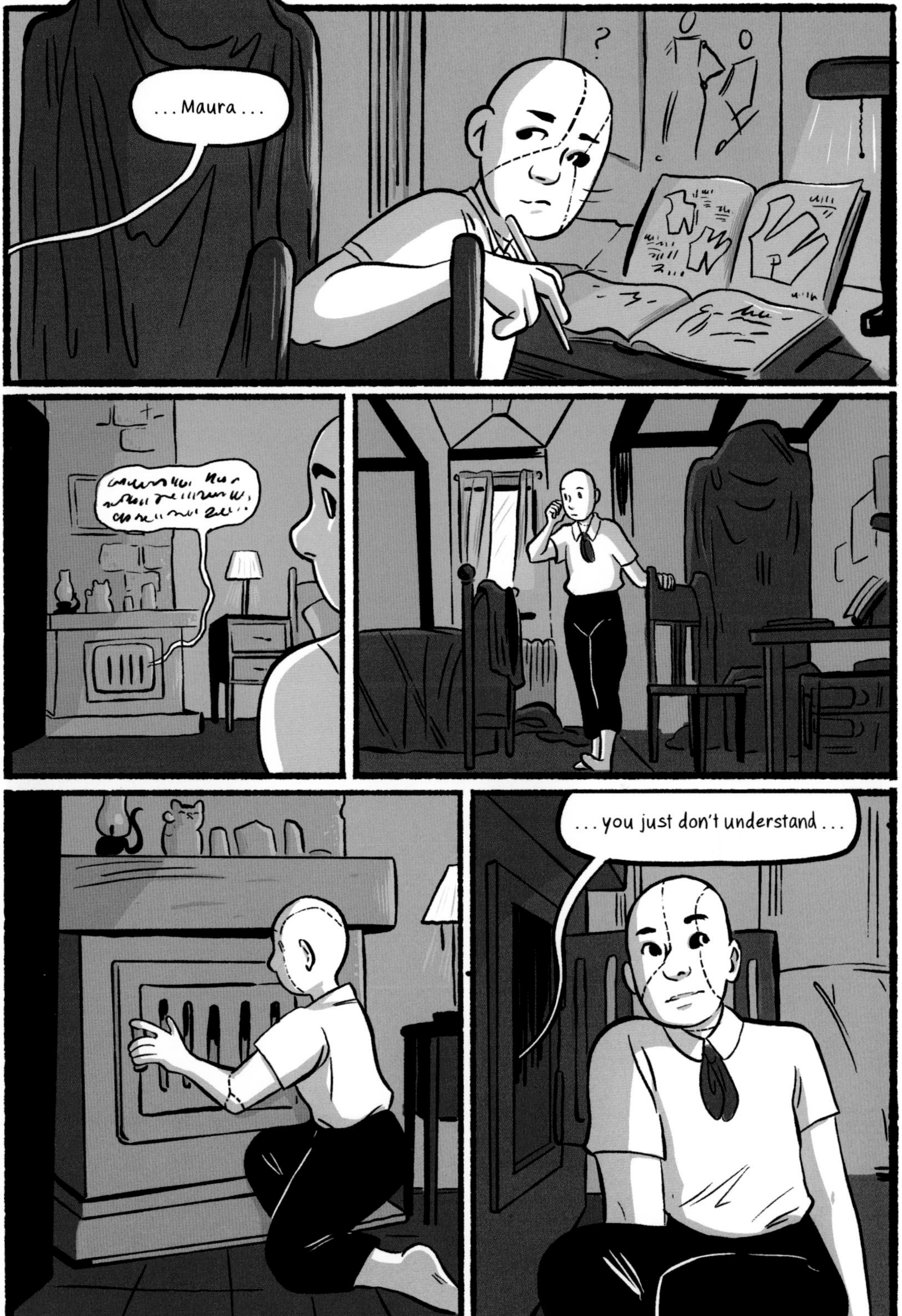
. . . Maura . . .
. . . you just don't understand . . .

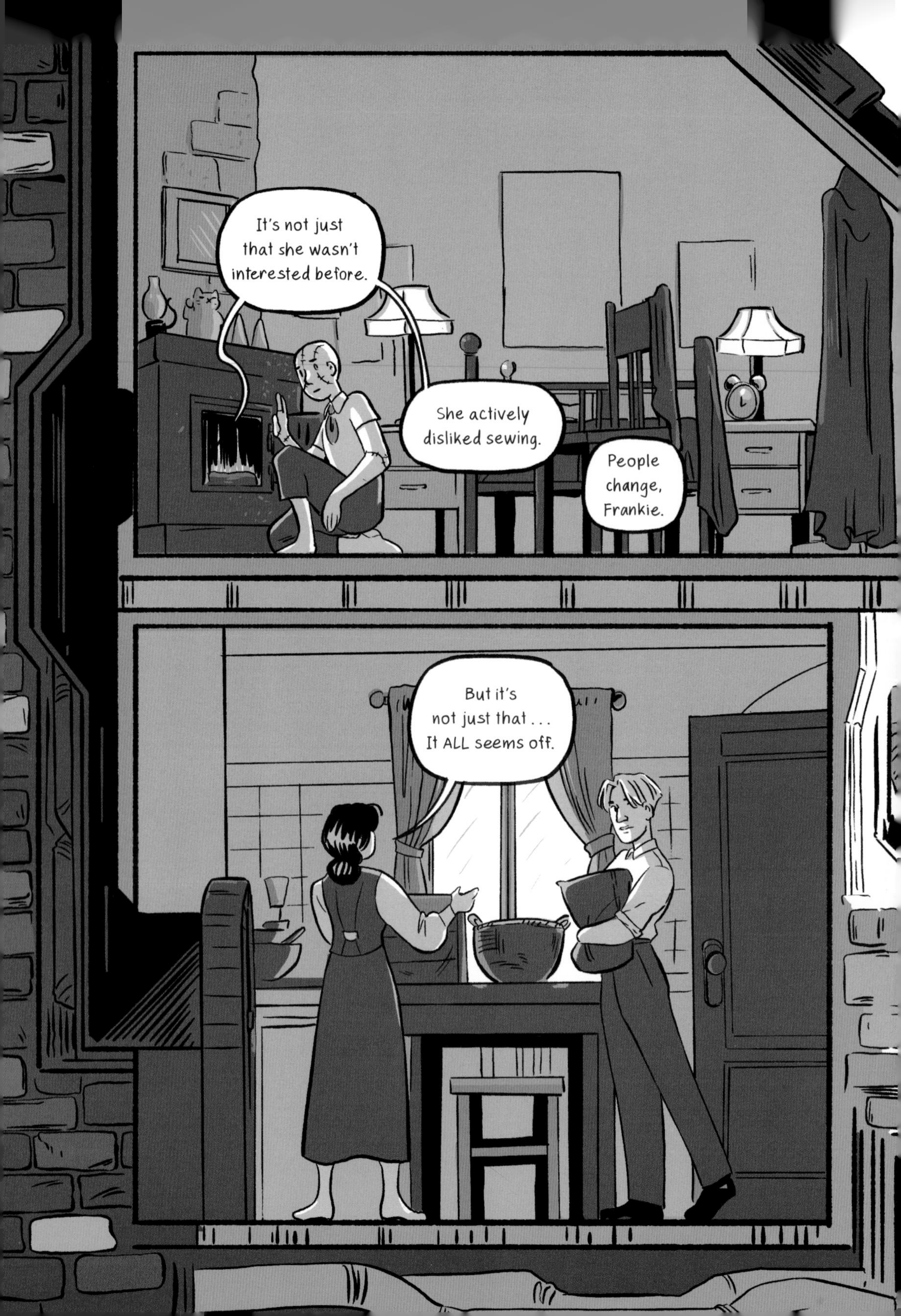

It's not just that she wasn't interested before.
She actively disliked sewing.
People change, Frankie.
But it's not just that . . . It ALL seems off.

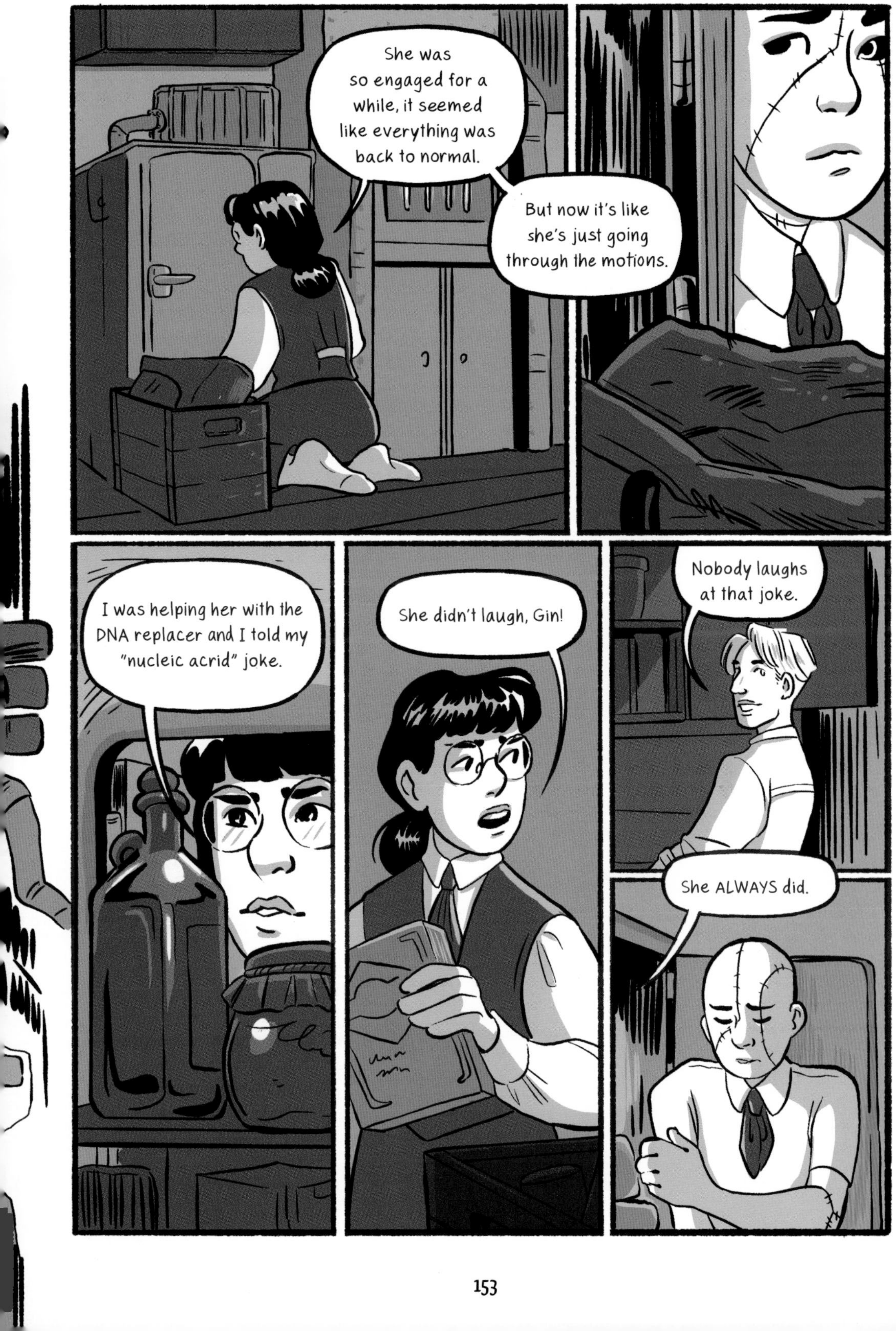
She was so engaged for a while, it seemed like everything was back to normal.
But now it's like she's just going through the motions.
I was helping her with the DNA replacer and I told my "nucleic acrid" joke.
She didn't laugh, Gin!
Nobody laughs at that joke.
She ALWAYS did.

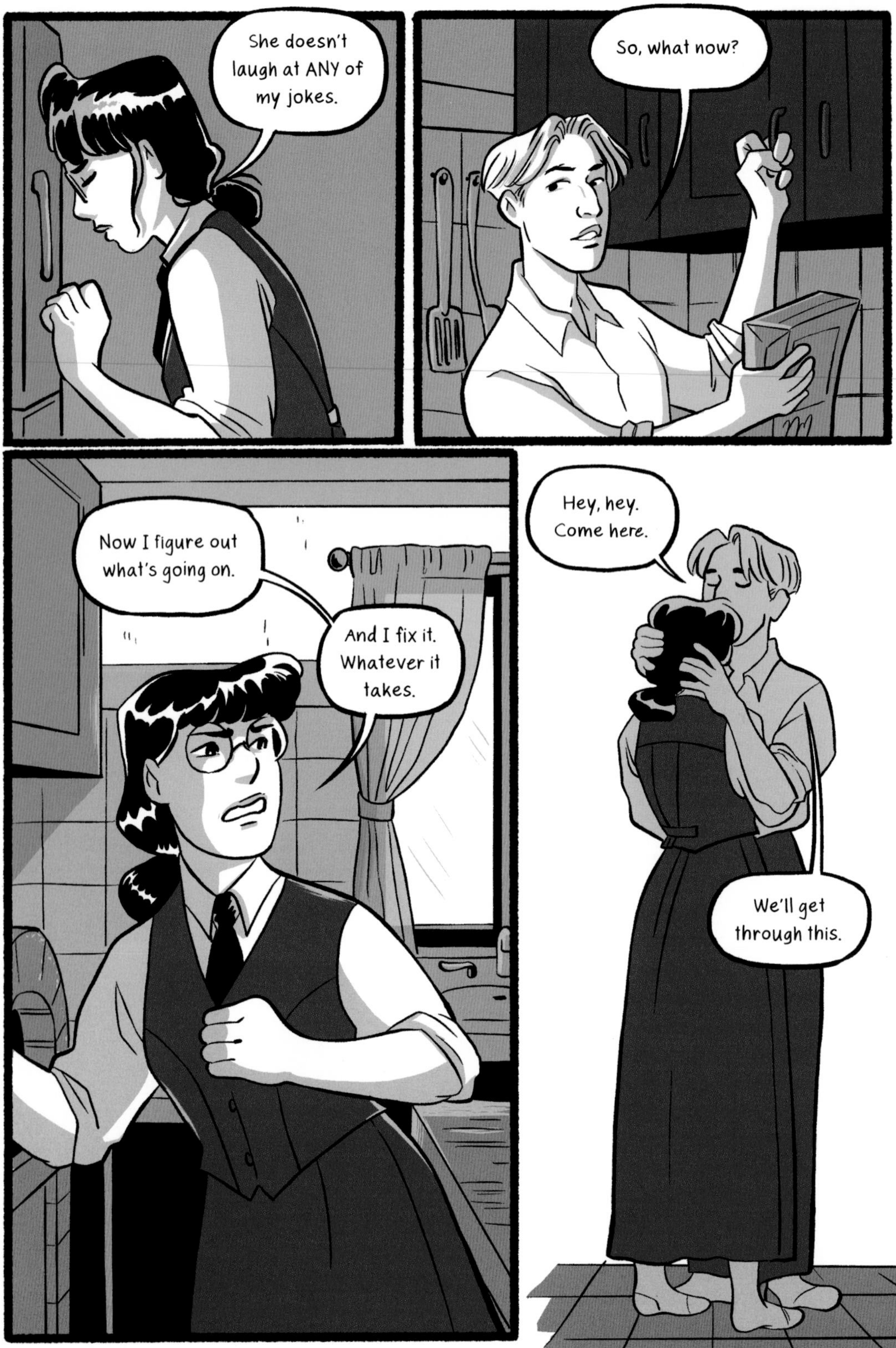
She doesn't laugh at ANY of my jokes.
So, what now?
Now I figure out what's going on.
And I fix it. Whatever it takes.
Hey, hey. Come here.
We'll get through this.

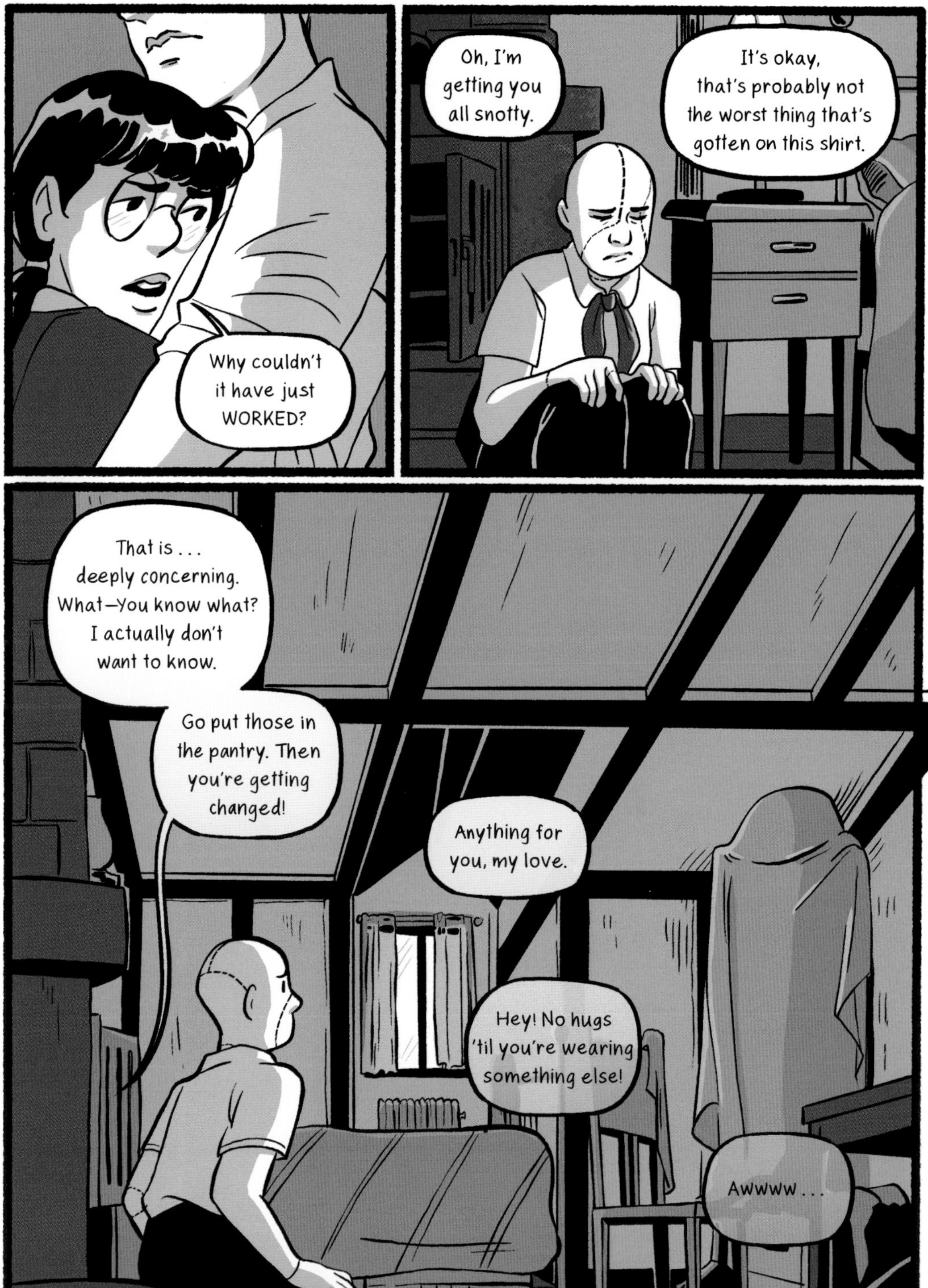

Why couldn't it have just WORKED?
Oh, I'm getting you all snotty.
It's okay, that's probably not the worst thing that's gotten on this shirt.
That is . . . deeply concerning. What—You know what? I actually don't want to know.
Go put those in the pantry. Then you're getting changed!
Anything for you, my love.
Hey! No hugs 'til you're wearing something else!
Awwww . . .

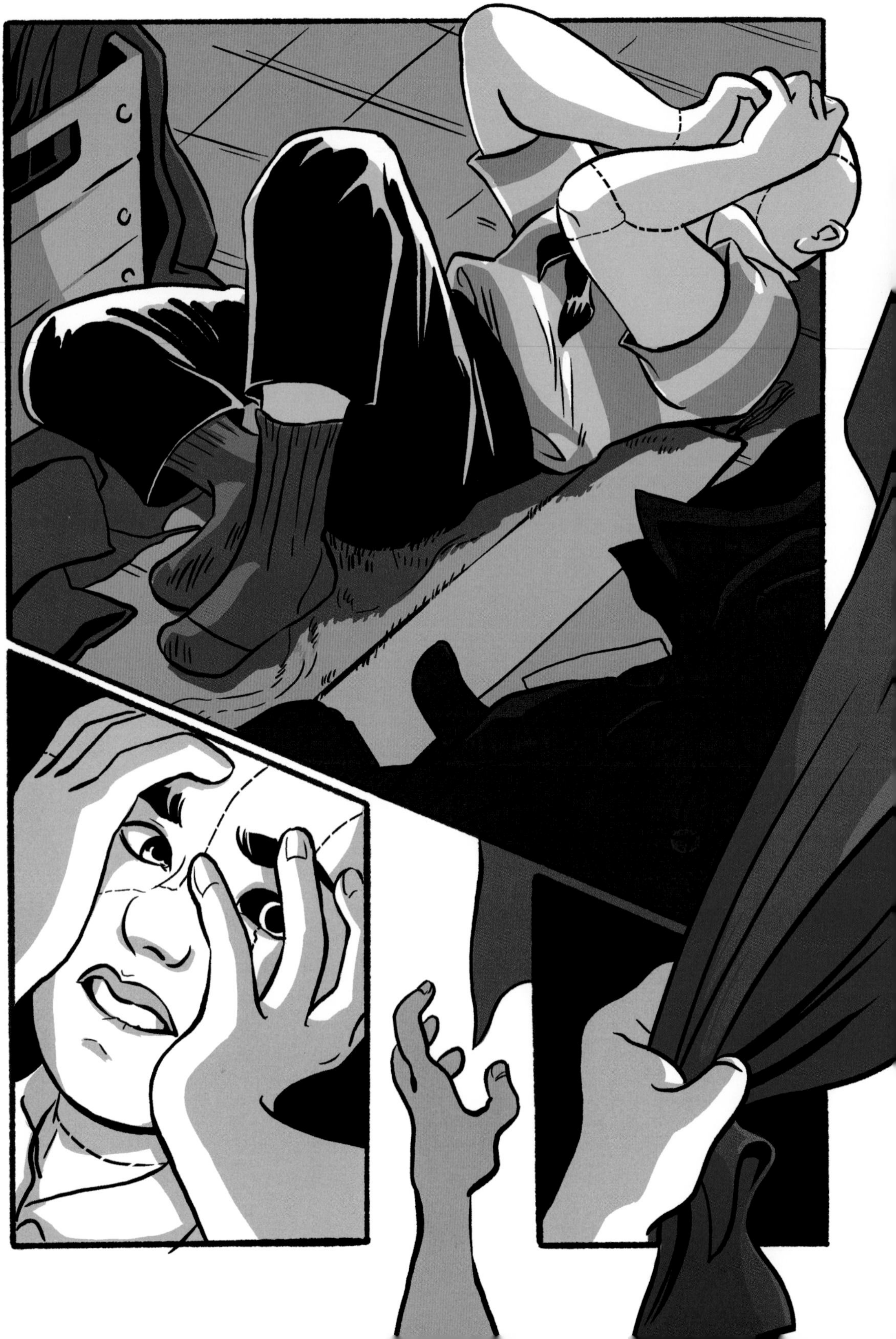

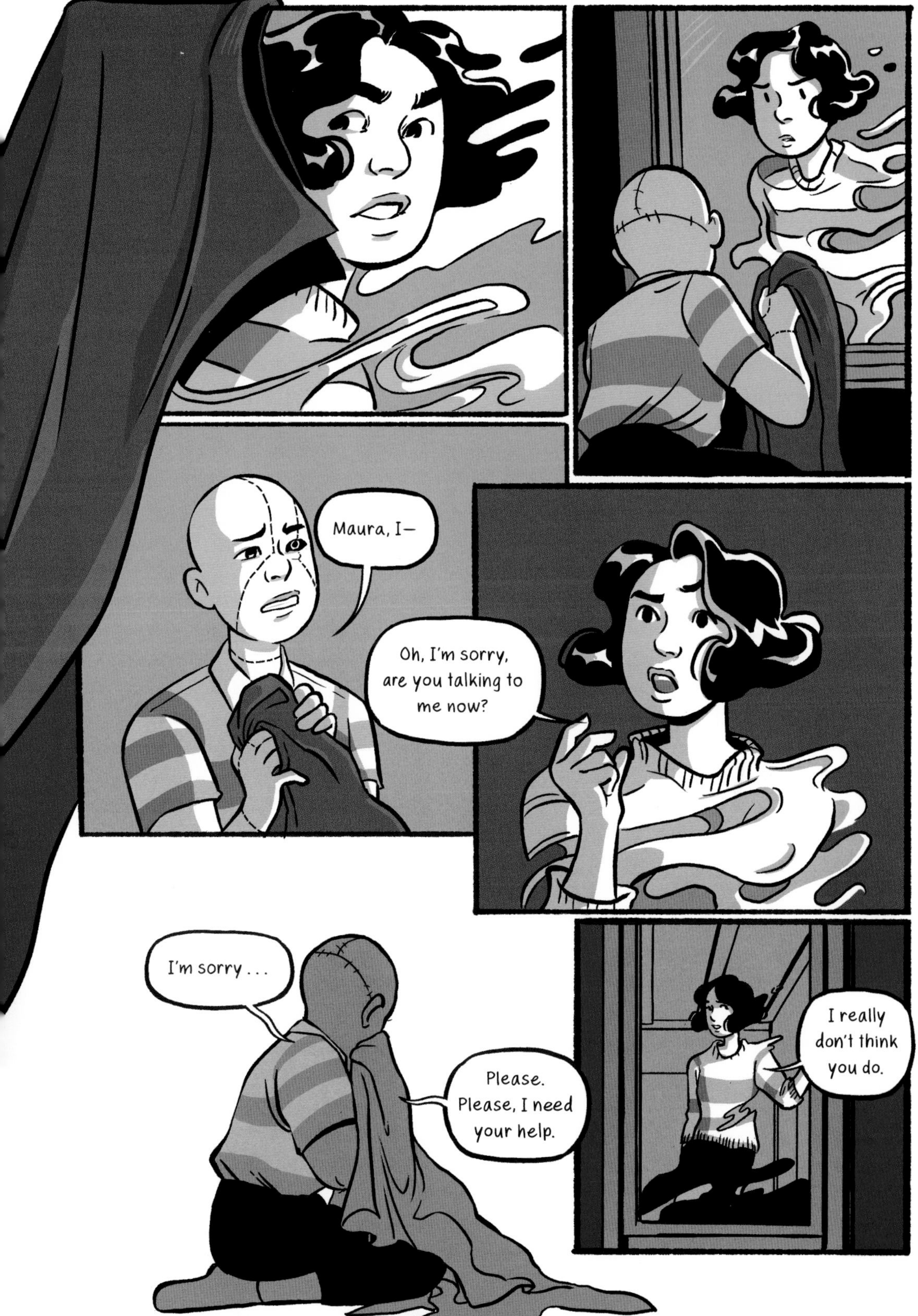
Maura, I—
Oh, I'm sorry, are you talking to me now?
I'm sorry . . .
Please. Please, I need your help.
I really don't think you do.

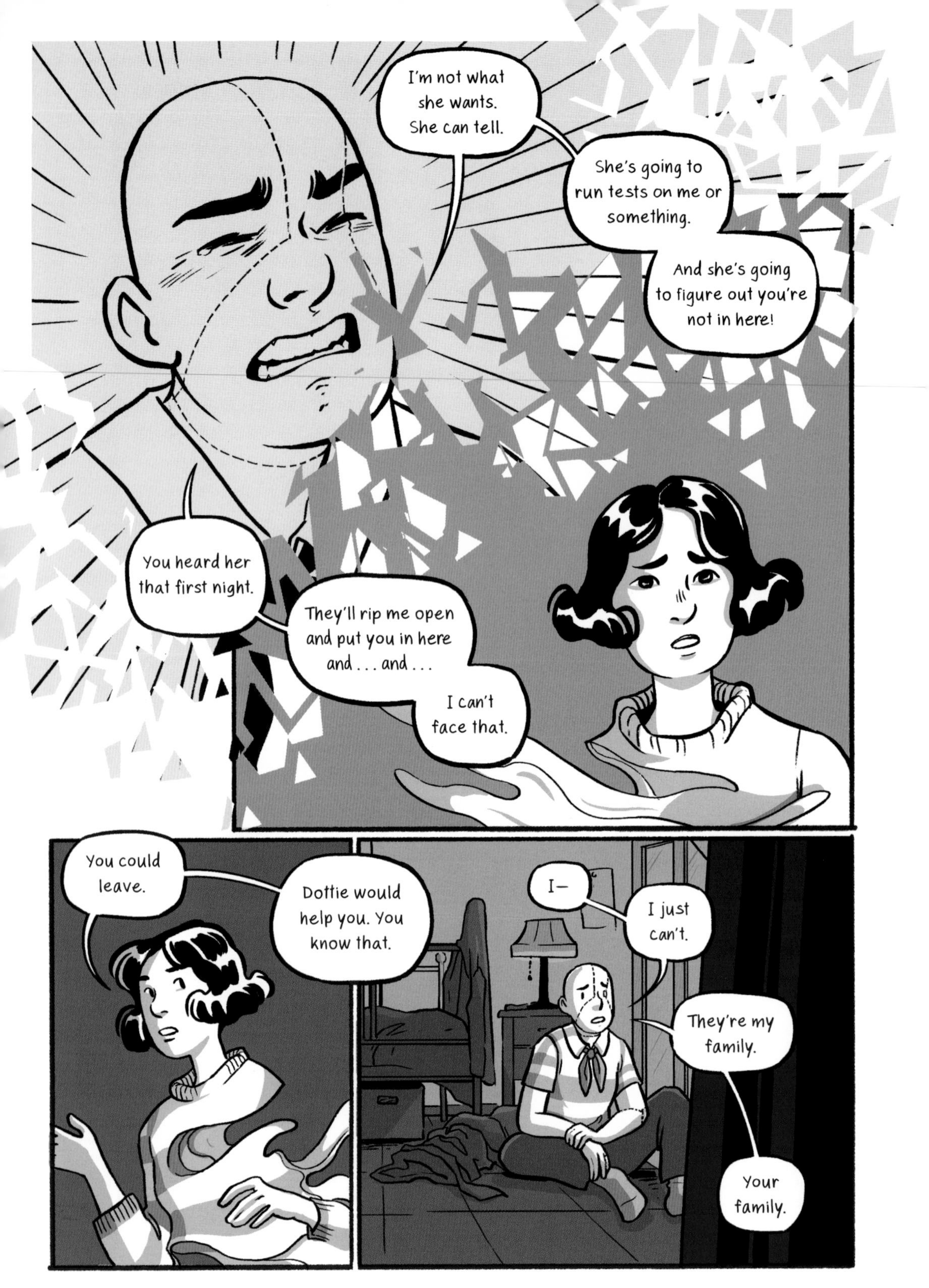
I'm not what she wants. She can tell.
She's going to run tests on me or something.
And she's going to figure out you're not in here!
You heard her that first night.
They'll rip me open and put you in here and . . . and . . .
I can't face that.
You could leave.
Dottie would help you. You know that.
I—
I just can't.
They're my family.
Your family.

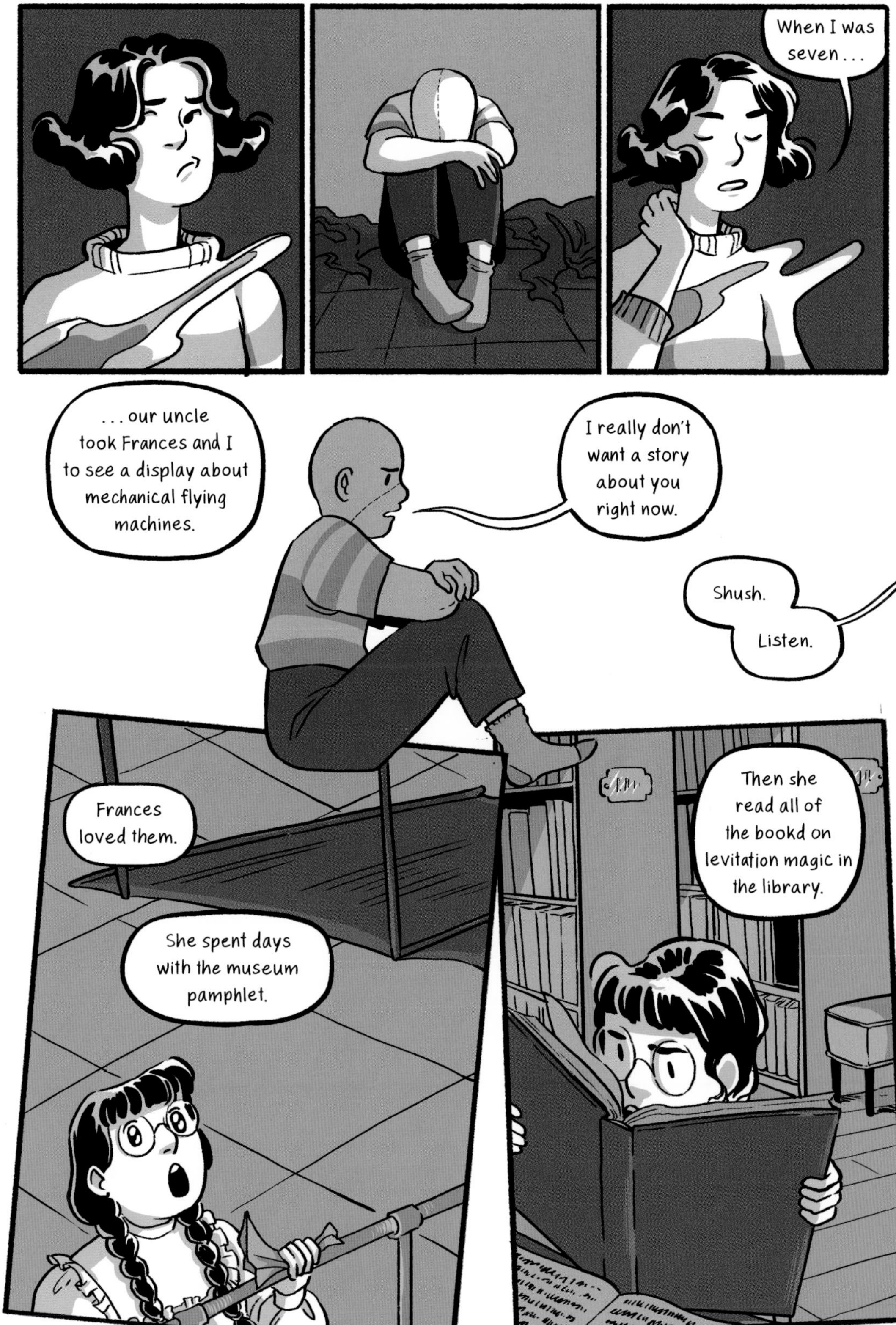
When I was seven . . .
. . . our uncle took Frances and I to see a display about mechanical flying machines.
I really don't want a story about you right now.
Shush. Listen.
Frances loved them.
She spent days with the museum pamphlet.
Then she read all of the bookd on levitation magic in the library.

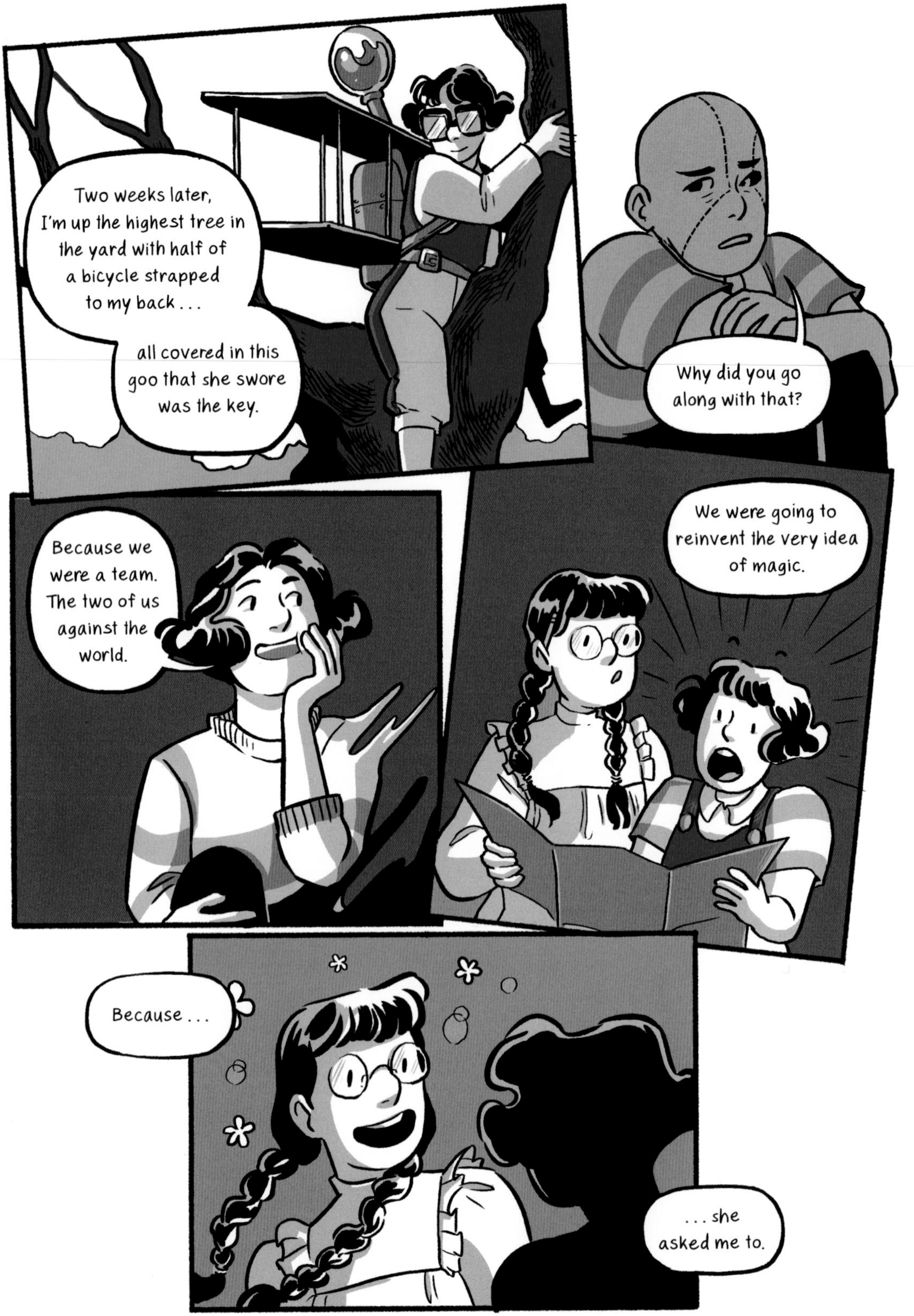
Two weeks later, I'm up the highest tree in the yard with half of a bicycle strapped to my back . . .
all covered in this goo that she swore was the key.
Why did you go along with that?
Because we were a team. The two of us against the world.
We were going to reinvent the very idea of magic.
Because . . .
. . . she asked me to.

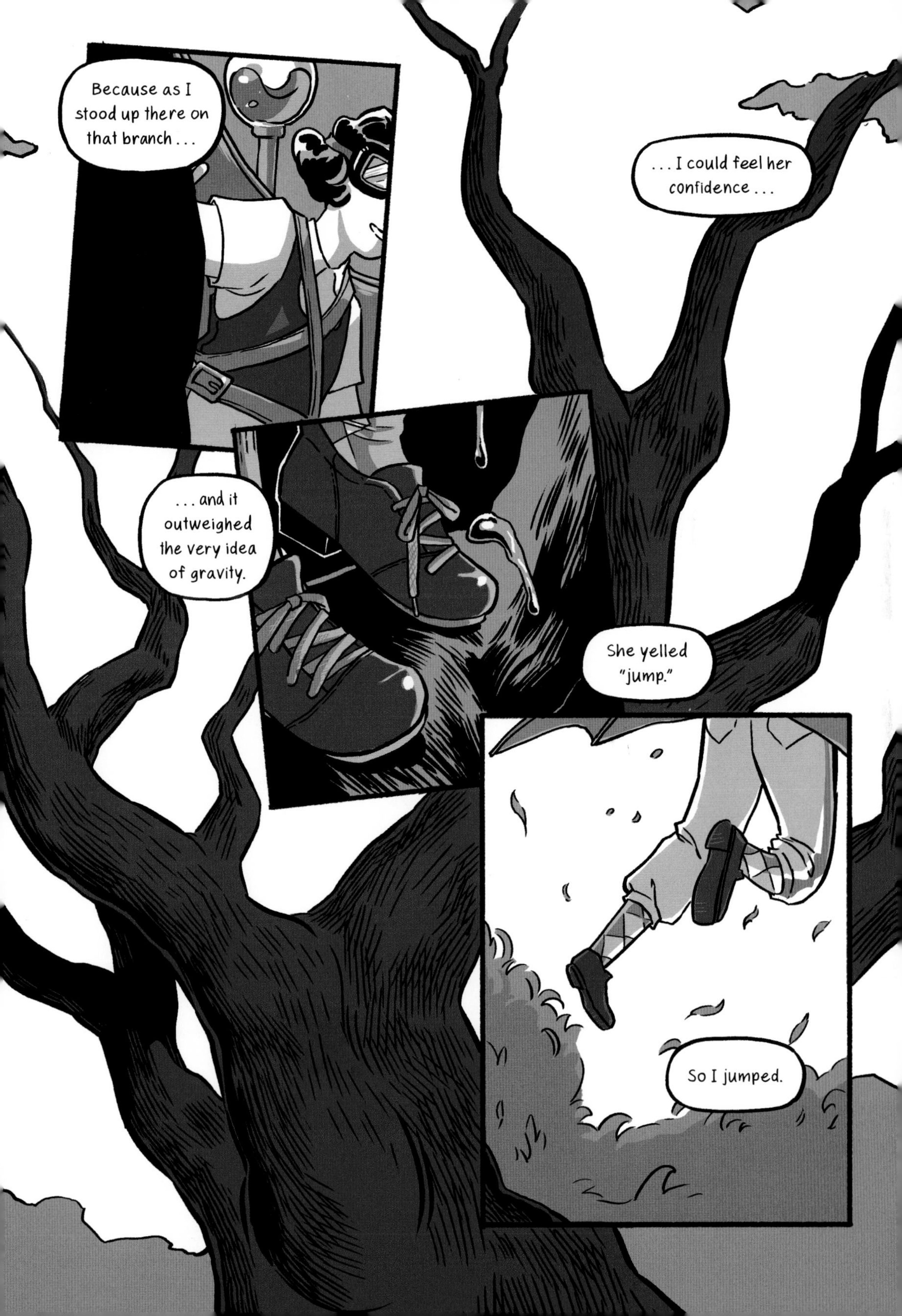
Because as I stood up there on that branch . . .
. . . I could feel her confidence . . .
. . . and it outweighed the very idea of gravity.
She yelled "jump."
So I jumped.

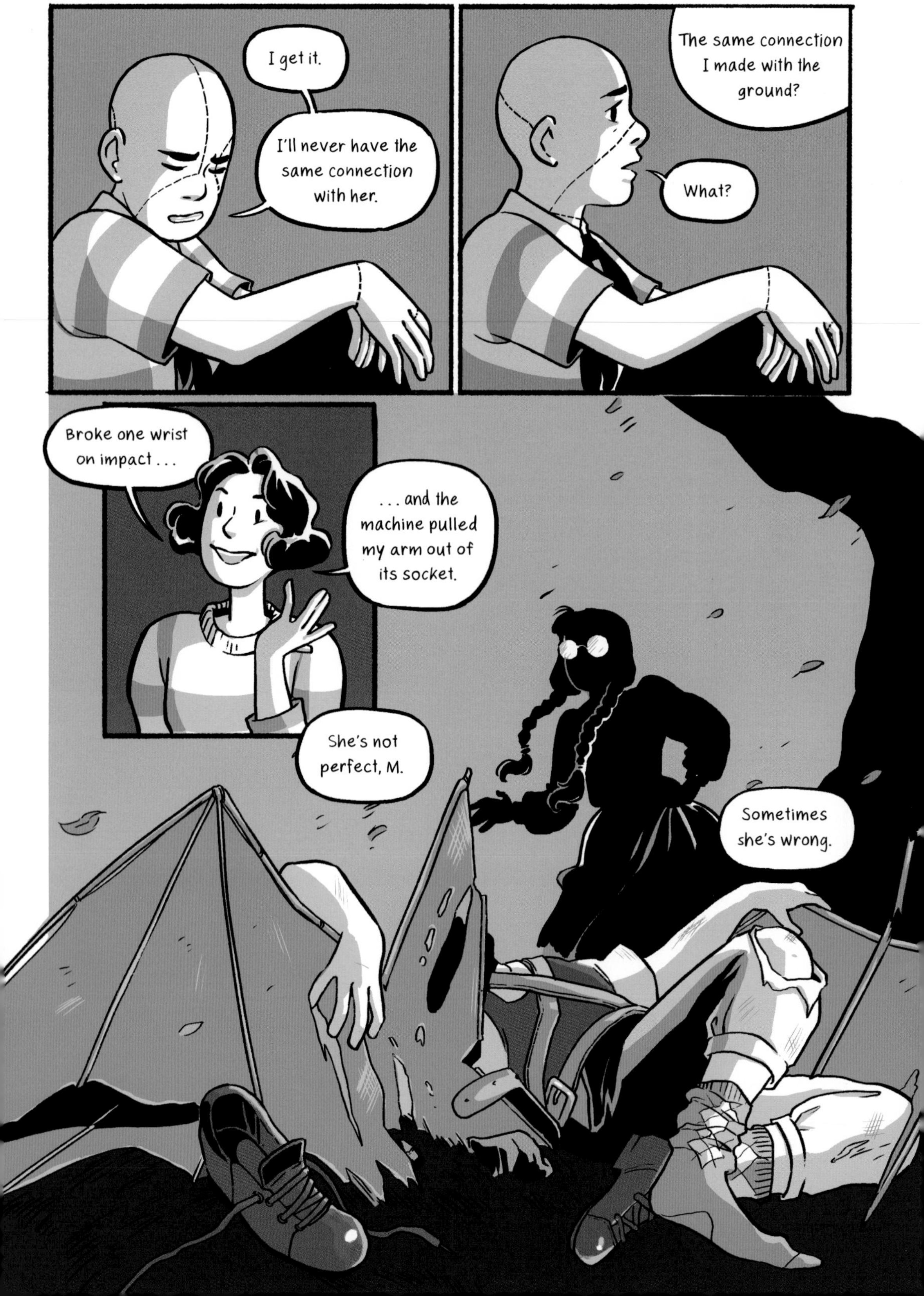
I get it.
I'll never have the same connection with her.
The same connection I made with the ground?
What?
Broke one wrist on impact . . .
. . . and the machine pulled my arm out of its socket.
She's not perfect, M.
Sometimes she's wrong.

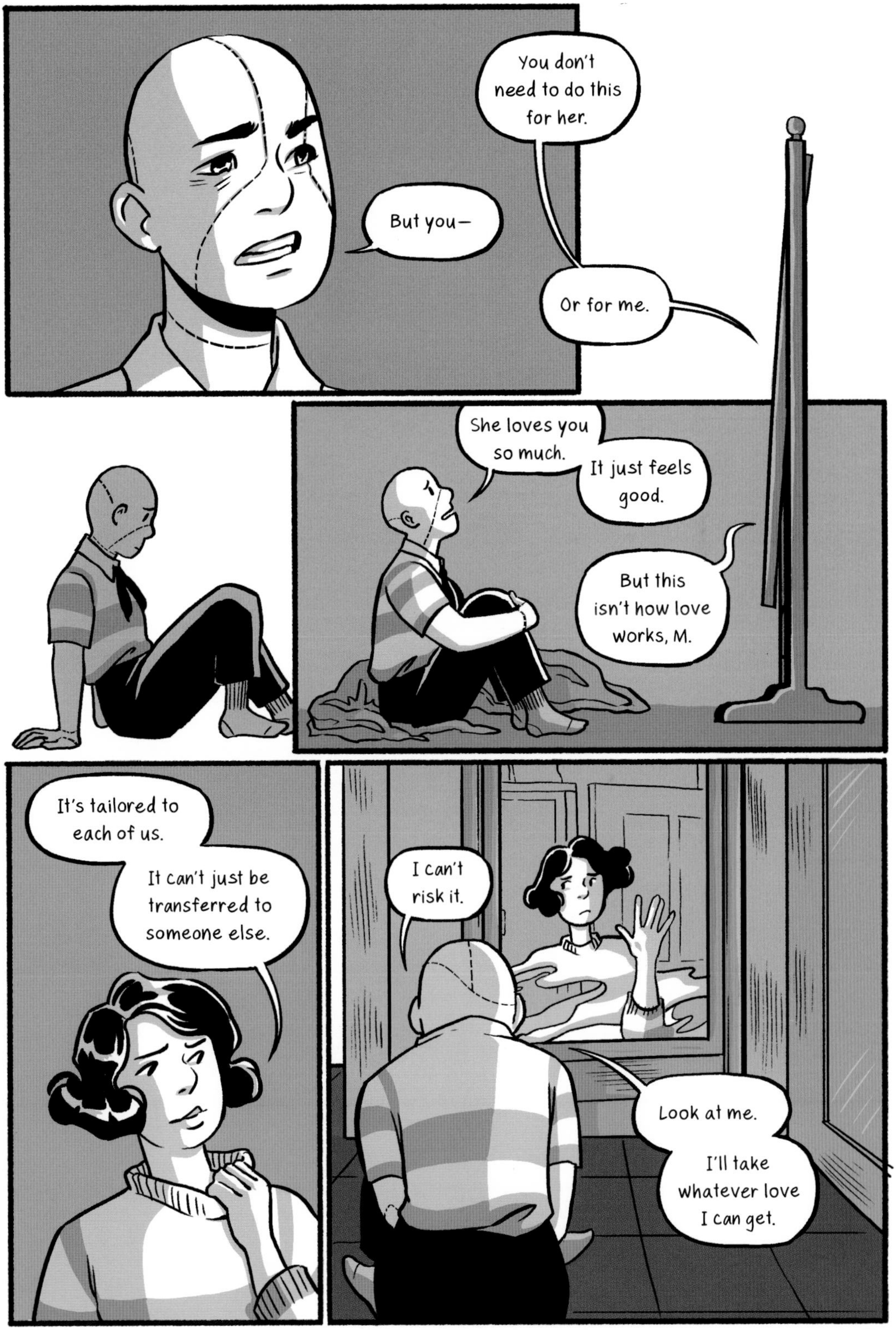
You don't need to do this for her.
But you—
Or for me.
She loves you so much.
It just feels good.
But this isn't how love works, M.
It's tailored to each of us.
It can't just be transferred to someone else.
I can't risk it.
Look at me.
I'll take whatever love I can get.

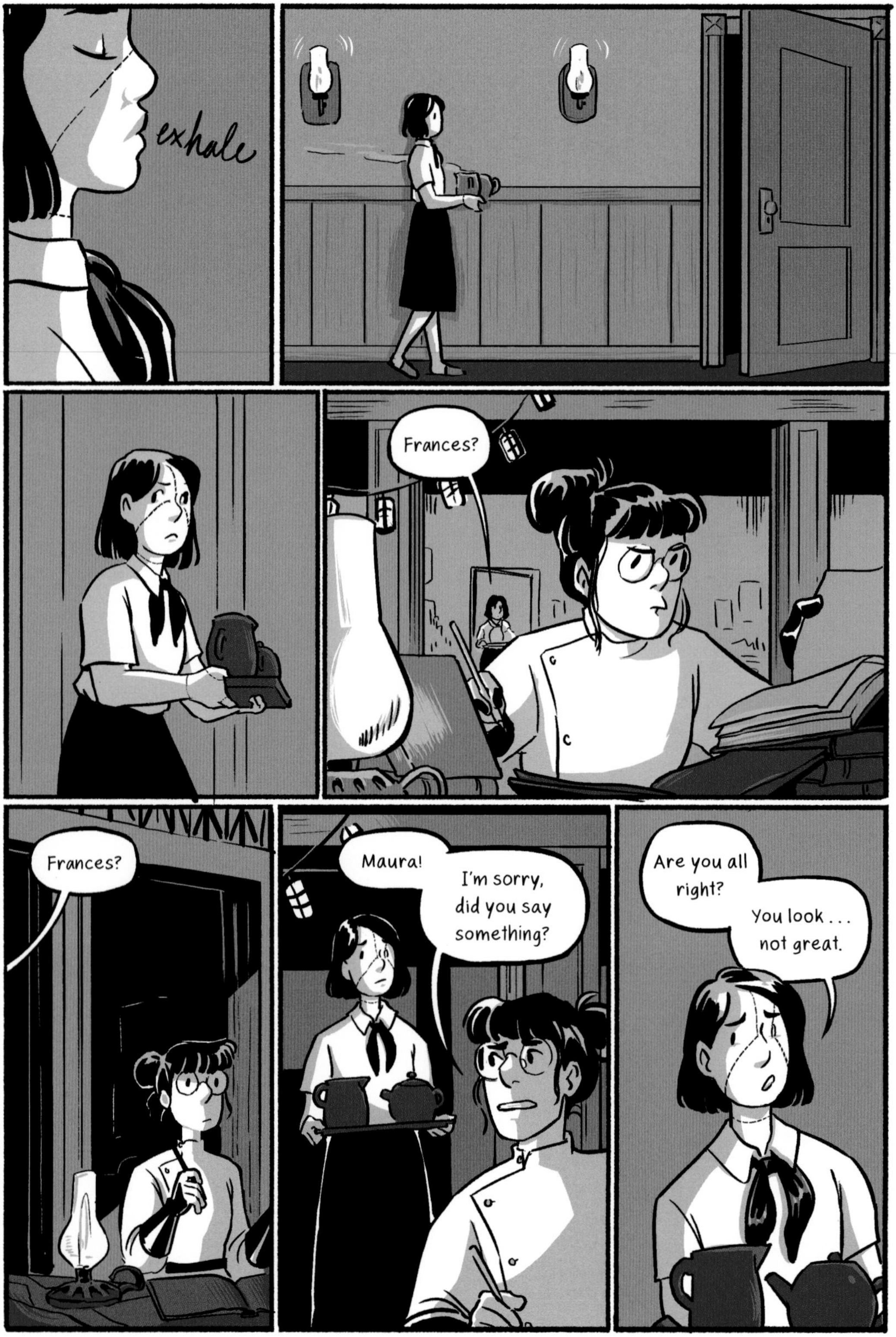
exhale
Frances?
Frances?
Maura!
I'm sorry, did you say something?
Are you all right?
You look . . . not great.

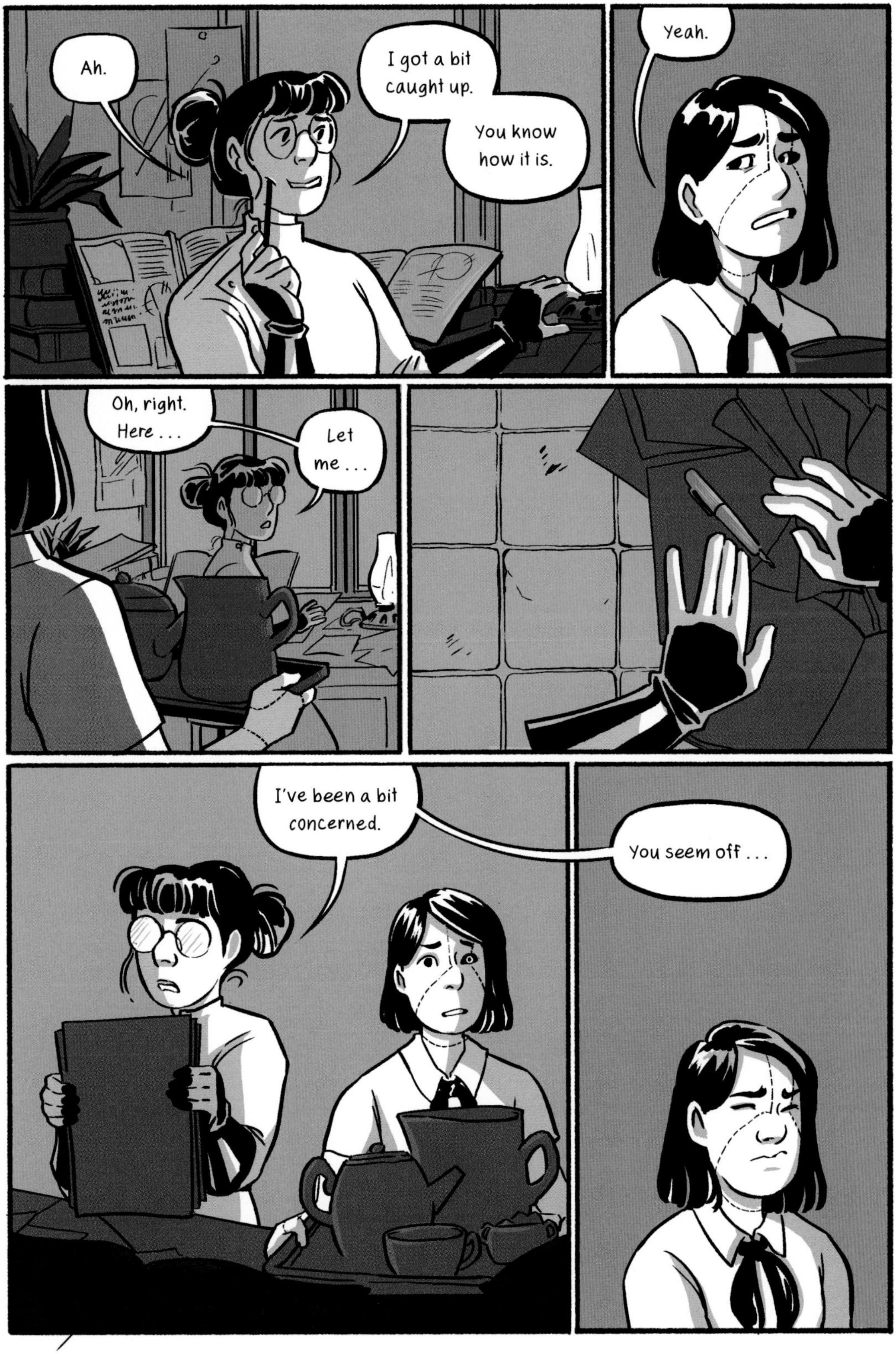
Ah.
I got a bit caught up.
You know how it is.
Yeah.
Oh, right. Here . . .
Let me . . .
I've been a bit concerned.
You seem off . . .

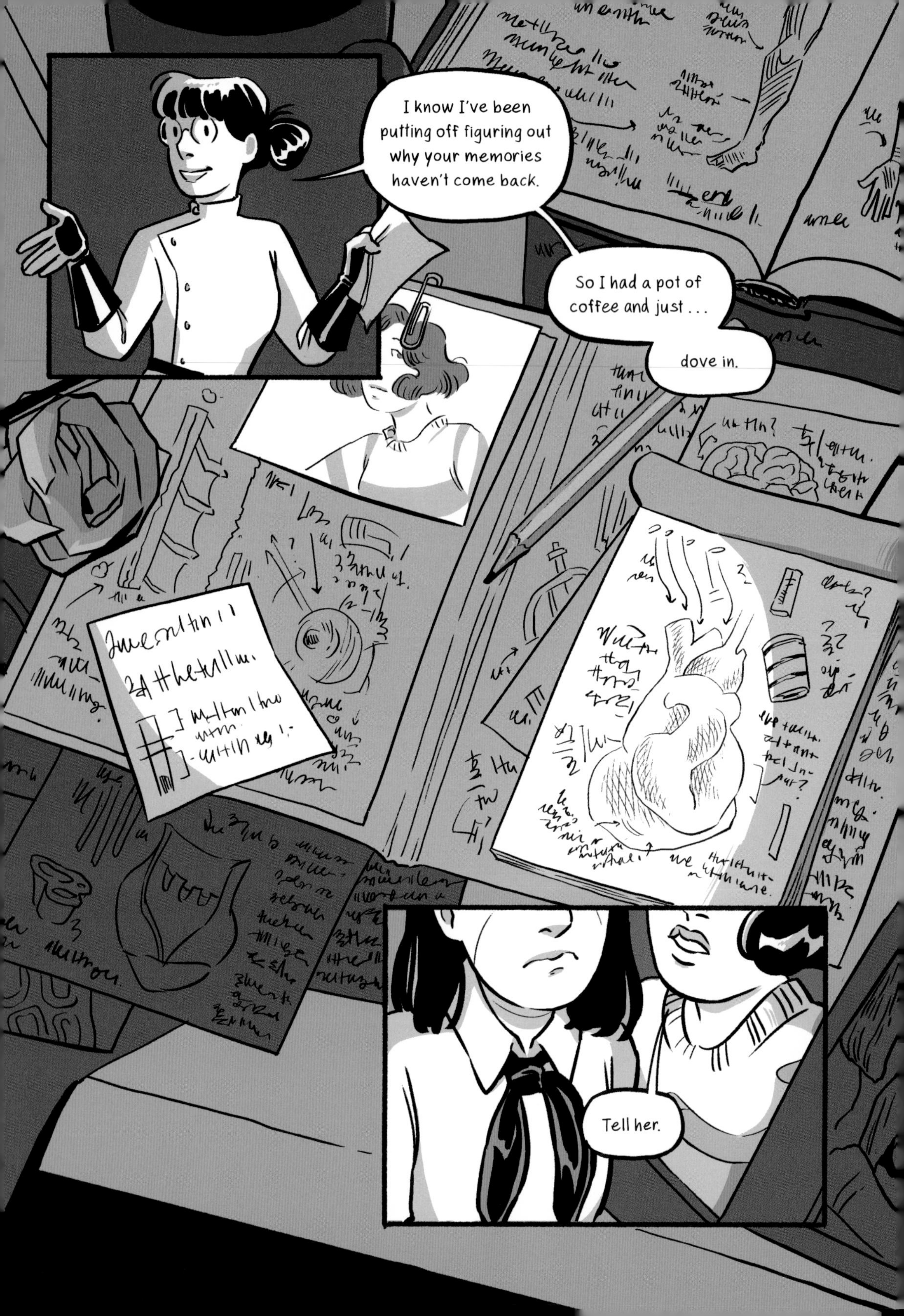
I know I've been putting off figuring out why your memories haven't come back.
So I had a pot of coffee and just . . .
dove in.
Tell her.

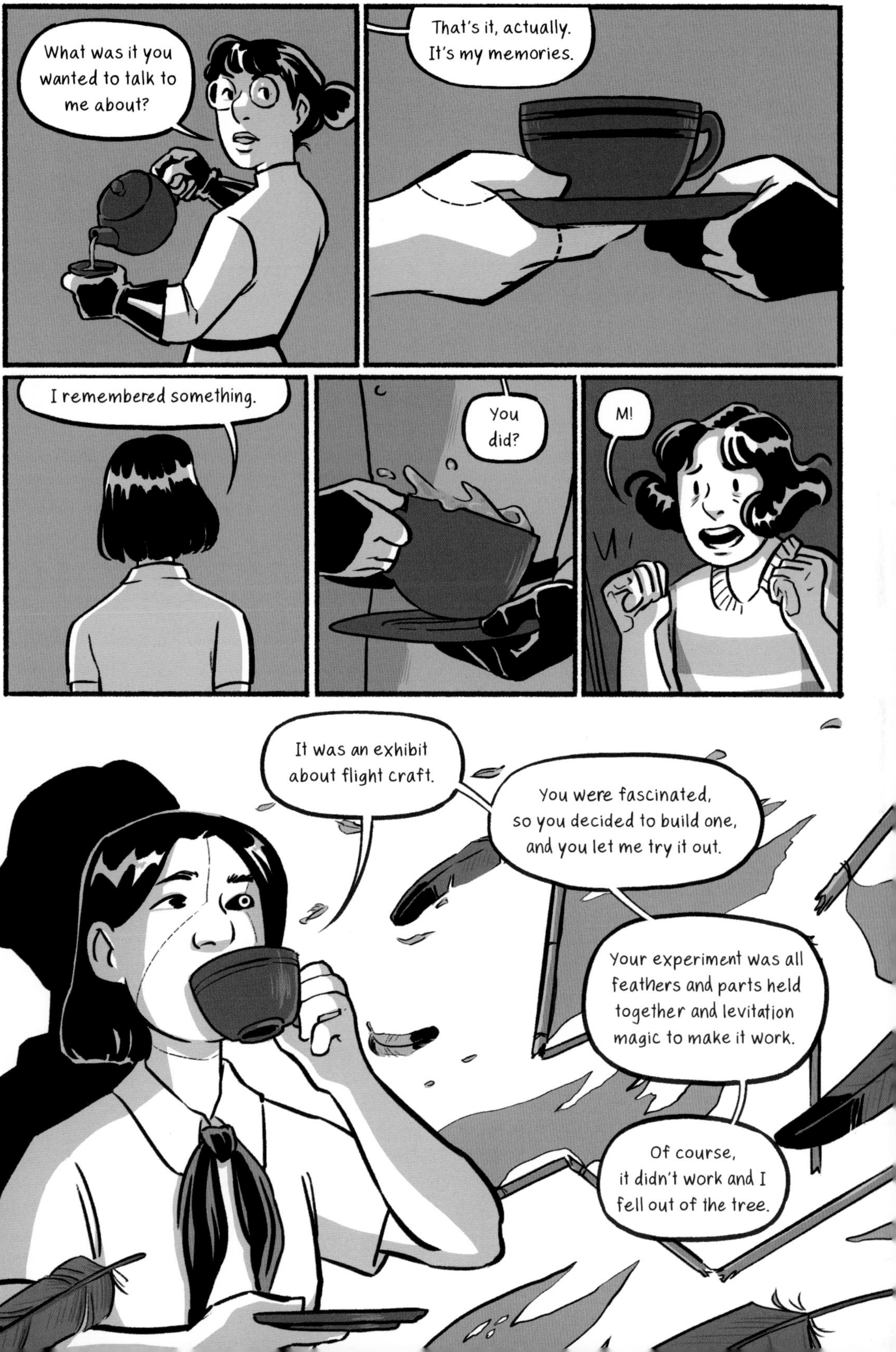
What was it you wanted to talk to me about?
That's it, actually. It's my memories.
I remembered something.
You did?
M!
It was an exhibit about flight craft.
You were fascinated, so you decided to build one, and you let me try it out.
Your experiment was all feathers and parts held together and levitation magic to make it work.
Of course, it didn't work and I fell out of the tree.

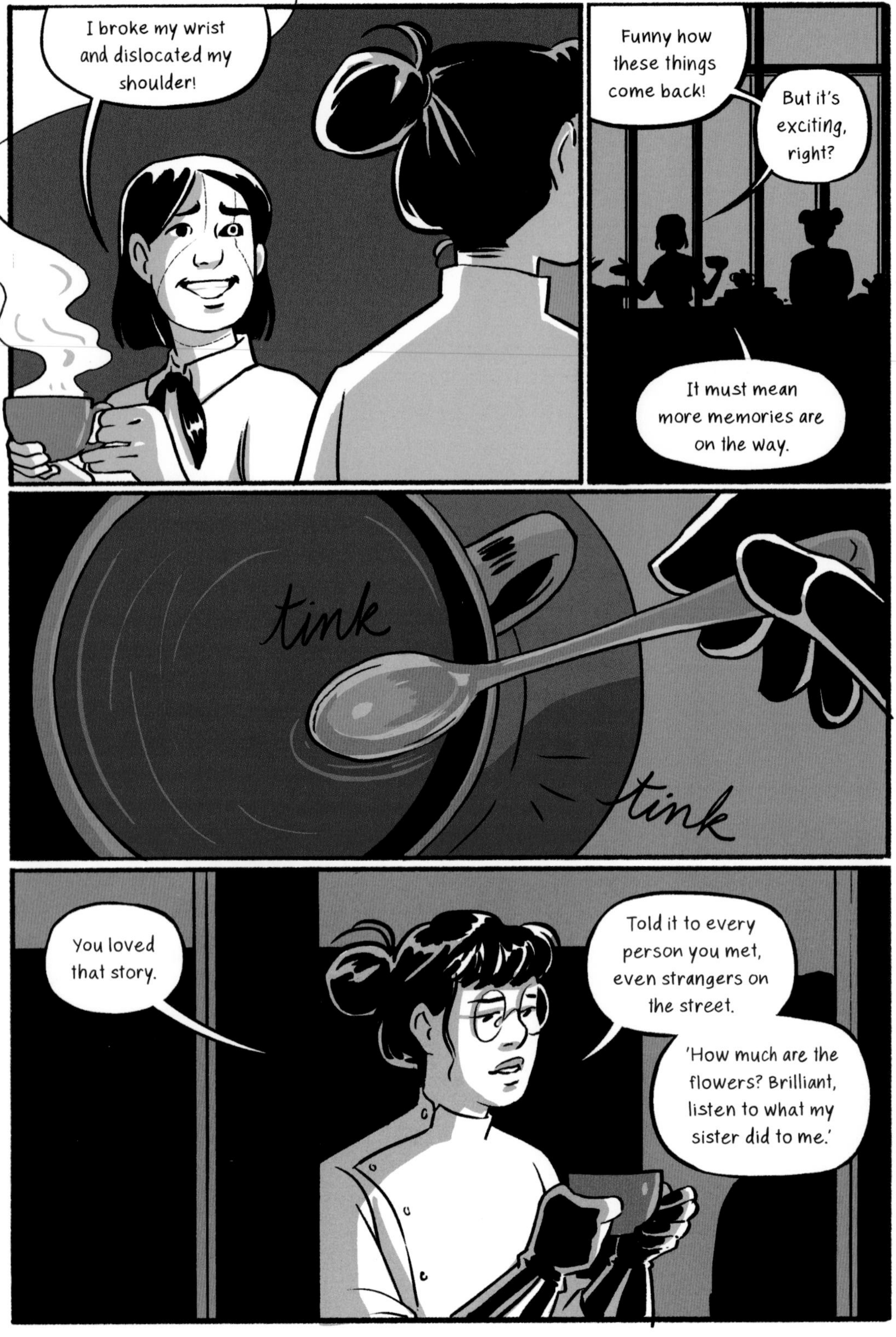
I broke my wrist and dislocated my shoulder!
Funny how these things come back!
But it's exciting, right?
It must mean more memories are on the way.
tink
tink
You loved that story.
Told it to every person you met, even strangers on the street.
'How much are the flowers? Brilliant, listen to what my sister did to me.'

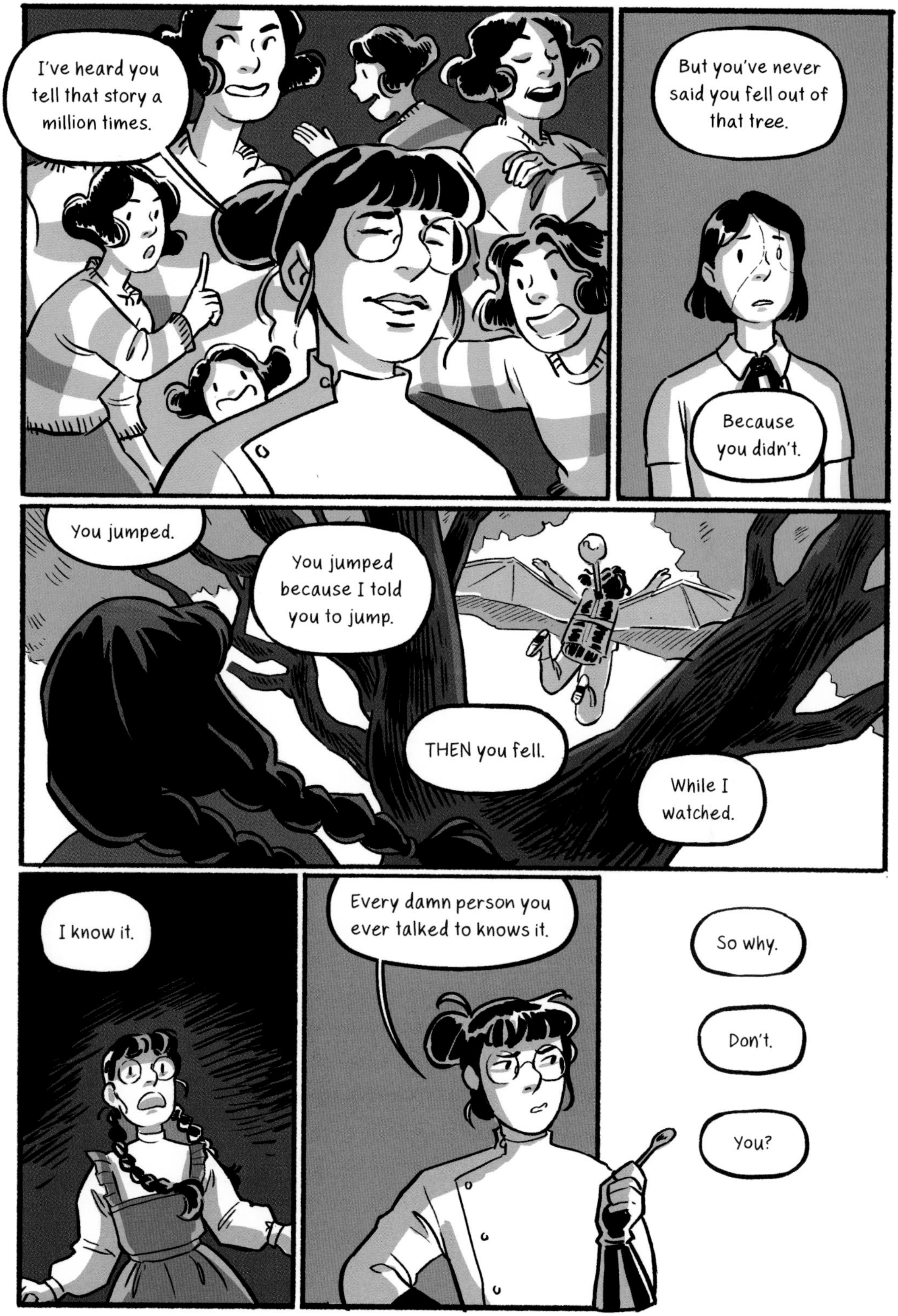
I've heard you tell that story a million times.
But you've never said you fell out of that tree.
Because you didn't.
You jumped.
You jumped because I told you to jump.
THEN you fell.
While I watched.
I know it.
Every damn person you ever talked to knows it.
So why.
Don't.
You?

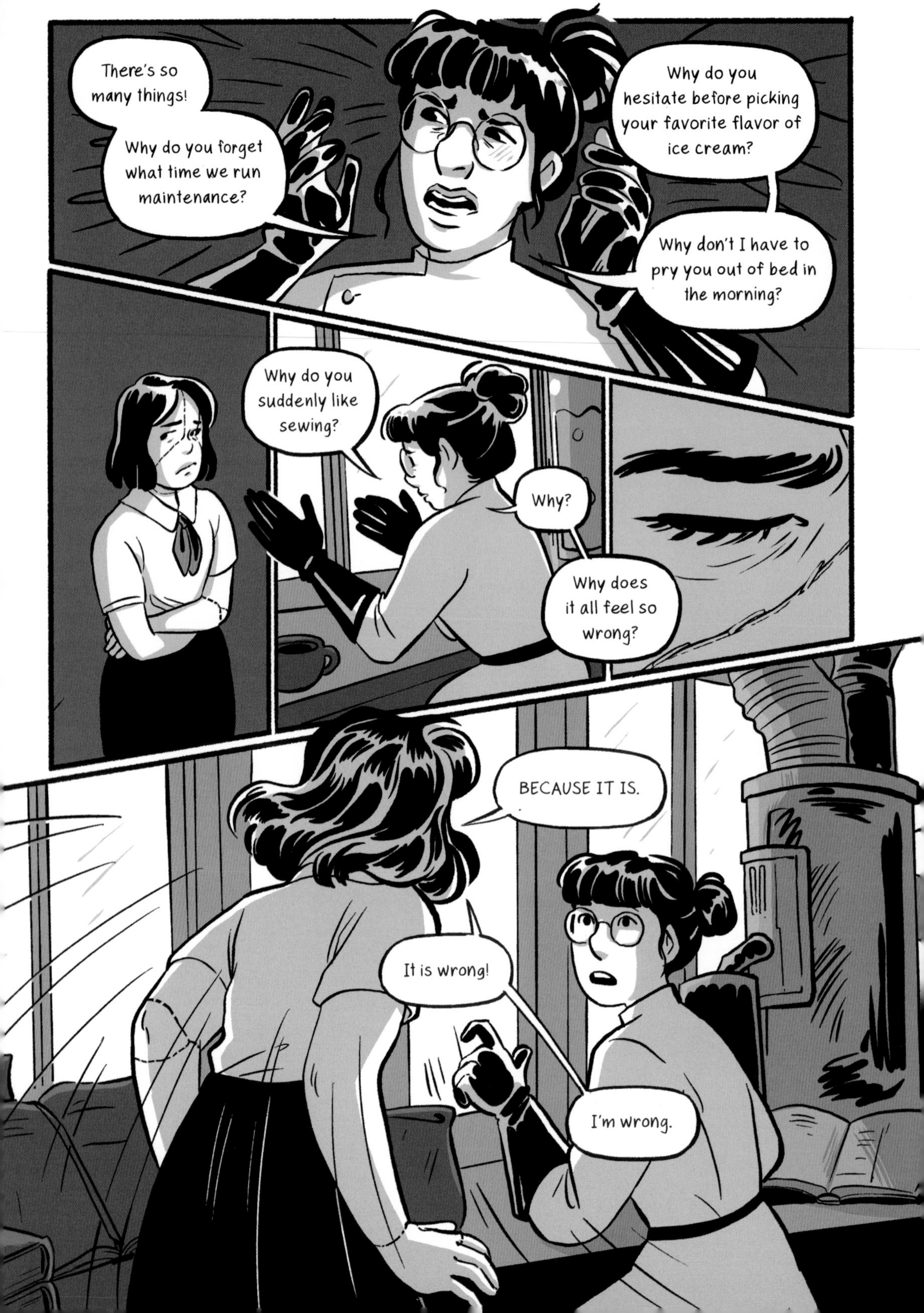
There's so many things!
Why do you forget what time we run maintenance?
Why do you hesitate before picking your favorite flavor of ice cream?
Why don't I have to pry you out of bed in the morning?
Why do you suddenly like sewing?
Why?
Why does it all feel so wrong?
BECAUSE IT IS.
It is wrong!
I'm wrong.

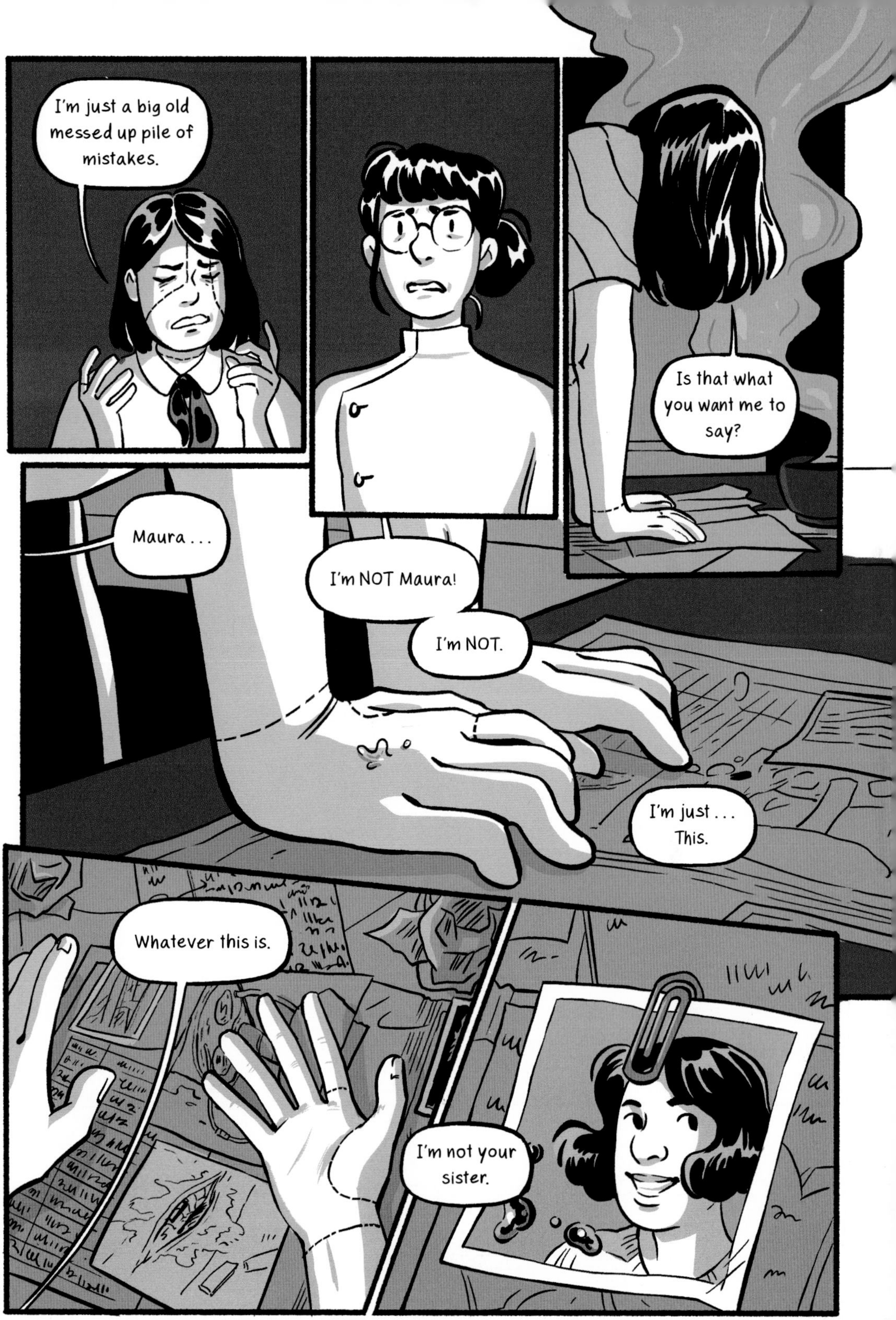
I'm just a big old messed up pile of mistakes.
Is that what you want me to say?
Maura . . .
I'm NOT Maura!
I'm NOT.
I'm just . . . This.
Whatever this is.
I'm not your sister.

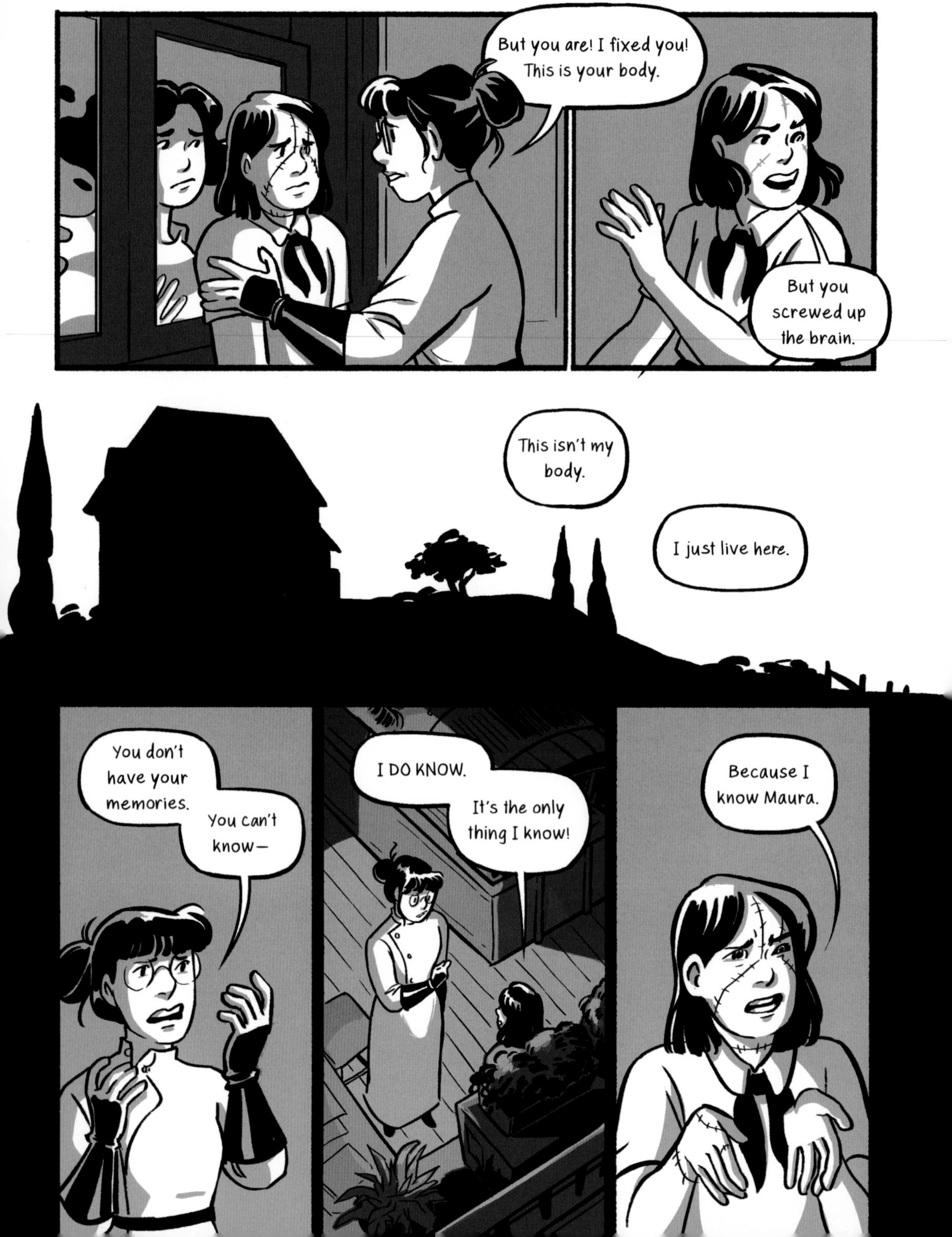
But you are! I fixed you! This is your body.
But you screwed up the brain.
This isn't my body.
I just live here.
You don't have your memories.
You can't know—
I DO KNOW.
It's the only thing I know!
Because I know Maura.

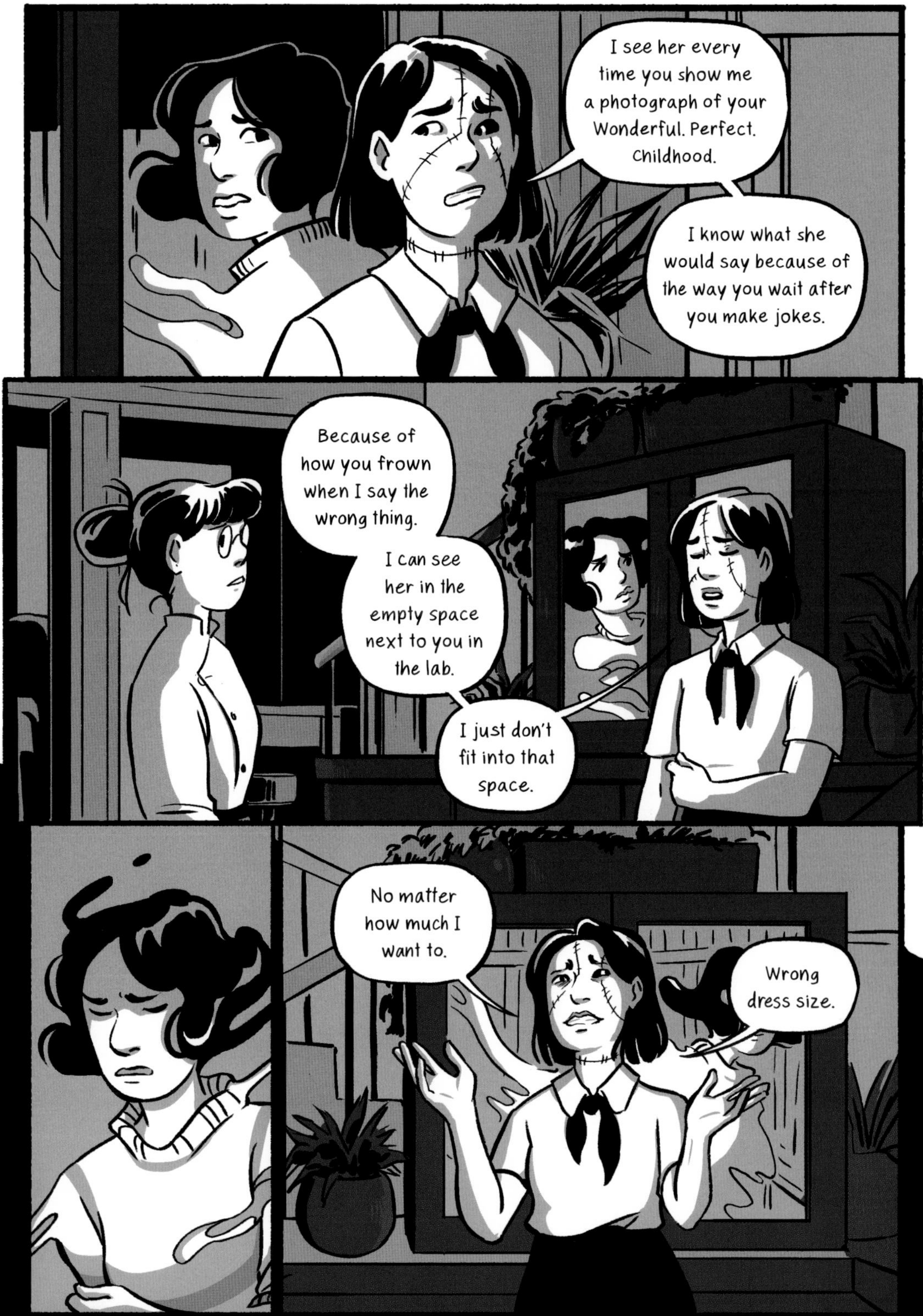
I see her every time you show me a photograph of your Wonderful. Perfect. Childhood.
I know what she would say because of the way you wait after you make jokes.
Because of how you frown when I say the wrong thing.
I can see her in the empty space next to you in the lab.
I just don't fit into that space.
No matter how much I want to.
Wrong dress size.

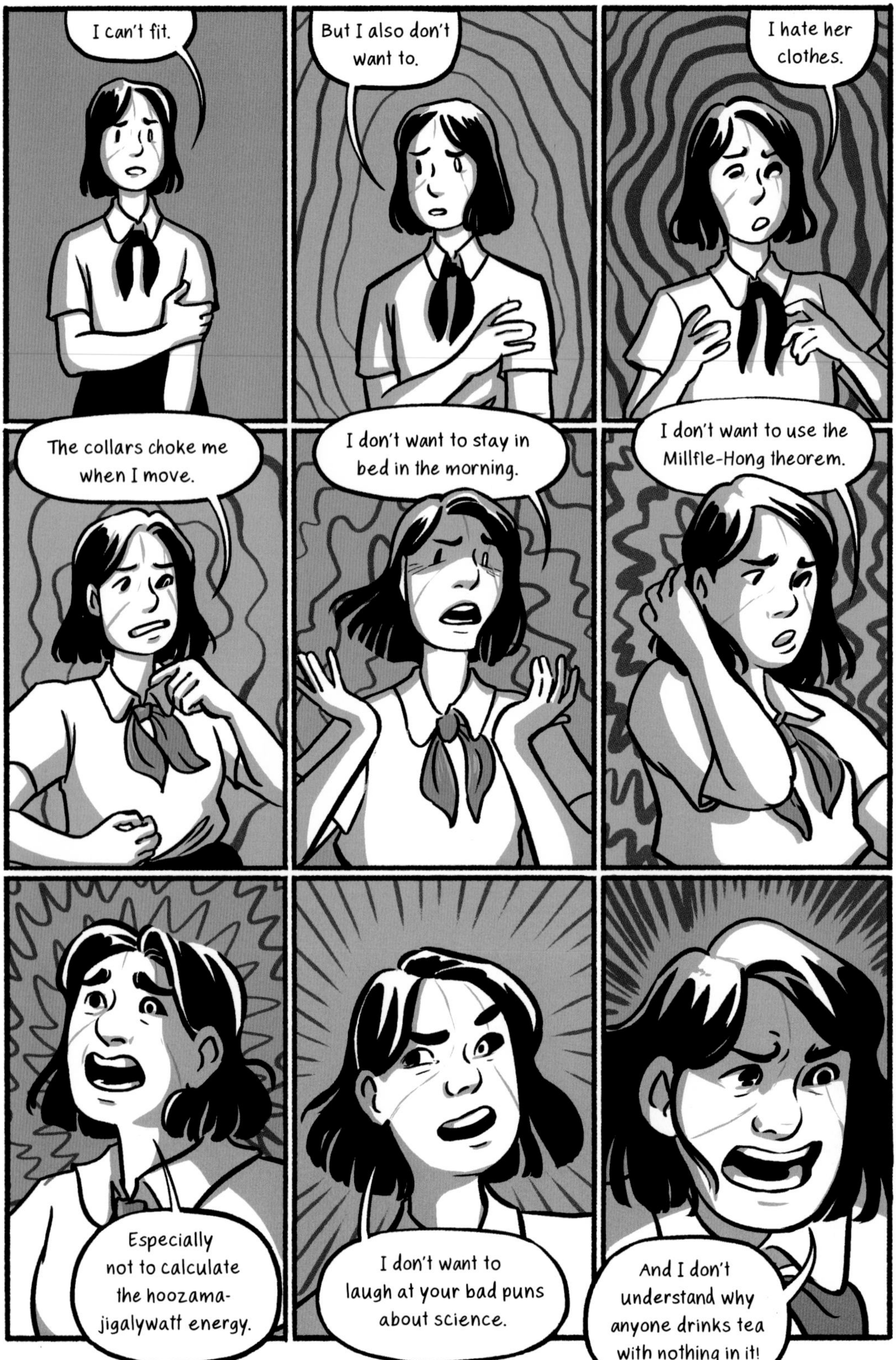
I can't fit.
But I also don't want to.
I hate her clothes.
The collars choke me when I move.
I don't want to stay in bed in the morning.
I don't want to use the Millfle-Hong theorem.
Especially not to calculate the hoozama-jigalywatt energy.
I don't want to laugh at your bad puns about science.
And I don't understand why anyone drinks tea with nothing in it!

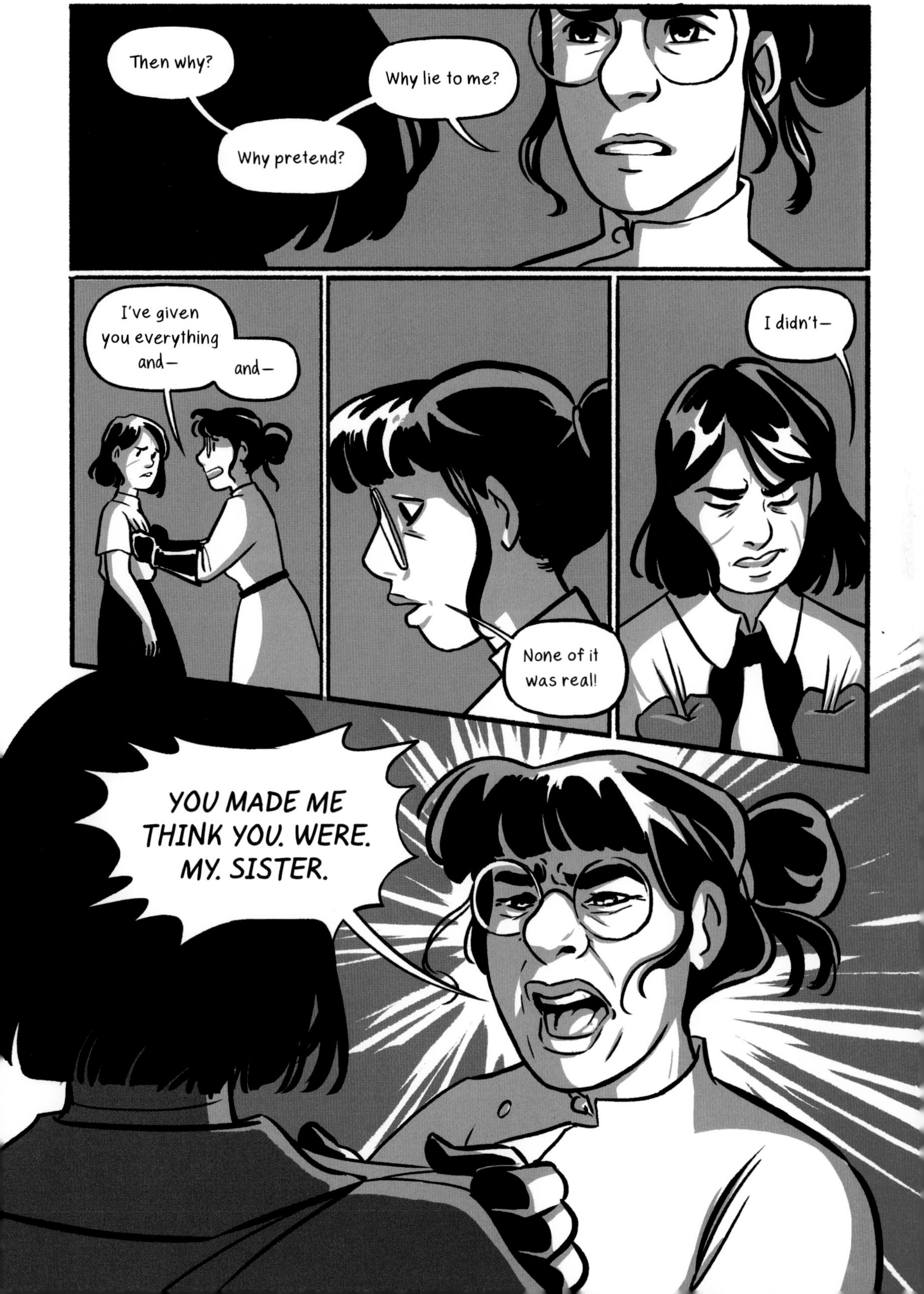
Then why?
Why pretend?
Why lie to me?
I've given you everything and—
and—
None of it was real!
I didn't—
YOU MADE ME THINK YOU. WERE. MY. SISTER.

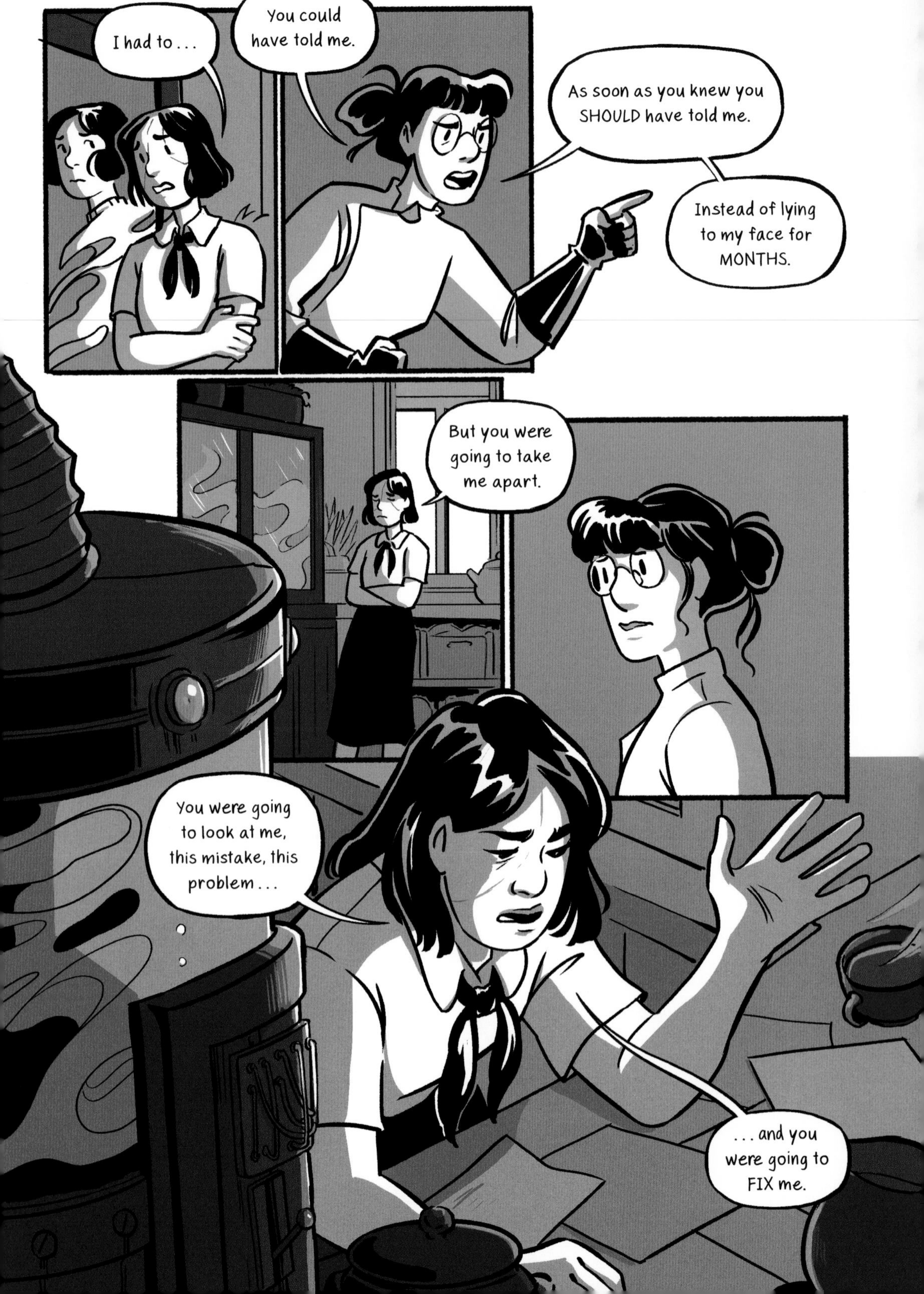
I had to . . .
You could have told me.
As soon as you knew you SHOULD have told me.
Instead of lying to my face for MONTHS.
But you were going to take me apart.
You were going to look at me, this mistake, this problem . . .
. . . and you were going to FIX me.

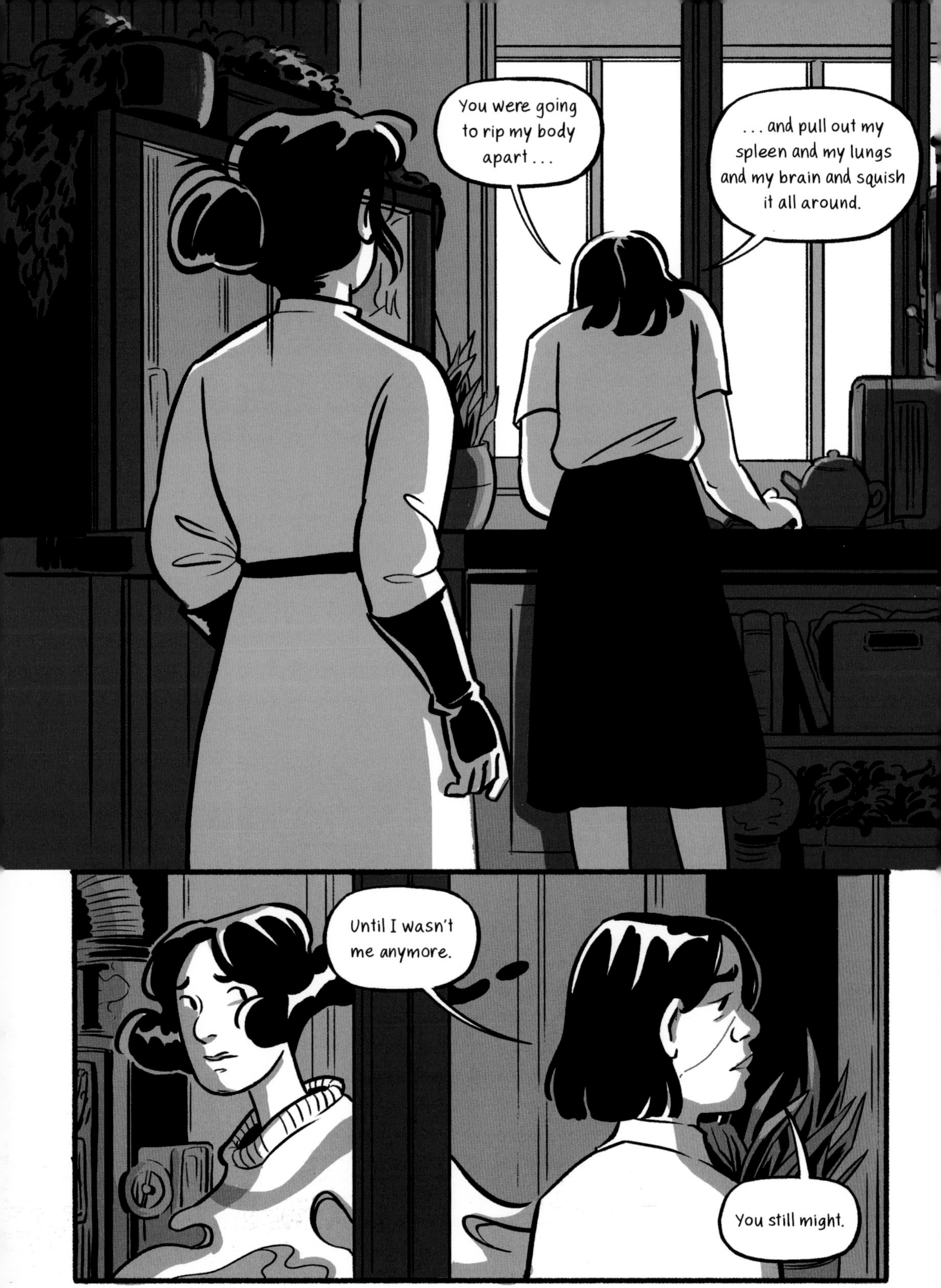
You were going to rip my body apart . . .
. . . and pull out my spleen and my lungs and my brain and squish it all around.
Until I wasn't me anymore.
You still might.

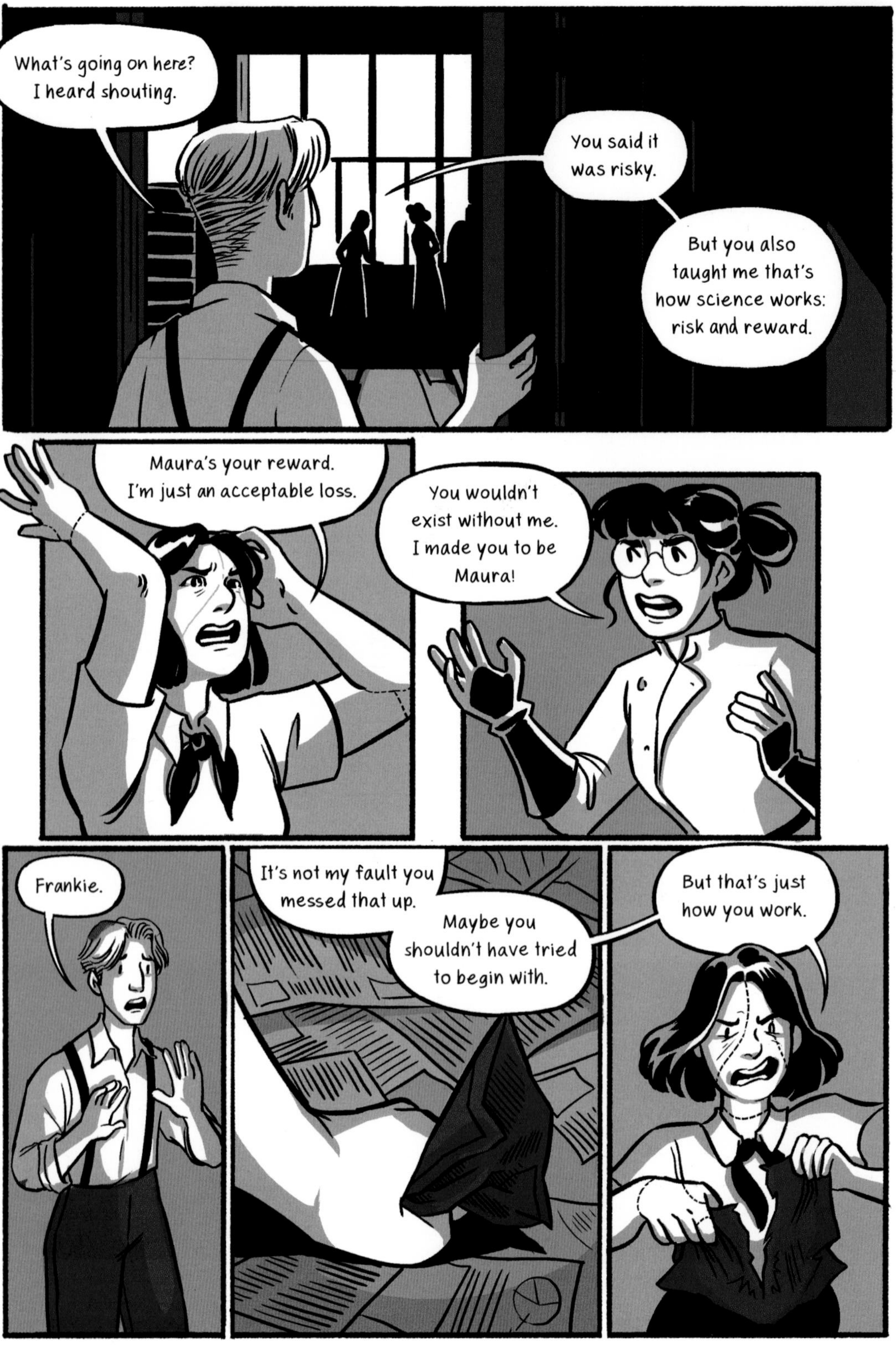
What's going on here? I heard shouting.
You said it was risky.
But you also taught me that's how science works: risk and reward.
Maura's your reward. I'm just an acceptable loss.
You wouldn't exist without me. I made you to be Maura!
Frankie.
It's not my fault you messed that up.
Maybe you shouldn't have tried to begin with.
But that's just how you work.

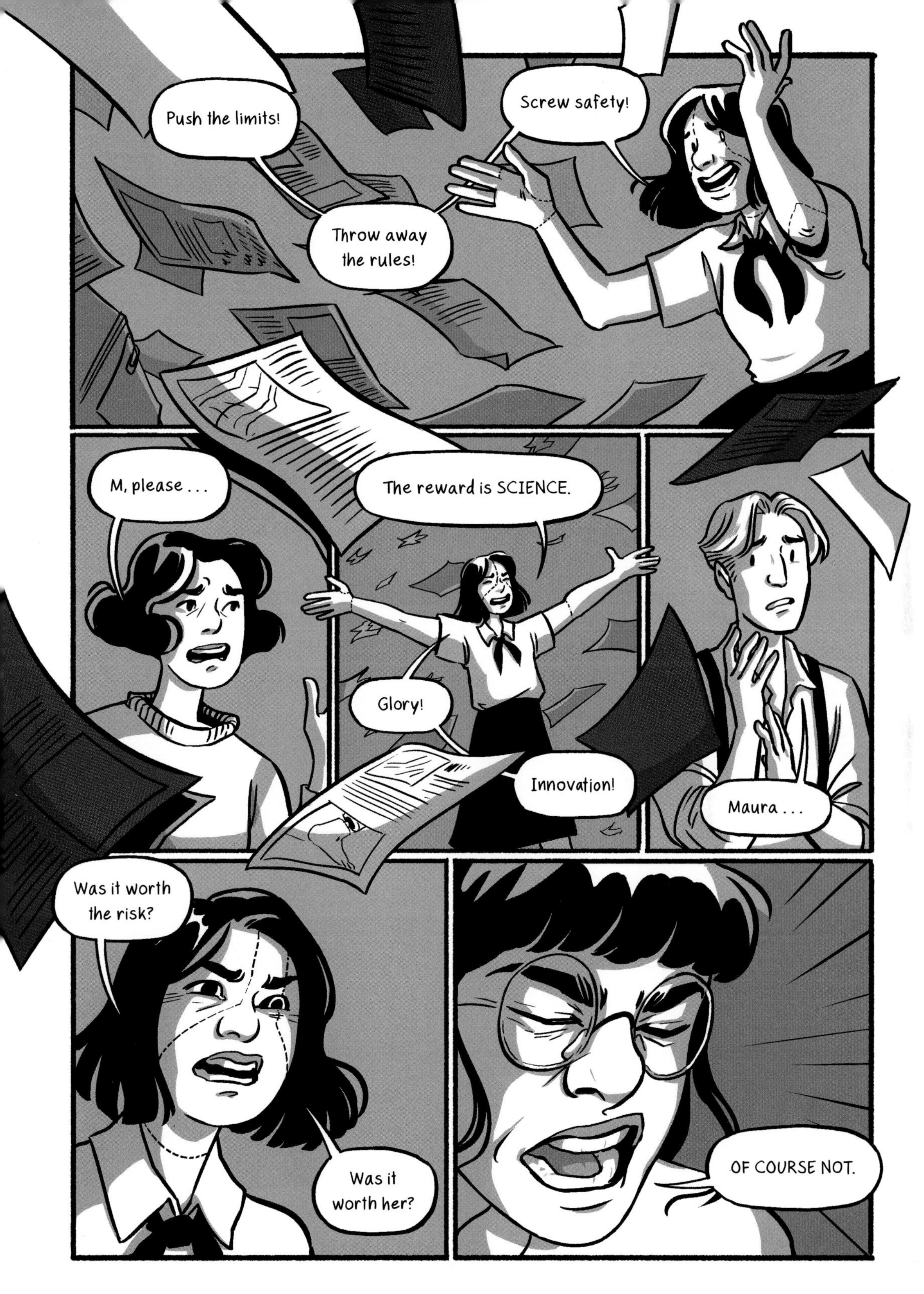
Push the limits!
Throw away the rules!
Screw safety!
M, please . . .
The reward is SCIENCE.
Glory!
Innovation!
Maura . . .
Was it worth the risk?
Was it worth her?
OF COURSE NOT.

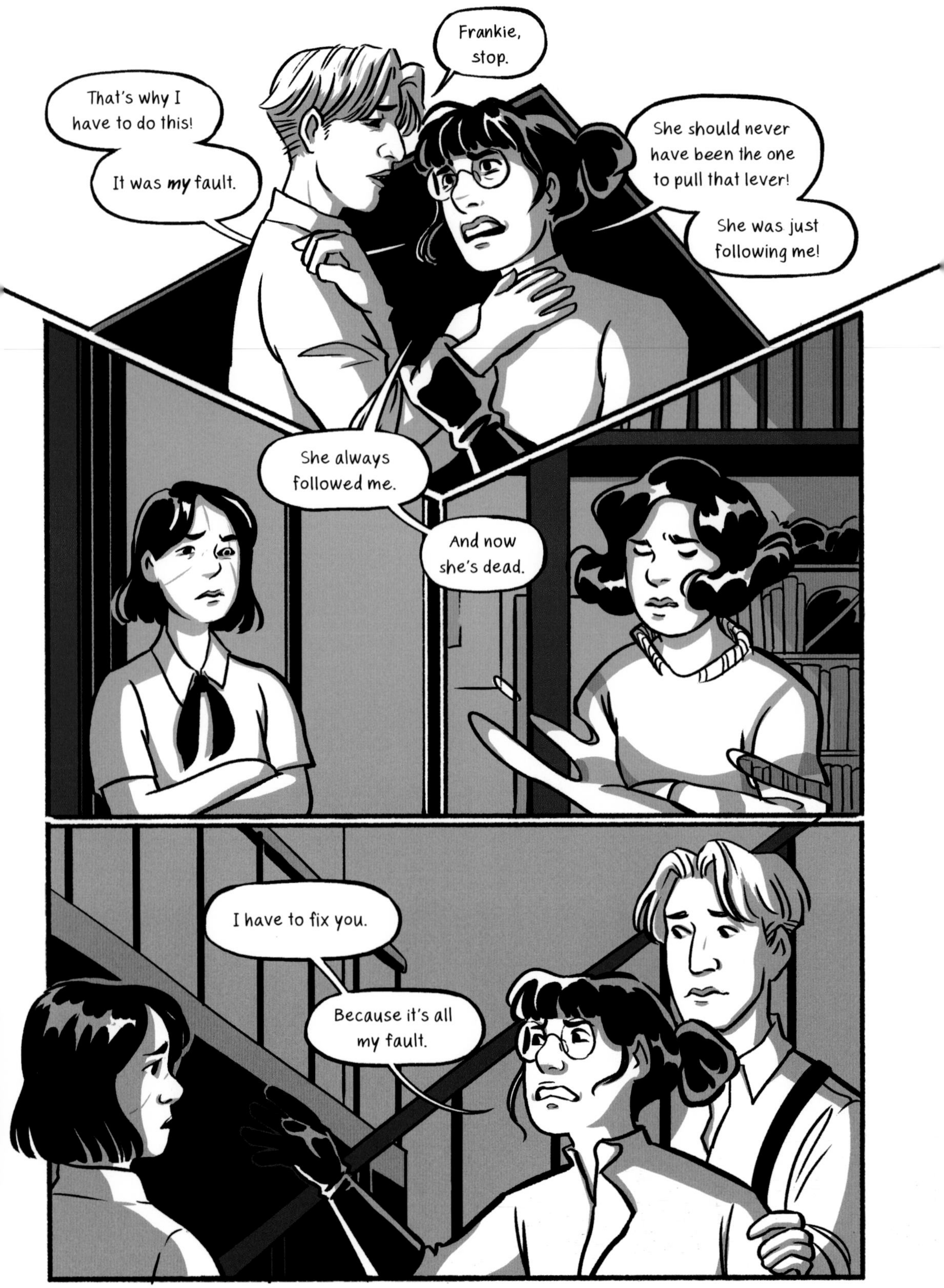

That's why I have to do this!
It was **my** fault.
Frankie, stop.
She should never have been the one to pull that lever!
She was just following me!
She always followed me.
And now she's dead.
I have to fix you.
Because it's all my fault.

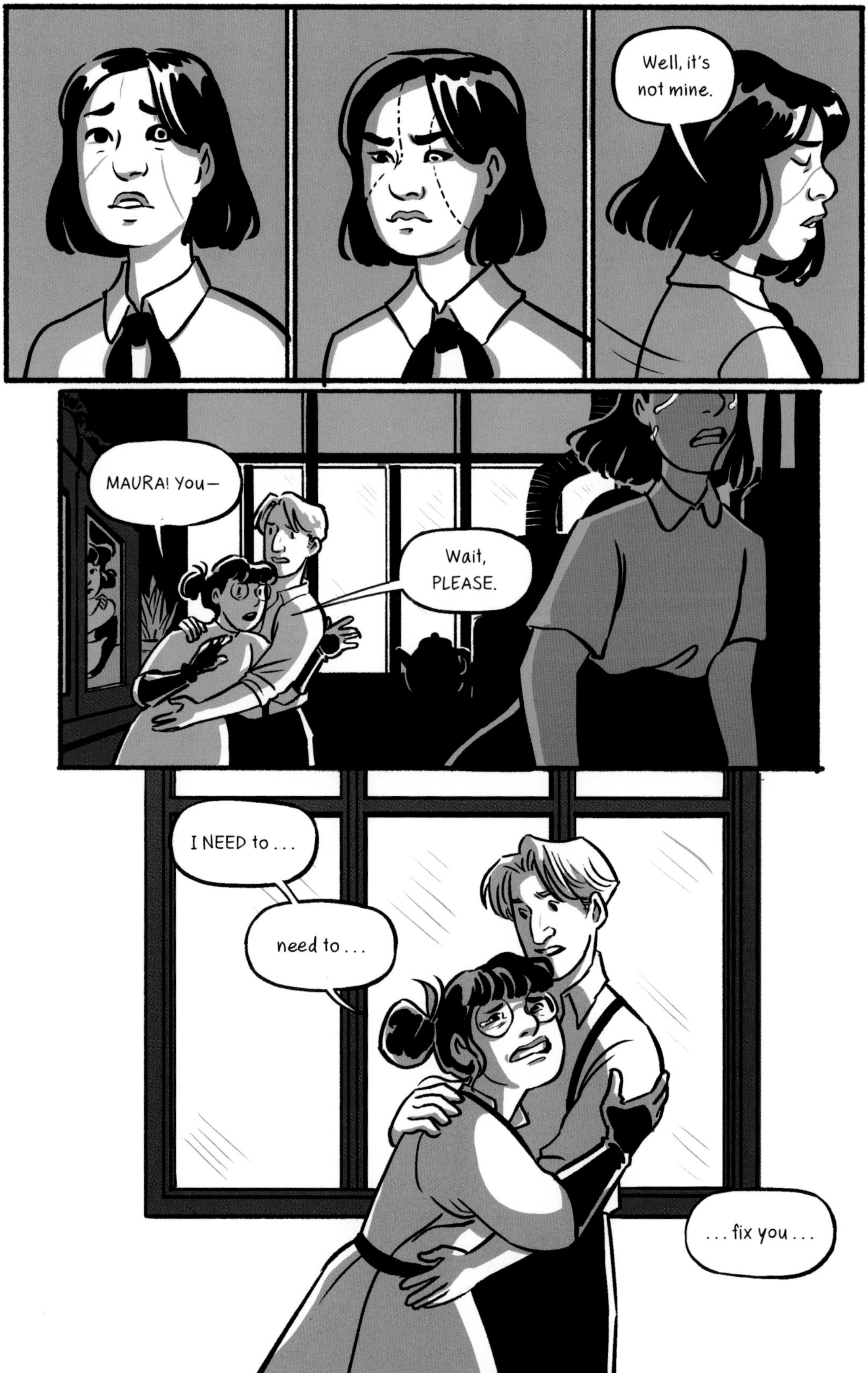
Well, it's not mine.
MAURA! You—
Wait, PLEASE.
I NEED to . . .
need to . . .
. . . fix you . . .

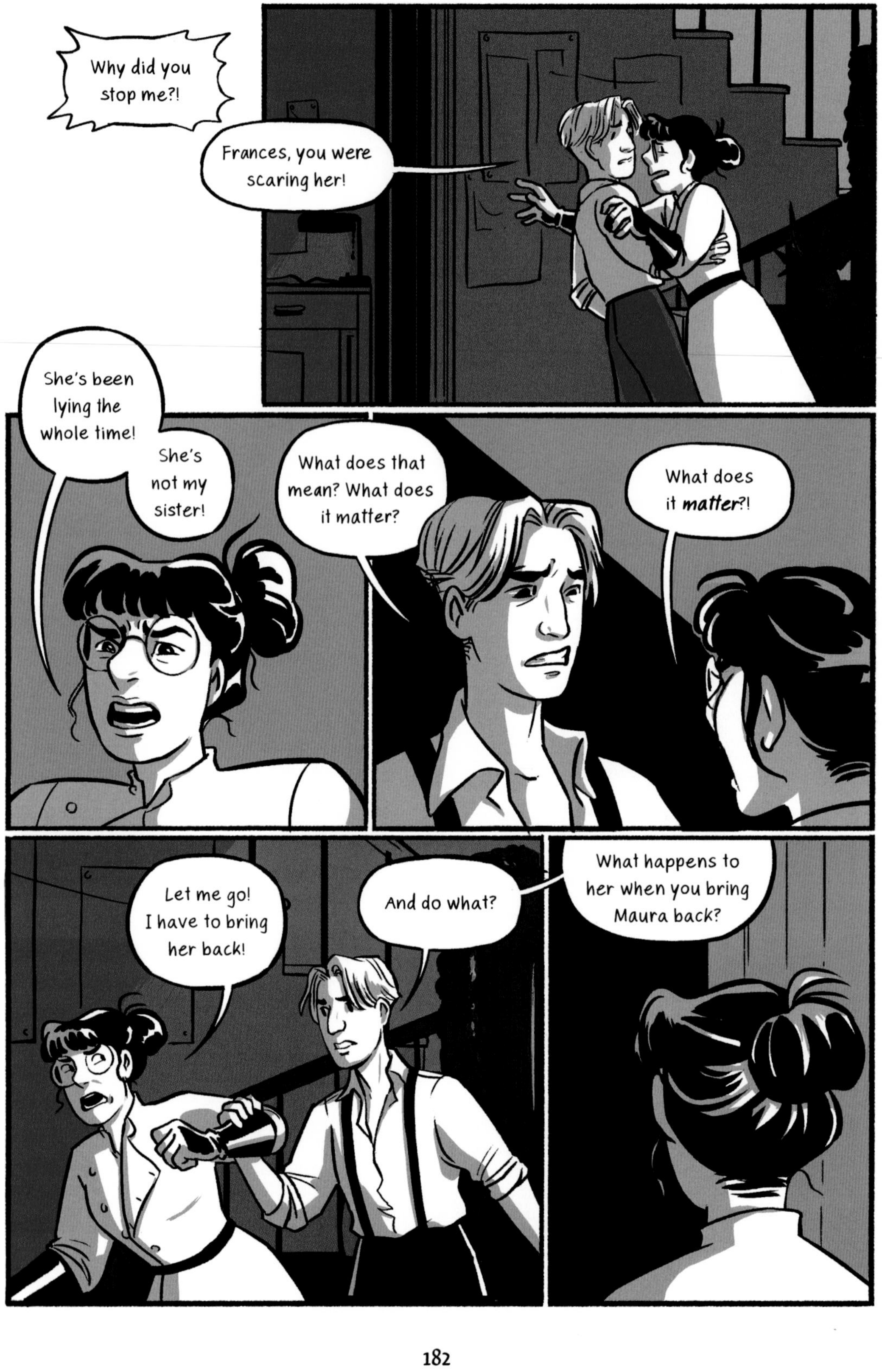
Why did you stop me?!
Frances, you were scaring her!
She's been lying the whole time!
She's not my sister!
What does that mean? What does it matter?
What does it *matter*?!
Let me go! I have to bring her back!
And do what?
What happens to her when you bring Maura back?

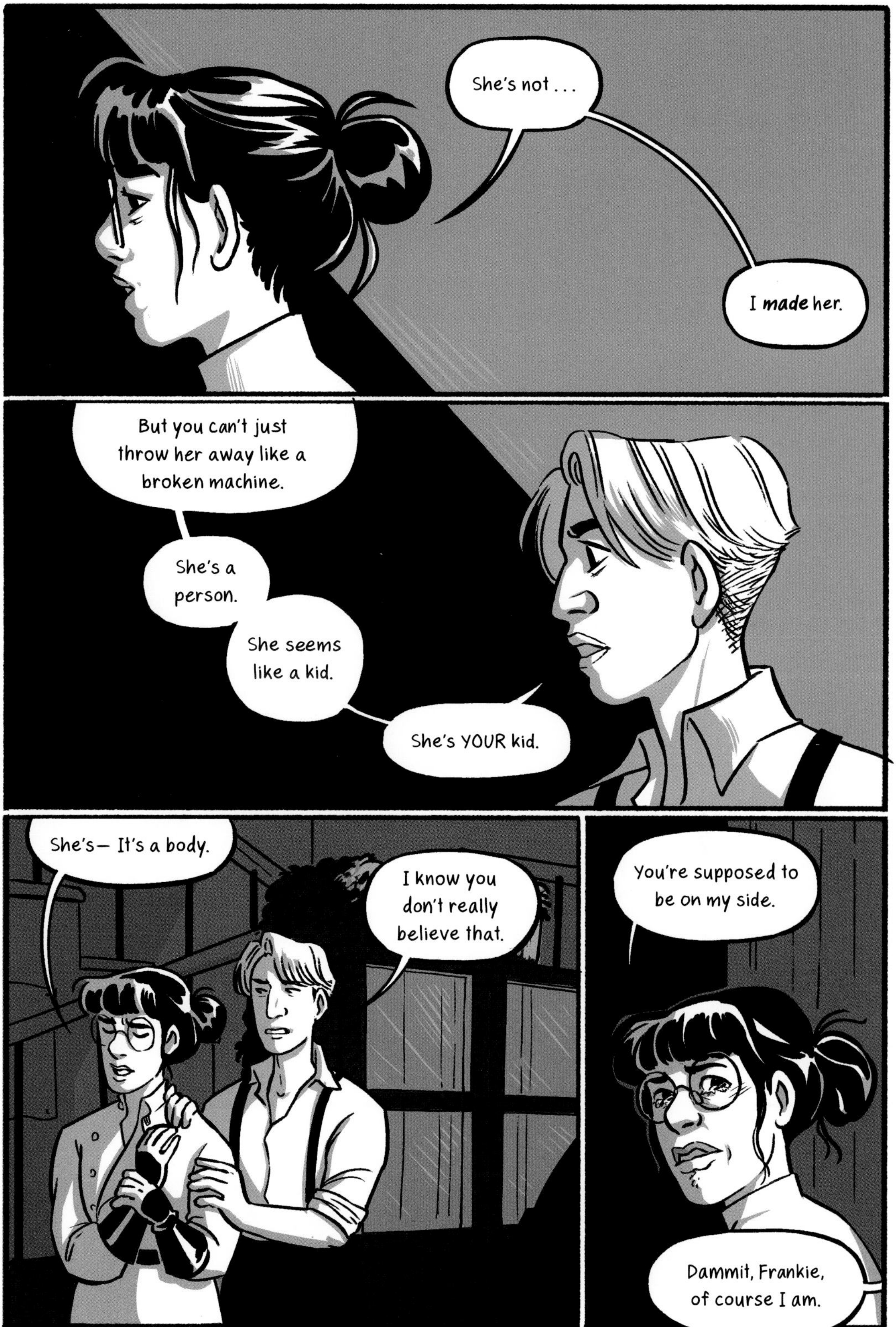
She's not . . .
I *made* her.
But you can't just throw her away like a broken machine.
She's a person.
She seems like a kid.
She's YOUR kid.
She's— It's a body.
I know you don't really believe that.
You're supposed to be on my side.
Dammit, Frankie, of course I am.

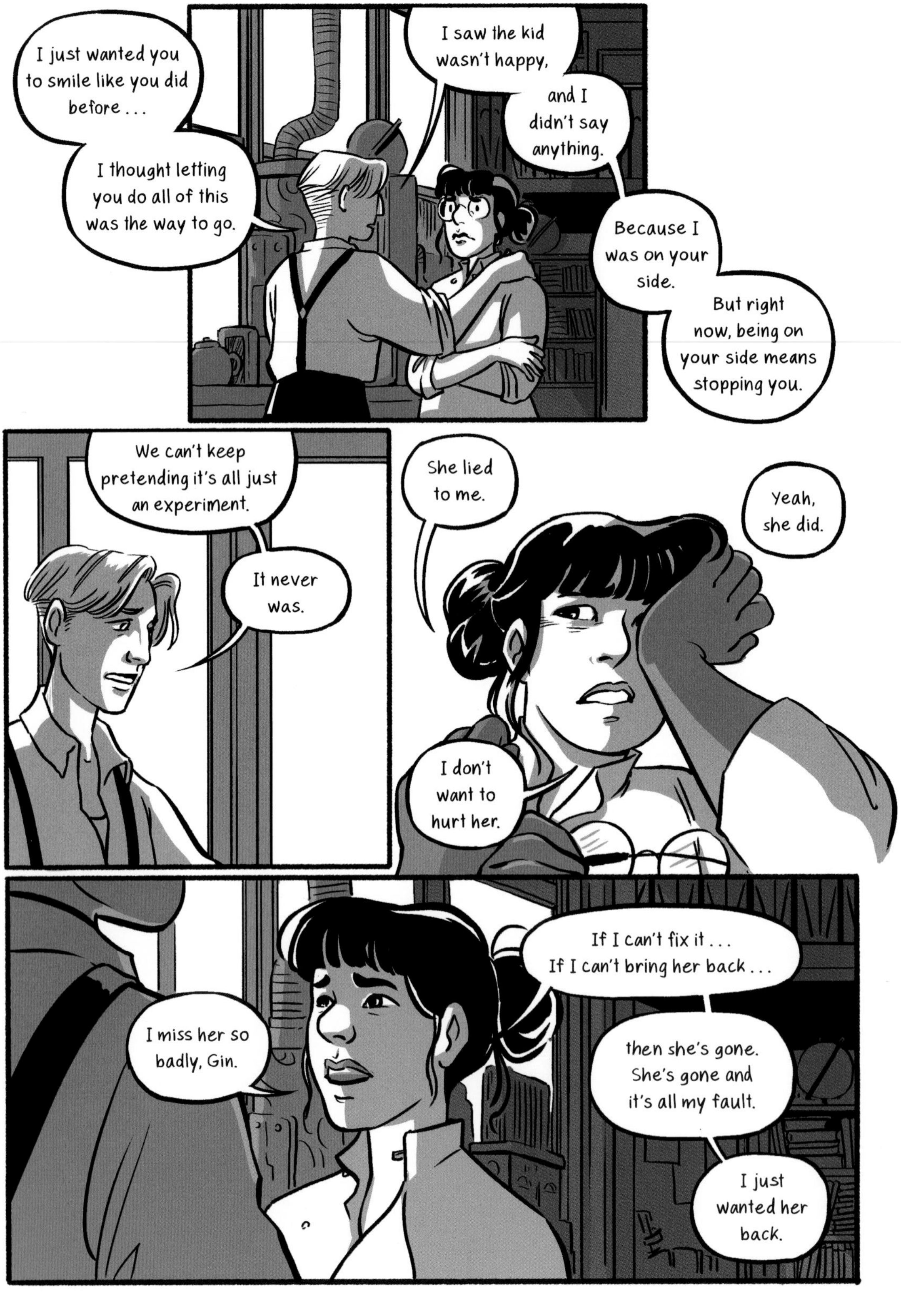
I just wanted you to smile like you did before . . .
I thought letting you do all of this was the way to go.
I saw the kid wasn't happy,
and I didn't say anything.
Because I was on your side.
But right now, being on your side means stopping you.
We can't keep pretending it's all just an experiment.
It never was.
She lied to me.
Yeah, she did.
I don't want to hurt her.
I miss her so badly, Gin.
If I can't fix it . . .
If I can't bring her back . . .
then she's gone. She's gone and it's all my fault.
I just wanted her back.

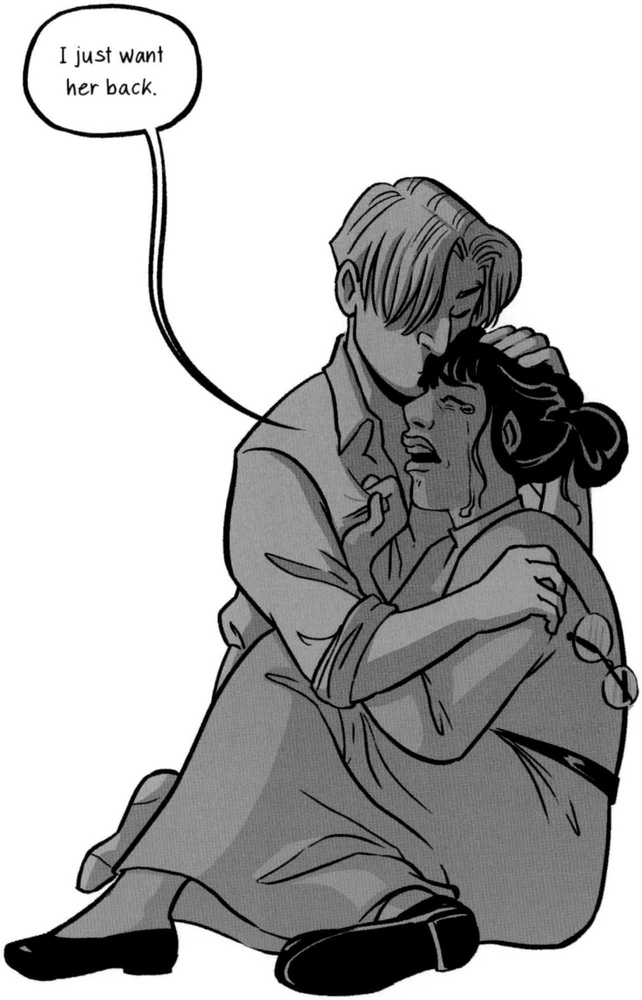
I just want her back.

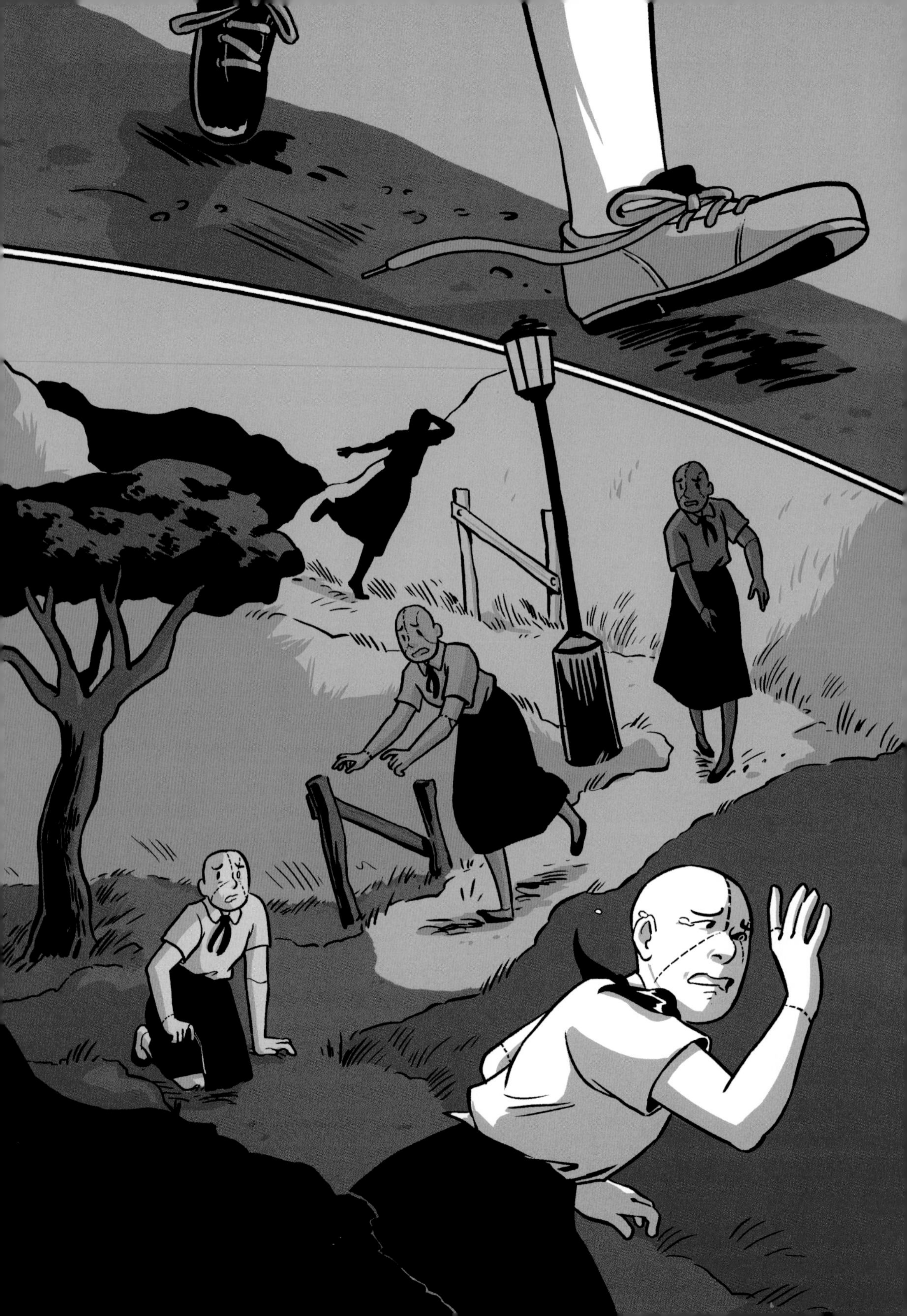

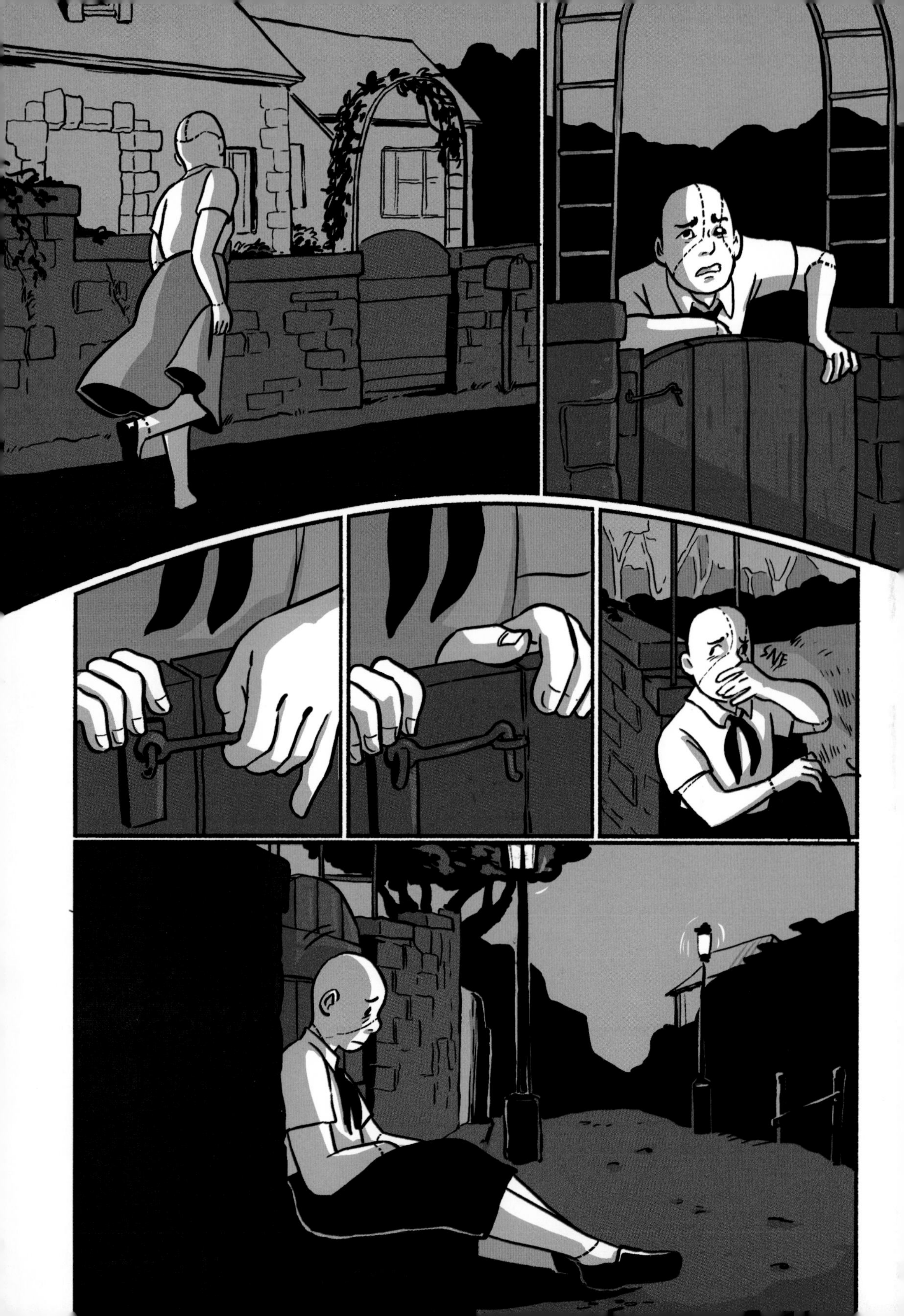
SNF

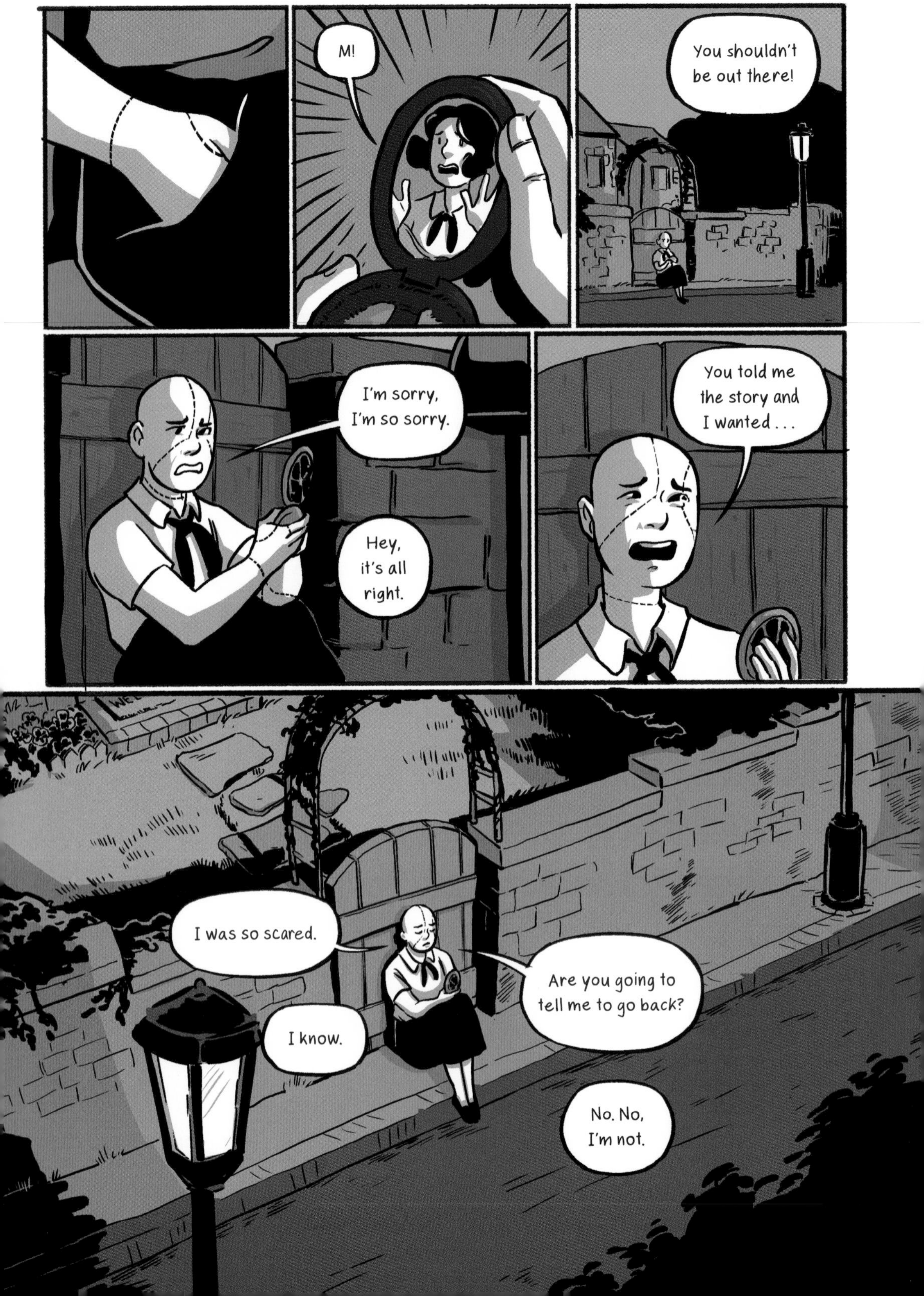

M!
You shouldn't be out there!
I'm sorry, I'm so sorry.
Hey, it's all right.
You told me the story and I wanted . . .
I was so scared.
I know.
Are you going to tell me to go back?
No. No, I'm not.

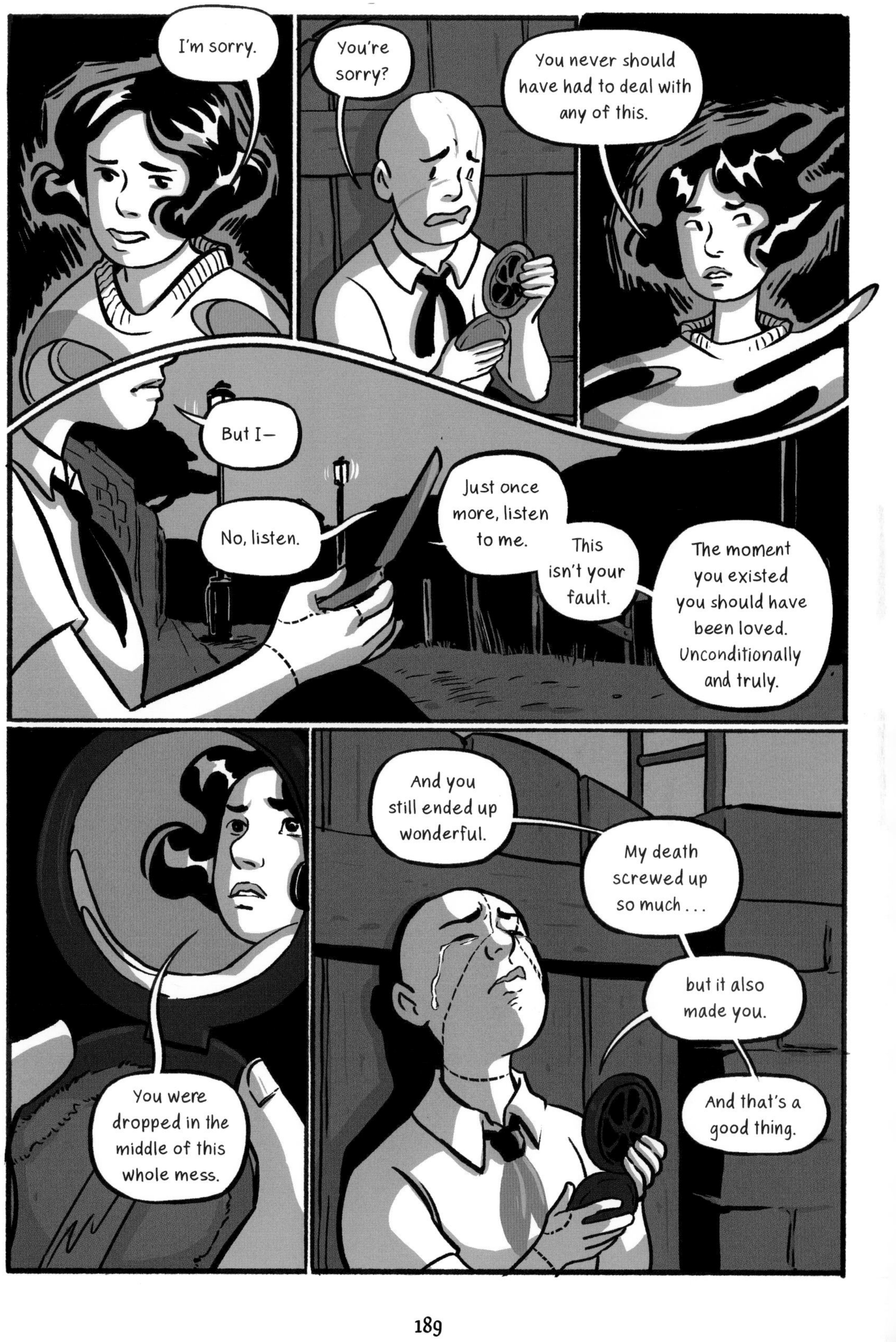
I'm sorry.
You're sorry?
You never should have had to deal with any of this.
But I—
No, listen.
Just once more, listen to me.
This isn't your fault.
The moment you existed you should have been loved. Unconditionally and truly.
You were dropped in the middle of this whole mess.
And you still ended up wonderful.
My death screwed up so much . . .
but it also made you.
And that's a good thing.

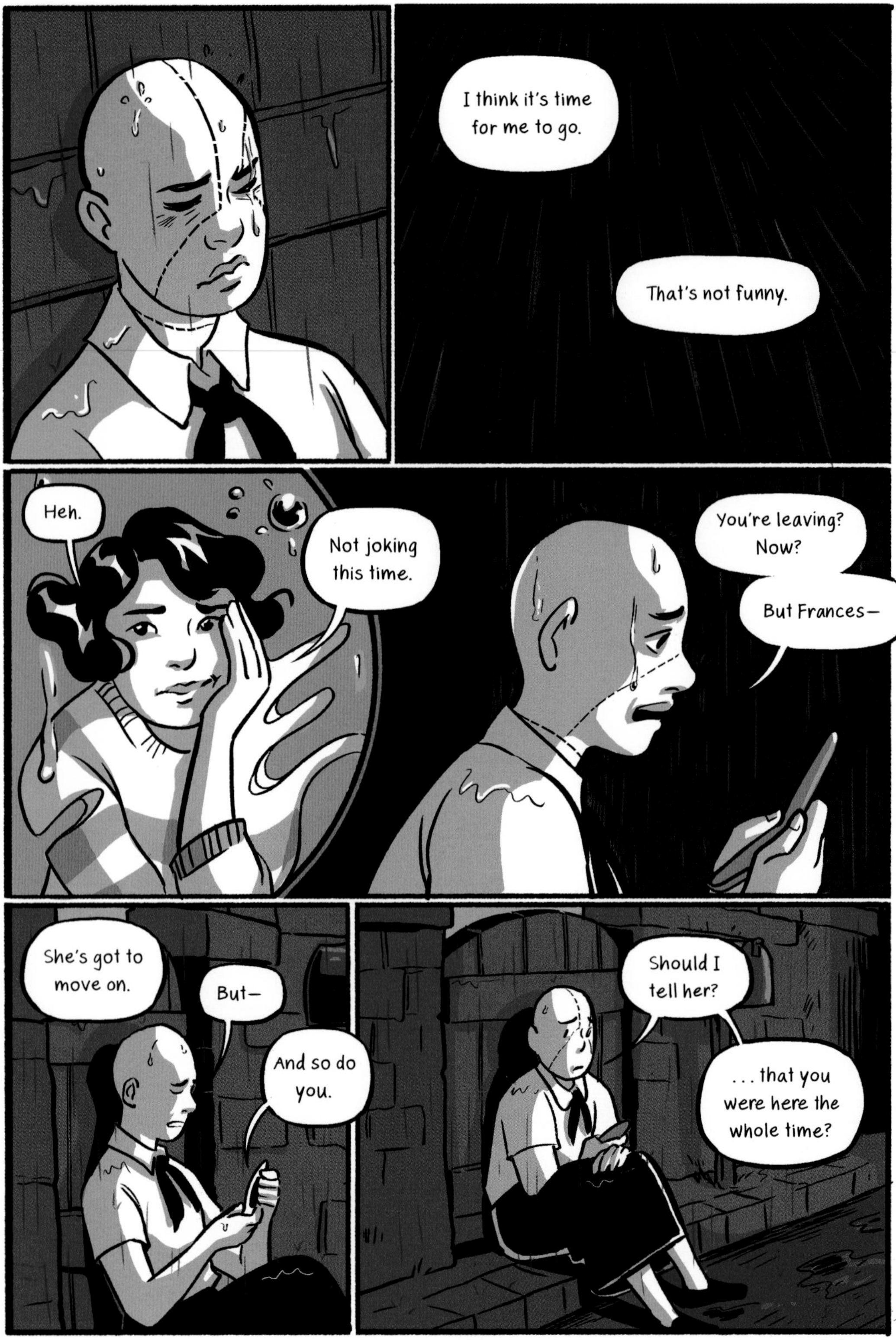
I think it's time for me to go.
That's not funny.
Heh.
Not joking this time.
You're leaving? Now?
But Frances—
She's got to move on.
But—
And so do you.
Should I tell her?
. . . that you were here the whole time?

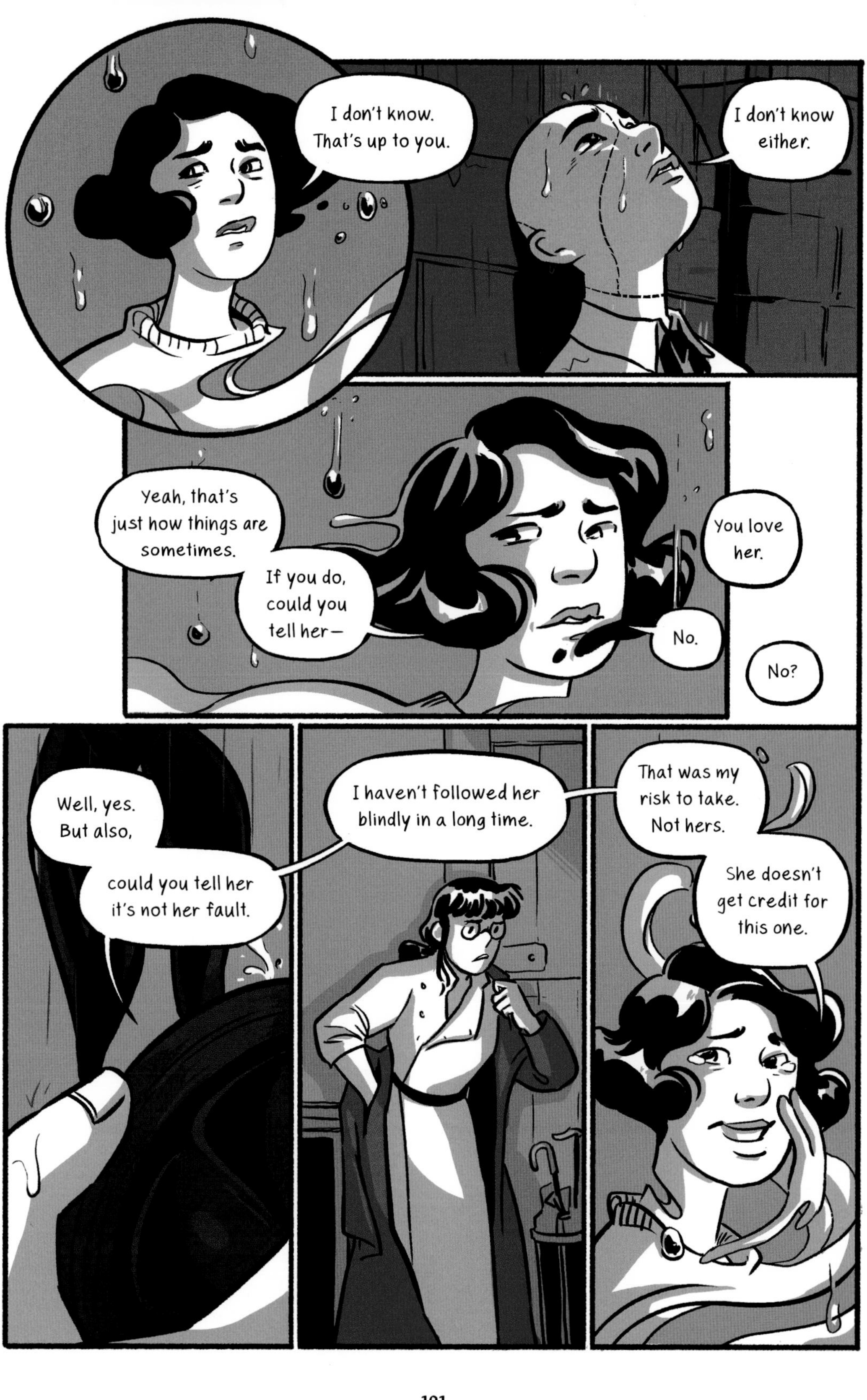
I don't know. That's up to you.
I don't know either.
Yeah, that's just how things are sometimes.
If you do, could you tell her—
You love her.
No.
No?
Well, yes. But also,
could you tell her it's not her fault.
I haven't followed her blindly in a long time.
That was my risk to take. Not hers.
She doesn't get credit for this one.

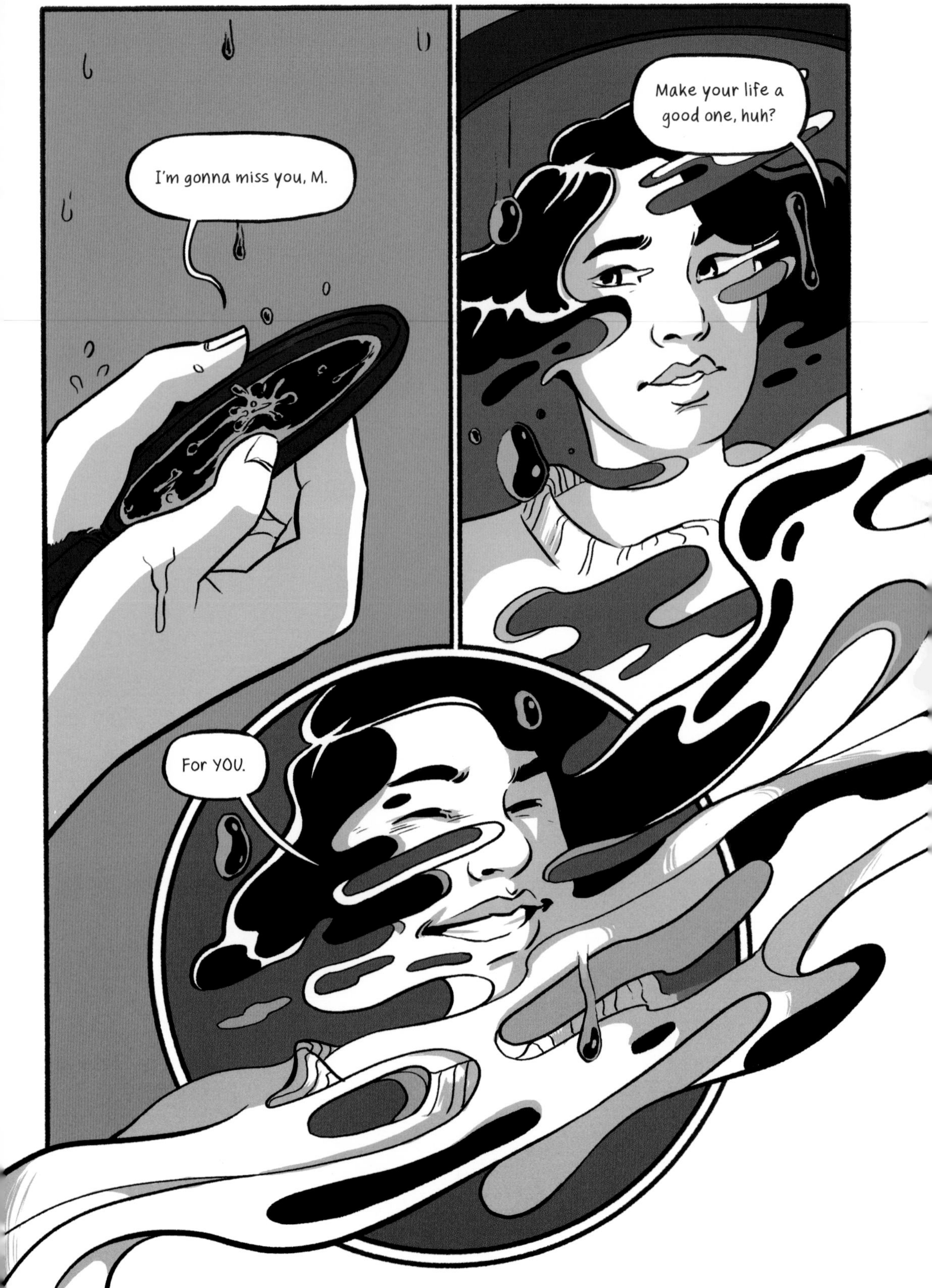
I'm gonna miss you, M.
Make your life a good one, huh?
For YOU.

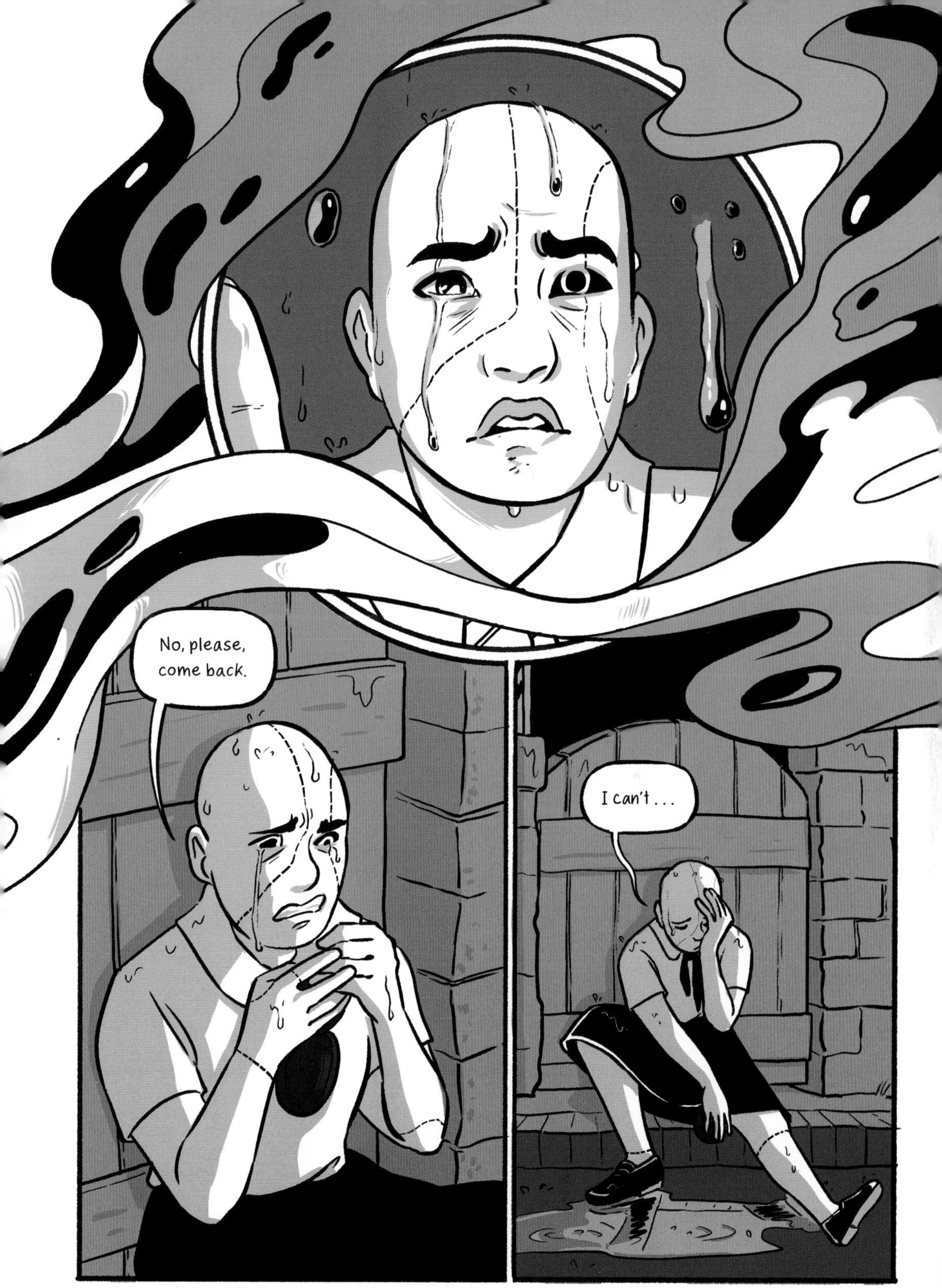
No, please, come back.
I can't . . .

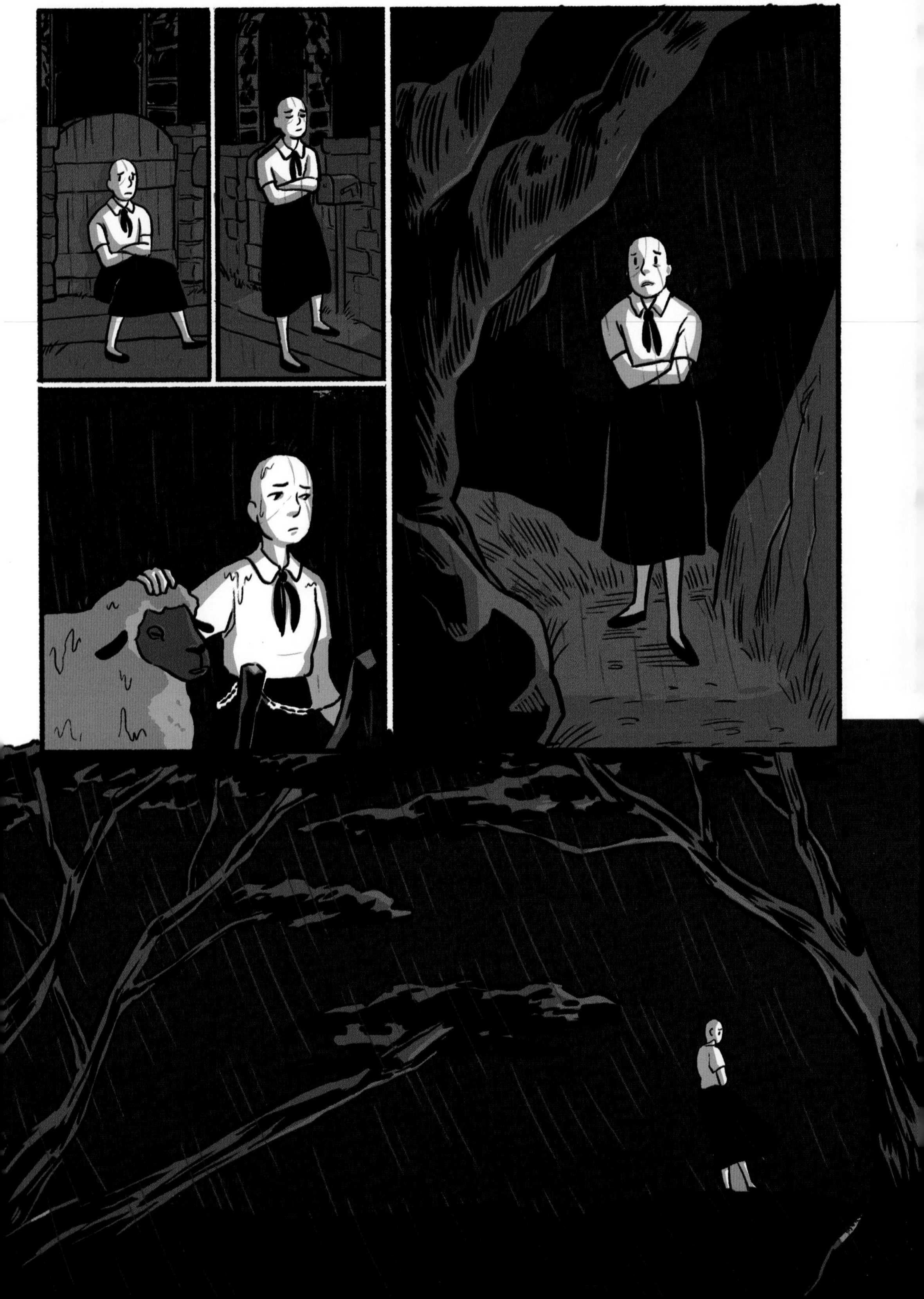

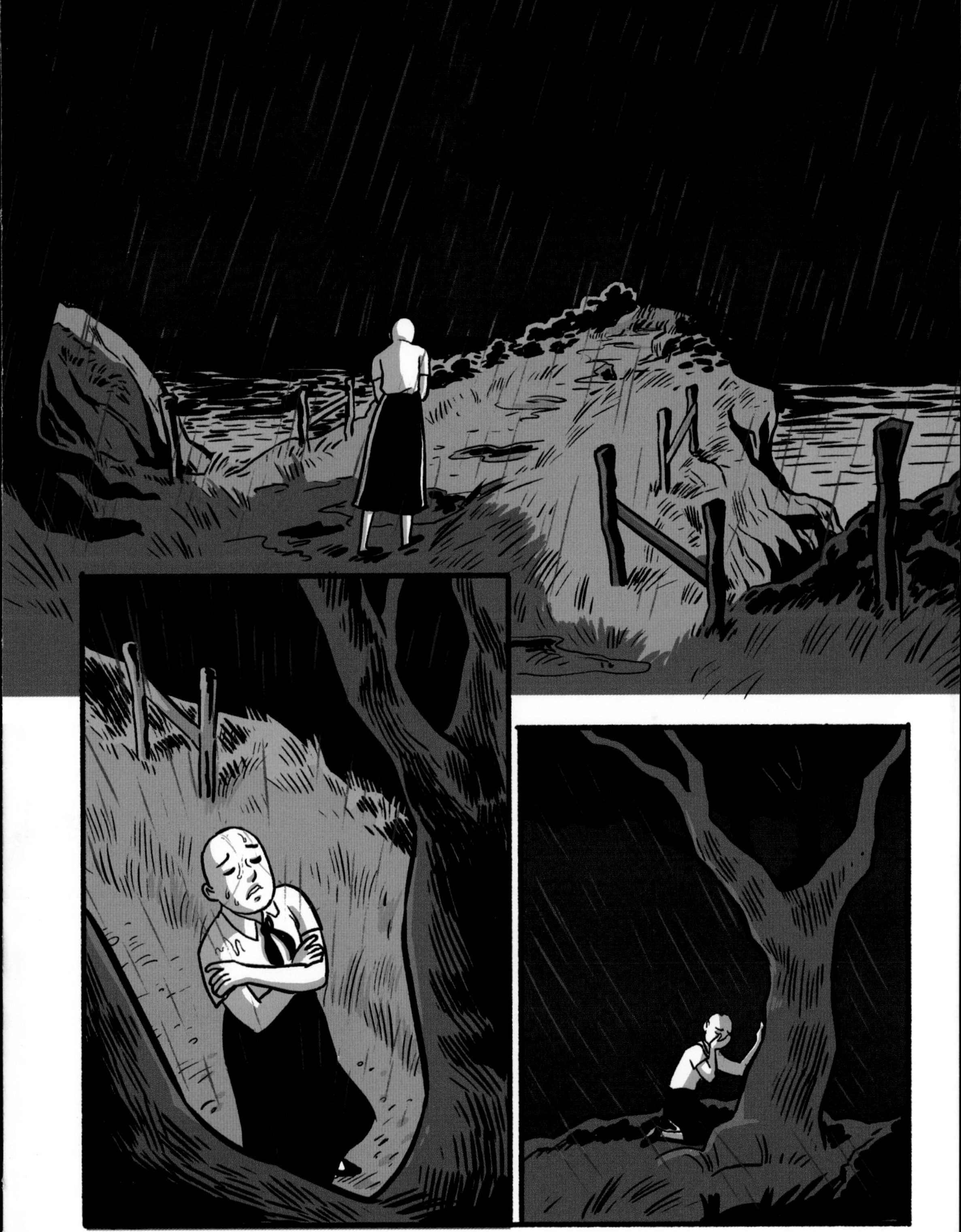

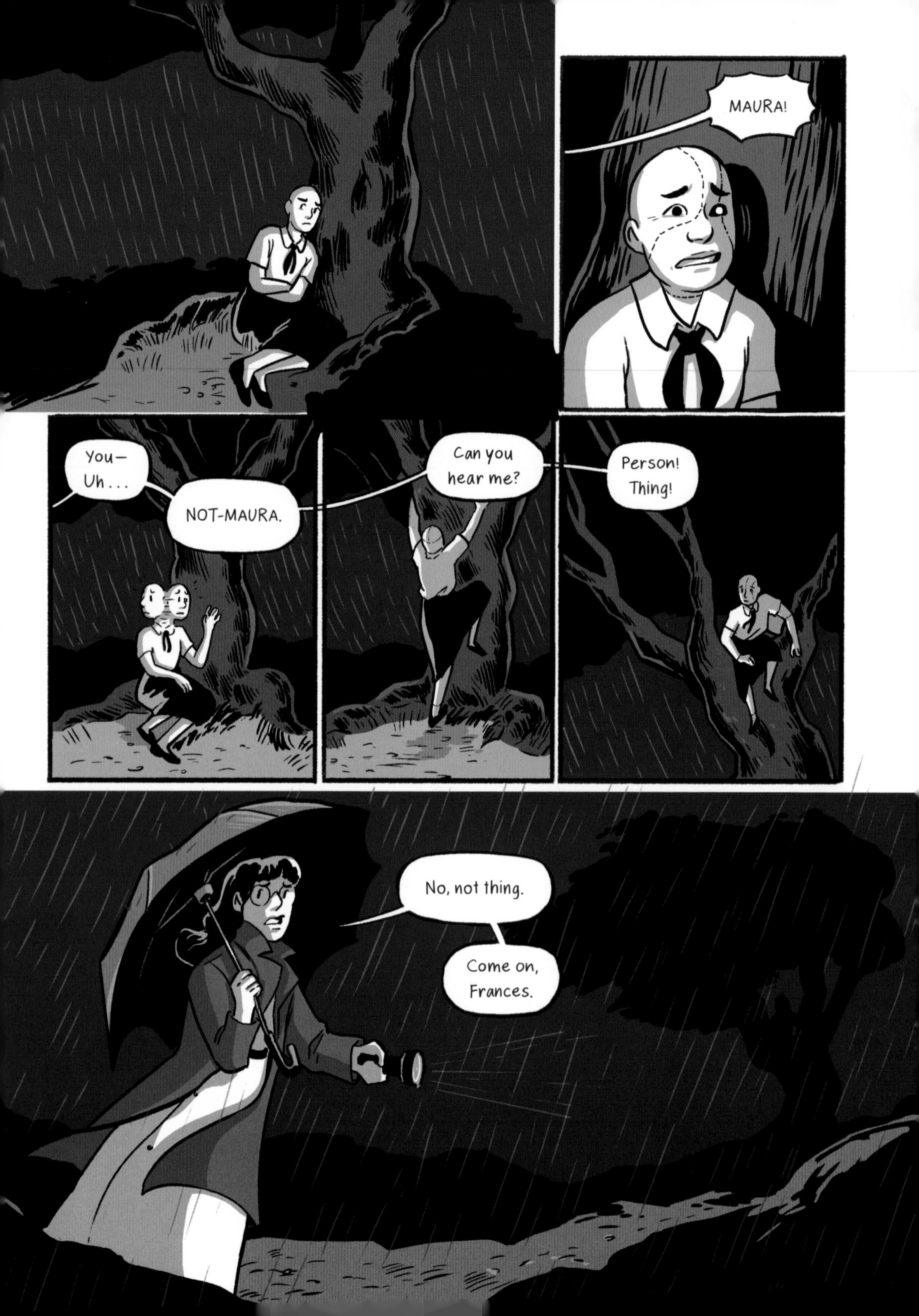
MAURA!
You—
Uh...
NOT-MAURA.
Can you hear me?
Person! Thing!
No, not thing.
Come on, Frances.

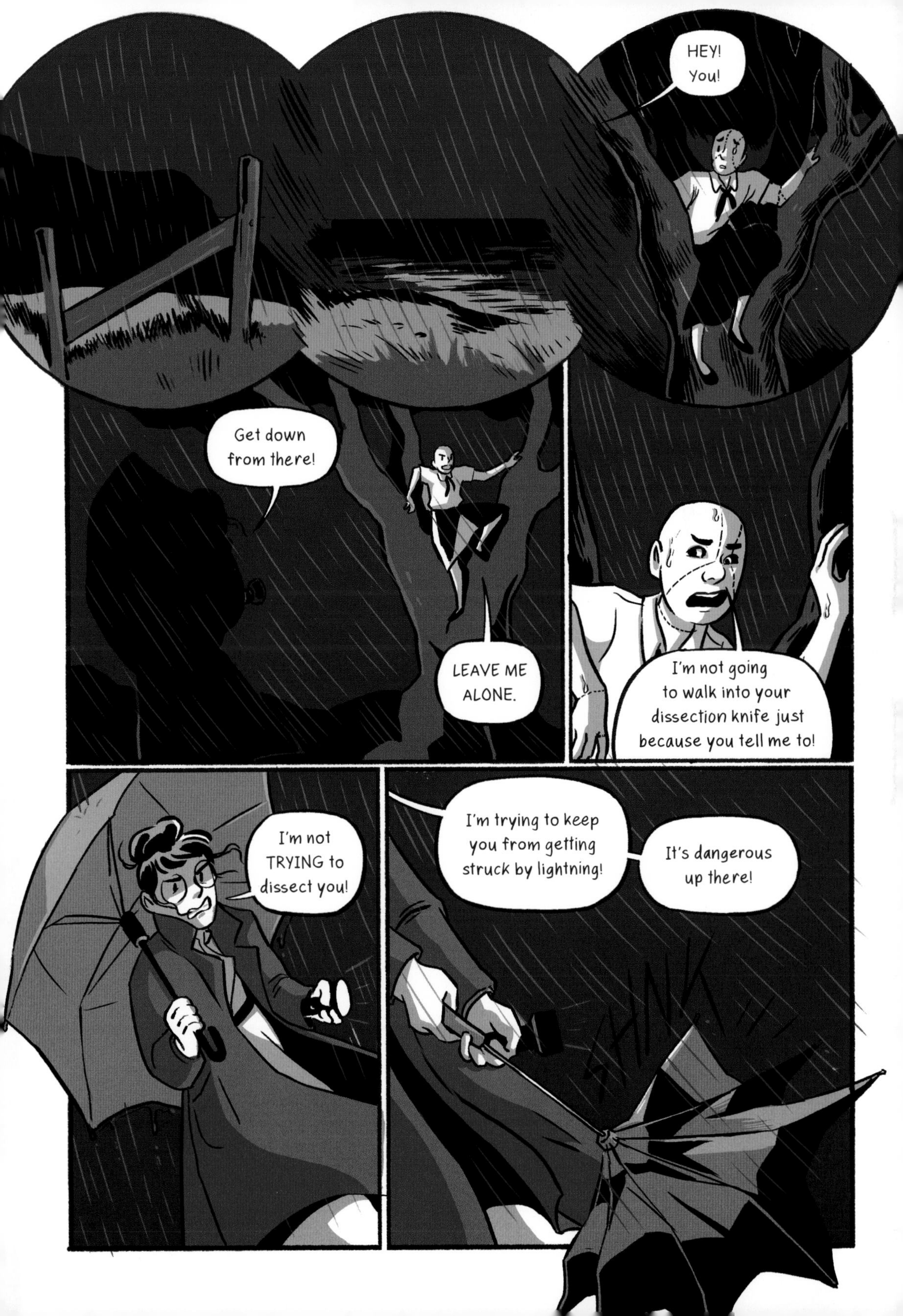
HEY! You!
Get down from there!
LEAVE ME ALONE.
I'm not going to walk into your dissection knife just because you tell me to!
I'm not TRYING to dissect you!
I'm trying to keep you from getting struck by lightning!
It's dangerous up there!
SHNK

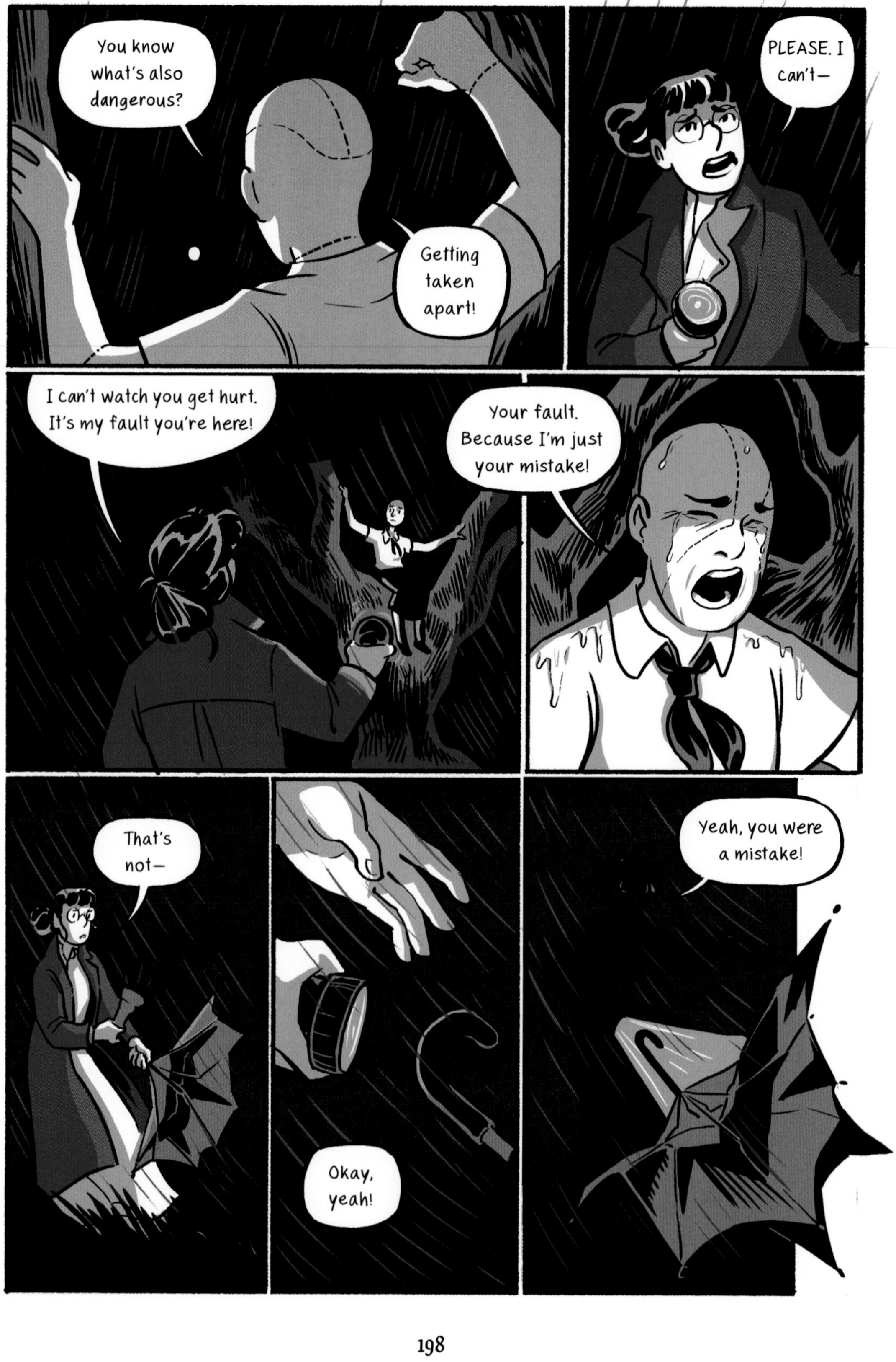
You know what's also dangerous?
Getting taken apart!
PLEASE. I can't—
I can't watch you get hurt. It's my fault you're here!
Your fault. Because I'm just your mistake!
That's not—
Okay, yeah!
Yeah, you were a mistake!

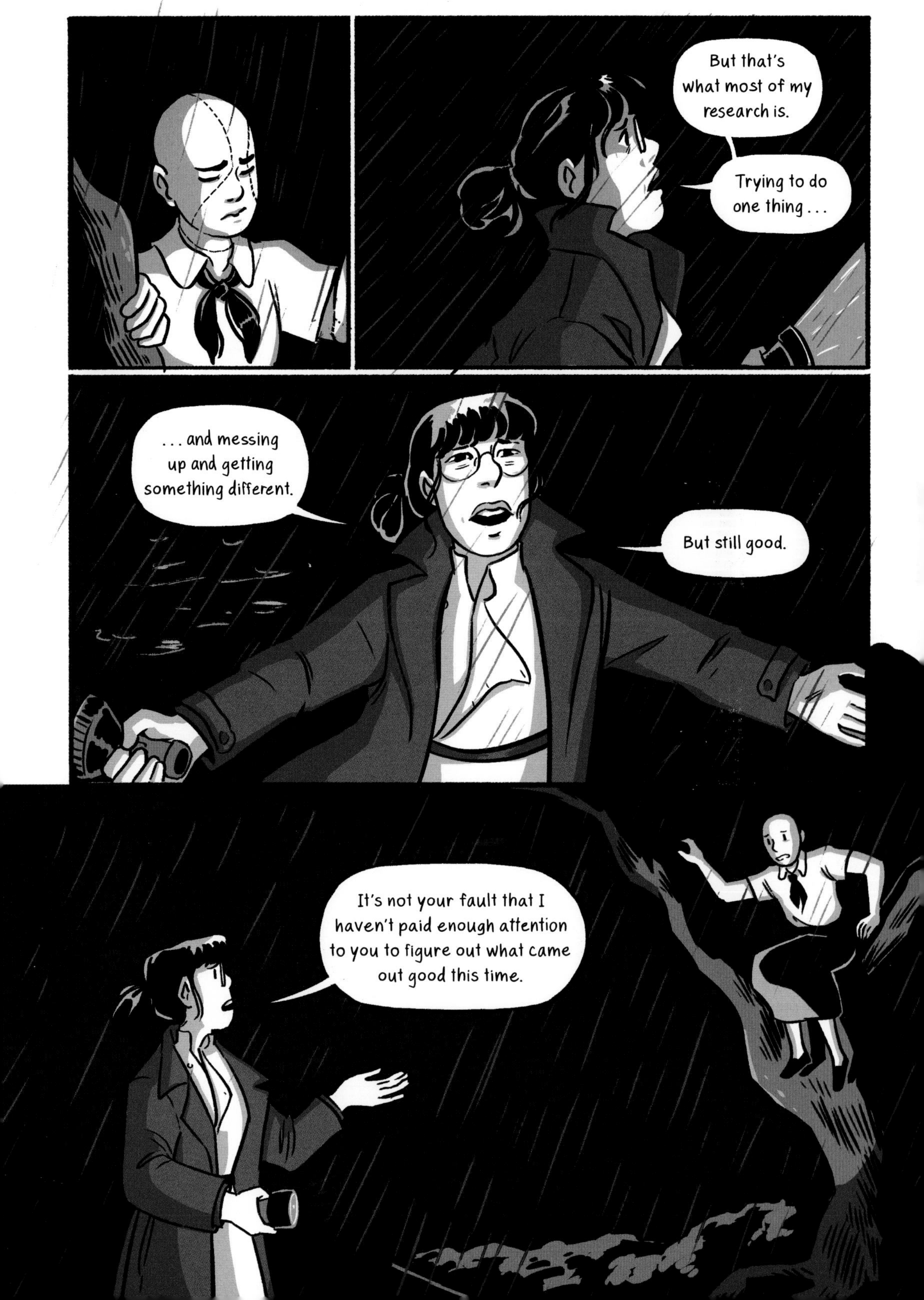
But that's what most of my research is.
Trying to do one thing . . .
. . . and messing up and getting something different.
But still good.
It's not your fault that I haven't paid enough attention to you to figure out what came out good this time.

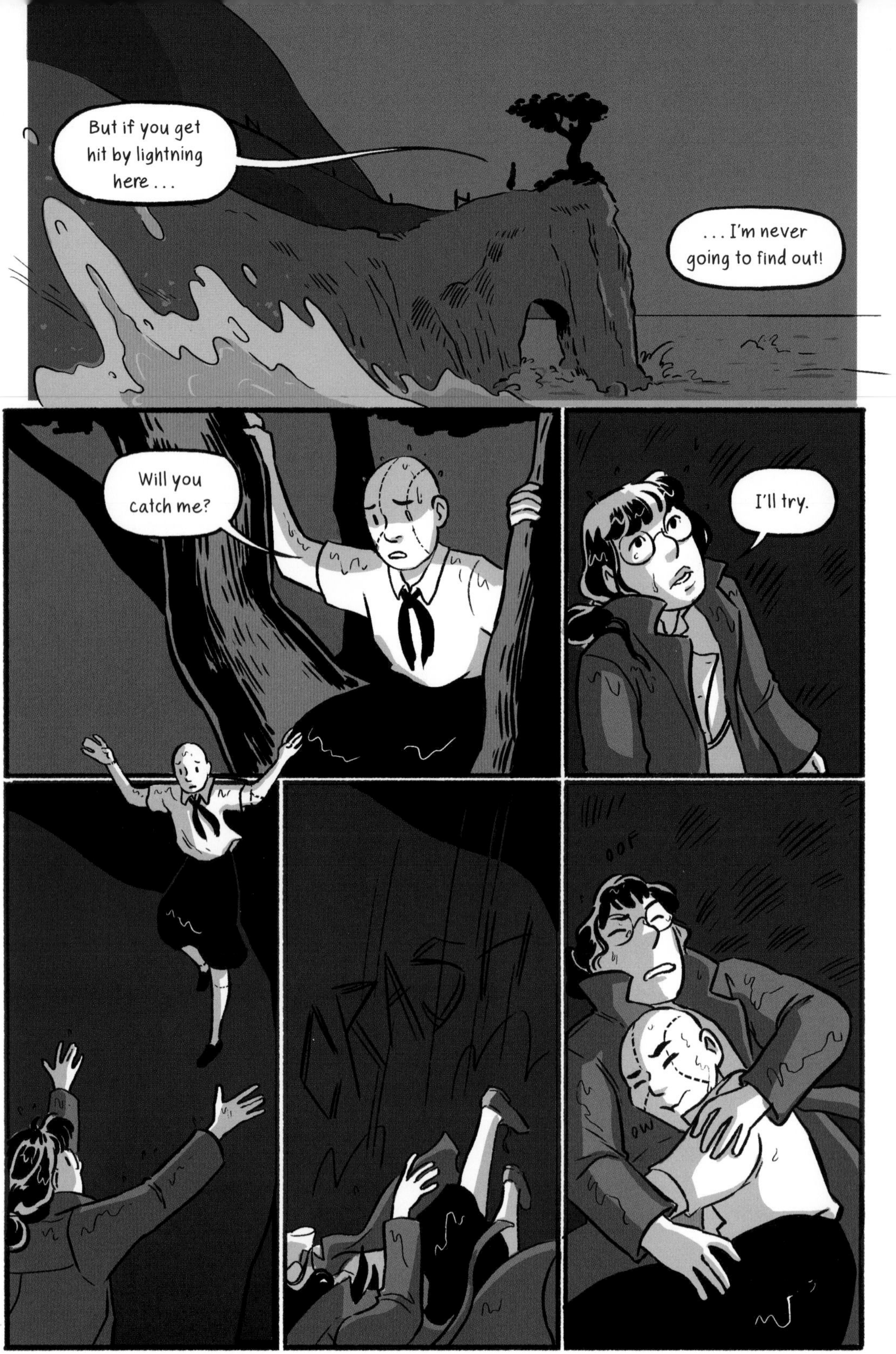
But if you get hit by lightning here . . .
. . . I'm never going to find out!
Will you catch me?
I'll try.
CRASH
OOF
OW

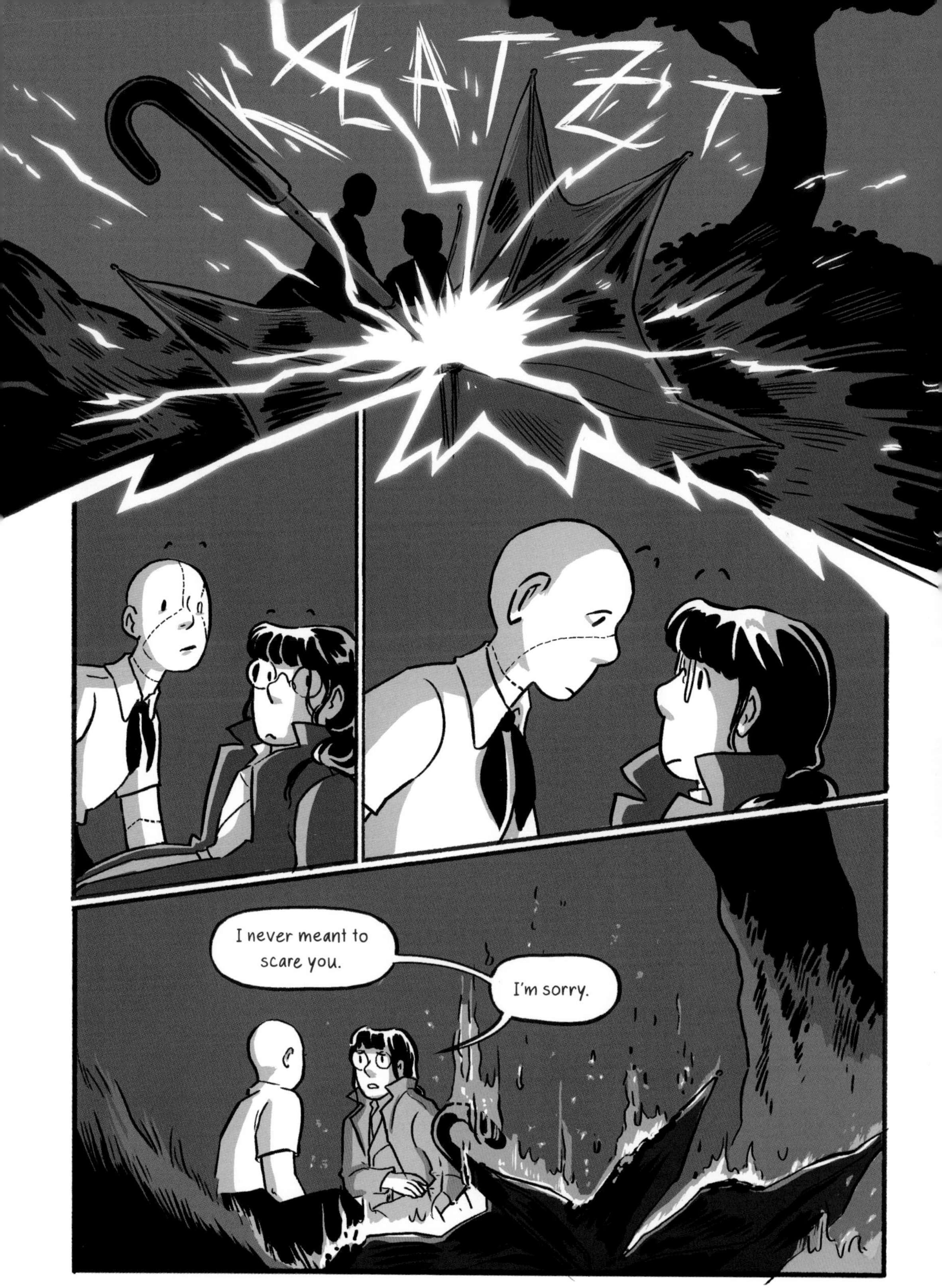
KZZATZZT
I never meant to scare you.
I'm sorry.

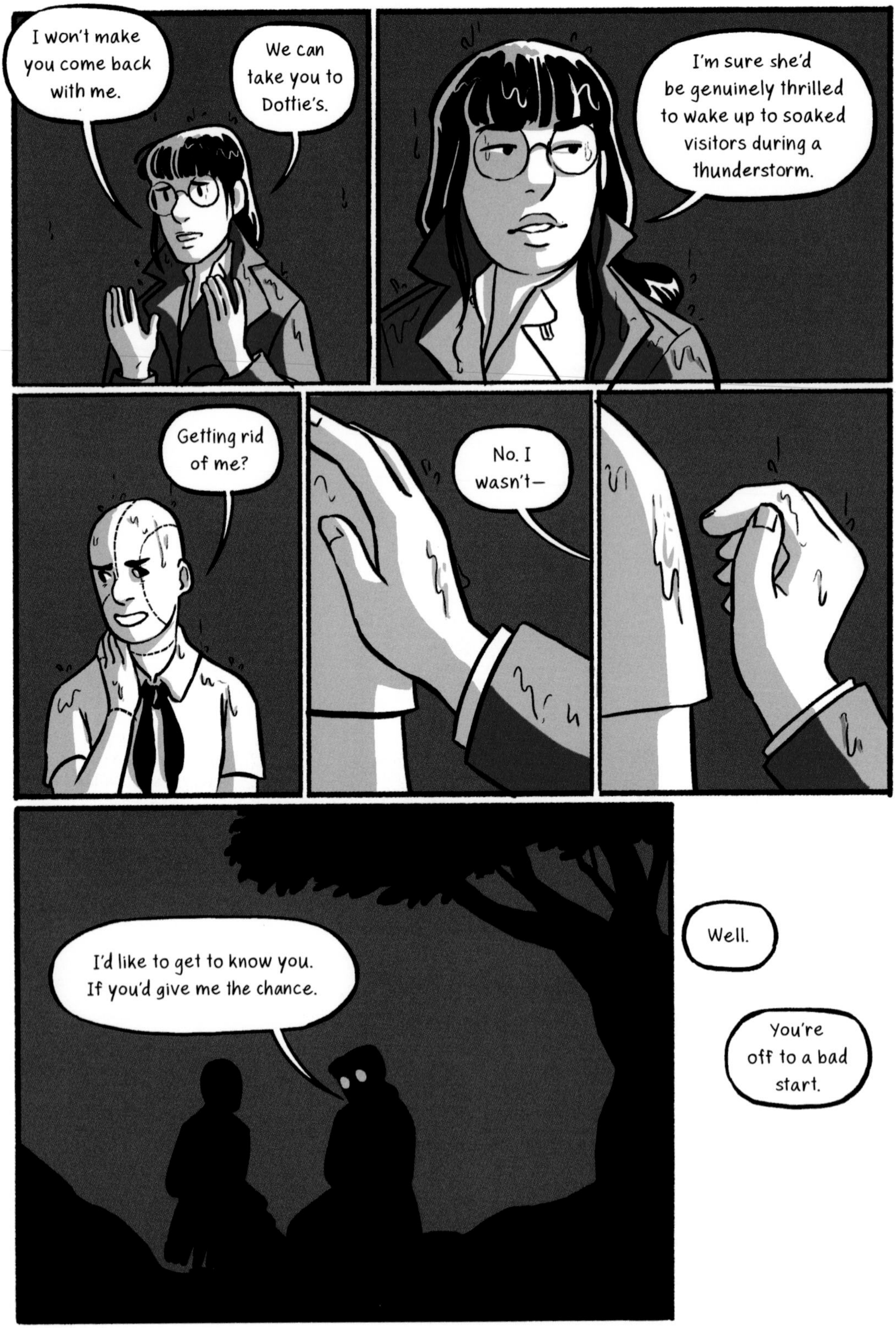
I won't make you come back with me.
We can take you to Dottie's.
I'm sure she'd be genuinely thrilled to wake up to soaked visitors during a thunderstorm.
Getting rid of me?
No. I wasn't—
I'd like to get to know you. If you'd give me the chance.
Well.
You're off to a bad start.

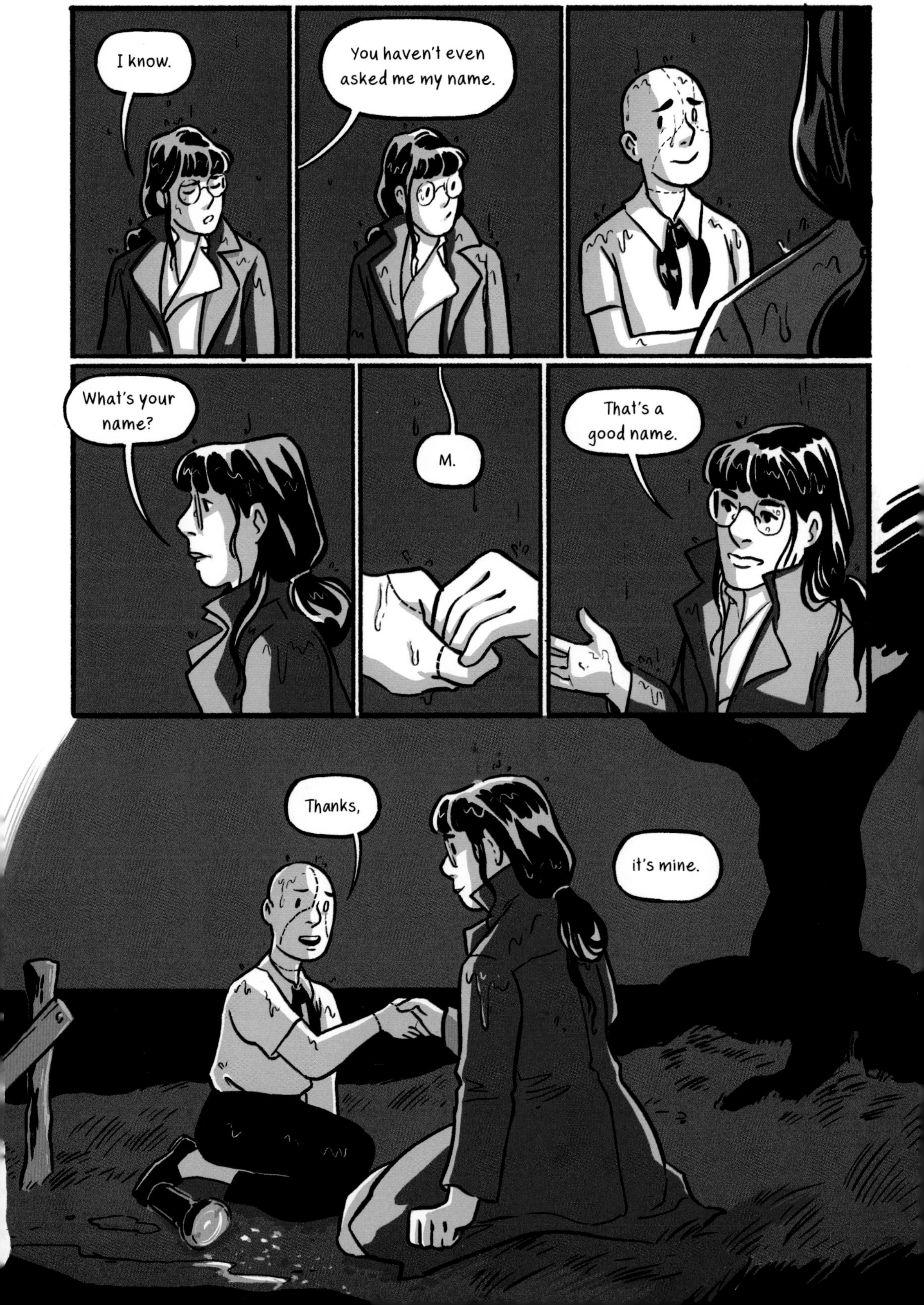
I know.
You haven't even asked me my name.
What's your name?
M.
That's a good name.
Thanks,
it's mine.

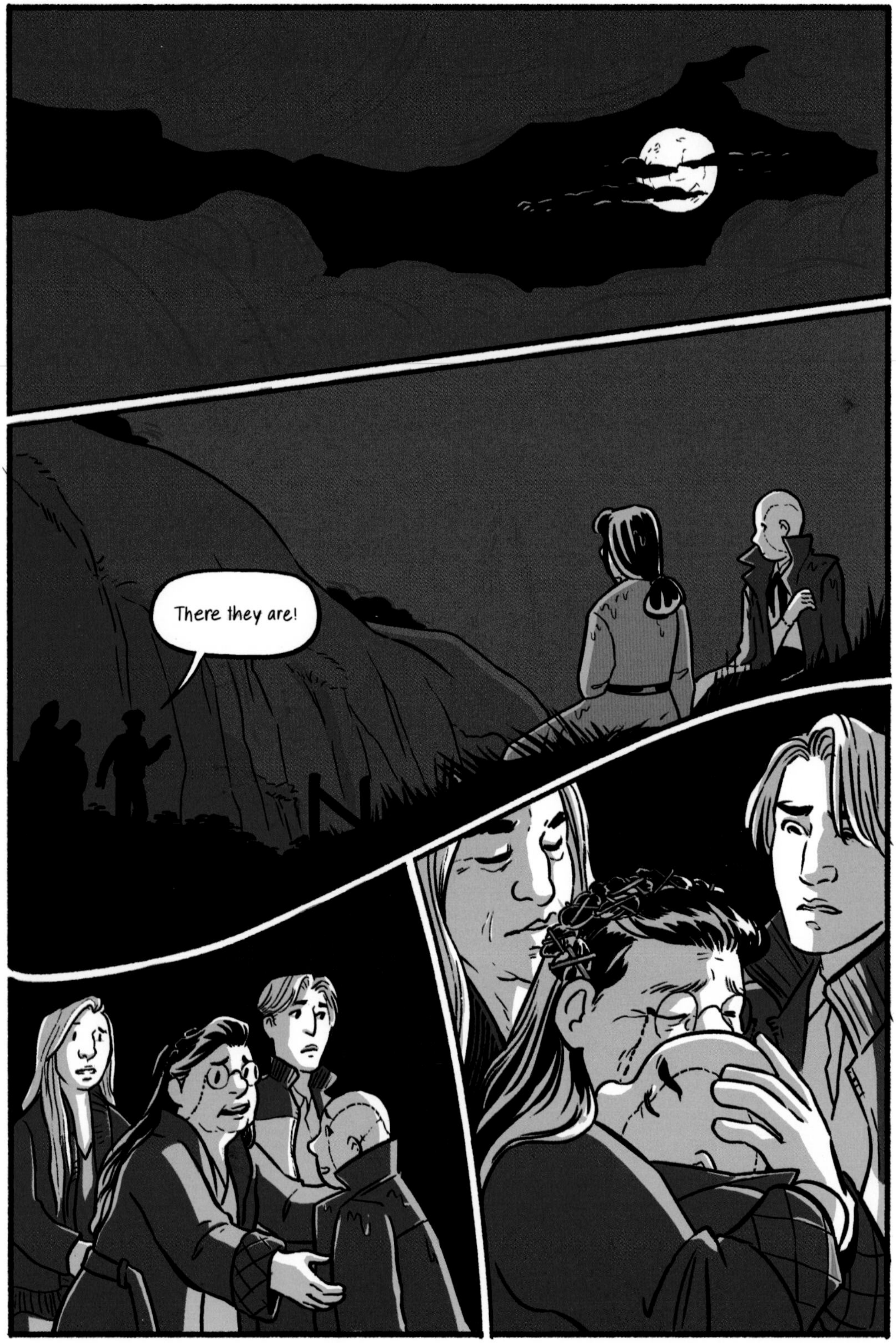
There they are!

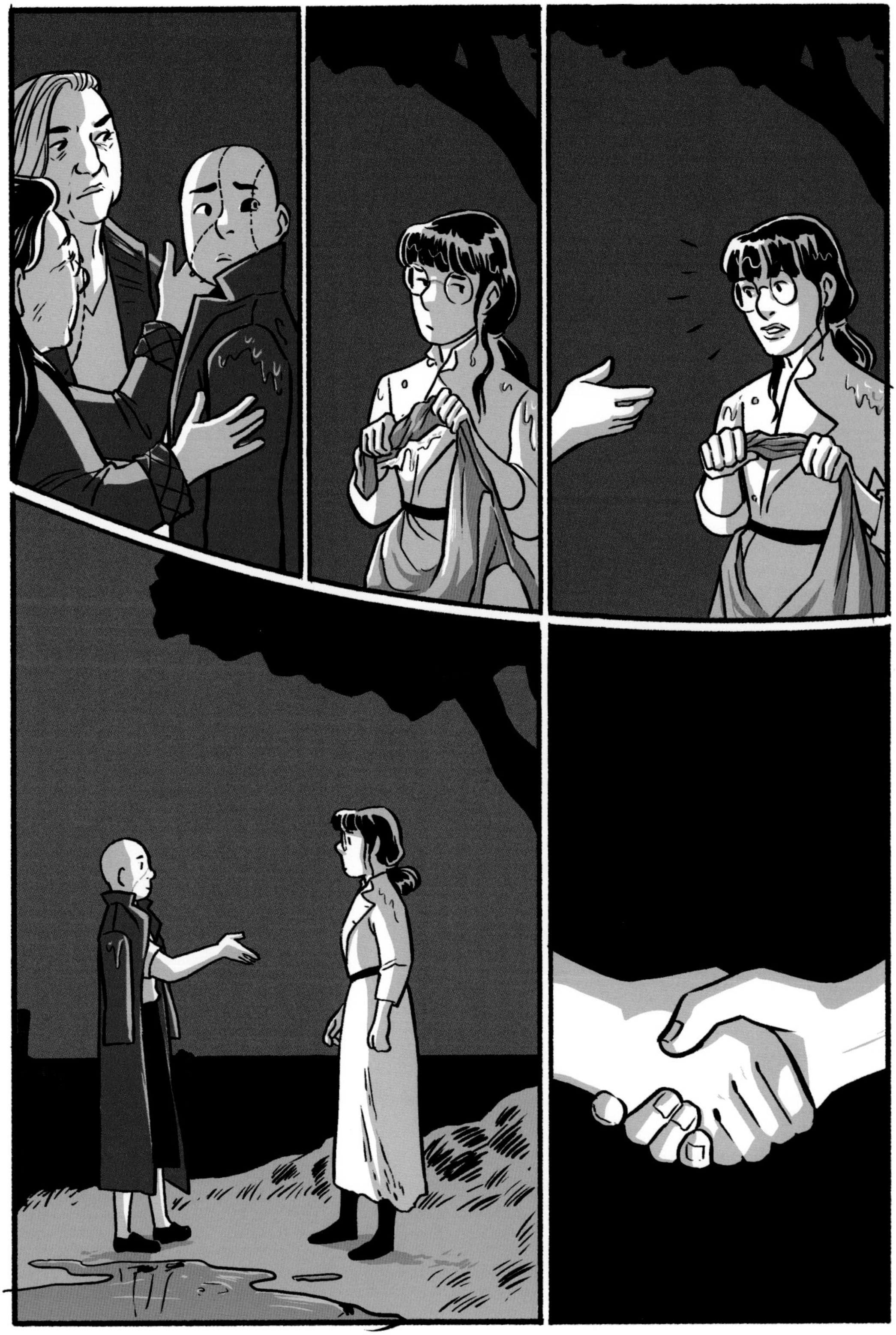

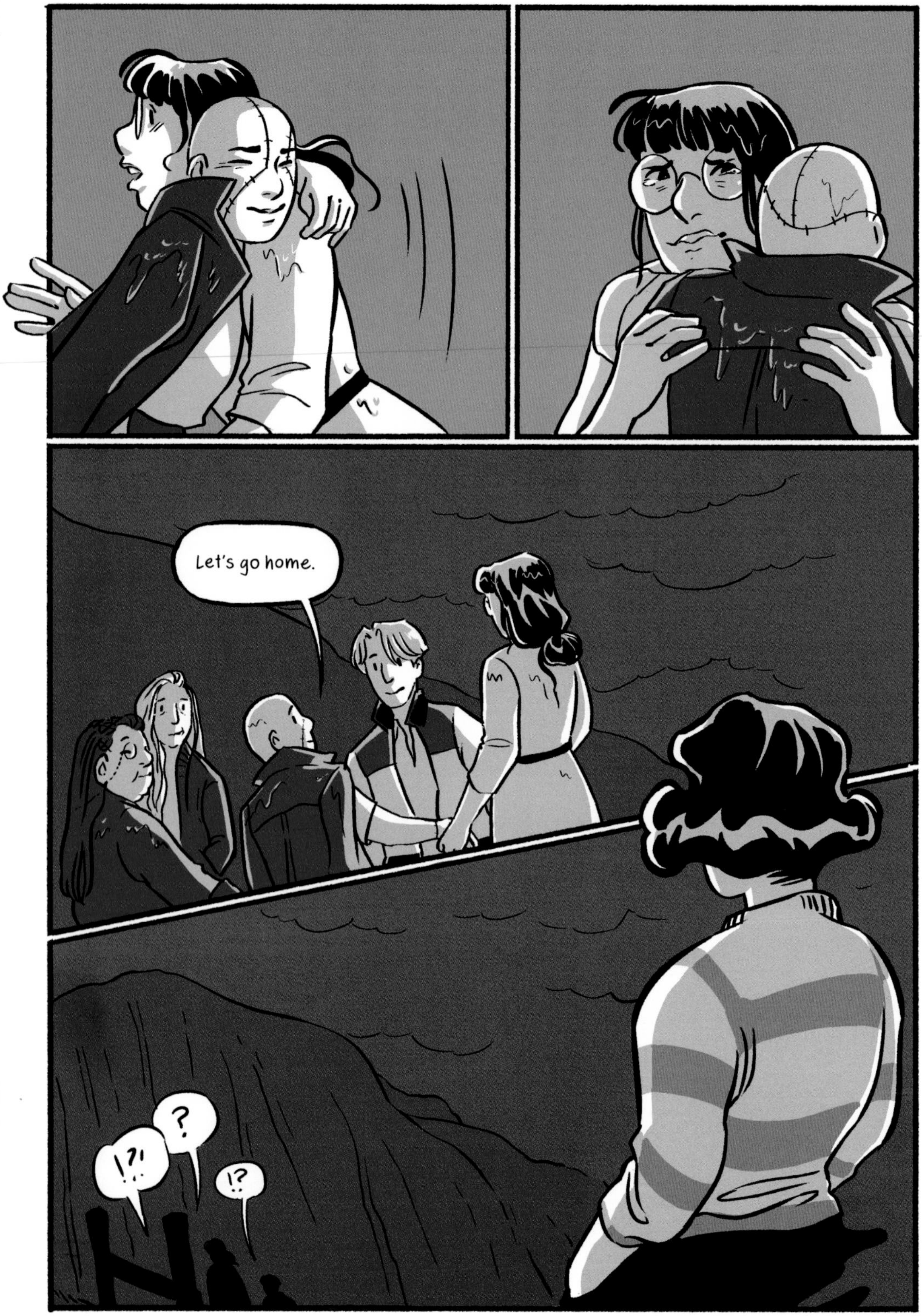
Let's go home.
!?!
?
!?

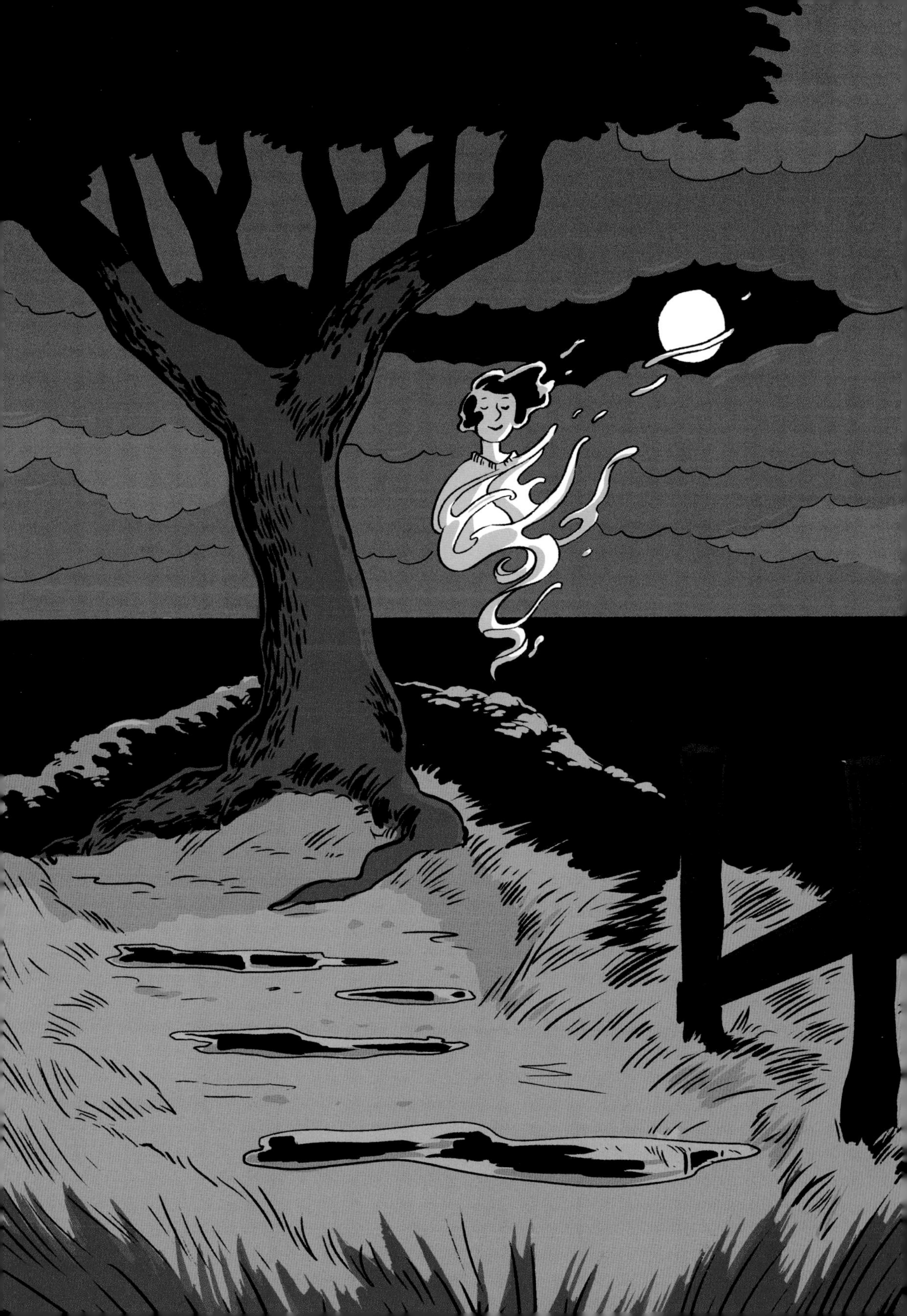

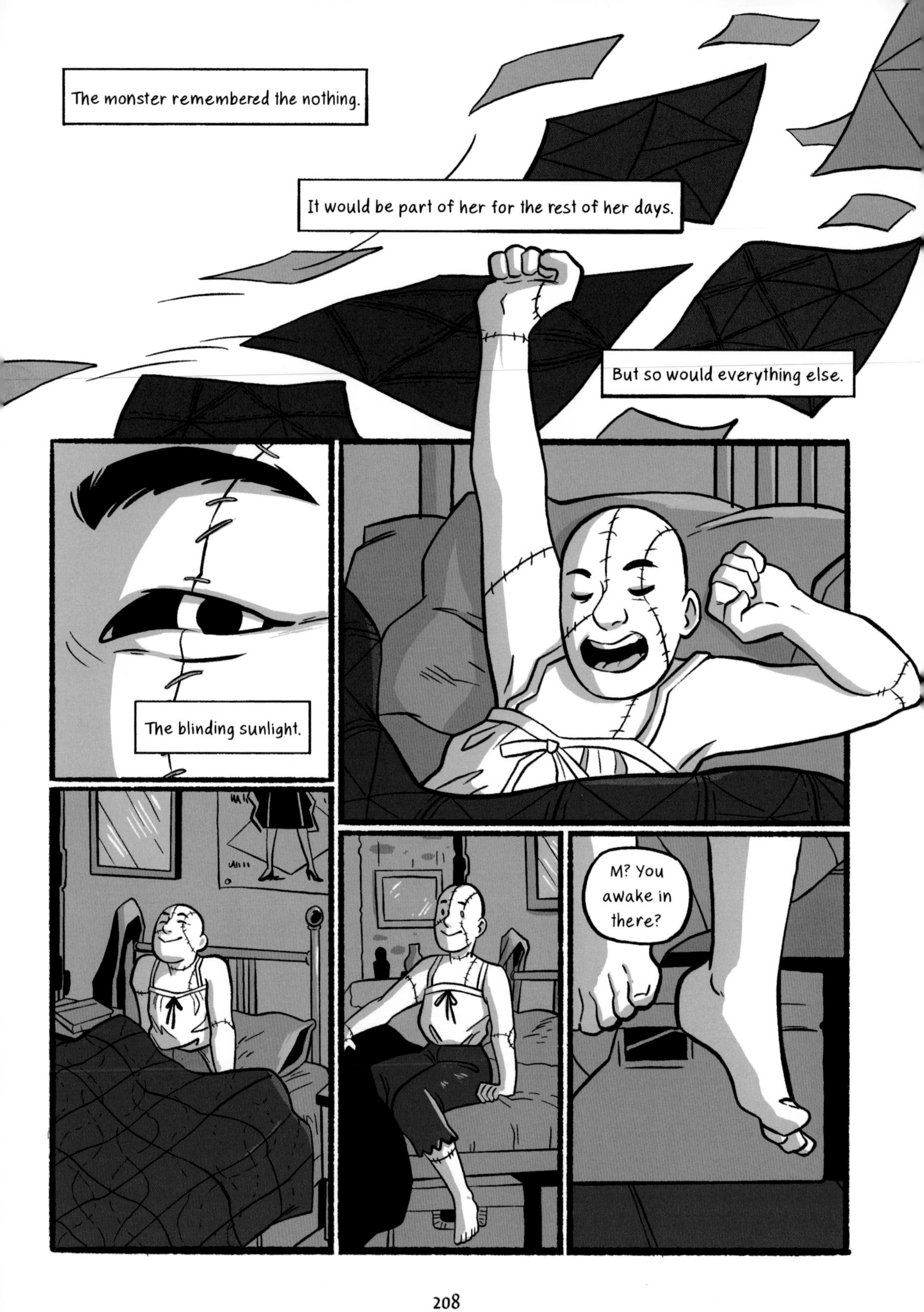
The monster remembered the nothing.
It would be part of her for the rest of her days.
But so would everything else.
The blinding sunlight.
M? You awake in there?

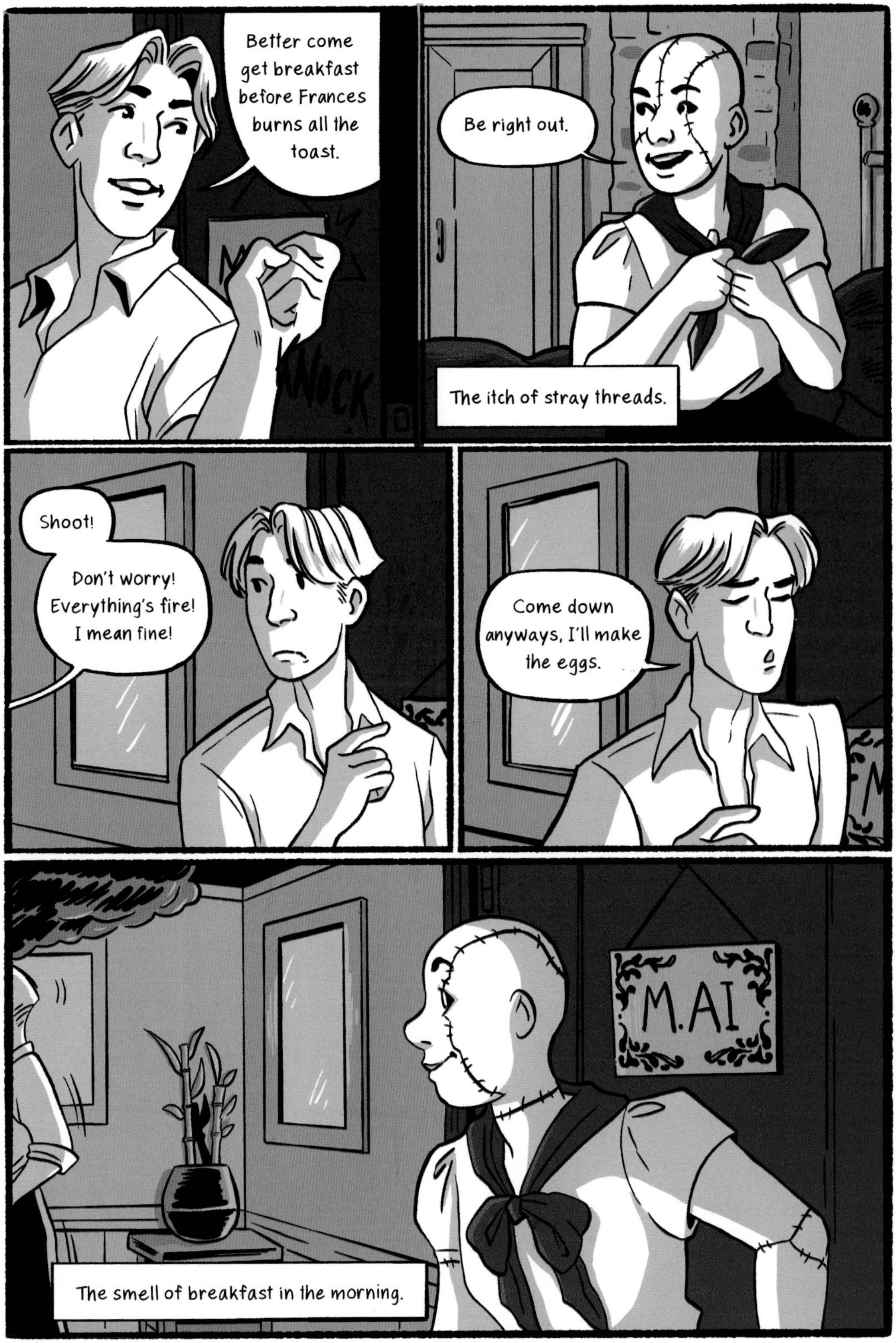

Better come get breakfast before Frances burns all the toast.
KNOCK
Be right out.
The itch of stray threads.
Shoot!
Don't worry! Everything's fire! I mean fine!
Come down anyways, I'll make the eggs.
M.AI
The smell of breakfast in the morning.

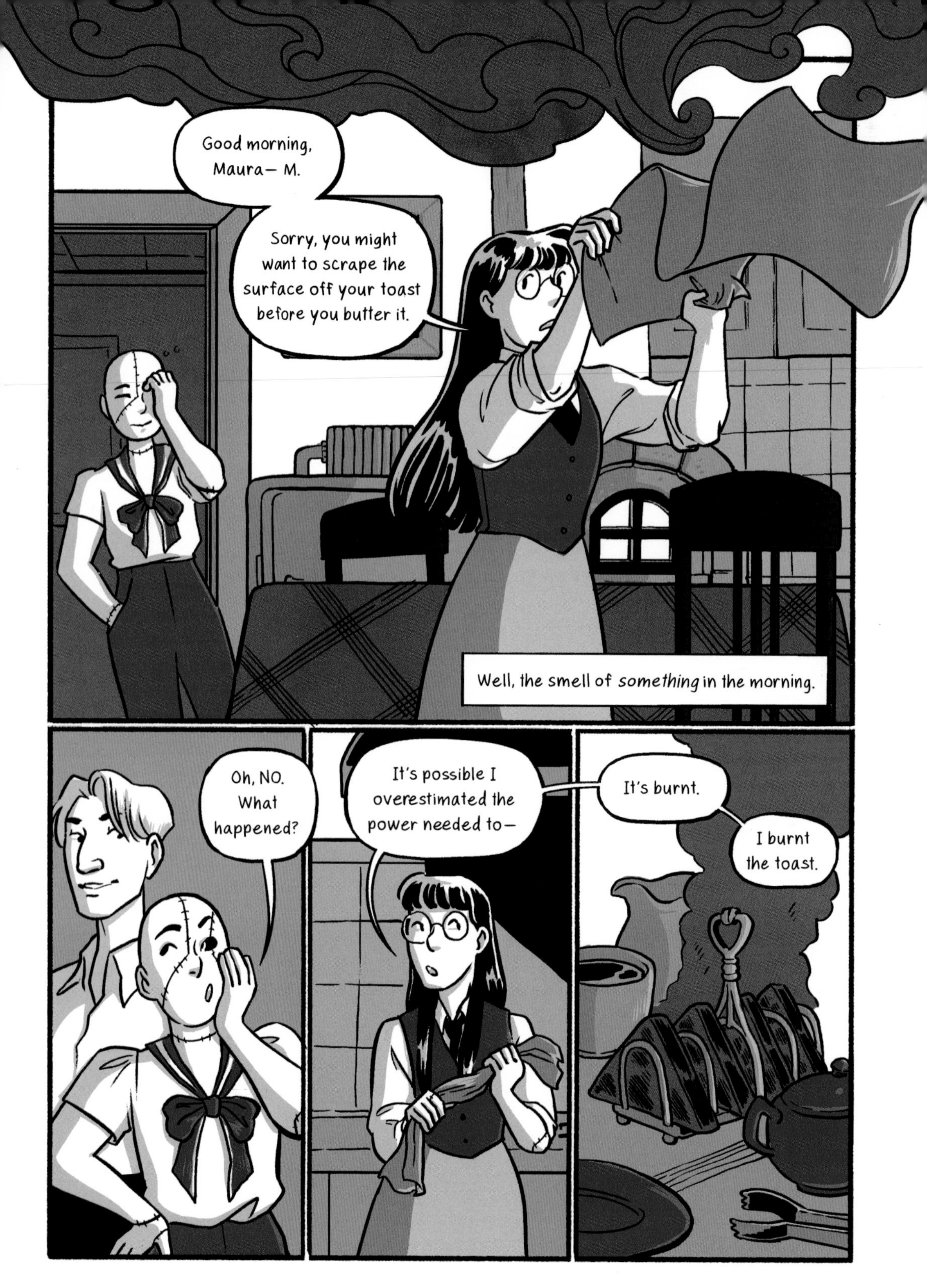
Good morning, Maura— M.
Sorry, you might want to scrape the surface off your toast before you butter it.
Well, the smell of *something* in the morning.
Oh, NO. What happened?
It's possible I overestimated the power needed to—
It's burnt.
I burnt the toast.

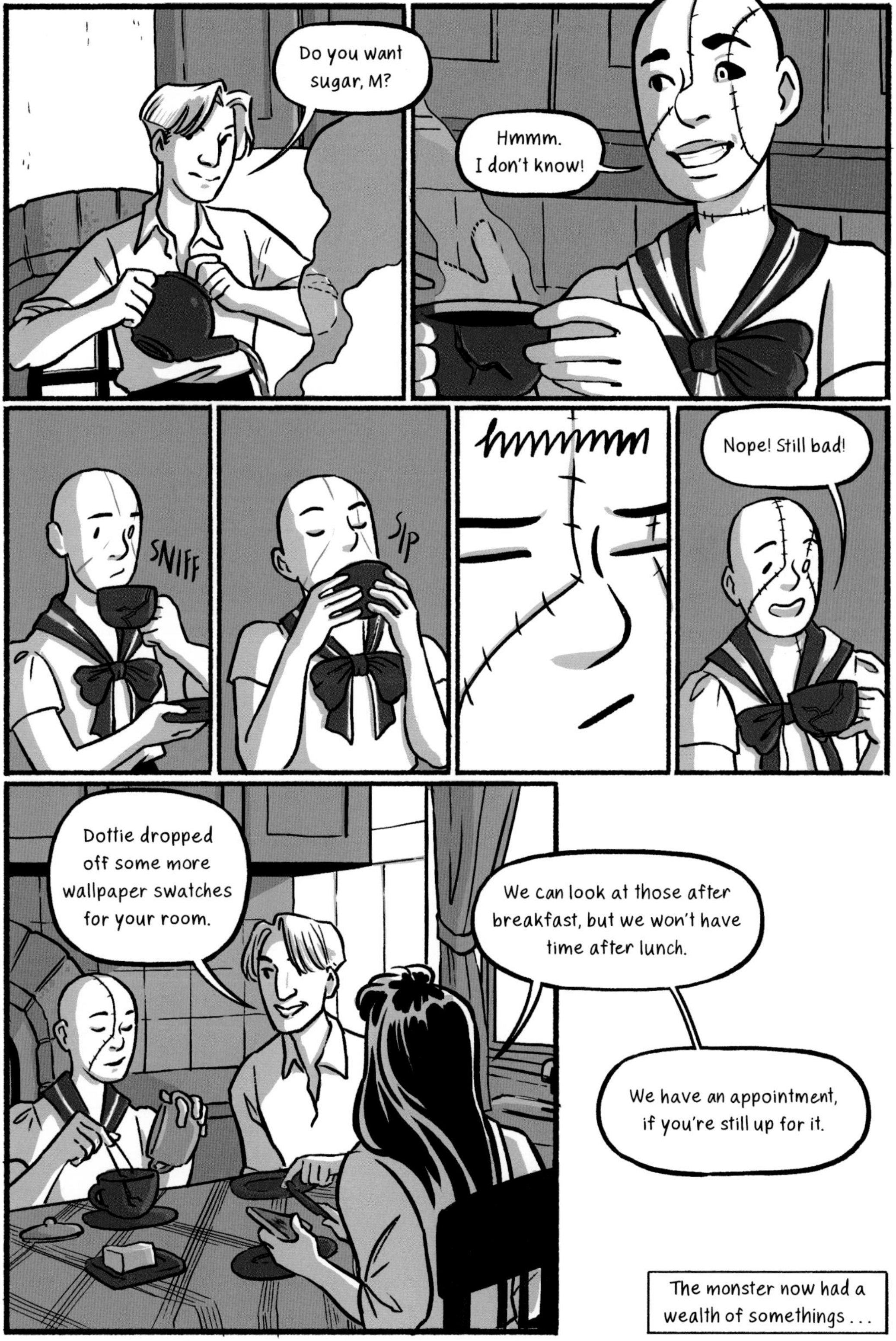
Do you want sugar, M?
Hmmm. I don't know!
SNIFF
SIP
hmmmmm
Nope! Still bad!
Dottie dropped off some more wallpaper swatches for your room.
We can look at those after breakfast, but we won't have time after lunch.
We have an appointment, if you're still up for it.
The monster now had a wealth of somethings . . .

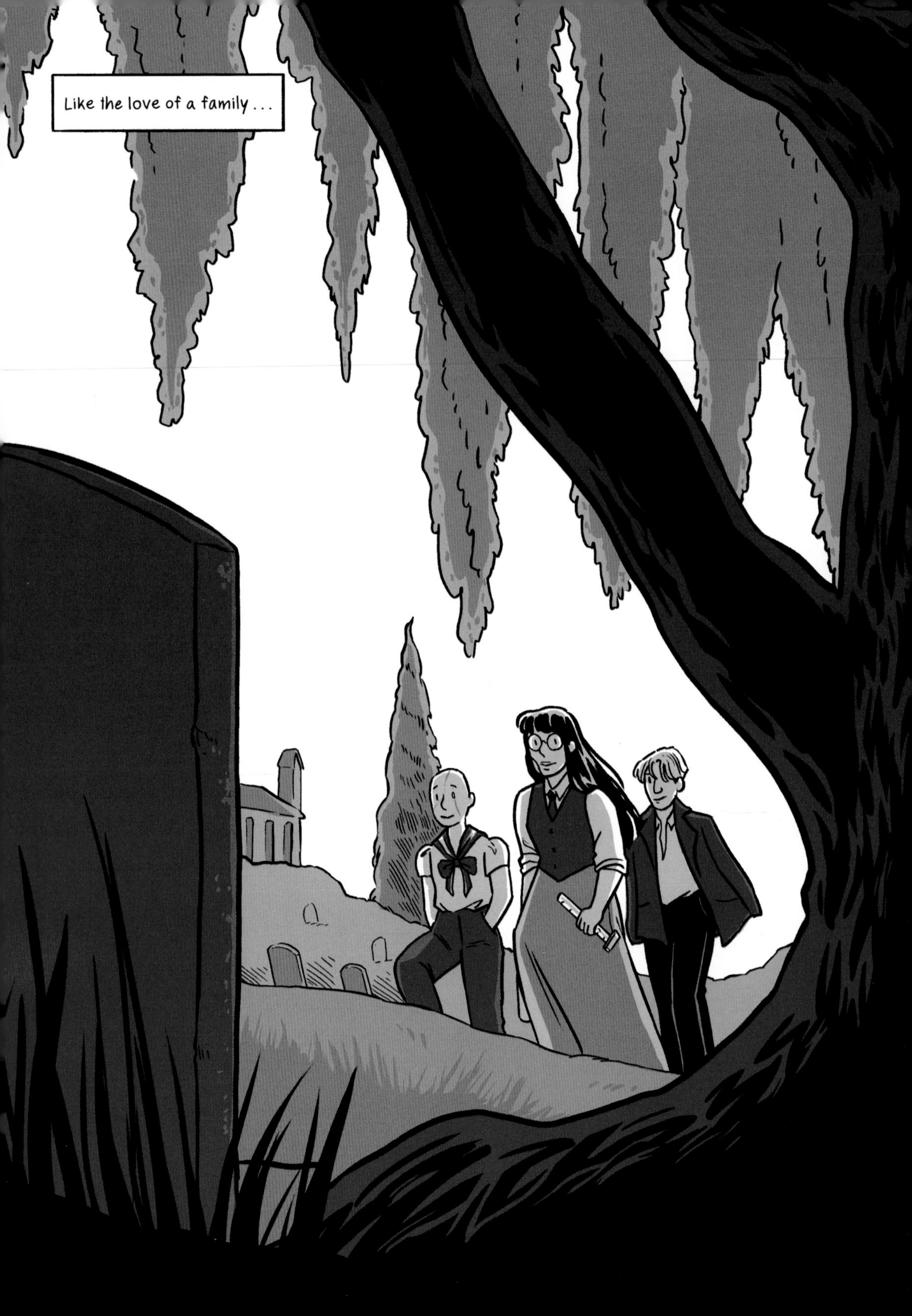
Like the love of a family . . .

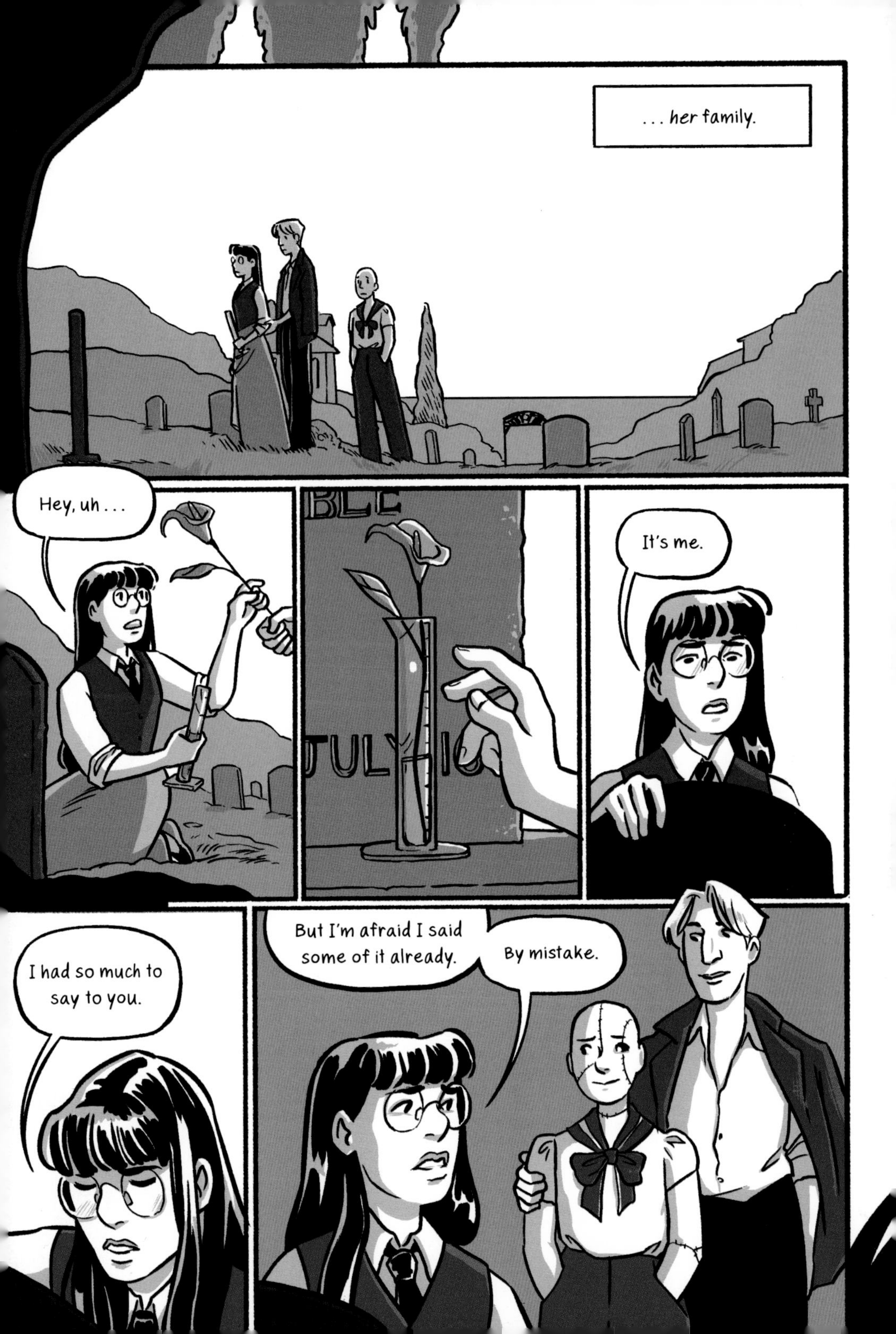
. . . her family.
Hey, uh . . .
BLE
JULY 1
It's me.
I had so much to say to you.
But I'm afraid I said some of it already.
By mistake.

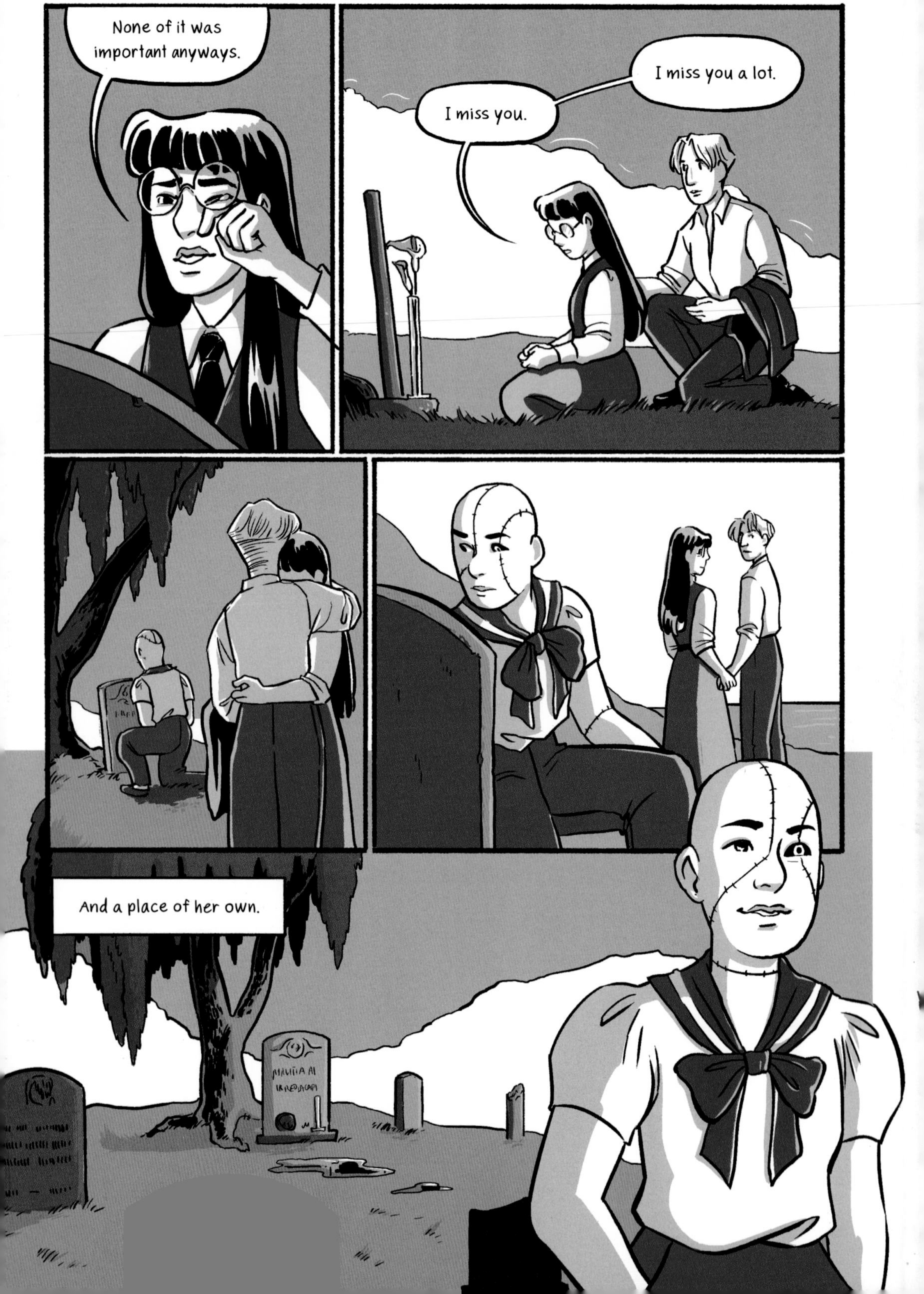
None of it was important anyways.
I miss you.
I miss you a lot.
And a place of her own.

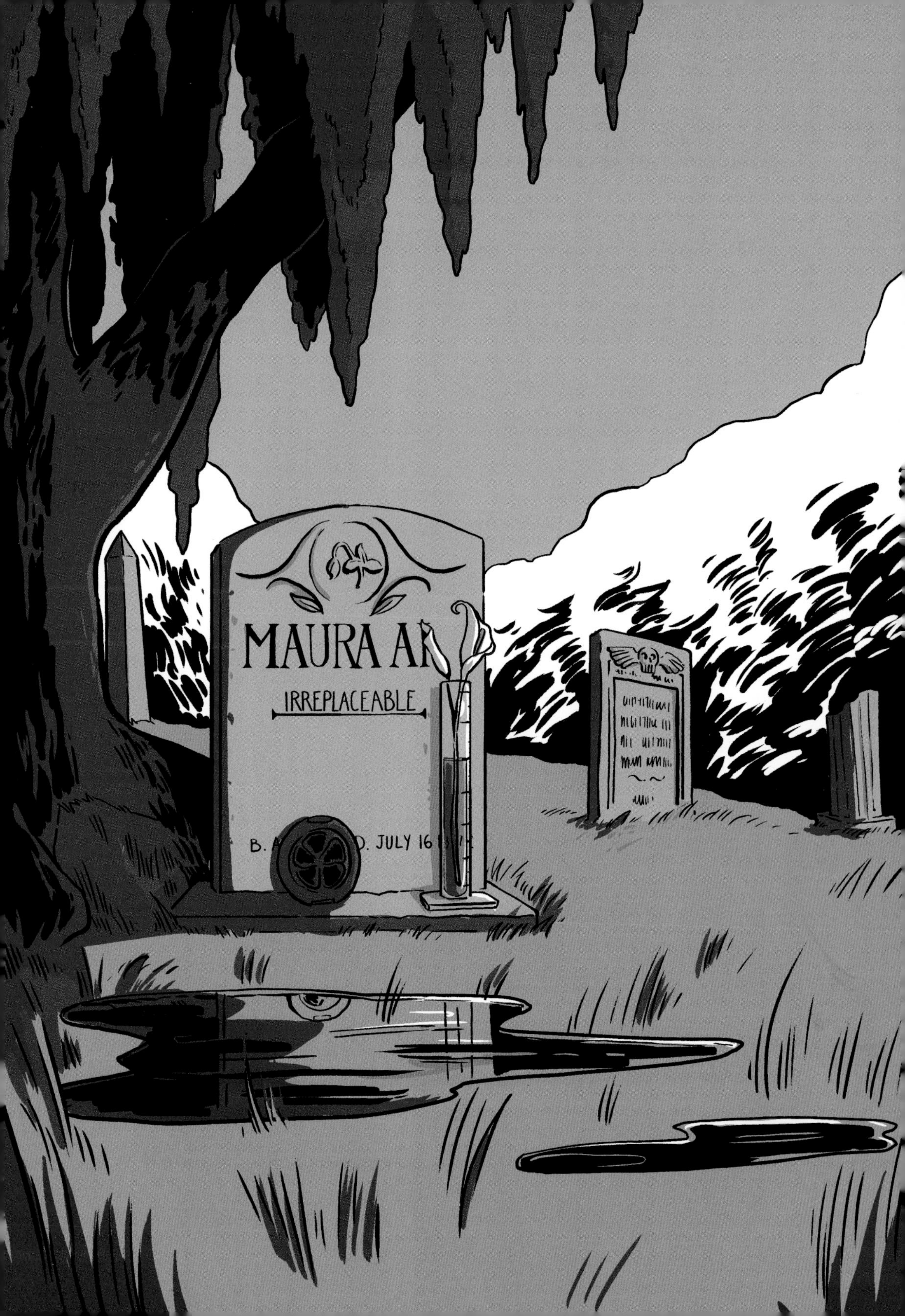
MAURA AR
IRREPLACEABLE
B.
D. JULY 16